Lily Herne divides her time between Cape Town and Norwich, UK, and can sometimes be found in both places at once. Her interests include chainsaws, steampunk and cake. You can follow her on Twitter at @Herne13 or friend her on Facebook - she'd love to hear from you.

Also by Lily Herne

Deadlands

DeATh
OF A
SAint

A Deadlands Novel

LILY
HERNE

Much-in-Little

Constable & Robinson Ltd
55–56 Russell Square
London WC1B 4HP
www.constablerobinson.com

First published by Penguin Books (South Africa) (Pty) Ltd 2012

First published in the UK by Corsair,
an imprint of Constable & Robinson Ltd, 2013

A copy of the British Library Cataloguing in
Publication Data is available from the British Library

ISBN: 978-1-47210-092-4 (paperback)
ISBN: 978-1-47210-093-1 (ebook)

Printed and bound in the UK

1 3 5 7 9 10 8 6 4 2

DeAth
OF A
SAint

A Short History of Cape Town City Enclave

(Transcripts of the War and its aftermath)

Name: Yolanda Visser (not her real name)

Previous occupation: Mortuary make-up artist

Current occupation: Resurrectionist amulet trader

Age: 27

Nationality: South African

(Date transcribed: July, 2015 [aka Year 5].)

Note: Yolanda is reported to be one of the first to have encountered a reanimate at her place of work.

Interviewer: Thank you for sharing your story with us today, Yolanda.

Yolanda: Are you sure it's cool for me to talk to you? 'Cos, like, I've heard that the Resurrectionists don't like us to talk about what happened during the War.

Interviewer: Your identity will be kept confidential.

Yolanda: Uh. Okay then. Where do you want me to start?

Interviewer: Can you start on the day when you first encountered a reanimate?

Yolanda: Cool. So, at first it was, like, just a normal day. I was working at the Peaceful Sleep Funeral Home on Buitenkant Street, and I only had a couple of decedents to deal with that morning – that's what we called the dead back then; it's like an industry word, you know. Anyway, I started on Mrs de Beer. Totally straightforward. She'd died of natural causes, basically because she was, like, really old, and I was just going to add a bit of blusher. Anyway, after a bit I popped out for a smoke break, and when I came back in there was this young guy, couldn't have been more than twenty, in the preparation room. I could tell straight away that there was something wrong with him. I thought he was probably on tik or something, 'cos, like, although he was really cute, his eyes were just blank and he didn't blink or anything.

Interviewer: Were you frightened?

Yolanda: Nah. I knew Eric, my supervisor, was just down the hall, and so I said to the guy: 'You're not supposed to be in here.' But he didn't answer, just cocked his head to one side in a lank creepy way and lurched out. So, anyway, I was about to sound the alarm, let Eric know that another one of the freaks who were into dead people had broken into the funeral home, when Mrs de Beer started moaning.

Interviewer: How did you react to this?

Yolanda: How do you think I reacted? I totally freaked out. Look, sometimes the decedents used to burp and groan and fart and stuff – but that was just air escaping from their guts or whatever. This was different; it went on and on. And then Mrs de Beer sat up and started sliding off the gurney. So I was like, oh no, someone's made a serious mistake – like maybe she hadn't been dead, just in a coma or something. But then I remembered that she'd been in the cooler room for, like, I dunno, a day at least, and so I knew it couldn't be that. I was really scared by now – at first I just froze, it was like my brain couldn't deal with what it was seeing, you know? But then she started reaching towards me, trying to touch me, and there was this weird white stuff snaking out of her mouth.

Interviewer: Can you describe it in more detail?

Yolanda: You've seen it, haven't you? Like this thin, wormy stuff. It sounds gross, but it reminded me of ... I dunno ... Thai noodles or something. It's what turns people into Rotters, isn't it? Part of the virus that infects them, right? Or keeps them alive and stops them decaying totally or whatever.

So I pushed my make-up trolley towards her, bashing it into her legs, and this gave me enough time to get out of there. I ran straight to Eric and told him about Mrs de Beer, but by now I was totally hysterical, and he was like, 'Yessus, Yolanda, what you been smoking?' And I swear I did my best to stop him going into the preparation room, but he was like, 'What*ever*.' Of course he didn't come out of there, or if he did, he wasn't, you know, *alive*.

Anyway, there was no way I was hanging around, so I just ran for my car. I tried to call my boyfriend at work – he was in IT, although not any more obviously – but the network was down. So I went home, had a shower and few drinks to calm me down, and then I had a nap. I guess at that stage I was thinking that maybe Mrs de Beer *had* been in a coma or something, that there had to be a rational explanation.

I woke up hours later – three a.m., I think it was – the vodka and the shock must've knocked me out, you know. The first thing I did was switch on CNN. And I immediately noticed that the newsreaders looked really scared and lost – like when the whole 9/11 thing happened – and they were babbling about a virus and stuff. And then, suddenly, the screen went black.

I didn't know what to do. I was about to try and call my boyfriend again when I heard the screaming and I looked out of the window. It was chaos out there. I mean, I lived fairly close to the stadium, and with the FIFA World Cup going on and everything, all those vuvuzelas and tourists everywhere, it was usually fairly crazy, but this was different. People were running everywhere, and everything was lit up, bright as day. I finally figured out that it was because the city was on fire, like *totally* on fire, but that was only when I opened the window and smelled the smoke.

I didn't want to stay in my flat – there were these weird banging and groaning noises coming from next door – so I ran outside. Everyone was screaming: 'Get to the stadium! Get to the stadium!' So I followed this crowd, and it was just like doing the FIFA Fan Walk, only, you know, more hectic and panicked and stuff. I mean, I was used to seeing dead people, but not them walking and running and attacking people.

But by then the stadium was totally full, and there were hundreds of infected people lurching around. There was no way I could get back to my flat, and so a bunch of us got together and made a break for it. We ended up in this restaurant in Green Point and we hid out in the kitchen, which was in the basement of this huge building. There were twenty of us or so, and we were there for weeks. It was horrible. We could hear the city burning around us, and the air force planes crashing, and then it was all, like, quiet, and then we just heard the moans of the Rotters. We had plenty to eat, of course, but with so many people and only one toilet … Well, you can imagine. It was just like one of those zombie movies – you know, the one where they're all trapped in the mall – only, like, way more hectic and disgusting.

Anyway, so we were all sure we were going to die, and then we heard someone banging on the door. We'd boarded it up and stuff, but a couple of the guys looked out and there was this figure dressed in this long brown robe like priests or monks wear. Well, we didn't know what to think. We couldn't tell if it was a person with freaky dress sense or one of the Rotters. But it didn't take us long to figure out that it was going to help us. They're not called Guardians for nothing, you know.

Interviewer: How did you know it was going to help you?

Yolanda: The Guardian had brought us food, and it was keeping the Rotters away.

Interviewer: How did it do this?

Yolanda: I dunno. No one knows, do they? It's the Guardians' thing, isn't it? Probably with its mind … Who knows? All I know is that when it was around us the Rotters kept their distance, like they were scared or whatever. Anyway, there were these really cute six-year-old twin girls with us, and the Guardian kind of gestured towards them. It didn't speak or anything, but we assumed it was going to take them to safety first. The kids' parents freaked out a bit, but they were also relieved to get the kids out of there – the place really stank.

The Guardian left us where we were for a few days. *That* was hectic; we were scared it wouldn't return, that we'd starve to death or whatever. But then it came back, and there were more Guardians with it. They gave us some clean clothes and food and stuff, and we followed them out.

It was really freaky being outside again. I couldn't believe it! The whole of Cape Town was trashed, with, like, Long Street and even the Waterfront just *gone*.

How much more do you need?

Interviewer: Can you describe the beginnings of the enclave?

Yolanda: Oh, right. Okay, so the Guardians took us in these big wagons to this huge empty space, keeping the dead ones from attacking us. One of the guys, this cute Malawian kid, said that it was where Khayelitsha used to be, but you couldn't tell for sure 'cos, like, most of the shacks and houses were all burned to the ground.

So we camped out for, like, ages, and then the Guardians started getting us to build this huge fence, and they brought us wood and bricks and stuff so that we could build shelters and toilets and things. And for the first few months we had this whole shanty-town vibe going on, you know.

I work on a market stall now. I know, crazy, right? Well, it's not as if I can go back to my former career. With all the decedents being thrown outside the fence so that they'll get infected and turn into more Rotters, no one does proper funerals anymore. (She laughs.)

Interviewer: Are you happy?

Yolanda: I guess it's okay. I mean, the Guardians look after us, right? Bring us food and stuff from the agricultural enclaves.

5

Interviewer: Are you a Resurrectionist?

Yolanda: Kind of. I mean, I'm not sure I buy into the whole worshipping the Rotters thing, but after seeing what happened during the War, I'm not really surprised that people worship the Guardians. They saved us. And the Resurrectionists say that everything's better now that we've all got a fresh start. They've kind of got a point. Before the War there was all this violence – hijackings and rape and stuff - and now there's none of that – no crime or HIV or anything like that. I mean, don't get me wrong, I miss *American Idol* and Friday night drinks and clothes shopping and stuff, but it could be worse.

Interviewer: Do you ever wonder what is happening out there in the rest of the world, the rest of South Africa?

Yolanda: Sometimes. But, I mean, what's the point thinking about that? It's not as if we can go outside and check it out, is it? (She holds up one of the carved Resurrectionist amulets she sells.) And who am I to complain? Business is good, right?

WANTED

For Crimes Against the Resurrectionist State

THE 'MALL RATS'

Name: Leletia (Lele) de la Fontein
Age: 17
Nationality: South African
Description: 5 ft 2, short (possibly shorn) hair, slight build.

Name: Saint (real name not known at this time)
Age: Approx. 19
Nationality: Motswana (assumed to be of Tswana origin)
Description: 5 ft 10, well built, unruly hair, known to use chains and fire as weapons.

Name: Ash (real name not known at this time)
Age: Approx. 20
Nationality: South African
Description: 6 ft 2, longish black hair, different-coloured eyes (grey/black).

Name: Ginger (real name not known at this time)
Age: Not known at this time
Nationality: British
Description: 6 ft 5, extra-large build, red (ginger) hair. Speaks with a pronounced British accent. Carries a chainsaw.

DO NOT ATTEMPT TO APPREHEND THESE
CRIMINALS AS THEY ARE ARMED AND EXTREMELY
DANGEROUS. IF SEEN CONTACT THE RESURRECTIONIST
GUARD IMMEDIATELY.

By order the Cape Town City Enclave.

Dear Jack,

The illness I have been hiding for so many months is now eating me up, and I know I do not have much time left.

I have many regrets, some of them trivial – that I will never again get to taste honey; that I will never again listen to you, Ginger, Ntombi and Lele bickering about which of Ginger's awful horror movies to watch; that I will never leave Cape Town and see what is happening beyond the enclave's walls. But the biggest regret I have concerns you.

I know I have not been a good person. I trained you – I trained all of you Mall Rats – to fight and defend yourselves, but I did not teach you what is important: I exploited your talents for my own gain, sending you out into the Deadlands to bring back what Lele calls 'worthless crap' from the mall to sell in the enclave.

You see, I always thought it was the dead – the Rotters – who were our enemies. You and I saw first-hand how they ravaged the population, turning our friends into empty, dead-eyed monsters. But now I know that it is not the dead who we should fear, but the living. The Resurrectionists who manipulate and feed the population their dangerous lies must be stopped AT ALL COSTS. This city is sick. It is corrupt; it is rotting; it is eating itself from the inside.

It is too late for me, but it is not too late for you.

The others are out there somewhere. You must find them; you must ask them to come back and help to stop this.

Please, tell them that I know now that they were right.

And tell them that I am sorry.

I love you, and I always have. Please give my love to Ginger, Ntombi and Lele.

Hester

Part One:
Cape Town

LELE

We smell it before we see it.

'Oh, man, not another one,' Saint says, propping herself up on one elbow. 'Whose turn is it?'

We both look over at Ginger, who's lying nearest to the fire, his orange hair curling out of the top of his sleeping bag. He rolls over and snores, but I can tell he's faking. I grab my sketchbook out of my rucksack and chuck it at him. 'Nice try, Ginger, but I know you're not really sleeping.'

'Am so,' he mumbles.

'Seriously, Ginger, it's your turn. And get a move on – it's stinking up the place.'

'All right, all right.' He sits up and kicks his sleeping bag off his legs. The Rotter is stumbling towards the campfire, its raggedy arms hanging at its sides. 'Yuk,' Ginger says. 'It's one of the soggy ones. I *hate* the soggy ones.'

It reeks of that old book odour that all the Rotters stink of, and something else, something *dead*.

'Just get on with it,' Saint sighs, flapping a hand in front of her face. 'It's rolled in something disgusting.'

Grabbing a smouldering log from the edge of the campfire, Ginger prods the Rotter in the leg, herding it away from the clearing. It turns its head in Ginger's direction and blindly thrashes out one of its bony arms. The suit it must have died in clings to its limbs, but its eyes are nothing but holes in its skull. 'Go on, fella,' Ginger says. 'Go and find your mates.'

The Rotter lurches out of camp, but it doesn't go far before it throws back its head and lets out a low, mournful moan. The sound echoes through the bush. There's a pause of a few seconds, and then there's a louder, answering chorus. *Crap.* There must be a pack close by. I know they won't harm us, but still, it's not really what you want to hear in the dark. It was one thing coming across a bunch of the walking dead on our excursions to fetch supplies from the mall, quite another to encounter them staggering into our camp. Saint thinks they must be attracted to the warmth of the fire, which creeps me out. I don't like to think of them as still human, as things that might have feelings or whatever.

Saint groans. 'I'm getting *so* sick of this crap.'

'Really, Saint? I never would have known, you only mention it every single day.'

'*Whatever*, Zombie Bait.'

I don't really blame her for whingeing. Being at one with nature is all very well, but it's not much fun waking up with a wolf spider inches away from your face. Not to mention the fact that we all stink – it doesn't matter how often we wash in the freshwater streams, the odour of wood smoke seems ingrained in our pores.

I shiver and shuffle deeper into my sleeping bag. We've been out here for weeks, and although summer is on its way the nights can still be chilly. We should really scrounge some tents from the mall, but there's no way we can risk going back there.

Another group moan floats towards us from the direction of the enclave. It's louder this time, and Saint and I share a glance. The Rotters are usually only this vocal when they sense there's going to be a relocation or a funeral – fresh meat to add to their numbers.

'What time do you think it is?' I ask.

'Dunno,' Saint says. 'Four, five a.m., maybe?'

I wriggle out of my sleeping bag, check my boots for scorpions and pull them on.

'Where are you going? You've already done lookout duty.'

'Yeah, I know. Can't sleep.'

Ginger nods knowingly at Saint.

'It's not like that, Ginger,' I snap at him. 'I'm just going to see if Ash needs anything.'

'Yeah, like some *lurrrrve*,' Ginger says.

'Ha ha, guys. We're just friends. How many more times?'

Saint stretches her arms behind her head and yawns. 'You might be fooling yourself, Zombie Bait, but you're not fooling us.'

'What's that supposed to mean?'

'Hurry up and get it on already. There's only so much lovesick *Twilight* crap me and Ginger can stand.' She holds out a hand and Ginger slaps her palm.

'Whatever. Give me your torch, Ginger.'

He leans forward and I snatch it out of his hand. 'Come on, Lele, don't be like that,' he says.

Giving them both the finger I start pushing my way through the fynbos and head towards the lookout point. I hate it when they tease me about Ash. It's a seriously sore point and they know it.

Early-morning light bathes everything in a bluish glow, and

I don't actually need the torch's beam to light my way. The top of Table Mountain appears in front of me and the occasional light from the enclave below winks through gaps in the trees. A porcupine snuffles out from behind a bush and bumbles across the path.

Ash is leaning against the large boulder that provides the best vantage point up here, and for a second I'm able to watch him without him being aware of me. It looks like he's reading something by torchlight. But that's nothing new. He's always reading.

I take a step forward and a branch cracks under my boot. He whirls around, shoving something into his pocket.

'Sorry! It's only me ... What's that?'

The shadow cast by the rock hides the expression on his face. 'Nothing. Why aren't you sleeping?' He sounds exhausted.

'Another Rotter came into camp. Woke me up.' In fact, it's been ages since I had a good night's shut-eye. *Thanks, guilty conscience.*

He sighs and runs a hand through his hair. It's growing long, and flops over his forehead. I can't remember the last time he smiled at me. Or smiled at all. Hester's death took its toll on all of us, but it hit Ash the hardest. She'd been a mother figure to every one of us, but he'd known her since he was seven years old, and they'd had a bond that the rest of us didn't – and couldn't – share.

I climb up onto the boulder and perch next to him. From this distance it's easy to pretend that the enclave is a peaceful place, all its citizens happy and equal. I swing round and let my legs dangle. It's a long way down, but we chose this spot on purpose. Saint had wanted us to camp out on the beach at Blouberg, but an oil tanker had run aground there, a decade's worth of pollution still clogging up the sand. And none of us wanted to find refuge in the crumbling, overgrown buildings that used to make up Cape Town's metropolis. The blackened shells of the hotels and convention centre are way too spooky and dangerous.

So we'd set up camp on a koppie with a good view of the enclave, and far enough away from the mall to feel safe. Looking down at the lights makes me feel closer to Jobe, and I know Ash feels the same way about his own twin, Sasha.

'You think they're okay?' I ask.

'Who?'

'Jobe and Sasha.'

'They have to be.'

Sometimes I think that Jobe and I share some kind of mental twin connection, but I know it's only wishful thinking. It sucks not being able to see him whenever I want to, but Ash and Saint insist that we should give it some time before we dare return to the enclave.

'So how will we know?' I ask.

'Know what?'

'When it's safe to go back?'

He shrugs. 'I don't know, Lele.'

'But we can't stay out here forever –'

He turns on me. 'I *said* I don't know. What more do you want from me?'

'Sheesh, sorry, okay . . . '

He scrubs a hand over his face. 'Yeah. Me too. I didn't mean to snap at you.'

I'm reluctant to leave, but it's pretty clear I'm not wanted here. Ash has never been one to witter on about kak – that's Ginger's forte – but since the fire at the mall an awkwardness has crept in between us. And after what happened with Thabo, I'm not sure he even thinks of me in that way any more. If he ever did.

The worst of it is that it's partly my fault. Ash isn't an idiot, and I reckon he knows I'm keeping something from him.

And he's right.

I *am* keeping something from him. I'm keeping something from all of them.

The secret burns inside me, but I've left it so long, *too* long, and I don't know how to even start to tell them what I know.

Ash suddenly reaches over and grips my arm. 'Did you hear that?'

'What?'

'Listen!'

All I can hear are the moans of the Rotters and the hoot of an eagle owl. Then I catch it – a faint rumbling sound. A wagon? This early?

'You think it's Guardians, Ash? They don't usually –'

But my words are cut off as a piercing scream carries towards us. A human scream.

Oh *crap*.

'Come on!' Ash holds out a hand to help me down – I don't need it, but take it anyway – and together we hare through the bushes, back to camp.

Ginger and Saint are booted up and waiting for us. Saint has tied a bandanna over her wild mop of hair and is attaching spiky metal weights to the chains wrapped around her wrists; Ginger is hefting the axe he's been using since he lost his chainsaw. I can barely lift it, but it looks like a toy in his hands. He swings it once around his head. 'Sounds like it's time to party!' He grins.

Another scream cuts through the bush.

'Save your breath, Ginger,' Ash says, sliding his panga out of the holster on his back. 'Sounds like you're going to need it.'

———

'This isn't a relocation,' Saint says. 'What do they think they're doing?'

We're hiding behind a thatch of wattle trees, twenty metres from the enclave fence, and the scene in front of us is made even more chilling by the shadows the Port Jacksons are casting around the clearing.

An elderly man, a woman about the same age as Dad and a teenage boy are cowering on top of the roof of a high, covered wagon. The family – if it is a family and not just a random bunch of escapees – are clustered in a tight, terrified bunch. There's no sign of the horse – it must have panicked and broken free of its harness. And who could blame it? There are at least twenty Rotters surrounding the wagon, bashing their bodies against the cart's sides and rocking it dangerously. And more are heading towards it, moving with that eerie speed they always find when they get the scent of blood in their manky nostrils.

Ash peers around us. 'See any Hatchlings?'

'Doesn't look like it, mate,' Ginger replies. 'We'd know about it if there were.'

'Okay, guys,' Ash says. 'Ginger, you go first – cut a path through to them. Lele, you hang back, check for Hatchlings and catch the stragglers. Saint, you're with me. Let's go!'

Ginger doesn't need asking twice. Raising his axe above his head he runs towards the pack. 'Come and get it, zombie freaks!' he yells as he swipes his axe in a clean arc, and heads tumble and bounce over the fynbos. But the Rotters aren't even slightly deterred. They seem intent on only one thing – tipping over the wagon.

I watch as Saint shakes out her wrists and throws her arms forward, her chains rocking through the air and wrapping around the necks of the two Rotters closest to her, Ash slices through their necks with his panga, and another two bite the dust. Scanning the bushes for Hatchlings, I grip the throwing stars Hester gave me before she died. My heart rate speeds up, the familiar flood of adrenalin coursing through my veins. I know the Rotters won't attack us, but where there's a wagon there are often Hatchlings around, and our immunity against Rotter attack doesn't extend to the newly zombiefied. It takes days for their senses to dull.

The woman spots us first. 'Help us!' she screams.

'Up here!' the man yells. 'Help! Nceda!'

'That's what we're here for, mate!' Ginger calls to them, dispatching another Rotter. This one's head rolls towards me and I kick it away, trying not to look at the spaghetti tendrils twitching and curling out of its severed neck.

One of the Rotters has managed to find a foothold on the wheel of the wagon, its arms flailing up at the woman and the teenager. I pick out a throwing star, weigh it in my hand and skim it towards the wagon. My aim is true and it hits the sweet spot at the back of the thing's neck. It jerks forward, twitches, and then slumps to the ground.

Ginger is making short work of the Rotters with his axe and Saint and Ash are working together seamlessly, easily polishing off two particularly ripe specimens, but even as they do the moans of another pack float towards us. They sound close. 'Lele!' Ash shouts. 'Get them down from there!'

'I'm on it!' Ducking to avoid Ginger's flailing axe, I race towards the wagon, jump up onto the wheel and hold my hand out to the woman. 'Come on!'

'No! The dead ones will get us!'

'You can't stay up there!'

Another moan echoes through the bushes. She glances around her and the elderly man nods. 'Take Thokozani first!' she says to me.

Ignoring my hand the teenager slides his legs over the edge and then tumbles onto the ground. The elderly man follows. He is way more athletic than he looks, and before I can stop him he picks up a large branch and drops to a crouch, waving it in front of him. 'Get the others away!' he shouts.

'Get back,' I yell as the woman finally takes my hand. 'We can handle it!'

Ignoring me, the old man runs over to where Ginger, Saint and Ash are finishing off the stragglers. We don't have time for this – we have to get them all as far away from here as possible before the next lot catch their scent. Luckily Ginger notices the old man, grabs him around the waist and drags him out of the danger zone before the last of the Rotters can get to him – though for some reason they seem to be more intent on getting to the woman and the boy. 'Blimey, you were lucky, mate,' Ginger says to the old man as Ash and Saint dispatch the last two Rotters. 'You shouldn't have done that.'

'I thought I would distract them. Give the others time to get away.'

'Yeah, well, all's well that ends well.'

The boy shudders, eyes glassy with shock. Ginger smiles down at him. 'Don't worry, we'll look after you.'

Ash wipes the blade of his panga on the grass. 'That was close.'

'You're telling me,' Saint says. 'I think that's the lot –'

But she's spoken too soon.

There's the *whip-crack* of branches breaking, and all of us freeze. I pull out another throwing star, weigh it in my hand, and only just manage to stop myself from skimming it as a herd of springbok leap into the clearing. They scatter in every direction, a youngster darting straight for us in its panicked state. It's so close I can make out the whites of its eyes – then it doubles back and shoots off through the trees.

'Not good,' Ash says. 'Something's spooked them.'

The trees shake as if there's a gale blowing through them, and a shadowy mass lurches towards us. It's impossible to tell exactly how many there are, but there have to be at least ten.

'Get them out of here!' Ash yells as the woman screams, grabs the boy's hand and starts scrabbling towards the fence.

Our only choice is to try and outrun them and though most look to be thoroughly rotted and decrepit I know from experience that they can move fast when they want to, and they clearly want to.

'I'll catch the first wave!' Ash calls. 'Ginger! You –'

'Huh?' Ginger pauses mid axe-swing. 'What are they doing?'

The pack has stopped metres from where we're standing. The one closest to us throws its head back and moans. It's missing its jaw bone, so the sound isn't as amplified as it normally is, but the others soon follow suit. Then, moving almost as one, they start backing up, bumping into each other as if they're a crowd of shoppers who've just got wind that there's a bomb in the supermarket.

'What are they *doing*?' Saint says.

But there can be only one explanation.

'There must be a Guardian around here somewhere,' Ash says, voicing what all of us are thinking.

'I don't get it,' Saint says as we scan the trees and fynbos – there is no sign of anyone, but there are plenty of places to hide in the gloom. 'If it *is* a Guardian, why would it help us?'

'Maybe there's another explanation,' Ginger says.

'Like what?'

'I dunno. A funeral or relocation going on somewhere else or summut.'

'Get real,' Saint snaps. 'This early?'

Ginger drops his eyes, clearly hurt.

'Sorry,' Saint says. 'It's just … you know. I thought it might be Ripley.'

'It's cool, Saint,' he says. 'I was looking for her, too.'

Ash slides his panga back into the holster on his back. 'Whatever the reason, let's get the hell away from here.'

'Where should we take them, Ash?' Ginger asks.

'Where do you think?' he says. 'There's only one option.'

Our secret entrance into the enclave is still a good few kilometres away and there's no way we'll be able to keep up the pace Ash has set all the way there. As the adrenalin ebbs out of my system the effects of too many sleepless nights start creeping up on me, and a stitch gnaws at my side. I glance back at the others. The teenager and the elderly man refused any help, but behind them I see Saint clutching the woman's arm, steering her around the obstacles in our way.

'Guys!' Saint calls. 'Let's stop for a quick breather.'

'You think we should?' Ash asks.

'They're not following.'

Ash gazes back the way we came. The moans sound far behind us now. And we can easily deal with any stragglers that approach. 'Five minutes.'

The elderly man sinks to his knees, struggling to regain his breath.

'Here,' Ginger says, passing him his thermos. 'Just water I'm afraid, mate.'

The man takes a huge gulp. 'Siyabonga. Thank you.' He looks at each of us in turn. Apart from gratitude there's something else in his expression: fear. And it's mirrored in the woman's eyes.

'Don't worry,' Saint says. 'We're not going to harm you.'

'But why is it that the dead ones do not attack you?'

Ginger grins. 'It's like our special talent, innit?'

'I do not understand.'

'Well, see, we're not really sure why they don't go for us, mate. But we think it's got something to do with the fact that Ash and Lele have twins – Saint's got one too but we don't know where he is – and like –'

Saint nudges him. 'TMI,' she hisses.

Ash holds up his hand. 'Thank you, Ginger.' I'm suddenly reminded of Hester. It's the same kind of affectionate, slightly exasperated tone of voice she always used with him. 'Your turn,' Ash says to the man. 'Why did you leave the enclave? You must have known the dead would attack, that it would be dangerous.' He points to the spine-shaped amulets around their necks. 'You're believers, aren't you? Resurrectionists?'

The woman drops her head. She looks almost ashamed. 'We played along, said that we were. It's just … ' She hunches into herself, looking like she's about to start crying. 'My husband was relocated.'

Ash shoots me a significant look. Both of us know that the odds are good her husband is out here somewhere, though no longer recognisable as the man she once knew.

'Why was he relocated?' Ash asks. 'What did he do?'

'Nothing! All he did was refuse to join one of the Resurrectionist marches – I was sick, and he needed to tend our stall – and then they came in the night and took him away from us.'

'I'm sorry,' Saint says.

The woman nods. She still looks distraught but no tears are actually rolling down her cheeks.

'But where were you going to go?'

'We have some family in the agricultural enclaves. We were going to go there.'

'It's just as bad there,' I say.

'You have been there?' the man asks.

I nod. After what happened at the mall I'd been hoping we could hide out in the Agriculturals – my old home – but the Resurrectionists were one step ahead of us, already threatening to relocate the farmers and citizens who didn't buy into their beliefs.

'And it is not just that,' the woman says. 'Thokozani will be sixteen soon.'

Without further explanation she hands me a crumpled piece of paper. I smooth it out so that we can all read it.

RESURRECTIONIST BULLETIN
(Number 608)

Spreading the Good News!

A message from your Cape Town Enclave Embassy CEO,
Comrade Vuyo Nkosi.

Greetings Comrades,

What a happy day this is for all of us! It is nearly eleven years since our saviours, the Guardians, came among us and gave us a new start in life, and what happiness and contentment they have brought to us all!

As you now know, the Guardians have blessed certain of our youth with a supreme honour – the honour of joining their ranks. Yes, Brothers and Sisters, several favoured teenagers have become Guardians! I know some of you are ambivalent about this development, but let me assure you, the chosen youth are far happier in their new, exalted state of being! And we hope that more will soon be added to their ranks. What an honour to have our own flesh and blood watching over us! And as a sign of their good faith and their boundless generosity, the Guardians have decreed that all who worship them will be provided with electricity, fresh running water and food for the stomach and the soul!

And let us treat our youth with love, respect and reverence, for they are tomorrow's Guardians!

Remember, if you are not with us, you are against us! REPORT THOSE WHO COME AMONG US SOWING SEEDS OF UNREST.

'Dammit,' Ash says.

'They're buying it,' Saint says. 'They're really just accepting it. Why am I not more surprised?'

Even Ginger looks gutted.

After our showdown at the mall we knew that the Guardians would be forced to reveal exactly what it was they'd been doing to the selected teenagers they'd been transporting into the Deadlands. We'd hoped this would fuel an uprising and that even the Resurrectionists would find this too much to swallow, but it looks like the opposite has happened.

'What can we do?' the woman asks. 'I will die before I let them take Thokozani and turn him into one of those ... demons.'

'Your only choice is to go back into the enclave,' Ash says. 'And hide out.'

'Can't we stay with you?' Thokozani says to Ginger.

'Sorry, mate,' Ginger says. 'But the Rotters won't have that. They'll be after you before you can say "you've got red on you."' (Ginger's *Shaun of the Dead* movie reference falls flat – he's always forgetting that unlike him the majority of citizens haven't had access to DVDs since the War.) 'But don't worry, the Anti-Zombians will help you out, mate. They'll take you underground, make sure the Ressers don't get their sweaty hands on you.'

'But we've heard stories about the ANZ,' the old man says. 'They are not to be trusted. They are violent, barbaric.'

'Yeah. But you've heard stories about the ANZ from the Ressers, right?' Ginger grins. 'You don't want to believe that load of old rubbish.'

'But won't the guards find us?'

'You'd be surprised how many places there are to hide, mate.'

'No ways, Ash,' Saint says. 'You're not going by yourself. It's too dangerous. You need us. We have no idea if they're going to be on the lookout for us or not.'

Ash and Saint have been arguing for the last five minutes, and Ginger and I have decided to let them get on with it.

Ash pulls the Resurrectionist robes we use as disguises out of their storage bag. Gross. After weeks of being hidden under a bush next to out secret entrance they stink of mildew. 'There aren't enough robes for all of us to go. The family will have to wear them in case the guards have their descriptions. That leaves one over.'

'So why you?'

Ash doesn't have an answer for that.

The family is huddled next to the fence, the woman clearly on edge, shifting uneasily at the slightest sound, the elderly man sitting cross-legged, his breathing ragged and his face slack from exhaustion. Only Thokozani looks like he's getting over the ordeal. He's scraping a stick through the earth and his eyes have lost their shell-shocked glaze.

25

'Oh, come on, Ash,' Ginger says. 'What's the worst that's going to happen? Say we do run into trouble, they'll only relocate us, right? Big deal. We *live* out in the Deadlands. And in any case we need to get supplies. We're totally out of biltong.'

'And what if they decide we'll make perfect Guardians?'

'No chance, mate. Anyway, aren't we all past the due date?'

'Huh?' Saint says.

'We're too old. They can't turn us into them things if we're no longer teenagers.'

'How do you know you're too old?' Saint says. 'You don't even know how old you are, exactly.'

'I'm nineteen. No, hang on ... ' He counts on his fingers. 'Twenty.' He pauses. 'I think. Eighteen's the cut-off, isn't it?'

'We don't know that for sure, Ginger,' Ash says. 'And besides, Lele's seventeen.'

I don't comment, but I can feel my face growing hot. I know more about becoming a Guardian than they're aware of. And I'm pretty sure that age is not a factor – at least for us.

'Come on, mate,' Ginger says. 'We'll be ultra careful. Pretty please?'

Ash sighs. 'Okay, but you'll have to keep your heads down.'

'Awesome!' Ginger says, giving me a high five.

'And you'll have to wear the spare robe, Ginger,' Saint says.

'Aw, why me?'

I nudge him in the ribs. Ash is clearly at the end of his tether, and could easily change his mind. And besides, Saint's right about Ginger. If they are on the lookout for us there's no way he can get away with entering the enclave without a disguise. With his uncommon height and wild red hair he's not exactly forgettable.

Ash hands three of the robes to the family, and passes the last one to Ginger, who pulls it over his head. 'I look like a giant

Ewok.'

'What's an Ewok?' Thokozani asks.

'Don't worry about it,' Saint says, rolling her eyes in Ginger's direction. 'He's just a freak.'

'Am not!'

'Are so!'

'Guys!' Ash says. 'Come on. Let's be serious.' He places his panga against the fence. 'You're going to have to leave your axe behind, Ginger.'

'But she's my baby.'

'How many axe-wielding Resurrectionists do you know?'

'Yeah, all right, fair play.'

Ash turns to the family. The woman is holding the teenager's hand so tightly her knuckles are white. 'Just keep quiet and follow me. And if anything happens, let me do the talking.'

Ginger claps Thokozani on the back, almost sending him flying. 'Don't worry, mate. You're in good hands.'

Ash hauls up the dead tree trunk that covers the secret entrance to our old home and climbs down into the tunnel, disappearing into darkness.

———————

'Where's all our stuff?' Ginger says as the light of his torch dances over the earthen walls. Our underground lair has been gutted. The kitchen, training room and lounge are empty of furniture – even the clunky old fridge, the generator and the ancient sink are missing. 'Oh no, man. This sucks. Where are my DVDs? And my comics?'

'They even took Hester's couch,' Saint says. 'Bastards.'

The place smells musty and unused – what was once a welcoming sanctuary now feels like a cold, oppressive hole.

'We should get out of here,' Ash says. 'And fast.' He jogs over to the hatchway that opens out into the enclave. 'If I say run,' he adds, turning back to us, 'then don't ask questions, okay?'

'You think the guards could be waiting for us?' I ask.

Ash doesn't answer. It was a stupid question anyway. Of course they could be waiting for us.

Ash pulls himself up, and I keep my eyes focused on the exit, every muscle tense. I'm so on edge that I can hear my blood pounding in my ears.

'Okay!' he calls after what seems like an eternity, his voice muffled.

Saint ushers the family through first, Ginger following on behind. We climb up and out into the alleyway. The wood-and-corrugated-iron shacks around the exit look exactly the same as I remember, and apart from a field mouse, which squeaks angrily at us and scurries to hide under a deflated tyre, the area is deserted.

Ash shoves a hand though his hair. 'Look, I reckon we should split up. You guys get the supplies, and I'll take the family to Lungi.'

'Shouldn't we all go?' Saint asks.

'No, Ash is right,' Ginger says. 'It's safer if we split up.' It's obvious he's already imagining stuffing biltong into his face.

Ash nods and then turns to lead the three robed figures out into the light. Thokozani and the woman follow him almost at once, but the old man hesitates. He pulls the hood from his head and turns to look at us. 'Thank you,' he says. 'You have saved our lives.'

'Don't thank us,' Saint mutters under her breath. 'You're not out of the woods yet, grandpa.'

———————

Ash needn't have worried. No one gives us any hassle as we head towards the marketplace – the stallholders are only just beginning to set out their wares, and the muddy alleyways and narrow winding streets are still relatively quiet. After weeks of camping out in the Deadlands, with just the Mall Rats for company, it's freaky to be around other people, and I've forgotten how much the enclave stinks. As we head deeper into the market I'm hit with the stench of sewage, damp washing, boiled chicken's feet and curried lambs' tails.

'It feels different, innit?' Ginger says.

'What do you mean?' Saint asks.

He shrugs. 'Last time we were here it felt way more ... I dunno, happier, more relaxed.'

'It's still very early, Ginger,' Saint says, but I can tell that she agrees with him. And he's right. There *is* something subdued about the atmosphere. People seem to be keeping more to themselves, and several drop their heads as we pass as if they're reluctant to catch our eyes.

'You cool to get the veggies, Ginger?' Saint asks. 'Lele and I will get the rest.'

'Aye aye, captain.'

'And don't spend all the credits on junk food,' Saint says. 'No biltong.'

'Aw, what?'

'Seriously, Ginger. We're low on funds, you know that.'

'You're not the boss of me,' he says, but he grins at Saint all the same before moving towards a row of vegetable stalls.

'Let's go,' Saint says, shouldering her rucksack and striding off.

It's always difficult to read Saint's moods – she has the same talent for hiding her feelings as Ash – but I suspect she's still dwelling on the Rotters' peculiar behaviour out in the

Deadlands. Something (or someone) either spooked them or deflected them away from their goal, but I don't know how to approach the subject without riling her. She never talks about Ripley, her old girlfriend. She's made it clear that *that* subject is seriously out of bounds. 'You okay?' I ask.

'Yeah. Why wouldn't I be?'

'Just asking.'

I hang back. We're a few streets away from Mandela House. It would only take a minute to slip away and catch a glimpse of Jobe.

'I tell you what, Saint. How about you get the supplies and I'll check out the area, see what's brewing?'

Turning, she puts a hand on her hip and looks me up and down. 'You think I'm stupid? I know where you want to go, Zombie Bait, and it's not going to happen.'

'I'll be really quick, okay? C'mon, he's my brother. I'll be careful.'

'Yeah, right.'

'C'mon, Saint. I'll do your washing for a week.'

'Seriously, Lele, if Ash finds out ... '

'He won't. I won't get too close or anything.'

She sighs. 'Look, it's your call, but as far as Ash is concerned, I didn't see you sneak off, 'kay?'

'Saint, you're a –'

She rolls her eyes. 'Yeah, yeah. I know, I know. A saint.'

I slip away before she can change her mind.

———

Just great.

There are two Resurrectionist guards lounging next to the fence on the far right-hand side of Mandela House. Fortunately they don't look like they're on high alert – one appears to be dozing, the other is picking his nose. Still, there's no way I can risk getting any closer. I bend down and pretend to search in my backpack, and when a rickshaw bumps to a stop, its driver disappearing into the tenement opposite, I sneak behind it and use it as cover.

Mandela House looks exactly the same: a comforting building with a wrap-around porch. One of the few original structures that survived the fires that swept through the city during the War, it looks way more substantial than the shacks and hastily built breeze-block houses that surround it. I'm disappointed that the sun-bleached lawn is deserted – it would've been cool to find the children playing outside – but just the sight of it makes me feel more at ease, more connected to my brother.

Something touches my leg, making me jump. I look down to find a cat snaking its way around my boots.

'Chinwag!' She looks up at me and mews. Jobe's kitten is now fully grown, and it's clear from her size and gleaming condition that she doesn't go hungry. I pick her up and bury my face in her fur. 'Hey girl,' I whisper to her. She was never out of Jobe's sight when she was a kitten.

'Thought I'd find you here,' a voice says close to my ear, making me jump.

'Ash!'

'I told you this wasn't a good idea.'

'Look who's talking.' I catch a whiff of a familiar odour wafting off his clothes. 'Have you been smoking? Saint will kill you!'

'Then don't tell her.' He reaches over to stroke Chinwag's back, and for a second his fingers touch my arm. For the first time in forever he smiles at me, and blood rushes to my cheeks. *Pathetic*.

'How's that family doing?' I ask, trying unsuccessfully to hide my burning face in Chinwag's fur.

'Still freaked,' Ash says as the cat wriggles out of my grasp and onto the ground. 'But Lungi will sort them out.'

'Lungi was cool with you just showing up?'

'She wasn't there. I left them with Jean-Paul. He'll get a message to her.' He doesn't speak for several seconds. 'It's bad, Lele. The ANZ is overrun with refugees. Jean-Paul says that they're setting up safe houses all over the city.'

'Who would have thought you'd be on their side?' I say.

'Whose side?'

'The ANZ's. You used to say that they were nothing but terrorists making everything worse.'

'Things change, Lele.'

I look up at him, struck as always by his eyes – one grey, the other so dark it's almost black. And I can't help asking myself, would I still have feelings for him if he wasn't so hot? I mean, since Hester's death he's hardly been the most approachable guy in the world.

We watch as Chinwag sashays across the street, leaps over the fence and wanders into the front garden of Mandela House.

The door opens and a woman's laugh floats towards us.

Ash grips my arm with such force it hurts. 'Look!'

Naomi, the children's carer, steps out onto the porch. She's lost weight since the last time I saw her, and I can't be sure from here but it looks as if she's glaring in the guards' direction. She turns to motion behind her, and Ash drops his hand from my arm. Several children shuffle out of the front door, and although they're all dressed identically in brown woollen smocks I spot Jobe immediately.

'How cool is that?' Ash whispers.

Jobe looks exactly the same as the last time I saw him – he hasn't grown an inch. I watch him make his way towards the front steps with a mix of emotions. Whatever the Guardians did to him (did to *us*) at the beginning of the War, it's still casting its spell over him, trapping him inside his seven-year-old body.

Jobe holds out a hand and a small girl takes it.

'Sasha,' Ash breathes.

The pair stands still at the top of the steps, and for an instant I'm almost positive that they're looking straight at us. They bow their heads together, and although I know that Jobe isn't capable of conversation – he hasn't spoken more than a single word since the War – I try and imagine that they're sharing some form of communication. Then the moment is broken and, taking each step carefully, they trundle towards the sandpit.

'I wish we could talk to them.'

'Yeah. So do I, Lele.'

The nose-picking guard stands up and stretches.

'Come on,' Ash says. 'We'd better get out of here.'

'A few more minutes?'

'We can't. It's too risky.'

'But –'

'Come on.'

It's a wrench to leave them, but Ash is right.

We walk in silence back to the market. The streets are filling up as more and more traders set up their stalls and set out their wares, but although it's busier, with shoppers haggling and rickshaws weaving their way through the alleyways, I'm struck again by the subdued atmosphere. There's no music, laughter or catcalling, and the stallholders aren't lobbing insults at each other like they used to do.

'Typical,' Ash says, casting around for any sign of Ginger and Saint. 'Where are they?'

'Chill out. They'll be around here somewhere. Just look for the biltong stall.'

There's a sudden burst of laughter from behind us. Two

teenage boys and a girl are swaggering through the market. They're dressed in clothes from before the War, and good ones at that – the kind of kick-ass gear we used to bring back from the mall to sell. I look down at my threadbare jeans and old army boots and can't help but feel a spike of envy. One of the boys, a hefty kid with his hair styled in cornrows is wearing the same kind of low-top Converse sneakers Thabo used to favour; the other boy, a well-built white guy with hectic acne, has a denim jacket slung around his waist. And Saint would kill for the girl's red skinny jeans.

Cornrows pauses at a market stall. It's one of the smaller ones, basically just an upturned wooden packing crate displaying a couple of apples, a few lemons and some mealies. He picks up one of the apples, throws it into the air and catches it. 'How much?' he says to the woman behind the stall.

She drops her head. 'One credit,' she mumbles.

'One credit?' Cornrows looks over to his friends, who nudge each other and snigger. He drops the apple on the floor and crushes it under his boot. 'How about now, mama?'

The woman winces and shakes her head. 'Please, I have to feed my children, I –'

'Oh boo hoo,' Cornrows says, and the girl shrieks with laughter.

I glance around to see if anyone's going to intervene, but the other stallholders are all pretending to be busy and the shoppers lower their heads and scurry past.

I make a move to approach, but Ash grabs my arm. 'Check,' he says nodding to his left. A couple of guards wearing Resurrectionist robes wander past. They nod at the teenagers, but do nothing to help the woman.

'Unbelievable!' I whisper to Ash.

'You know,' Cornrows says. 'I'm still hungry.' He grabs

another apple and drop-kicks it towards his friends. The girl smacks it with the side of her foot and lobs it into an overturned metal drum. 'Goal!' she screeches.

'Please!' the stallholder begs.

'We can't just let this happen, Ash.'

'We've got no choice,' he hisses. 'We can't risk it.'

'Why not?' I nod towards the two guards who are disappearing around the side of the large amulet stall at the end of the row. 'They've gone.'

'Yeah. But they could be back at any time.'

Cornrows and Denim Jacket edge nearer to the woman. She shrinks back, and even from here, several metres away, I can see tears glistening in her eyes. The words explode out of my mouth before I can stop them. 'Hey! Assholes!'

Cornrows and Denim Jacket literally do a double take. 'You talking to us?'

'Yeah.' I move to approach them, but Ash holds me back.

'Lele, *no.*'

I pull my arm out of his grip. All I can see is the stallholder's traumatised face. There's no way I can stand back and let this happen, guards or no guards. I stride towards the stall.

'Heita, girl,' Cornrows says. 'Don't I know you?'

I shrug. He doesn't look familiar, but he could well be one of the kids from my short time at Malema High – let's face it, I only had eyes for Thabo back then.

'Nice hair, sister,' the girl sneers at me.

'Nice face,' I snap back at her, staring her down, 'but it won't be for much longer if you don't stop what you're doing.'

'Ooooh,' Cornrows says, leaving the stallholder and approaching me. 'Chutzpah. I like that in a chick.' He picks up a mealie and chucks it into the air.

'You need to pay for that,' I say.

The woman shakes her head at me. 'Don't worry, sisi. It's fine. Everything's fine.'

'No it isn't,' I say, directing this at Cornrows.

'Don't you know the rules, girl?' he says to me.

'What rules are those? Whoever is the biggest asshole wins?'

'Oh *snap*!' Denim Jacket says, and the girl shoots daggers at him.

Cornrows smirks at me. 'You know, if you were wearing something half-decent, you'd be pretty hot.'

I smile sweetly. 'Thank you. If you had a different face, you'd be pretty hot, too.' My anger is under control now and all I feel is a cold wash of calm. 'Now. Last chance. Pay for what you have stolen or you'll be sorry.'

'You can make me sorry any time, baby.' Cornrows reaches over to stroke my cheek.

'If you insist,' I say, stepping forward and elbowing him in the solar plexus. He drops to his knees with an 'oof', and then crumples into the mud, clutching his stomach.

'Bitch!' the girl shrieks, lashing out with her fist. I catch it, bend her wrist back and force her onto her knees. 'Ow! Let me go!'

'Not until you've paid for what you've stolen!'

She spits at me, but her aim is crap and it lands on the back of Cornrows's head.

An arm snakes around my throat. I haven't been paying attention to Denim Jacket and he's snuck around behind me. 'You're mine now, girly,' he hisses.

Twisting her hand out of my grip the girl gets to her feet. 'Now you'll be sorry,' she says. But it's not the first time I've been in this position and as she draws back her fist I kick up with my legs and whack her in the stomach.

Squealing like a trapped warthog she drops to the ground.

Denim Jacket tightens his grip.

'Let her go,' Ash says.

'It's under control,' I say, fighting for breath.

'Make me,' Denim Jacket says, but his voice is wavering.

'If you insist.'

There's the sound of a fist hitting flesh, a gasp of pain and then the hold around my neck loosens and I'm free. I look down to see that Denim Jacket has joined his friends in the mud.

'Thanks,' I say to Ash, rubbing my throat.

'What the hell am I going to do with you, Lele?'

I'm about to say that I've got a few ideas, when Cornrows gets to his feet and kicks out wildly. Instead of stepping back to avoid being booted, Ash moves forward, blocks the swipe, then grasps Cornrows's lower leg, pulls it towards him and abruptly lets it go. Unbalanced, Cornrows falls heavily on his tail bone.

I place a boot on his stomach. 'Now,' I say. 'Apologise to the nice lady and hand over the credits.'

'Really, it's fine,' the stallholder says. 'I don't want any trouble.'

I reach down, dig in Cornrows's pockets and haul out his wallet. 'Hey!' he whines. 'That's mine.'

'Shut up,' Ash says.

I pull out several coins, chuck the wallet in the mud and hand the money to the stallholder. 'This should cover it.'

'Really, sisi, it's fine.'

'It's not fine. They were stealing from you.'

She shakes her head and looks down at her feet. I glance around. Thankfully there's no sign of the guards, but the other stallholders are still busily ignoring the scene.

'Let's go, Lele,' Ash says and I let him take my arm and draw me away.

'You'll be sorry!' the girl screeches after us.

We increase our pace and cut through into the parallel aisle.

'Sorry, Ash. I guess I just lost it.' I'm expecting him to be furious, but it actually looks like he's doing his best not to smile.

'We'd better get out of here sharpish.' He scans the stalls. 'Where the hell are they?'

'Check!' I catch sight of Ginger's hooded head looming over the crowd. He's at least five inches taller than anyone in the vicinity.

'About time,' Ash says.

Saint and Ginger are standing next to a stall selling stuffed vegetables. Ginger's tucking into a huge cabbage, nuts and mealie kernels peppering his face. Saint looks like she's struggling not to throw up.

'You get what we need?' Ash asks her.

Saint nudges the rucksack at her feet with her boot. 'Course.' She looks down at my mud-caked boots and peers closely at me. 'What have you two been up to?'

'Nothing,' Ash says.

'Ooooh, have you two been having a lover's tiff?' Ginger says, chucking the rest of the cabbage head in a dumpster.

'Leave it, Ginger,' I say to him. 'Seriously.'

'Let's get out of here,' Ash says. 'You guys ready?'

'Born ready,' Ginger says.

We take a circular route towards the fence, slipping through alleyways at random.

'Come on, Zombie Bait, what's going on?' Saint asks. 'You look like you've been in a fight.'

'Had a run-in with some wannabe Guardians.'

Saint raises an eyebrow. 'Was it fun?'

'You could say that. It's freaking me out though, Saint. How everyone has just accepted that for years the Guardians have been secretly turning their kids into monsters. Now they know the truth they just seem to be going along with it.'

Saint snorts. 'Why does that surprise you, Zombie Bait? Why is that any different to the other crap the Ressers have been spouting for years? Get with the programme; most people are basically sheep.' She sighs. 'Hey, you get to see your brother?'

'Yeah! It was so –'

'Shit,' Ash says, stopping dead in his tracks so abruptly that I almost bang into him.

'What?' Saint says. 'Oh shit!'

'Try and blend in,' Ash hisses.

A group of ten or so guards is marching through the alleyway towards us. Crap. My run-in with the teenagers might have screwed us all. I peer back the way we came, but there's another, albeit smaller, bunch of guards, approaching from that direction. They appear to be checking the stallholder's credentials, so if we act natural we should be cool. Saint and I immediately start admiring the amulets on a nearby stall, and Ash slings his arm around my shoulders, pretending to be a bored boyfriend.

'Howzit,' the seller says to Saint. 'You want to try them on? I made them myself.'

'Hey! You! Comrade!' a man's voice shouts behind us.

Ash drops his arm. Trying not to make it too obvious I peer over my shoulder. Two guards are standing in front of Ginger.

'Take off your hood,' one of them says to him. 'You know the rules. Heads must be uncovered at all times.'

They must have finally figured out that the robes they all stupidly wear make convenient disguises. It took them long enough, but it's bad news for us.

Out of the corner of my eye I see Ash stiffen. I stick my hand in my jacket pocket and curl my fingers around my throwing stars.

'But I'm a Resurrectionist!' Ginger is saying. 'Doing my

bit to worship ... you know ... the Guardians and Rotters and that.' Just great. Ginger may be a movie fundi, but his acting chops need serious work. 'And ... hey! That's it. I'm a teenager. Don't I get special treatment and stuff?'

The guards look at each other and shake their heads. I don't like the way they're checking us out. They're giving me and Ash special attention – the kids we dealt with must have squealed.

'You think we can take them?' Saint murmurs to me, eyeing a huge guy with thinning brown hair. 'Mine's the one on the left.'

'Name?' a guard with messy dreadlocks barks at Ginger.

'David,' Ginger says, ramping up his English accent. 'David Beckham. But my friends call me Becks.'

'Think you're funny, do you?' Dreads says.

'Yeah, I do actually.'

The guard places a hand on Ginger's chest and shoves him backwards. Ginger stumbles slightly, but he's way too big to push around. The guard reaches for the club slung in his belt.

'Hey!' Saint yells. 'Leave him alone! We haven't done anything.'

As if drawn by invisible strings the shoppers around us melt away, leaving me, Saint, Ginger and Ash surrounded by guards.

'All of yous,' the balding guard says in a strong Afrikaans accent. 'Hands on your heads and surrender your weapons.'

'No,' Ash says.

'What was that?'

Ash takes a step forward. 'I said, *no.*'

'Well then,' the guard says, 'I'll be forced to make you.'

I catch a glimpse of something metallic in the guard's hand, and Ash backs up, arms in the air.

Oh double crap. It's a gun.

So the Guardians have relaxed their ban on weapons. Not

good for us. Not good at all.

Ginger opens his mouth to protest, but Ash looks at him meaningfully and chucks his bowie knife into the mud.

'Search them,' the balding guard says to a giant of a woman sporting several extra chins.

'Sorry, but you're not my type,' Saint says to her as she begins to pat her down roughly.

'Sies, man,' the guard says. 'What is this?' She's missed the chains concealed under Saint's jacket, but she's found the spiked weights attached to her belt.

'Fashion accessories,' Saint says with a straight face. 'They're all the rage.'

The large woman sucks her teeth, gestures for another hard-faced female guard to keep an eye on Saint, and moves on to me. I carefully palm the throwing stars, feeling the sharp metal digging into my skin, praying that she'll miss them. She takes her time dragging her hands over my torso, arms and thighs, but doesn't bother checking my hands.

'Let's move out,' the balding guy commands.

The woman grabs my left arm and pulls it behind my back; my shoulder muscles scream. 'That hurt, sisi?' she says in my ear. She sounds like she's smiling.

'No,' I lie.

Ash, Saint and Ginger are being similarly manhandled – Ginger getting the dubious honour of two guards, one on either side of him.

Passers-by give us a wide berth as we're herded through the market. I'll only have one shot at this and I need to get it right. I wait until the guard relaxes her grip – it's not easy dragging me along in this position – and we're almost opposite one of the sector's trademark winding alleyways. Then I dart forwards, pulling my arms free of my jacket.

'Huh?' the woman says, looking down stupidly at the empty jacket in her hands.

I don't hesitate. I hook my left leg under her right calf and, using the momentum of her weight, send her sprawling onto her back.

'No, Lele!' Ash yells as I turn to kick the guard closest to him. 'Just run!'

'But –'

'Go, Lele!' Saint screams.

The balding guard is raising the gun and I don't stop to think. I hare into the alleyway, ducking as a bullet thucks into the breeze-block wall next to me. I run as if my life depends on it (which it does – of course it does) and I don't look back.

SAINT

'Get in there, sisi.' The guard releases her grip on the back of my neck and shoves me forward into the gloom. I whirl around, but stop myself from kicking out just in time. I can tell by the smirk on her face that this is what she *wants* me to do – it will give her the perfect excuse to use the gun in her belt. She might not actually shoot me, but I wouldn't put it past her to whack me over the head with it. She's still covered in mud from when Lele floored her and I'm sure she'd happily revenge herself on me.

A male guard – one I don't remember seeing during the skirmish in the marketplace – stands in the doorway, almost blocking out the weak light floating in from the corridor outside. It's impossible to tell how large the cell is – the areas untouched by the small pool of light are nothing but blocks of inky blackness – but the smell of the place tells its own story. There's a vile stench coming from my left, most likely from a toilet bucket, but even that doesn't hide the reek of nervous sweat, the smell of fear that's bled into the cell's floors and walls. The parts of the Embassy I glimpsed as we were pulled through the bowels of the building looked elegant and comfortable. Not so this room. This *cell*. The saliva dries in my mouth. When the door clangs shut it will be pitch black in here.

'Hands up, sisi,' the fat female guard barks. 'I know you're hiding something. I can see it in your eyes.'

'We've been through this before,' I say, adding sugar to my voice. 'You aren't my type. Don't take rejection very well do you, *sisi?*'

The male guard takes a step forward. He's as wide and well padded as the woman, but I suspect his bulk is more muscle than fat.

With as much insolence as I can muster, I slowly raise my arms.

She pats me down roughly, slapping her meaty hands down my thighs and over my sides. *Please let her miss them. Please let her miss them. Please let her miss them.* She checks my arms, pausing as her fingers fumble over the chains hidden beneath my jacket. *Dammit.* She grins in triumph, revealing that several of her bottom teeth are missing. 'Lift up your sleeves, sisi.'

'Ever heard of a toothbrush? Your breath stinks.'

'Watch it, girl,' she hisses.

'Do as she says, Saint,' Ash says.

I know he's right and it's not worth baiting her any more than I already have, but for a few seconds I keep her guessing, holding her gaze until she gives in and blinks. Still staring straight at her I roll up my sleeves, taking my time. There is just enough light floating in from the cell's open door to make the chains glint like silver.

'Hand them over.'

'Aren't you going to say please?'

She sighs and places her hand on the gun slung in her belt.

'Okay, okay.' I unwrap the coiled metal from my forearms

and shove the chains into her hands. They're heavier than they look and they slither through her fingers as she scrambles not to drop them.

'Take good care of those,' Ginger calls from the back of the cell. 'We'll be taking them back soon.'

'In your dreams, boy,' she says, turning to leave.

'What are you going to do with us?' Ash asks, directing this at the male guard at the door. I know he's fishing to find out how much they know.

'What do you think, bru?' The guard snorts. 'What we do with all the skelms. You're going to get a little holiday outside the enclave.' Adjusting his belt and squaring his shoulders the guard steps back to let the woman pass. 'Sweet dreams,' he says, slamming the heavy door behind him.

I back up against the wall and slide down until I'm sitting on the cement. My eyes are beginning to adjust, but the darkness isn't giving up without a fight. After living underground for so long I thought I'd lost my fear of enclosed spaces, but my palms are tingling and my breath is not coming easily.

I cannot allow myself to give into the claustrophobia. I would rather die than reveal my weakness to anyone – even Ginger and Ash. One of the first things Hester taught me when I came to live with her was an exercise to control my fear and vanquish the nightmares that used to plague me. She told me to choose a line from a song or a poem that had meaning for me, and repeat it like a mantra until the bad thoughts were washed from my mind. I never told her which song I'd picked. I think she assumed that I'd chosen some childhood Tswana folk song, but the one that my brain stuck on was from a cheesy Chumbawamba CD Atang and I had both loved. We'd played that CD over and over at full volume for days, trying to punish Dad after he told us what he had planned for me: that I was to be shipped off to

Cape Town and shoved into boarding school. Of course, after the rise of the Rotters, the song now has another meaning. But I don't care. It is still *mine*, and I've used it so often that it no longer seems ridiculous.

I get knocked down, but I get up again, you're never going keep me down. I repeat this line in my head three times, very quickly.

It helps a little.

I can breathe again.

Ash sighs. I can just about make out his shape crouched on the floor to my right.

'You think they know who we are?' I ask.

'I don't think so. If they did they'd be interrogating us right now, wouldn't they? It's more likely that they picked us up after what happened at the market.'

'What did happen exactly?'

'Lele and her sense of justice again. A bunch of kids were picking on a stallholder. She took offence.'

Typical Zombie Bait behaviour.

'We *so* could have taken those guards,' Ginger says.

'In case you didn't notice, Ginger, they were packing guns,' Ash replies.

'Takes more than a few bullets to stop me.'

'Yeah, right. Ginger, the bulletproof boy,' I say, trying to sound upbeat.

'The Guardians must be getting seriously overconfident if they're handing guns out to all and sundry,' Ash says.

'A few guns are hardly going to keep the Rotters at bay.'

'Yeah, but think about it, Saint,' he says slowly, as if explaining something very simple to an idiot. 'If there are weapons floating around in the enclave it makes an uprising against the Guardians a real possibility.'

I don't like being treated like an idiot, but I let it pass. 'It wasn't the Guardians who put us here, Ash. It was *the people*. The Resurrectionists. Do they look like they're about to revolt?'

Ash drops the subject, but I know he's chewing it over in his mind. And the answer is obvious. Without the Guardians the Resurrectionists have no power. There is no way that they will attempt to overthrow them. And without the Guardians the people in the enclave would starve. After all, they are the ones who ferry food back and forth from the Agriculturals and keep the Rotters at bay.

'So, when do we make our great escape?' Ginger asks.

'We don't.' Ash sighs again. 'They're just going to relocate us. It's easier than sneaking back out again.'

'Yeah!' Ginger says. 'We'll arrive back at camp in style. I like it. You think they'll put us in one of those big wagons? I've always wanted to ride in one of them.'

I hope that relocation is all they have planned for us. 'Whose turn is it to make the fire?' I say, hoping that casual chit-chat will stop the next wave of claustrophobia.

'Not it!' Ginger and Ash say in unison.

'Fine. We'll make Lele do it. It's the least she can do since she doesn't have to endure all this shi –'

'Quiet,' Ash says. 'We've got company.'

He's right. I can make out what sounds like the rustle of fabric and a muffled sob. It seems to be coming from the far right-hand corner of the cell.

'Who's there?' Ash asks.

There's a moment of tense silence as we scan the cell. My eyes have now almost fully adjusted to the darkness and I can just about make out two shapes hunched in the corner. There's another muffled sob.

'It's all right,' Ash says, softening his voice – or at least making it as soft as it ever gets. 'We're not going to hurt you.

What are your names?'

'I'm ... My name is Washeila,' a girl stutters. 'And I'm with my sister, Amina.'

'How long have you been here?'

'Not long. A day – something like that.'

'What are you in for?' Ginger asks.

Washeila clears her throat. 'How do we know you're not spies?' she says, a hint of defiance in her voice. Good for her.

'Do we sound like spies, mate?' Ginger asks, almost hopefully.

'No,' Washeila says. 'I guess not.'

'So, go on, then,' Ginger says. 'You can trust us.'

The girls' shapes move as they bend their heads together and share a quick whispered conversation. I cannot catch what they're saying.

'Our home was raided,' Washeila says finally. 'The guards came last night. Busted in while we were sleeping.' She pauses. 'They searched the place, trashed it. And then they found our copy of the Qur'an.' Her voice has grown defensive, as if she's expecting us to start hurling insults at her because of her religion. 'It was my father's. All we had left of him.'

'Sorry,' Ginger says. 'He die in the War, did he?'

'No. Our parents ... They were taken when the Rotters broke into the enclave. Five years ago.'

I stiffen.

'Go on,' Ash says, glancing in my direction.

'They had a market stall in New Arrivals – shoe repairs ... and ... ' Her voice cracks. 'I don't like to talk about it.'

I don't blame her. I don't like to talk about it either. Images of that terrible day flash into my mind before I can stop them: that first scream and the sound of splintering wood as the fence split open; the Rotters' moans, sounding louder than I had ever heard them; the panic as people fled, slipping in the mud, pushing each other over, trampling over fallen bodies in their haste to get away. The feeling of not being able to move. Of being frozen with terror, like in a nightmare where you know you have to run but cannot. Catching sight of the first one, still dressed in its funeral suit. Squeezing my eyes shut, and the sense of disbelief as it ran right past me, knocking my shoulder as it passed.

Before the Guardians arrived to keep them at bay the Rotters had taken scores of citizens, but unlike Washeila's parents' story mine had a happy ending, if you can call it that. If that horrible incident hadn't occurred I might never have hooked up with Hester and the Mall Rats. She'd found me wandering through the chaos, shell-shocked and traumatised, the only survivor the Rotters didn't try and attack.

'I'm sorry for your loss,' I say.

Washeila sniffs loudly. 'Thank you.' She sounds like she's making a real effort to get her emotions under control. 'What about you three?'

'Long story,' I say. 'Hey, how old are you?'

'Twenty-two. Amina's twenty.'

So they are both probably too old to be used as Guardian fodder.

'They're going to relocate us,' a huskier girl's voice says – it must be the sister, Amina.

'No they aren't,' Ash says. 'Because we're going to get you out of here.'

'How?' the sisters ask together.

'Yeah, how, Ash?' Ginger asks.

But I know what Ash is thinking. 'Plan A,' I say without missing a beat.

'No, that won't work,' Ash says. 'We'll do Plan B.'

'I'm telling you, Plan A. It's our best chance.'

'What you talking about, guys?' Ginger asks.

'Plan B and that's final,' Ash says, ignoring Ginger.

'Who died and made you leader?' I snap back.

Ash goes very quiet. Have I gone too far?

Not even Ginger breaks the miserable silence that settles around us. It's up to me. 'I hope Zombie Bait got out okay.'

'Yeah, well,' Ash says, 'if she tries playing the hero I'm going to kick her ass.'

'I thought that was what you liked about her?'

'Her ass?' Ginger pipes in.

'No, Ginger. Her spirit,' I say. 'Or are strong women a bit too much for you to handle, Ash?'

'Saint, I am so not in the mood for another one of your Lele lectures.'

'I thought once Thabo was out of the picture you'd make your move.'

'Saint, I'm serious. Drop it.'

'The angst act is getting old, Ash,' I say. 'Lele is only going to put up with so much of it.'

'Saint, I'm warning you.'

'Lele's hot. It's not going to be long before someone else moves in for the kill.'

'At least I'm not the one who's in love with a Guardian.'

I feel myself go cold. 'What did you just say?'

'You heard me.'

'Say it again. I dare you.'

'She's gone, Saint. There's nothing left of the old Ripley in her.'

'Low blow, mate,' Ginger says.

'I'm just telling it like it is,' Ash says.

Before I can second-guess myself I swing my fist in the

direction of his voice. There's a satisfying thwack as my knuckles connect with his cheek. We both scramble to our feet, desperate to get the advantage. I aim for another head shot, suddenly aware that I actually really do want to hurt him. I don't hold back, but he ducks just in time, my fist slicing though the air. And Ash, never one to disappoint, doesn't hold back either – he spins around and catches the side of my head with his boot. I stagger back into the door as Ginger and the sisters shriek in unison, my cheekbone an explosion of pain. Shaking my head to clear it, I go to hit him again, my other senses kicking into high gear to make up for the poor visibility. Ash catches my fist, but before he can throw me off balance I knee him in his stomach. He grunts, but doesn't drop. Instead he pulls me out of the way as the door bursts open.

The male guard hesitates at the cell's entrance, his gun drawn. 'Hey! What's all this blerrie noise?'

He's alone – I can't see any sign of the fat woman. I use the sudden blast of light to my advantage, easily dodging Ash's next swipe.

'Hey! You want me to shoot you? Stop that!' The guard rushes forward to separate us, but we're ready for him. We both spin, and instead of hitting each other, kick him in the gut simultaneously. Ash follows up with a straight-armed punch to his nose, and the guard knocks his head on the edge of the open door and goes down like a sack of samp, the gun clattering to the floor.

Ginger leaps to his feet and joins us. 'Is he ... a goner?' he asks as Ash picks up the guard's weapon and tucks it into his waistband.

I drop to my knees to check the guard's pulse. 'No,' I say. 'He's still breathing.'

I help Ash drag the dead weight into the shadows at the back of the cell. 'Told you Plan A would work.'

Ash shrugs. 'Fair enough,' he says, making quick work of unhooking the guard's keys from his belt and stripping the robe from his body.

'You two were just acting?' Washeila asks, stepping into the pool of light created by the open door. We might be in the middle of a life-or-death situation, but I still have time to notice that she's not bad-looking. A bit buxom for my taste, but under other circumstances I might have flirted a little.

'Pretty much,' Ash says, also checking her out. He is human, after all. 'Here, put this on.' He hands her the robe and turns to glare at me. 'You didn't have to whack me so hard.'

'Like you can talk. That kick almost put me into a coma.'

'And the Oscar goes to the Emo Kid and the Angry Lesbian.' Ginger grins at Amina, who has joined her sister in the light. She matches Washeila blow for blow in the looks department, but this is not the time to get distracted.

Ash turns to the sisters. 'The rest is up to you. You're going to have to be quick, and it's not going to be easy getting out of the Embassy without being challenged. Do you remember how they brought you here?'

Washeila shakes her head.

'I do,' Amina says. 'We go left, up three flights of stairs, and then ... ' She scrunches up her nose. 'I think I'll know where to go from there.'

'Good. When you get out of the Embassy, head to New Arrivals. Look for the soup kitchen and ask for Lungi. She'll find you. Tell her that Ash sent you and she'll help you out. Got all that?'

Washeila nods. She must have thousands of questions, but she keeps them to herself. 'What about you three? Aren't you going to come with us?'

'Don't worry about us,' Ginger says. 'You'll have a far better chance if it's just you two.'

'And shut the cell door behind you,' Ash says. 'We need to keep up the pretence that everything's cool for as long as we can.' He hands Washeila the bunch of keys and the gun. 'And take this.'

'Aw, what?' Ginger says.

Ash ignores him. 'Only use it if you have to and give it to Lungi when you see her.' Washeila takes it gingerly. 'And be careful with it.'

'How ... how does it work?'

'Point and pull the trigger,' I say.

She nods. I'm pretty sure that if push comes to shove she'll handle herself all right.

'You'd better get out of here before that other guard pitches up,' I say.

'Thank you,' Amina says softly but with feeling. Then they hurry out, quietly shutting the door behind them and leaving us in the dark again.

'So, why couldn't we keep the gun?' Ginger asks as I lean back against the wall, trying to ignore my throbbing head.

'We don't need it,' Ash says. 'The guard said that they're going to relocate us. And besides, I hate guns.'

'I thought you were like a child soldier or summut during the War?'

'Yeah. That's why I hate them.'

We sit in silence for a few minutes, listening for any sounds of a scuffle, any sign that the two girls might have run into trouble. Nothing. I start to relax.

'Oh well,' Ginger says. (I knew he wouldn't be able to keep quiet for too long.) 'That was easy, innit? I wonder how long it's going to take them before they realise that –'

But he doesn't have time to finish his sentence because at that very moment the door flies open and there's the click of a pistol hammer being cocked.

I get knocked down, but I get up again, they're never going to keep me down.

Good. My hands have stopped trembling.

The man behind the desk sighs and leans back in his chair as the armed guard standing behind him shifts his weight from one foot to the other. Thanks to the name plaque helpfully placed in front of me I know full well who my adversary is: Comrade Nkosi – CEO of the Embassy and head Resurrectionist. If someone this high up is interested in us they must have some idea of who we are.

Nkosi hasn't said a word since I was dragged in here five minutes ago. I know he is trying to intimidate me, hoping I'll crack and break the silence first. I suspect he's picked me instead of Ash or Ginger because he assumes I'm the weak link, that because I'm a girl I'll crumble and tell him everything. But he has made an error in judgement if he thinks I'm overawed by the plush furnishings. The room's dark wood panelling and thick carpeting instantly reminded me of the principal's office at Saint Agnes's School for Girls – where I'd spent hour after mind-numbing hour listening to lectures about 'fitting in'. This room might be the kind of place designed to make a visitor feel inferior, but I refused to feel intimidated back then, at age seven, and I refuse to be intimidated now.

I thought Nkosi would be older, but it is obvious that he spends a great deal of time on his appearance – his fingernails are polished and his hair is clipped close to his scalp. I toy with the idea of telling him that if it wasn't for me and the other Mall Rats that sharp designer suit he's hiding behind would still be stuck on its hanger, mouldering in the mall. Instead I yawn, crack my knuckles and sling my boots up onto the desk, knocking the name plaque onto the carpet. The guard steps forward, but Nkosi casually waves him away. 'It's fine.'

Good. He spoke first. Score one to me.

Nkosi steeples his fingers together and smiles icily at me. 'I suppose you're wondering why you're here?'

'Nope,' I say, relieved that my voice sounds even. 'I know why I'm here.'

'Oh, really?'

'You brought me here to show off, right? Impress me with your luxurious office. Intimidate me with your power and influence.' I roll my eyes. 'Well, consider me impressed and intimidated. Now bring on the relocation.'

'No need to be so defensive, Sister, I just wish to have a little chat.'

'I'm not your sister, Comrade.'

He blinks. I bet it has been a long time since someone spoke to him like that. 'You *do* know who I am?'

'Yeah. You're the head psycho.'

He smiles again. 'You still have a trace of your original accent.' He glances down at the papers littering his desk. 'Botswana, am I right?'

'How did you know?' The words slip out before I can stop them. I'll have to be more careful.

'I'm assuming you were stranded here when the War broke out?'

'It doesn't take a genius to figure that out.'

'Must have been hard. I hope you didn't suffer many personal losses? Family members, perhaps? Parents? Brothers? Sisters?'

I do my best to shrug nonchalantly, as if his question hasn't hit a sore spot, but the walls I've built up around those memories aren't the strongest. I cannot allow myself to think about Atang now. I will not let Nkosi hurt me with old memories, old ghosts.

But he can see he's scored a hit. 'What were you doing in South Africa? Were you at school, perhaps?'

Another hit, but this one doesn't sting so much. After the horror of being whisked away to an unfamiliar country, ripped away from my brother and best friend and shoved into a boarding school with a bunch of stuck-up bullies, the outbreak of War was almost a relief.

A flicker of frustration flashes in Nkosi's eyes, but he tries to hide it by turning in his chair to open a small fridge next to the desk. 'You seem eager to be relocated. I imagine it wouldn't be a very pleasant way to go.'

'It's got to be better than sitting in here with your ego.'

The guard looks down to hide a smirk.

Nkosi keeps very still for a second as if he's struggling to control his temper, but when he turns back to face me his soulless smile is back in place. 'Try this, Sister,' he says, placing a can of Coke in front of me. 'It's a delicacy. Very hard to come by these days.'

'I know what it is.' I can't stand the stuff. Thank goodness they didn't pick Ginger for this cosy chat – he'd have spilled his guts for one sip.

'You seem like a smart girl. We could always do with an insider.'

I yawn again and Nkosi clenches his jaw. I'm getting to him. Good.

'Any information you could give us about the ANZ would be greatly rewarded. If you prove valuable and cooperative we will spare your life. The lives of your friends.'

'The AN who?'

'I am making you a once-off offer, Sister. You might want to consider it a little more carefully.'

'Oh, well, if you put it like that ... ' I pause for several seconds. 'Nope. You can shove it.'

His cheeks shimmer as he struggles to hold onto his self-control. He sighs, grits his teeth and gives the smarm offensive one last try. 'Would it really be so bad, working for the Embassy, for the good of the people?'

'The good of the people? Are you serious?'

'Very.' He picks through the papers on his desk. 'Now, let's talk about the two girls.'

I breathe out very slowly. 'What girls?'

'The girls you tried to help escape.'

Keep it together, Saint. You don't know for sure that they haven't got away.

He glances down at the papers again. 'Washeila and Amina Masood.'

I shrug. 'Don't sound familiar.'

'I believe one of our guards was very seriously injured by you and your ... friends. Your violent actions have only made things worse for these two young women.'

'How could things be worse?' I'm finding it hard to swallow. 'You were going to throw them to the Rotters!'

He winces at this. 'Reanimates, please. Let's be civilised.'

'Civilised? Are you serious? You're sending people out to their deaths daily! You worship those who caused the War in the first place! I'm not the one who is uncivilised here. The only thing those girls are guilty of is having the good sense not to buy into the madness that you have spread throughout the enclave.'

'Death is a natural part of life. When we find them –' He

snaps his mouth shut.

'*When* you find them?' So they did get away.

Nkosi's eyes narrow. 'You will eventually come round to our way of thinking. It is the will of the people.'

'Put it this way, I would sooner be ripped to pieces by a horde of rotting corpses than help you bunch of murdering psychopaths.'

He slams his fist on the desk. I don't even flinch. Anger I can handle. But before he can start hurling insults at me, there's a knock on the door.

'What is it?' he snaps.

'Apologies for the interruption, Comrade,' a woman's voice says. 'But I have just heard about our new detainees.'

A tall, slender woman with straightened black hair glides towards the desk. Her clothes are tailored and she's carrying a fine-tooled leather briefcase. There's something about her rigid body language and flawless appearance that makes me suspect that she could be a far more dangerous adversary than Nkosi.

She peers down at me. 'I believe you know my stepdaughter.'

'I know a lot of people.'

'I'm sure you do. But I think you know her better than most. Leletia de la Fontein? Lele?'

'You're the Mantis!'

Nkosi frowns in confusion, but the woman's expression doesn't waver for an instant. I'm not surprised at her nickname, there's definitely something inhuman about her, something insectile – she hasn't blinked once since she entered the room. Lele said her stepmother worked at the Embassy, but she didn't mention she was one of the puppet masters.

'And you must be Saint, although I'm assuming that isn't the name you were born with?'

I was right. They know who I am. I can only hope that they

don't know *what* I am. 'How do you know my name?'

'You'd be surprised how much we know about you and your friends.' She gazes into the distance. 'What do you call yourselves? The Mall Rats? Rather a juvenile name, isn't it?'

Well, there goes my last little shred of hope. The question is, how do they know so much? Have they got a claw hold in the ANZ? Surely not. *Hopefully* not. Lungi's careful. Very careful. Almost paranoid. No. The information must have come from one of the friendly neighbourhood Guardians we ran into at the mall all those weeks ago.

My own poker face must have slipped again because the smirk is back on Comrade Nkosi's face. 'Show her,' he snaps at the Mantis.

She rummages in her briefcase, pulls out a piece of paper and hands it to me. Not good. It's a 'Wanted' poster, detailing our names and descriptions. 'You have good timing,' the Mantis says. 'Comrade Nkosi was about to post these all over the enclave. Thank you for saving us the trouble.'

I glance up at her. 'What's with this "well built" stuff? Are you calling me fat?'

She finally blinks. 'Where is Lele?'

'Haven't seen her for months.'

'You're lying.'

'And you and Comrade Nkosi here are dangerously deluded, but we can't all be perfect, can we?'

'We could make life very comfortable for you if you see sense, Saint,' the Mantis says. 'We know that you can leave the enclave. That there are more ... *resources* ... outside the fence than we suspected.'

I shrug again.

'We know you have been bringing contraband back into the enclave to sell,' Nkosi says.

'So what?' I glance at his suit. 'It's you lot, the holier-than-thou Resurrectionists who are our main customers. What are you going to do? Arrest yourselves?'

'You have a choice,' the Mantis says. 'Work with us against the insurgents, join with those of us who are building a better life in the enclave –'

I snort. 'Yeah, like that's going to happen.'

But the Mantis continues, undeterred. 'Or, if you choose to continue with this frankly rather childish behaviour, life could become very uncomfortable indeed.'

I let the silence drag on for another couple of minutes. 'Thanks, that's sweet, but I think I'll take the second option.'

'Very well.' Nkosi gestures behind him to the guard.

'I'm so scared.' I lay the sarcasm on thick, mostly because I really *am* scared.

———

'Well, look on the bright side,' Ginger says. 'It can't get much worse than this.'

'Shut up, Ginger,' Ash groans.

'Oh, wait, it *has* just got worse! My nose is itching like crazy. Saint, can you just reach over and –'

'Does it *look* like I can just reach over?' There's a loud *thwack* as something hits the wood an inch away from my face. The sickening smell of vrot fruit washes over me. Glancing up I see a second piece of fruit flying towards me. I dodge it, or, at least, I dodge it as much as I can – the wooden planks sandwiching my neck don't allow for much movement, and my hands are similarly pinioned at the wrists.

'What are these things called again?' Ginger asks, wiggling his fingers.

'Stocks,' Ash mumbles. 'Or pillories. I can't remember which is which.'

'Yeah, well, mate, whatever they are it's all a bit too medieval for my taste.'

'I think that's the idea, Ginger,' I say.

'So what's next? The iron whatsit? Thumbscrews? The comfy chair?'

I'm trying to catch some of Ginger's levity, but it's not working. I remember flicking through the banned history books Hester had smuggled into our hideout, squeamishly drawn to the sketches of ancient torture devices. Even after all the horrendous things I'd seen during the War and its aftermath, after checking out the illustrations depicting iron maidens and stretching racks I remember thinking: there's no way people were *actually* that cruel to each other.

But now I know better.

They've placed us on an elevated stage just outside the Embassy's entrance; the three of us imprisoned separately a couple of feet apart. I've tried pushing against the hinged wooden planks locked around my neck and wrists, but while I suspect they were hastily built, whoever constructed them knew what he or she was doing. My back is killing me from being bent at such an awkward angle for so long, but physical discomfort I can stand. It's the humiliation and powerlessness that's really getting to me. In the time we've been trapped here a crowd has gathered. Not content with just chucking insults at us (and there have been lots of those), our audience has started to lob rotten fruit and veg our way. And I know Ash feels the same way. Although it hurts to do so, I crane my neck to check him out. His eyes are trained on the ground, his thick fringe masking his burning face.

An overly ripe tomato hits Ginger square in the face,

spattering red flesh and seeds all over him. He twitches his nose. 'Almost, mate!' he yells. 'A little to the left this time!' A second tomato follows. 'Perfect! Ta! Got any bananas?'

It doesn't take long for a small group of children to crowd around the bottom of the stage. They throw small pieces of fruit at Ginger and giggle shrilly as he catches them in his mouth.

Good old Ginger. It takes more than medieval torture to get him down.

The rickety wood beneath our feet vibrates as footsteps thump across the stage. A familiar sharp-suited figure strides in front of us.

'Comrades!' Nkosi calls out. 'My Brothers! My Sisters!' The mob instantly quietens. 'Today is a glorious day indeed!' He pauses dramatically, keeping the horde hanging. 'How wonderful it is to see so many of you today!' He raises his arms as if he wishes he could hug each and every member of the crowd. Every eye is trained on him, gazing up at him with rapt attention. 'We have here, right before your eyes, three known rebels, three *terrorists*.' He shakes his head and lowers his voice. 'Three enemies of the state. Yes, my Brothers and Sisters! Enemies of the Guardians who keep your sons and daughters safe! Enemies of our saviours! Enemies of every man, woman and child who calls this enclave home –'

I try and block out the rhetoric, wishing I was anywhere else but here, even back in that stinking cell. I search the crowd for any sign of a friendly face – just one person who isn't wearing an expression of self-righteous indignation or malicious delight. No luck. Nothing but a sea of Resurrectionist robes, vertebra amulets and pseudo-religious fervour.

I don't want to think about what Nkosi and his crew might be planning for us next. They obviously know it's pointless to relocate us, and if we're not going to talk we're of no use to them.

In our current form, that is.

At the far edge of the crowd, someone catches my eye. I strain my neck, scanning the faces for another glimpse of that familiar shaven head. But she's gone. If it *was* her in the first place. I hope she's had the good sense to get the hell out of the enclave. But then again, I know Lele; she can't resist playing the hero.

Another set of footsteps, lighter this time, clump over the wood behind us. The crowd falls silent. No whispering or coughing, not even the rustle of clothing.

I cannot peer behind me to see who it is, but I know it can't be good for us.

Then a hooded figure glides into my eyeline. Comrade Nkosi turns around and bows towards it, a look of maniacal joy on his face, as the figure slowly lifts its pale hands and pulls the cowl of its robe down. It turns to glance down at us and I recognise the flawless skin, and, of course, the blank, black eyes. Lele says that the teenage Guardians are just like those Terminator robot things out of Ginger's movies – all traces of humanity absent from them, leaving nothing but a cold, human-shaped shell. But I hope this isn't true. For Ripley's sake. For *my* sake.

'Oh, look!' Ginger says, still resolutely sticking to his cheerfulness. 'It's what's-his-face. The Guardian fella. The one we ran into at the mall. What's his name again?'

'Paul,' Ash mutters. 'His name is Paul.'

'What an honour!' Nkosi gasps. 'To be joined by a Guardian. Brothers and Sisters! Feast your eyes! May I say –'

Nkosi's words are cut off as a scream ricochets through the crowd.

A plump woman with matted grey hair is shoving her way through the centre of the mob. 'Paul!' she screams. 'Paul!'

People struggle to move back and let her through as if she's contagious. 'Paul! Why won't you look at me! It's me! It's Ma!'

I try to concentrate on the boards beneath my feet – I don't want to see this – but I cannot stop myself from looking up again. Nkosi is waving to the guards patrolling the edges of the crowd, and several start making their way to the front, roughly shoving people out of their way.

The woman finally makes it to the edge of the stage. 'Paul! Why won't you look at me!'

'Just look at her!' I yell at him.

He turns to face me and for a split second I'm almost certain that something shifts in his eyes, then it dies and he takes a step back, out of her reach.

The woman screams again. 'Paul!'

Two hefty guards each grab one of her arms and drag her backwards. She fights them with each step, still screaming: 'No! That's my baby! My baby! Paul!'

Her cries are finally drowned out by the murmuring of the crowd.

Nkosi clears his throat. I can't see his face, but I hope he's lost some of his bluster. 'Settle down, my Brothers and Sisters. We will make sure that this poor deluded soul gets all the help she needs.'

I can guess exactly what sort of help Paul's mother will be getting. I glare at Paul's back – if I wasn't trapped in this wooden prison I wouldn't be able to hold back.

As if he can feel the weight of my gaze, he turns to face me once again. Then he smiles – a smile as dead as his eyes.

Comrade Nkosi rattles on, whipping the crowd into a religious fervour, but his words are lost on me.

'That was your mother,' I hiss at Paul. 'Your *mother*.' He doesn't react. 'You didn't even look her in the eye.'

'Cold, mate. Very cold.' Ginger says. 'Bloody disgusting behaviour.'

'What do you want with us?' Ash asks.

'Yeah, mate,' Ginger says. 'Don't you have places to go, zombies to see, small furry creatures to rip to pieces with your teeth?'

Paul cocks his head to the side. 'Listen,' he says, gesturing to where Nkosi is still holding forth.

'Yes! Brothers and Sisters!' Comrade Nkosi's voice rings out. 'Next time you lay your eyes on these insurgents it will be in their new role as protectors of your way of life!'

'What's he on about now?' Ginger says. 'We can't be turned into Guardians. We're too old.'

Paul smiles that dead smile again. He leans close to me. 'When you die,' he whispers, 'you will live.'

Then he pulls his hood over his head and slips off the stage, the crowd parting to let him through.

LELE

Oh crap.

Double crap.

Triple crap.

I elbow my way through the crowd, ignoring the glares and grunts of irritation thrown my way. If I let myself give into the panic, then we're all screwed. I'm still reeling from the sight of Ash, Ginger and Saint imprisoned in those cruel contraptions, and, of course, from catching a glimpse of Paul. I still remember him as the self-conscious spotty kid I'd once nicknamed Zit Face, a far cry from the blank-faced, unfeeling Guardian he is now. And that scene with his mother was *hectic*.

I can't let what happened to Paul happen to my friends. But how am I going to stop it?

Hideous images keep popping into my head, and I can't make them quit. I keep picturing Ginger as a remote automaton, his wisecracks silenced forever, Saint's no nonsense attitude and the sensitivity she tries so hard to hide replaced by a cold mask. And Ash ... Ash who would no longer think of me as anything but just another disposable human, another pawn in the complicated game the Guardians are playing with us.

I need help. There's no way I can do this on my own.

Lungi's out of the question – there's no way I can get the ANZ involved. They're all that stands between the Resurrectionists' madness and some sort of normality – the last resort for citizens who need help – and I can't risk their underground network being discovered.

Dad and the Mantis? Forget it. They have their own agendas, and the Mantis was useless last time I needed help.

Then I have it. There *is* one person who might hold the key to springing Ash, Ginger and Saint.

And I think I know where to find him.

Time to go back to school.

'Well, well, well, if it isn't Cape Town's Most Wanted. Howzit, Farm Girl.'

'Great to see you again, Zyed. Like what you've done with the place.'

I'm trying to mirror Zyed's world-weary tone, but the truth is I'm rattled. I hardly recognise Malema High. My old school looks as if it's been overrun by a pack of feral animals (which it kind of has if you think about it). The crap sun sculpture in the main courtyard has been spray-painted bright pink, and underwear and toilet paper are draped over its rusty metal rays. The small window in Acid Face Pelosi's old office is smashed, and the courtyard is strewn with rubbish: ripped magazines, rotten fruit, crumpled notebooks and broken glass. Several of the wooden tables we used to sit around at break have been moved out here and most of them look as if they've been cannibalised for firewood. Still, some things don't change. The school may have morphed into a cesspit, but Zyed's dress sense is much the same. He's wearing clothes from before the War – stuff that must have cost a fortune – and his trademark guineafowl feathers are woven through the lapels of his jacket.

Trying not to make it too obvious, I check out the rest of Zyed's gang. Groups of kids my age and younger are lounging around, some of them smoking pungent hand-rolled joints, most of them watching me distrustfully. I scan their faces, just in case the group I ran into at the New Arrivals market is around – the last thing I need right now – but I don't spot them.

'Where's Comrade Xhati?' I ask, focusing my attention back on Zyed. He's sitting at the base of the sun sculpture, a pretty blond boy of about my age slumped at his feet. 'And the other teachers?'

'We fired them, of course,' Zyed says, smirking.

'What?'

'Sheesh, don't you know anything? We have the power now. We can do what we like.'

'All this comes at a price, though, doesn't it?'

'Not getting you, Farm Girl.'

I wish he'd stop calling me that, but I can't allow my irritation to get the better of me. I have to remind myself that last time I was in kak he helped me out. 'Aren't you worried that you'll all be turned into Guardians?'

'Have you forgotten who my father is?'

I haven't forgotten. That's why I'm here.

'So, Farm Girl, haven't seen you around lately,' Zyed says, reaching down and stroking the blond boy's hair. He reminds me of one of those crazed James Bond villains in Ginger's DVDs.

'I've been busy,' I say.

'So I see.'

'What's that supposed to mean?'

'You know you're famous, right?' He kicks at one of the many crumpled pieces of paper scattered all over the floor.

'What?'

'Look for yourself.'

I bend down and pick one of them up. Crap. It's a 'Wanted' flier. A wanted flier for us – for the Mall Rats – and the descriptions are uncannily accurate. 'Where did you get this?'

'Dad gave them to me. Asked me to hand them round.'

'And did you?'

'Nah. Why should I? He can't tell me what to do. Not any more.' He flicks his hair. 'I like the sound of Ash. He your new boyfriend?'

'No!'

'Ja, right. You're a fast worker, I'll give you that. Did you dump Thabo or did he give you the push?'

'You can talk,' I say, nodding at the blond kid.

'They've even got your hairstyle right,' he says, wrinkling his nose in distaste.

I shrug, but my heart is racing. No wonder the guards were so forceful. But who could have grassed us up? It can only have been Paul.

Unless it was Thabo.

But I don't want to get into *that* right now.

Zyed fakes a yawn. 'So, any reason why I shouldn't just hand you over, get myself the reward?'

'If you do I'll kick your ass.'

He laughs, and the blond boy looks up at him uncertainly before giggling along. 'I'd like to see you try.'

'Name the time and place.'

Zyed fakes another yawn. 'So, what is it you want? I'm honestly curious.'

There's no sugar-coating it. 'I need help.'

He sneers. 'Well, well, well. Talk about déjà vu.'

'Day jer what?' the blond kid asks.

Zyed rolls his eyes and gets to his feet. 'Come on,' he says to me. The blond boy gets up as if to follow, but Zyed dismisses him. 'Not you.'

'Where are we going?'

'Where we can talk privately.'

I follow him towards Acid Face Pelosi's old office, and he opens the door and waves me in. 'What do you think?'

My first thought is that I want to thump him, and it's a struggle to hold myself back.

Unbelievable.

The office is filled with our stuff – the fixtures and fittings from our old hideout. The generator is dumped in one corner and Ginger's movie posters are tacked up on the walls. He'd freak out if he caught sight of this place: his vast collection of DVDs is littered over Acid Face's old desk, his beloved DVD player balancing precariously on a pile of Ash's books. I spot Hester's couch pushed up against one of the walls, and a lump forms in my throat. She was lying on it when she said goodbye to me that last time – the last time I saw her alive. Zyed has even managed to get his hands on the wooden man we used to use during our training sessions, although someone's scrawled a moustache and eyes on its face. The irony of this doesn't escape me. I hated practising blocking and kicking on that thing, and had named it after him.

I pretend to fiddle with a DVD case (*Dawn of the Dead*, one of Ginger's favourites) so that my burning face is hidden. 'Where did you get all this stuff?'

'Gift from dear old Dad.' He slumps down on Hester's couch and I have to clench my fists to stop myself from lashing out at him. 'Lele, what happened to Thabo?' he asks, toying with a strand of hair. The arrogance has left his voice, and he sounds like the Zyed who helped me out the last time. But I really, really don't want to discuss Thabo with him. 'Last time you said ... you said he was in trouble. That he was going to be relocated.' I wasn't the only one who'd had a thing for Thabo. 'Is he ... Is he still alive?'

'In a manner of speaking.'

'What do you mean?'

What can it hurt? 'He's a Guardian.' I don't mention that this is the best-case scenario.

'No ways! Seriously? I haven't seen him around.'

I shrug. 'Maybe he's working in the Agriculturals.'

'Hmm. Maybe.'

My palms are starting to sweat. Thinking about Thabo and that awful day is making me feel physically sick.

He seems to shake himself mentally. 'So, you want my help. What's in it for me?'

'Knowing that you'd be annoying your father. Annoying the Resurrectionists.'

'Not good enough, Farm Girl.'

'Fine. I'll go somewhere else then,' I bluff, heading for the door. 'See ya. Next time I head out of the enclave to fetch supplies I'll leave you off my Christmas list.' Zyed isn't to know that we can't return to the mall, and I know he's well aware that I can leave the enclave.

'Wait!'

I turn around.

'There *is* something you can do for me.'

'Oh yeah? What?'

Zyed gets up off the couch, moves to the desk and pokes around in a drawer. He chucks a familiar-looking can at me.

'Catch.'

'Spray paint?'

'Ja. You can draw, can't you?'

'So?'

'So, I've always wanted my portrait done. I was thinking on the outside wall of the school, or do you think that would be too much?'

'You're joking!'

'Do I look like I am?'

'Zyed, this is serious! I haven't got time for this!'

'Take it or leave it, Farm Girl. You want my help? You got to pay for it.'

Crap.

The other kids follow us out of the gates, and arrange themselves in a tight circle around me. I catch sight of Summer, Zyed's old sidekick, but she doesn't show any sign of recognising me. She never was the sharpest tool in the box.

I'll have to work fast, but I haven't drawn anything in the weeks I've been living out in the Deadlands, so I'm out of practise.

'How shall I pose?' Zyed asks, lapping up the attention.

'Just be yourself,' I say. But I'm not sure he knows who that is. He tries out several positions before finally arranging himself with his hand on his hip.

I shake the can and make my first line. Thankfully old habits die hard, and it gets easier with every stroke. For a few minutes I forget where I am, and I almost start enjoying myself.

I put the finishing touches to the crown I've spray-painted on Zyed's head and stand back. Not bad, considering I only had pink, black and yellow. 'What do you think?' I ask.

'It's okay,' Zyed says, but I can tell he's stoked.

I've deliberately strengthened his slightly weak chin, but I couldn't help the evil glint I'd added to his eyes.

'Your turn, Zyed,' I say.

'Shoot, Farm Girl. What do you need?'

I count to three. 'I need you to get me into the Embassy. I need to get to the cells.'

Zyed looks shocked for a second, but then he fixes his haughty expression back on his face. 'What makes you think I can do that?'

'Your father is the CEO of the Embassy, right?'

'So?'

'So make a plan.' I glance at the crowd of kids around us. 'Unless you can't do it. Am I right? Are you all talk and no action, Zyed?' I stare meaningfully at the blond boy. 'So? We have a deal?' I pick up the can of black spray paint and aim it at the graffiti portrait. 'Or does the painting get it?'

Zyed sighs. 'All right, Farm Girl. But there's no way I'm going anywhere with you looking like that. I've got my rep to consider.'

––––––––––––

Night is falling as we head towards the Embassy, but the streets are still packed, the new electric street lights extending business hours well into the night.

A band of passing teenagers shoots me approving glances, and one of the guys looks me up and down. I stop myself from giving him the finger, choosing to ignore him instead. Zyed may be a total egomaniac, but I'll say something for him – he's got great taste in clothes. The outfit he insisted I change into is almost as kick-ass as the kind of gear we used to bring back from the mall in the good old days: a tight-fitting long-sleeved T-shirt with a raven logo, skinny jeans and a short army-style jacket. I'd refused the high heels he offered me – I'm not *that* willing to compromise for the sake of Zyed's rep, and they'd be a serious hindrance if I have to make a quick getaway.

As we stride through the marketplace people automatically bow out of our way. Zyed reaches over and grabs a roti from a stall, takes a bite and chucks the rest onto the ground. I hate the thought that everyone assumes that I share his values; that I'm going to take advantage of the Resurrectionists' bizarre belief that teenagers are above the law and can do whatever they like.

'So what's the plan?' I ask Zyed.

He slams into an elderly man pushing a wheelbarrow. 'Watch it,' Zyed snaps.

'I'm sorry,' I murmur to the man. He looks up at me with an expression so hate-filled it takes my breath away.

'I don't need a plan, Farm Girl,' Zyed says. 'We can go anywhere we choose.'

'Oh ha ha, Zyed, like we can just walk in there.'

'Why not?'

'I'm the enclave's most wanted, remember?'

'Chillax, Farm Girl. I've thought of everything.' He digs in his bag and pulls out a long, dark, curly wig. He throws at me. *Gross.* It's slippery and synthetic.

'Charming.'

'Go on, Farm Girl, try it on for size.'

I slip it on. It feels even worse than it looks – itchy and uncomfortable – and I instantly regret getting Saint to shave my hair so close to my scalp.

'Stunning,' Zyed says with a high-pitched giggle.

'Zyed, seriously, this isn't going to work.'

'Trust me.'

'As if.'

But it's not like I have much choice.

A line of hard-core, robe-wearing Resurrectionists snakes its way towards us. None of them have their heads hidden beneath hoods. If only we'd known about this new rule then we might have avoided being arrested.

More wishful thinking. Just great, Lele. *Very* helpful.

We're close to the Embassy now – its intricate wrought-iron gates towering above passers-by – and my gut squirms with nerves.

Hang on ... Zyed's heading straight for the main gate. I grab his arm to hold him back. He can't seriously think we can just walk in there, can he? I know he's full of himself, but that's suicidal.

'What?' he says.

'What do you think you're doing?'

'Like I said, chill out, Farm Girl. Far as they're concerned, you're just my girlfriend – my girlfriend with tragically kak hair – who's coming with me to meet dear old dad.'

Crap. I have to make a decision. Trust him, or get the hell out of here.

But Zyed's already chatting to the two stone-faced guards outside the entrance. 'Howzit,' he says. 'We're here to see my father.'

Without even glancing in my direction they unlatch one side of the gate and usher us through.

'See?' Zyed says as soon as we're out of earshot. 'I told you. Couldn't be easier.'

The Resurrectionists are clearly in the middle of building another wing onto the already sprawling Embassy, this one constructed out of white stone. A bunch of exhausted workmen and women are stirring cement in the corner of the courtyard, watched over by a couple of bored guards. This place has always creeped me out, but as the windows gleam down at us, reflecting the last of the day's light, I have to admit it's impressive. Then it hits me – somewhere inside the Embassy the Mantis is probably preparing to head home after a hard day working for the enemy. What would she say – what would *Dad* say – if either of them knew where I was and what I was about to do? Whose side would they be on if push came to shove?

'Earth to Lele,' Zyed says, sashaying straight towards one of the wooden entrance doors. 'Come on.'

I grab his arm again. 'We can't just walk straight in!'

'Why not? No one's going to stop us.'

'But this is madness. I'll get caught!'

He shrugs. 'You want to go in or not? I've got better things to do than hang out with a farm girl in a bad wig.'

'This is serious, Zyed.'

'Oh boo hoo. Now, come on, or I'm out of here.'

'Can't we slip in a side entrance?'

One of the guards is watching us from her post next to the door's marbled archway. She's frowning and looks as if she's about to click on the walkie-talkie she's holding.

'Ja, right,' Zyed says, tossing his hair. 'Like that wouldn't look suspicious. Last chance. You in or out?'

I can't believe it's this easy. I'd formed some half-baked idea of sneaking in, maybe through a disused office bathroom or whatever, disabling a guard, grabbing her weapon and springing the others, but this ...

'Doesn't look like I've got much choice,' I say, praying that I won't be too late, praying that my friends haven't already been turned into dead-eyed Guardians.

Zyed rolls his eyes. 'We're here to see my father,' he says to the guard. She shoots me a sceptical glance, but unlocks the door to let us through.

The interior immediately reminds me of the mall: the floors

are polished marble, the walls stark white and the ceilings are two storeys high. A gold replica of the crap sun sculpture is plonked in the centre of the entrance area. It makes me think of Thabo again – one of the things that really got him about the Resurrectionists was the amount of credits they squandered on the Embassy while ordinary people in the enclave went hungry.

Not that it's ever going to worry him again.

A snooty-looking woman sitting behind a desk the size of a vegetable wagon smiles and nods at Zyed, but he doesn't give her a second glance.

'Where now?' I hiss in his ear.

'Up to you, Farm Girl.'

'Where are the cells? Can you take me there?'

'Follow me,' he says.

A curved stone staircase sweeps up in front of us, and we head up to the first floor. Zyed takes a right into a long, carpeted corridor. The walls are lined with framed pencil sketches depicting the Resurrectionists' emblem: a sun with a small child gazing rapturously up at its rays. Talk about overkill.

Zyed's heading for the only door – a carved monstrosity at the end of the corridor.

This can't be right. I'd imagined the cells would be bare concrete blocks in the basement somewhere – a far cry from all this pre-War style luxury.

'Hang on. How do you know where the cells are, Zyed?'

'I don't,' he says, knocking on the door. 'But I know someone who does.'

He pokes his head around the door, says something and then steps back. I don't like the way he's smiling.

A tall figure wearing a suit appears in the doorway. 'Hello, Leletia.'

Oh *crap*.

It's Comrade Nkosi.

'Hi, Dad,' Zyed says. 'Like I said. Brought you a present.'

I turn to run, but a group of guards is already approaching, cutting off my exit.

I shoot daggers at Zyed. 'How could you?'

He rolls his eyes and pouts. 'Oh, don't look so surprised, Farm Girl. What did you expect? I can't believe you actually fell for it.'

'But ... but ... they'll turn you into a Guardian!'

'Don't you get it? I *want* to be a Guardian. Imagine the power.' He giggles shrilly. 'Adios, Farm Girl. Enjoy the afterlife.'

Comrade Nkosi waves his hand languidly in the air. He actually looks bored. 'Take her away,' he says to the guards.

I recognise the large woman who I'd blindsided earlier. 'Howzit,' I say to her. 'Still eating those cakes, I see.'

She smiles at me humourlessly and shoves me into the wall.

———————

'Let go of me!'

I struggle as hard as I can but the two guards pulling me along are way stronger than I am, and clearly have some sort of martial arts training. I've tried every move in the book to wriggle free, but they've blocked everything.

I've lost all sense of direction. They've been dragging me through a labyrinth of dusty corridors, lit by smoky paraffin lamps and heavy with the smell of mould, sweat and fear; a far cry from the carpeted luxury of the upper floors of the Embassy. They wrestle me down a long flight of rickety wooden steps. I try and plant my feet firmly, but one of the guards slams his fist into my side, winding me. 'Give it up, sisi. Or next time I'll *really* hurt you.'

He bends my left arm up behind my back while the other unlocks a heavy wooden door. My arm is released and I'm shoved into blackness. The floor is uneven and I lose my balance, careening into something soft.

'Ow!'

I know that voice. 'Saint? Saint, is that you?' I'm almost dizzy with relief. I may have screwed up the rescue mission, but at least I made it here in time.

'Lele? I thought you'd bust us out of here.'

'Yeah. Sorry about that. I did try.'

'Not hard enough, Zombie Bait.'

'Sorry.'

'S'cool, Lele,' Ginger's voice floats my way. 'We've been in far worse situations than this.'

'No we haven't, Ginger,' Saint snaps. 'Like when?'

'Like when we were at the mall and Lele stole those condoms and all the other stuff and the Guardians turned off all the lights and I had to –'

'That wasn't anywhere near as dire as this!'

'Was so!'

'Guys!' I snap. 'Enough already. Is Ash here?'

'Yeah,' he says. 'I'm here all right.' Another stab of relief, but I don't like the defeated tone in his voice. 'Lele, I told you to get the hell away from here.'

'I'm hardly going to leave you guys to get turned into Guardians, am I?'

'I appreciate it, Lele,' Ginger says.

'Thanks, Ginger.'

'So, Zombie Bait,' Saint says. 'Where did they capture you?'

'They didn't.'

'So how did you get in here?'

'Seriously, Saint, you really don't want to know.' I'm too

embarrassed to tell them about the Zyed situation. How could I have been so stupid? Time to change the subject. And quickly. 'What's that smell?' The cell pongs of rotten fruit and decaying vegetables.

'Seriously, Lele,' Ginger says. '*You* don't want to know.'

'Is that from when they put you in those ... things?'

'Yeah,' Ginger says. 'Nice of them, wasn't it?'

'So, what now?' I ask.

'So now they're going to turn us into Guardians is what,' Saint says.

'But they can't,' Ginger says. 'Like I said, we're past the sell-by date, innit.'

'That Paul thing said otherwise, Ginger,' Saint says.

I have no choice. I have to tell the others what I know. That I know the real reason why the Rotters don't attack us. That there's something living and growing inside all of us that makes us more like the Guardians – more like the Rotters – than they could ever guess.

Thabo's last words float into my mind: '*When you die, you will live ...* '

I take a deep breath, knowing that they're not going to thank me for this. 'Look, guys, there's something you should know. Something that Thabo told me before he –'

There's the clack of heels from outside the door and then a light on the ceiling clicks on, blasting the room with brightness. I have to blink to stop my eyes from watering. So they do have electricity down here after all, but obviously only when it suits them.

'Whoa, girl,' Saint says, 'what you done to your hair?'

I've forgotten that I'm still wearing the wig. I pull it off and chuck it away.

'Nice threads though, Lele,' Ginger says. 'You look hot.

Doesn't she, Ash?'

Ash looks up at me, but his eyes are hidden behind his hair and I can't tell what he's thinking.

'Wish I could say the same, Ginger. You guys look like kak.'

Ginger's clothes and hair are spattered with rotten fruit and his jeans are ripped at the knees, there's a gash above Ash's eye which is already scabbing over and Saint's cheek is badly bruised.

The door clangs open and all of us leap to our feet. There's something familiar about the slim outline of the figure silhouetted in the doorway.

It can't be.

But it is. It's the Mantis. Last time I saw her she dropped the bombshell that she was pregnant with my half-brother or sister, but I can't see any sign of it. She looks just as slim and brittle as always.

'Hello, Leletia.'

Ginger is looking confused. 'You *know* this woman, Lele?' he says. 'And your real name's Leletia?'

'Yeah,' I say. 'She's my stepmother.'

'No ways!' Ginger says.

'You can introduce me to your friends later, Leletia,' the Mantis says. 'Saint I know, of course.'

I glance at Saint. 'How come?'

'We had a little chat earlier,' Saint says, shooting daggers at the Mantis.

'Does Dad know what you're doing? Does he know I'm here?'

'I don't have time for this, Leletia. Now, follow me.'

'Make me,' I say. 'If you think I'm going to let you turn all of us into Guardians without a fight, you can forget it.'

The Mantis sighs. 'Don't be ridiculous. I am here to get you out of here.'

'Yeah, right.'

'Have I ever lied to you, Leletia?'

'Why should we trust you?' Saint asks.

The Mantis sighs and smoothes her hair with her palms. 'Do you see any guards? You could easily overpower me if you wished. Now, quickly, we'll only have one shot at this. Keep quiet and follow me.'

I look over at Ash. He stares at the Mantis for several seconds, then comes to a decision and nods. We all follow her out into the corridor, but instead of heading back up the rickety wooden steps – into the heart of the Embassy – the Mantis strides in the opposite direction, pulling off her high heels as she walks so that they won't make a noise on the concrete floor.

At the end of the passageway the Mantis pulls a bunch of keys out of her pocket and unlocks the gate. 'Quiet as you can,' she says, leading us into another ill-lit service corridor, this one lined with bags of rubbish and trolleys stacked with dirty plates. It reeks of stale cooking and steam hisses out of a vent in the floor. We tiptoe past a pair of large swing doors, behind which we can hear the clatter of plates and someone singing loudly in Xhosa.

Moonlight filters through a barred metal gate at the end of the passageway; the Mantis wastes no time in unlocking it and ushering us through.

I immediately recognise where we are: dumpster alley – where the Embassy kitchen dumps its rubbish and where Thabo and I hung out all those weeks ago.

We're free.

'What are you going to do now, Cleo?' I ask the Mantis.

'What do you mean?'

'But ... they'll come after you, won't they? You helped us

escape.'

'You managed to help those girls escape, didn't you? It will be assumed that you are more resourceful than we realised. Besides, I'm about to be named head of security. Why would they suspect me?'

'Yeah. You were pretty convincing back in Nkosi's office,' Saint says.

'You're not really going to go back and work for those monsters are you?' I say. 'How can you?'

The Mantis smoothes her hair again. 'I am all that's standing between them and total depravity, Leletia.'

'Don't talk *kak*. You know what the Guardians are doing to teenagers – it's beyond sick. What's wrong with you? Dad would never support that. *Never*.'

The Mantis digs in her bag and hands me a piece of paper. It's dog-eared and ripped but it's still readable. It's one of the old fliers I'd drawn for the ANZ, in the days when Thabo was still Thabo and my biggest problem was dealing with the bitches at Malema High.

'So?'

'Do I need to spell it out?'

Then it dawns. 'No ways,' I breathe. 'You work for the ANZ?' Even Ash looks shocked.

'Wow,' Ginger says. 'You're like a ... a double whatsit? A mole? That's so cool.'

'I must go,' the Mantis says.

'Wait,' Saint says. 'Did that Paul thing – the Guardian – tell you about us? Those "Wanted" descriptions were pretty accurate.'

'It was not the Guardians,' the Mantis says.

'Then who?'

For the first time she looks slightly ill-at-ease.

Ash sighs. 'It was Lungi, wasn't it?'

'No ways,' Saint says. 'She'd never do that. She'd never betray us.'

'She wasn't betraying you,' the Mantis says. 'It was necessary. You'd hardly been discrete about your black market activities, and too many questions were being asked.'

Ash stares straight at her. 'I get it. You needed to give Nkosi something so that you'd be above suspicion. And if you'd betray your own stepdaughter, then how could he doubt you?'

'But you could have got us killed!' I say.

'Or worse,' Ginger mumbles.

'I honestly didn't think you'd be foolish enough to come back into the enclave, and neither did Lungi.' Her face hardens. 'It really was incredibly stupid, Leletia. Have you any idea what you've done? You *cannot* get caught again. Next time there is no way I will be able to risk getting you out.' This is more like the Mantis I know and loathe. 'I mean it, Leletia. You've put us all in a great deal of danger. You must leave immediately.'

'And go where?'

'Wherever it is that you have been all this time.'

'Don't worry about it, ma'am,' Ginger says. 'We hear you loud and clear.'

Saint steps forward. 'I can see where Lele gets her pig-headedness from.'

The Mantis ignores her. She reaches over and touches my cheek. 'I will give your father your love.' Then, without looking back, she disappears back inside the Embassy, the gate clanging behind her.

'Wow, Lele,' Ginger says. 'Your stepmother is *seriously* hard-core.'

'Yeah,' I whisper. 'I know.'

'Let's go,' Saint says, putting an arm around me.

A small clump of Rotters is bumbling around outside the tunnel's exit. They don't react at all as we climb up and out, brushing earth from our clothes.

Saint, Ash and I all slump down onto the grass, but Ginger heads straight to where he left his axe. He picks it up lovingly. 'Miss me, baby?'

'I cannot *believe* you, Ginger,' Saint says.

'So, now what, guys?' Ginger asks. 'What's our next move?'

'Isn't it obvious?' Ash says. 'We've got to get the hell out of here.'

'We *are* the hell out of here,' Saint says.

'It'll only be a matter of time before the Guardians come for us. We can't stay in the Deadlands.'

'What are you saying?' Ginger asks.

'There have to be other people out there, other survivors.'

'You mean leave Cape Town?' Saint asks.

'Yeah,' Ash says, deliberately not looking in my direction. 'That's exactly what I mean.'

'But what about Jobe and Sasha?' I say. 'We can't do that – we can't just go.'

'Look, Lele, I'm not saying that you have to come with me – that any of you have to come with me – but ... I don't think we have a choice.'

'Yes we do! We could go back in and rescue Jobe and Sasha! We could –'

'Could what?' Ash snaps. 'The whole enclave is going to be looking for us. They've got guns and numbers on their side. We have hardly any weapons, zero credits and next to no allies. Even if we did magically manage to spirit Sasha and Jobe away, we don't know for sure that the Rotters won't attack them. We could be putting them in even more danger than they are in already.'

'We could help the ANZ fight, Ash,' I insist. 'There have to be hundreds of citizens who don't want their kids turned into Guardians.'

'You want to start a war, Lele?' Ash says.

'Yeah. If that's what it takes. We could get weapons for the ANZ, we could –'

'The ANZ doesn't have the numbers to fight back anymore – they're overextended as it is. It would be suicide. We're the only people who are capable of leaving. We owe it to them to see if there are any survivors out there.'

'We owe it to them to stand and fight. It's what Thabo would have done!'

'Ouch,' Saint mutters.

Ash doesn't say anything for a few seconds and I wonder if I've gone too far. 'And what happened to him, Lele? He's a Guardian. They turned him against us.' I'm starting to feel sick. 'Look, don't you think I'd fight back if I could? But now that the terrorist wing of the ANZ is disbanded –'

'Don't call them that! They're not terrorists!'

'Freedom fighters – whatever you want to call them.' He sighs. 'Stay if you like, Lele. But think about this, if you do stay, and they *do* catch you, how long do you think it will be before they decide to use Jobe against you?'

'What do you mean?'

'You know exactly what I mean.'

'You mean leave forever, Ash?' Ginger pipes in.

'No. Of course not. Who knows what's out there? There could be people who've found a way to live without the Guardians, communities who are living normal lives, lives that don't involve oppressing other people and –'

'Yeah, right,' I say, cutting him off. 'And what about all the other people in the enclave here, our *home*, the other people we *won't* be helping? The other people who'll be relocated while we're off exploring?'

'What about them, Lele? You saw that crowd. You saw how they treated us. You saw everyone turning a blind eye in the marketplace.' He turns away. 'It's your choice, but I'm going and that's final.'

I know he's right, and I know that there's no way we can go back into the enclave, but for a second all I feel is a surge of hatred towards him.

SAINT

'It looks exactly the same,' Ginger says, staring up at the mall's high white walls. 'I thought it would have all burned down or summut.'

'It could be a whole different story inside, Ginger,' Ash says.

We're all reluctant to take the plunge and head inside the building, but if we're going to follow through with Ash's radical plan then we need supplies, and with the enclave out of bounds there's only one place to get them: the mall – the only building the Guardians didn't destroy when the dead took over the city.

Its walls and cylindrical glass doors hold nightmarish memories for all of us, but me and Lele especially.

'Why don't you guys wait out here,' Ash says. 'I'll go in alone.'

Lele snorts. 'Playing the hero again, Ash?'

It's the first time she's spoken since he told us of his decision – she might as well have a dark cloud floating above her head – and he doesn't answer her, which he knows will only make her more ornery. Not that she's alone in being more than a little cranky – none of us managed a wink of sleep last night and we're all exhausted and irritable. After a few uncomfortable hours we gave up on trying to get any rest and decided to make the long trek through the Deadlands in the dark, arriving at the mall's outskirts just before dawn.

'Well, I don't know about you lot,' Ginger says, chucking his axe on the ground (so much for it being his 'baby'). 'But I'm going chainsaw shopping.'

'We have to get other stuff as well, Ginger,' Ash says.

'Yeah. But we can get it all from the Game store, right? They sell everything.'

Ginger walks towards the entrance. The glass in the door is cracked and spider-webbed, and I don't have to see Lele's face to know what she's thinking. This is where her ex-boyfriend, Thabo, was shot.

But she's not the only one with an ex on her mind.

I miss my chains, my hands feel empty without them, and every muscle in my body is tense.

The lights are still on, but somehow it doesn't feel the same. When we used to come here on our weekly excursions to collect goods to sell back in the enclave, the mall had been a place frozen in time, complete with muzak and gleaming windows. I remember thinking that the clumps of Rotters that meandered aimlessly through the corridors were the War's version of browsing shoppers, complete with the brain-dead look of retail-therapy junkies.

Near the entrance the shops and off-white walls look much the same as when we were last here, but I can detect the faint stench of burnt plastic. It gets stronger as we make our way into the main passageway, and I pull the bandana down from the top of my head to cover my mouth and nose.

We all stop dead when we see the blackened maw of what used to be the bookstore's entrance.

'We did that,' Ginger says, a solemn expression on his face for once.

I glance at Lele and reach over to take her hand. 'You going to be okay with this?'

She doesn't reply. Her hand hangs limply in mine.

The shops either side of the store are also scorched wrecks. A mannequin buried in a pile of melted plastic limbs stares at us accusingly as we pass by, and the mixture of soot and water still smeared over the tiles looks horribly like blackened blood at the scene of some kind of crime.

Lele pauses outside the bookstore's entrance. The floor beyond the door's buckled glass is a sea of soot, paper, ash and warped metal where the shelves gave into the heat. She takes a step forward, but Ash grabs her upper arm. 'I wouldn't, Lele.'

Without looking at him, she shrugs out of his grip. 'Can I borrow your torch, Ginger?'

'Here you go, mate,' Ginger says gently, handing it over.

'Lele, don't,' I say.

'I have to *see*, Saint.'

I move as if to follow her, but she shakes her head and disappears into the dark interior.

She's gone for less than three minutes and when she reappears her face is expressionless.

'Well?' I say.

'Nothing,' she mumbles. Then, without another word, she walks quickly towards the escalators, and we hurry after her.

The level beneath us is untouched by the fire, but Ash hesitates when we reach the entrance to the Game store. 'We need to make this as quick as possible,' he says. 'We'll need tents, sleeping bags, batteries –'

'What about clothes?' I ask.

'Up to you. I don't want to hang around here any longer than we have to, though.'

'Lele?' I say. 'You want to come with me?'

She shrugs, face still shut down. 'Whatever.'

––––––––––

'Phew! Shopping's exhausting, innit?' Ginger says, taking a ride on the back of his trolley.

'Yeah, right, Ginger,' I say. His trolley contains nothing but clanking Coke bottles and a chainsaw. 'And you're going to carry all of that *how*?'

I eye the growing pile of stuff we've collected, which includes a bag of tinned goods, two lightweight tents, a small camping stove and a few collapsible water containers. I cannot see how on earth we'll manage to squash it all into our bags.

Ash clicks his fingers, jumps up and jogs off. He's gone for ages, but when he returns he's holding a map book. He flicks through it and then lays it out on the tiles. 'I think our best bet is to get to the next town.'

'Which is where?'

'Well, there are loads, but I reckon we should keep as close to the coast as possible – it's more likely that we'll find survivors where there's easy access to food and water. So we need to get onto this road – the N2. And then I'm thinking, maybe head towards Durban and then on to Johannesburg.'

'And then what?' Lele asks. 'Say we do find a settlement, do we breeze on in and say, "Hey, guys, we're from Cape Town, which is seriously screwed up, how about you join us to start a war?"'

'Sounds good to me,' Ginger says.

'You're forgetting something, Ash,' Lele says, ignoring Ginger.

'What?'

'As far as we know we're the only people the Rotters don't attack.'

Ash pauses. *Has* he forgotten that? 'I know, Lele, but there have to be other people like us out there, don't there? Besides, maybe we'll find some answers.'

'To what?'

'To why the Guardians are doing this in the first place, why they even started the War. What they *want*. Maybe there are other settlements that have figured this out.'

Lele opens her mouth to snap back at him, but before she can say anything the air is filled with a mechanical groaning sound.

'Uh-oh,' Ginger says.

The strip lights above us flicker, and then, suddenly, we're plunged into darkness.

'Ginger! Your torch!' Ash hisses.

'I can't find it ... hang on.'

The sound of footsteps clacking over tiles.

'That you, Lele?' Ginger asks, his voice higher than usual.

'No. I'm right next to you, Ginger –'

Then: 'Hello, Saint.'

———————

I'd know that voice anywhere. Even stripped of all inflection it's still recognisable as Ripley's. For a second I cannot breathe; all the air's vacuumed out of my lungs.

Ginger wobbles the light up to Ripley's face, but she doesn't flinch or even blink. Half of me hopes – the stupid, unrealistic half – that what happened to her had all been a fake-out, that she will suddenly quip, 'Yessus, guys, what took you so long? I've been waiting for you to come get me.' Or something. But a glance at her eyes quashes this stupid thought. They are flat black and empty; as dead as that Paul thing's eyes.

The old Ripley – the Ripley I knew before she was taken by the Guardians – wasn't perfect. Her teeth were crooked, the front one chipped after a run-in with some nunchakus, she bit her nails, and whenever she had a scrape she'd obsessively pick at the scab until it bled. She fidgeted continually, her jokes were even lamer than Ginger's and she giggled when she was nervous. The Ripley standing in front of me does not fidget once. She keeps absolutely still – unnaturally still. Her hair hangs to her waist in gleaming waves, her nails are long and polished, and it is impossible to read her.

'Hi, Ripley,' Ginger says, swallowing noisily. 'Looking good. Um ... you're not going to kill us are you?'

Still looking at me, she says, 'You must leave here.' Her voice is as dead as her eyes. 'Go to Exit 6. Now.'

'Why?' Ash asks. 'You got another bunch of Guardians waiting for us there?'

'No.'

'Why should we trust you?'

'It is your choice.'

'Do you have to be so cryptic, Ripley?' Ginger says. 'No offence, but it's really annoying.'

'Get out.'

'Come on,' Ash says.

The others gather the stuff and start heading for the exit. But I hang back. I have not finished with Ripley.

'Saint?' Lele says. 'Come on.'

'No,' I say. 'You go on.'

'I'm not leaving you –'

'Lele,' I say. 'Just do it. I won't be long. I promise.'

'Come on,' Ash says to her. 'We'll wait for you next to Woolworths, Saint. Shout if you need us.'

'Are you sure?' Lele says to me.

'Yes.'

As Lele reluctantly allows herself to be led away I move closer to Ripley. She doesn't smell like the old Ripley used to smell – this new version reeks of perfume and freshly washed hair, of cosmetics and creams. 'Was that you, Ripley?' I ask her. 'Back in the clearing. Did you stop the Rotters from attacking that family?'

No answer.

'How much of you is in there, Ripley?' I touch her hand. I'm expecting it to feel icy and ... dead, but her skin is warm. I have no idea if I'm talking to a Ripley-shaped shell that's been infected by an alien virus, or whatever it is that keeps the Rotters and Guardians from ageing, or if there's a part of her that's still alive in there.

I can't help it, I feel the hope growing in my chest. 'You could come with us! Yes, you could –'

She steps away from me. 'No.'

'Why not?'

I raise the torch and shine it straight into her eyes. I search them for a glimmer of humanity – the flicker that I am sure I saw in Paul's eyes.

She takes the torch out of my hand, her fingertips brushing my skin as she does so. She clicks off the light. 'Goodbye,' she says.

I hear her footsteps recede. 'Will I see you again?' I call after her.

Nothing, just the clack of her heels on the tiles. Then: 'We are all connected.'

And it's then that I start to shake.

No one speaks as we make our way to Exit 6 and head out into the sunlight, all of us blinking like moles after the gloom inside.

'What the hell?' Ash says.

There are two motorbikes resting on their stands outside the trolley bay. Next to them sits a sealed plastic container. On more than one occasion as we'd made out way out of the mall we'd heard the buzz of engines echoing through the aisles, a sure sign that there were Guardians in the vicinity – they may have banned technology in the enclave, but they're not above using it for their own benefit. As well as the bikes, we know that they must have a vast secret store of fuel hidden somewhere, how else could they power the mall's generators? Ash believes that they have kept several of the power plants maintained as well; using the promise of electricity to keep the Ressers on side, so that they will feed them more potential Guardians.

'No ways,' Ginger says. 'Did Ripley leave those for us?'

'It's a trap,' Lele says. 'It has to be a trap. I mean, why would she do this? And how did she know?'

'Know what?'

'About Ash's crazy plan? That we were leaving Cape Town? I mean, we've only just decided.'

'The Guardians move in mysterious way, I guess,' Ginger says.

'Don't call her that!'

'Call her what, Saint?'

'A Guardian.'

'But that's what she is.'

'I know, Ginger, it's just ... ' Just what? I don't even know what I'm trying to say.

'So why would Ripley leave the bikes here if she doesn't want us to leave the enclave?' Lele asks. 'Weird, especially when Paul seemed so keen to turn us into one of *them*.'

'No idea,' I say, 'but if she was going to hurt us she would have done so already. She had the perfect opportunity back there.'

'Hey!' Ginger says. 'Maybe she's fighting her Guardian nature, like the cyborg bloke in *Terminator Salvation*.'

'Enough, Ginger,' I snap at him.

'Sorry, Saint,' he mumbles. But what if he's right? What if there is still a spark of the old Ripley somewhere inside her?

'Forget it.' I take a closer look at the bikes. Their bodywork is spotless and even the tread on the tyres is free from stones and grit.

'What's that mean?' Ginger points at a shiny metal cap attached to the engine. There's a stylised picture of a spider below the word *Rekluse*, which is written in blocky letters. 'You think that's the bike's name?'

'How would I know?'

'Does anyone have any idea how to ride one of these?' Lele asks. 'Because if we're going to do this we'd better do it fast.'

'How hard can it be?' Ginger says. He climbs onto the bigger of the two bikes and fumbles with the ignition. 'I think what you do is –' The bike roars into life, its front wheel rising vertically into the air like a horse rearing up. Ginger falls backwards onto his bum, the bike landing next to him, wheels spinning.

He scrambles to his feet. 'See?' he says. 'Easy.'

It has taken us almost an hour to figure out how the bikes work; all of us spurred on by the fear that the Guardians could show up at any moment. Lele has bowed out. She has the skill, but not the strength – we'll need to double up and she'll struggle to control the machine with the weight of a passenger behind her. And after falling off for the third time, Ginger has given up, choosing to mope on the sidelines. He doesn't have the coordination to work the gears, accelerator and brakes. He either revs the bike too high, or brakes too hard, sending him tumbling over the handlebars. So it falls to me and Ash.

It takes all of my concentration and coordination to get it right, repeating instructions to myself over and over again: back brake, right foot; gear lever, left foot; accelerator and front brake, right hand. But I'm glad of this; it stops me obsessing about Ripley. I thought I had buried these feelings a long time ago, shut them away in the place I keep all the things I don't want to think about, my memories of Atang, of Dad and, now, Hester.

'Ginger, you ride with Saint,' Ash says. 'I'll take Lele.'

'I'm happy to go with Saint,' Lele says.

'No, Ash is right, Lele,' I say. 'We need to distribute the weight. I'm lighter than Ash, and you're way lighter than Ginger.'

'Everyone's lighter than me,' Ginger says, as if this is something to be proud of.

Although I'm not relishing the prospect of balancing the bike with a six-foot-five giant and all our equipment on the back, maybe if Lele and Ash travel together it will help bring about a thaw in the cold war raging between them.

Ginger and Lele get to work, tying the sleeping bags and other equipment onto the back and sides of the bikes. There's only enough space for essentials. We'll have to hope we can collect food along the way.

Ash spreads the map out on the bonnet of a rusty car in the parking lot.

'So, Ash, you really think this is our best option?' I keep my voice low so that Lele doesn't overhear.

'Yeah,' he says, keeping his eyes focused on the map. 'I do.'

'What if there are no survivors out there? What if this is all there is?'

'There are survivors out there, Saint.'

'How can you be so sure?'

'I just am.' Then, before I can quiz him further, he stalks off to help the others.

'So we're really doing this?' Ginger says. 'We're really going?'

'We really are, Ginger,' Ash says.

Lele has found herself a pair of huge sunglasses and she slips them on. But I don't need to see her eyes to gauge how she's feeling – she's obviously still battling with her decision to leave her brother in the enclave.

'There's no way you can take that with you,' I say to Ginger, pointing at the chainsaw he's sneaked onto the back of the bike.

'Please, Saint? Pretty please?'

'We can't spare any fuel for it ... '

'But it makes me feel better. You know, more secure.'

I sigh. 'Okay.'

'You're the bestest.'

I climb on the bike and Ginger hops on behind me, his weight squashing the rear tyre flat against the mudguard. 'So what are we waiting for?' he says. 'Zombie road trip! How awesome is this going to be?'

I look back at the mall, wondering if this is the last time I will ever see Ripley, if this is the last time we will ever see

Cape Town, but I don't voice what I'm thinking. That there's a serious flaw in Ash's plan. If there are capable survivors out there who are able to stop the Guardians and somehow deal with the Rotters, why haven't *they* come to find *us*?

Part Two:
On the Road

LELE

We're forced to double back towards the city ruins in order to hook up with the highway Ash wants to take, ending up so close to the enclave fence that I can see the top of it rising above the trees. I've been trying to avoid holding onto Ash's waist too tightly, but as we putter past the enclave's perimeter I bury my face in his back. The grumble of the bikes' engines sounds way too loud, and at any moment I'm expecting a group of Guardians to burst out of the gate, frogmarch us into the Embassy and throw us back into that foul-smelling cell.

The awful thing is that part of me *wants* the Guardians to stop us and take us back. Leaving the Deadlands feels so final, as if I'm betraying Jobe, abandoning him. But making a stand doesn't always work out, does it? Thabo found that out the hard way.

I peer over my shoulder to check how Saint and Ginger are doing. Saint looks like she's keeping the bike steady by will alone and every so often it wobbles drunkenly as it shudders over the uneven surface. Ginger's wildly grinning face peeks over her shoulder, his hair blowing around his head in a ginger halo. He gives me a thumbs-up, and I'm about to wave back at him when I feel the bike slowing down.

Holy *crap*.

Ash pulls over to the side of the road and we wait in silence for Saint and Ginger to catch up to us.

'Blimey,' Ginger says as Saint kills the engine. 'I saw the signs for the airport back there but I didn't expect this.'

A colossal tubular structure blocks both sides of the highway. Arum lilies and myrtle bushes have grown up around it, the greenery melding with thick nests of multicoloured wiring and concertinaed metal, but despite its camouflage it's clear what it is: a crashed plane – its once-white paint pitted and blackened in places where a fire's raged through it. It must've landed on its belly, and evenly spaced oblong windows are still visible along some sections, the glass cracked and opaque. I can't see any sign of the wings, but to our far left the tail towers above the tops of the trees. And even though it's covered in bird droppings I can still make out the faded colours of the South African flag.

'How on earth are we going to get past that?' Saint sighs.

Ash walks along next to it, disturbing a flock of guineafowl. They angrily dart away in different directions, fleeing into a plumbago thicket as he heads towards a jagged, gaping hole in the plane's side, more wires spilling from its edges. He steps up, then suddenly leaps back, catching himself before he trips over his feet, as a Rotter staggers out of the plane, letting out a long throaty moan. Its face is nothing more than large yellow teeth and empty eye sockets, but it still gives the impression of being annoyed that someone's gatecrashed its home.

'Like your new friend,' Ginger calls.

Giving Ginger the finger Ash disappears inside the plane.

Saint pulls out her water bottle and offers it around.

'I hope it was quick,' Ginger says. 'I hope they didn't suffer.'

'Who?' Saint asks.

'The tourists or whoever was on that plane.'

'I don't think there could have been any survivors, Ginger,' I say. And even if there were they wouldn't have lasted long out in the Deadlands.

Ash reappears, brushing cobwebs off his clothes. 'We can get through here. There's another opening on the other side.'

Saint looks at him dubiously. 'You serious? How are we going to get the bikes in there?'

'Easy,' Ash says. 'Ginger and I can lift them in, and you and Lele can carry the equipment.'

'Maybe it's a sign,' I say to Saint as Ginger and Ash wheel the bikes towards the plane.

Saint snorts. 'A sign of what? That flying is hazardous to your health?'

'No. A sign that we shouldn't even be doing this dumb-ass road trip.'

'Oh, chill out, Lele. You can still go back, it's not too late.'

Ash turns around. 'What was that?'

'Nothing,' I mutter.

Saint and I load ourselves up with the rucksacks, the spare fuel canister and Ginger's chainsaw and follow Ash and Ginger into the belly of the aircraft.

It's not as dark inside as I thought it would be, but it smells rank and musty, and fungi grows in meaty clumps over the curved sides. Thankfully the opening on the other side isn't too far away. Ash and Ginger heft the bikes past mangled seats, kicking rotting luggage out of their way. My boot crunches on the smashed remains of a laptop, and beneath one of the seats a plastic doll peeks out, one of its eyes missing. A large rat zips out of its backpack nest and squeaks indignantly at me as I pass.

I pick my way through the debris and out into the sunlight.

No *ways*.

Saint's struggling with the chainsaw and she thumps into my back as I stop abruptly.

'Oh *shit*,' she says.

Starting from a slip road, fifty metres or so ahead, the highway is clogged with lines of abandoned vehicles, their roofs laden with luggage, and in some cases furniture. I spot a kombi, a towering stack of widescreen televisions balanced on its roof; a yellow school bus, mattresses and a bed frame lashed to its sides; and some kind of fancy sports car, the head of a marble sculpture poking out of the driver's side window.

There's just enough space for us to manoeuvre the bikes between the vehicles, but I'm not looking forward to it. It's going to feel like driving through a rusted metal graveyard.

'Whoa,' Ginger says. 'Where did all these people think they were going?'

'That, Ginger, is what we're about to find out,' Ash says.

———

'What's weird about this scene?' Ginger asks, climbing off the back of the bike and stretching his legs. The wind has tangled his hair into an orange Afro.

'That we're even doing this in the first place?' I say, earning a disgusted look from Ash.

'No. *Listen*, guys.'

All I can hear is the chirruping of bird song. Then it hits me. Something really is missing.

'No Rotters,' Ginger says. 'Haven't seen – or heard – any since the plane. You guys noticed that?'

Ash pushes his sunglasses to the top of his head and stares

at Ginger in surprise. 'You're right, Ginger. I hadn't noticed.'

I hadn't either, but now that Ginger's mentioned it, it's all I can think about.

'It's creepy, don't you think?' Ginger says.

'It's creepy *without* the Rotters?'

He nods. But I know what he means. I've grown so used to seeing and hearing them that it feels odd without them. Thabo's old catchphase pops into my head: 'Everything's better with zombies, NOT.'

Saint rubs the back of her neck. 'I wish I could say this is fun.' She kicks the wheel of her bike. 'Still can't get the hang of this thing.'

'You're doing great, Saint,' Ginger says.

She snorts and rolls her eyes. 'Yeah, right. How many near misses have we had?'

She isn't the only one. Ash and I almost wiped out halfway up a winding mountain pass. He swerved to avoid a duiker that bounded out from behind a derelict truck, and the bike slewed dangerously to the side before magically righting itself.

Ginger grins ruefully. 'Wish I could take over from you, Saint.'

She manages to smile back at him. 'I know, I know, but it's not just that. My bum is completely numb.'

I wander away from the others and gaze out over the landscape around us. I reckon we've been on the road for at least four hours, and in that time it has changed radically. The Deadlands' rocky outcrops and Port Jackson bushes have morphed into forests of gum and pine trees, neglected farmland – which has been greedily reclaimed by fynbos – and clusters of spiky orange aloes. Thankfully the vehicle graveyard eventually petered out, and we were able to pick up the pace. Cape Town's outskirts were less devastated than I'd imagined they would be, but although the buildings were still standing there was absolutely no sign of human life in the fire-ravaged shells of the warehouses, strip malls and roadside hotels that were visible through bush that's had ten years to run riot.

Right now we can't be more than a couple of kilometres away from the edges of a sizeable town; I can make out the faraway shape of some kind of factory building, and across the road there's a corroded billboard advertising a casino and luxury spa.

Ginger nods into the distance. 'You think we'll find survivors there?'

'Only one way to find out,' Ash says.

Ginger stands in the middle of the street, cups his hands around his mouth and yells: 'Helllooooo!'

The only answer is the whisper of plastic as the wind picks up and a tatty bin bag pirouettes down the street, catching on the mudguard of Saint's bike. A few faded South African flags are stuck in the darkened windows of the trashed shops. The tattered remains of a large *Go Bafana!* banner billows sadly in the doorway of what was once a restaurant, and a Mr Video sign hangs at a skew angle above a shattered display window.

I peer inside the shell of a convenience store. The shelves are empty; the till on the counter smashed.

'I don't like it here, guys,' Ginger says. 'Where *is* everyone?'

'More importantly, where are all the Rotters?' Saint asks.

Ash nods at several bones lying next to the curb, debris piled around them. I step closer – the spaghetti stuff that keeps the Rotters 'alive' has solidified onto the bones; they look like sculptures made by a sick mind.

The burned and crumbling ruin that was once Cape Town

has its own atmosphere, and that's disturbing enough, but the buildings on either side of us are fairly intact, which is somehow worse. It feels ... lonely. Spooky. Too quiet. I step over a broken office chair that's lying on the pavement and stare down the street. The petrol station at the bottom of the road won't be of much use to us – the pumps are rusted and overgrown; the *24hr Open* sign on the store front cracked and peeling.

'There must be someone alive, somewhere,' Ginger insists. 'I mean, if there are no Rotters here, why shouldn't there be people?'

'Doesn't look like it, Ginger.'

'Yeah, but it won't hurt to explore a bit, will it?'

We climb back onto the bikes and whir towards what looks to be a residential area. Ash takes a turning at random, and we pass a row of silent houses, all painted different colours. He slows to a halt and switches off the engine.

'Hello!' Ginger calls again. 'Hello!' Leaping off the bike, he hurries up to one of the houses. He jumps over the gate – a *Pasop/Beware* sign tacked to the top of it – and strides through a yard containing an empty dog kennel, a mouldering tyre swing and a battered kid's tricycle.

Ginger hesitates outside the front door, allowing me time to jog over and join him. The security gate is unlocked, and although the door's wooden frame is swollen from moisture damage, it swings open when Ginger turns the handle. Together we take turns to peer inside. It's like looking at a museum exhibit: a couch, a coffee table and a mildewed Manchester United poster tacked on the wall. I look into the dusty black eye of a television, waiting forever for its owner to flump down in front of it and switch on the soccer.

'Blimey,' Ginger sighs. 'This sucks, doesn't it?'

I'm not sure what we were expecting to find, but I think all of us had some kind of crazy daydream that just outside the Deadlands we'd come across another enclave – this one full of sane, helpful people who had created an anti-Guardian device or something.

I shudder. 'What if the whole of South Africa is like this? I mean, what if the only survivors are left in Cape Town?'

'No way, Lele. Can't be,' Ginger says.

'We're not going back,' Ash calls.

'I *know*, Ash. I'm not saying that.'

He mumbles something under his breath, and I'm hit with a sharp jab of anger. 'Oh, why don't you just shove your self-righteous crap up your arse, Ash!'

Saint shoots me a 'chill out' glance.

'Hey!' Ginger calls. He points to the end of the street. 'Something moved back there!'

He runs off, disappearing around the corner, and I sprint after him. I find him crouched over, hands on his knees, trying to catch his breath. Just metres away there's a group of Cape Vultures, their hunched backs encircling the corpse of some kind of buck. They ignore us, which isn't a good sign. People have been absent for so long that they're no longer wary of us.

'Do you think they know?' Ginger asks.

'Know what?'

'That everyone is dead?'

'Everyone isn't dead, Ginger,' Ash says, appearing behind us. 'We're alive, aren't we? The people back in the enclave are alive, aren't they?'

No one answers him.

'Come on,' he says. 'Let's get the hell out of here.'

We trudge through the deserted streets back to the bikes. Ash guns the engine and the back tyre skids in the dust, but he slows as we pull back onto the main road. Directly in front of us there's a long, low building that looks like it was once a school, its walls covered in graffiti. It immediately makes me think of Zyed. What sort of place is the enclave going to become with people like him controlling everyone? A flash of bright blue paint catches my eye, and I make out the shape of a large star, one of the points longer than the others. It looks fresher than the other tags and slogans around it.

It also seems to have attracted Ash's attention.

'What is it?' I shout in his ear.

'Nothing,' he says, pressing the accelerator, and before I can ask him again the bike's engine screams and we shoot away, leaving the dead town far behind.

'That's it,' Ash says, upending the fuel canister into Saint's petrol tank. 'That's all we've got left.'

'How far will it take us?' Saint asks.

'How would I know?'

'Okay, okay, I'm only asking.'

'Sorry, Saint,' he says, pushing his hair out of his eyes. 'It's just ... I thought we'd have found *someone* by now.'

It feels like we're right out in the middle of nowheresville. For the last few kays the road has been flanked by flat yellow fields of mustard grass, woven with weeds and determined fynbos. And now that we have stopped, the only sound is the crackle of the plastic bags impaled on the tines of the barbed-wire fence next to us as the slight breeze buffets them. We're all exhausted and grimed with dust from the road. And worse than that, everyone looks defeated.

'We need to make camp,' Ash says. 'I don't think it's a good plan to travel at night.'

Ginger points to a gateway a few metres to our left. 'How about there?' There's a sun-bleached sign above it, and I can just about make out the words *Game Lodge*.

Ash sighs and scrubs a hand over his chin. 'Maybe.'

It's warm, but I shiver all the same. Since we left the ghost town behind us it's been the same depressing story for kilometre after kilometre. I'm trying not to obsess over what we've seen, but there are snapshots that just won't quit: A yellow police van, finger bones poking out of the rusted wire mesh at the back of it. An enormous cobra sunning itself in the middle of the road next to a rusting shopping trolley containing nothing but a small blonde doll. And, worst of all, coming across another ghost town, one that must have housed thousands of people. The shops and houses were plundered and crumbling, and packs of feral dogs slunk into the ruined buildings' shadows as we coasted through. We'd seen more Rotter bones, but no sign of human life. No one suggested stopping to search for supplies or fuel. We knew it was pointless. But on the way out of town, in among faded black graffiti on the side of a grain silo, I caught a glimpse of that blue star symbol I'd seen on the wall of the school.

'Did any of you see the graffiti?'

'The what?' Saint says. 'After everything we've seen you want to talk about graffiti?'

'I keep seeing this . . . I dunno, like, star symbol. Once in that first town, and then just back there.'

'So?' Saint yawns.

'It didn't look as old as the other tags.'

Ash turns abruptly and starts fiddling with the bike's petrol cap.

'Ash? Does it mean something to you?'

'Of course not.'

'Forget it, then,' I fire back at him.

'Guys,' Ginger says. 'Look!'

There's something moving in the copse of trees to our far right. I pull off my sunglasses and shield my eyes. Large silhouettes with impossibly long necks emerge from behind the branches.

'Are those ... No *way* ... Are those giraffes?' Ginger asks.

They're moving in our direction, and as we watch, they glide across the road in front of us, a baby gallomping to catch up with its parents.

'Whoa!' Ginger says. 'It's just like Africa, innit.'

'We're *in* Africa, Ginger,' Saint says.

'Yeah. I know. But, I mean, it's like *real* Africa.' He scuffs his boot in the dust. 'The folks were going to take me to a game farm place after the football. It's sad if you think about it, innit? I mean, I didn't even get to see if England would beat Germany in the World Cup. Didn't get to go up Table Mountain in the cable car. Didn't get to see any animals.'

Saint looks at me and raises her eyebrows, then reaches over and takes his hand. Ginger rarely speaks about his life before he met Hester. And he hardly ever mentions his family.

'Sorry, Ginger,' I say.

He shrugs. 'S'kay. If the War hadn't happened I wouldn't have met you guys, would I?'

Typical Ginger – the only person in the world who can put a positive spin on a zombie apocalypse.

'So, how about it?' he says. 'We have to stay somewhere tonight, right?' He looks at us eagerly.

'Fine by me,' Ash says.

'Awesometastic! Cheers, mate.'

Saint looks unsure. 'Shouldn't we stay by the road?'

'Giraffes won't eat you, Saint,' Ginger says.

'Yeah, but what if there are other animals down there? If this used to be a game farm there could be ones with sharp teeth.'

'They'd have moved on by now, wouldn't they? It has been ten years,' Ash says. 'Anyway, how can you be afraid of animals when you can kick Hatchling ass?'

'Watch me.'

We follow a dirt track that leads away from the road and down into a valley peppered with acacia trees. A sprawling thatched building sits next to a large waterhole fed by a stream, pepperpot rondavels set in a tight cluster behind it. From here – half a kay or so away – it looks fairly intact, welcoming even. But as we pull up outside the main structure it becomes clear that time has taken its toll. The thatch has collapsed in places, and is home to several large birds' nests, and the glass in the double entrance doors is shattered, grubby mosquito netting hanging across the frame. Still, it's way better than the ghost towns we have driven through.

We climb off the bikes and head towards the entrance, a carved *Welcome, Reception* sign still in place above the doors.

'Maybe we'll get lucky and find some petrol,' Ash says, picking his way through the broken glass. 'You think they'll be any usable supplies in here?'

'How would I know?' I say, sounding snarkier than I mean to.

'Okay, look, you guys,' Saint says. 'I've had enough. You either start talking to each other or I'm going to smash your heads together.'

She doesn't look like she's joking.

Ash glances at me. 'Peace?'

I nod. 'Okay. Peace.' Thinking, *for now.*

The door leads into a spacious dining and bar area packed with heavy wooden furniture. The room stinks of mould and rotten wood and by the weak light shining in through a ragged hole in the thatch I can see that everything's sprinkled with dust.

'Shit!' Saint yells as something moves under the table nearest to me. I step back just in time to see a mole snake as thick as my calf glide towards the front door.

'It won't hurt you,' Ginger says, watching the snake's exit with fascination.

'Yeah, right,' Saint says, backing towards the bar counter. 'I really don't like this, you guys.'

'They're more afraid of you than you are of them, Saint,' Ginger says.

Ash nudges me and I follow his gaze to the wall next to Saint's head.

'Um, Saint?' I say, trying to keep my voice bland.

'What?'

'Um ... Just so you know –'

But I don't even get to finish my sentence. She flies towards us. 'It's a spider, isn't it?'

It is a spider, and one large enough to give even me the creeps. Still, it does my head in that the girl who can kick Resurrectionist guard ass, and has probably killed more Hatchlings than all of us put together, gets freaked out by spiders.

'That's it,' Saint says. 'No *way* am I sleeping in this dump.'

'We can make camp out there,' Ginger says, pointing towards the stoep.

'Yeah. C'mon, Ginger, I prefer those giraffe things to spiders any day.'

Ash looks at me and grins. 'Saint: fearless zombie hunter,' he says, and I find myself smiling back at him.

I move as if to follow Saint outside but Ash grabs my arm. 'Look, Lele, I would have gone back to get Jobe and Sasha if I could.'

'I know. But ... after what we've seen so far, do you really think we're going to find any survivors?'

He shrugs. 'I don't know what we'll find. But we had to leave. You do see that, don't you?'

I can't make myself say 'yes', but I give a curt nod.

'Friends?' he says.

'Friends.'

Ash holds my gaze for a few seconds, and I hate myself for the way my stomach flips. He looks as if he's about to say something else, but before he can Ginger yells: 'Bloody hell, you guys! Come check it out!'

Saint and Ginger are standing together, staring out over the waterhole. A herd of giraffe are standing, splay-legged, drinking. The whole scene is bathed in golden light and looks as if it has been put on for our benefit. And for the first time since we left the Deadlands behind us I feel my heart lift.

The fire hisses and crackles, sparks spiralling up into the night. There's no moon, but although it's too dark to see the animals we have no trouble hearing them: a snort, a grunt, the swish of something large moving through the grass. Ginger insists we're safe on the stoep, but what does he know? Baboons and the odd pack of feral dogs were all we had to deal with animal-wise in the Deadlands.

'This is the life,' Ginger says, scraping the pot and spooning the last of the food into his mouth. He'd unearthed a potjie from the kitchen and made a surprisingly delicious concoction out of a few tins of butter beans and ancient vacuum-packed noodles. 'Good food, good company, but summut's missing.'

He grabs his torch and disappears inside the lodge. We hear him rummaging around, followed by the sound of something crashing over, and then he returns, arms full of glass bottles.

'What you got there?' Saint asks. 'Coke?'

'Nope.'

He hands one of the bottles to Ash, who looks at it and grins. 'Champagne? What we celebrating?'

'The fact that we're not locked in a cell about to be turned into Guardians, enough of an excuse?'

'I'll drink to that,' Saint says.

Ginger looks at the label on his bottle. '2010. A good year. The World Cup, a zombie apocalypse and certain death for most of the population.'

'Won't it have gone off?'

'Nah. Alcohol gets better with age. Like me, innit.' He shakes the bottle, rips the foil off the top of it and thumbs the cork. It shoots into the night, the bottle showering all of us with liquid.

'Ginger!' Saint shrieks.

He tips the champagne to his lips and drinks deeply, but it's way too fizzy and he ends up coughing and spluttering.

'Nice, Ginger,' Saint says. 'Very smooth.'

He passes the bottle to me. Bubbles explode in my mouth and shoot up my nose. The only alcohol I've had before is the sweet beer the farmers used to brew in the Agriculturals, and this is nothing like that – it tastes lighter and less heady. I take another, more careful sip and hand it on to Saint.

'So,' Ginger says. 'So far, no Rotters. And no people. But on the bright side, no Guardians.'

'What do you think would happen if one day the Guardians

just disappeared?' Saint asks. 'I mean, say they weren't around anymore, and we were left to look after ourselves.'

'The enclave would be screwed,' Ash says.

'Why?' Ginger asks. 'I mean, the Rotters will eventually rot away into nothingness, right?'

'We don't know that for sure, Ginger,' Saint says. 'I think it depends on how squishy they were in the first place. If they were old, or already dead when they were taken or whatever.'

'True. But we've seen loads of bones out here, so I reckon if that spaghetti stuff doesn't worm its way into fresh bodies it does eventually just dry up into nothingness.' Ginger takes another gargantuan gulp of champagne. 'And if there were more people like us, we wouldn't need the Guardians, would we? It would be, like, our job to go out and fetch supplies until all the Rotters had rotted, and then, after that, life could return to normal.'

'You think we *will* find other people like us?' Saint asks.

'Gotta be people out there who have twins like you lot,' Ginger says. 'It's what you've all got in common. Whereas I'm just a –'

'Freak of nature,' Ash and I say in unison. He grins at me. The alcohol is making me feel light and giggly. My worries about Jobe and what could be happening back in the enclave seem to have drifted to the back of my mind.

'Do you know what I'd say to Paul if I ever saw him again?' Ginger says.

'I can guess,' Saint says. 'You wouldn't be able to resist saying: "I'll be baaaaaack."'

I snort with laughter at Saint's dire Terminator impression, and the mouthful of champagne I've just taken goes down the wrong way. Ash moves closer and thumps me on the back. I take another sip and hand him the bottle. He looks relaxed, almost happy, the frown lines gone from between his eyes.

'Nah, Saint,' Ginger says. 'This.' And then he burps loudly.

It's lame and crass and stupid, but suddenly all of us are laughing and we can't stop, tears are actually rolling down Saint's face. My stomach aches, and just a glance at Ginger sets me off again. I fall to the side, right into Ash, and he steadies me, putting his arm around me. Part of me wants to push him away from me – I want to stay angry at him – but I don't. Instead I relax, letting him hold my weight, and it feels good. I reach for the bottle again, but Ash tugs me back, and his other hand reaches for my face, turning it towards him. I find my neck tipping back, my eyes closing. His mouth settles on mine, firm and warm, and then I'm kissing him, wrapping my arms around his neck and pressing against him. I'm aware of Saint saying 'Get a room, you guys!', but her voice is coming from miles away.

'Let's get out of here,' Ash whispers. He takes my hand, pulls me up onto wobbly legs and leads me towards the lodge.

SAINT

'About bloody time,' Ginger says, staring at the spot where Lele and Ash were sitting a few moments ago. 'I can't actually believe they've finally got their act together.'

I know what he means. The tension between Ash and Lele has been like an overfilled balloon. You know the bang is coming, but when it does you still jump. 'Took them long enough,' I say. 'Hopefully now we'll be able to have a hormone-free trip.'

'I'll drink to that.'

We clink the necks of our bottles together and the warm champagne fizzes up and runs over my hand. I shake it off, splattering my jeans which are matted with dead bug bodies. I'd do anything for a shower right now.

Ginger scrambles to his feet and lifts his bottle into the air as if he's about to make a toast at a wedding. He sways and for a moment I'm certain he is going to tumble into the fire. 'Lashle!' he slurs.

'What?'

'Ash and Lele! They're like the Brangelina of the zombie

apocalypse, innit! Lashle!'

I'm hit with a pang of longing for the copies of *Heat* magazine that used to be my guilty pleasure. They provided me with a glimpse of what the outside world used to be like; pieces of the past frozen on glossy pages full of celebrity gossip and scandals. Who knows, maybe everywhere else is still functioning as normal? The zombie apocalypse in South Africa might be nothing more than a byline underneath Lady Gaga's latest fashion faux pas. 'Yeah, Ginger. They're exactly like Brangelina. Apart from the movie deals of course, and the millions of dollars.'

'And the millions of adopted kids.'

I open my mouth to say that it is more than probable that Brangelina are now haunting Hollywood as members of the living dead, when I realise Ginger has stopped laughing. He slumps down on to a log and starts picking at the bottle's label.

'What's wrong, Ginger?'

'Nothing.'

'Come on. Spill.'

'Well ... Lele and Ash are finally getting it together.' He pauses as if he is choosing his words carefully, which isn't like him. 'And you ... you had ... *have* ... well, Ripley, innit?'

'Yeah? So?'

'I've never had that.' He gulps another mouthful of champagne.

Hearing Ginger talk like this is a slap in the face. He's never let on that he feels like he's missing out on something or someone. That he could be as lonely as the rest of us is a scary thought. He may come across as an overgrown child who rarely stops joking around, but of course he has feelings too.

Have I been so obsessed with my own relationship with Ripley that I haven't noticed that he felt this way? I've always known that Ginger had a bit of a crush on me, but I assumed it was harmless. Now I have to wonder if it was more because there was a lack of other viable options. The guy lived with an old woman, two lesbians and a child soldier for all of his teenage years, we are smack bang in the middle of a zombie apocalypse and it isn't as if he can bump into his soulmate at a sci-fi convention.

'Anyway, good champagne, innit?' Ginger says and grins. The shift back to his old self is seamless, but now that easy-going smile looks more like a mask than anything else.

I'm tempted to go along with him and pretend that his show of emotion never happened, but what kind of a friend would I be then? I wrack my brain to come up with something to say to him, the silence filled with the hoot of an owl and the distant call of some large-sounding animal.

'Sounds like *The Lion King* soundtrack out here,' Ginger says.

'Yeah, but I don't think these animals want to sing a duet with us. I think we need to – *what the hell is that?*'

Four small lights have appeared a short distance away from where we are sitting.

'Chill, Saint, it's only fireflies. Look like Java eyes don't they?'

'*What* eyes?'

'Like in *Star Wars*.'

Right. So why aren't they moving? 'Ginger ... those aren't fireflies.'

'Don't worry. It's just –'

A deep, throaty rumble that hits me in the pit of my stomach floats towards us from the direction of the lights. Not lights – *eyes*. And they do not belong to harmless *Star Wars* characters.

'Guys!' Ash calls from behind us.

'Stay inside!' I shout back at him. I grip Ginger's arm and haul him to his feet. We bolt for the lodge, Ash sweeping the curtain aside for us as we burst inside.

'I'm not going crazy, right?' Lele's busy dragging her jeans up over her legs, and she stares at us with wide eyes. 'You heard it as well?'

Ash swears under his breath and we turn to follow his gaze. The white curtain is backlit by the fire, reminding me of the times when Atang and I used to make shadow-puppet shows with a sheet and a torch, and the silhouettes of what can only be lions prowl around the flames. The shadows they cast are so distinct that I can make out their sloping shoulders, shaggy heads and long, sinuous bodies. All that is between them and us is a flimsy piece of fabric. 'Shit, Saint,' Ash whispers. 'I left my panga next to the fire.'

My heart judders and I'm hit with a primal fear that takes me back to the first time I ever saw a Rotter. I'd been staring out of the window during a boring maths lesson when a group lurched across the school car park. The horror I felt then was paralysing, my brain couldn't make sense of what I was seeing, but something instinctual kicked in, every nerve ending screaming that I was in danger.

We huddle in the darkness, flinching at the sound of ripping canvas. It has to be our stuff – in all the excitement we've left the bags by the fire – but it's hard to care about our supplies right now.

It is suddenly far too quiet. As if the world is holding its breath; even the insect noises have ceased. Then, a high-pitched cackle cuts though the night. Nothing human could make that sound. It comes again, and this time it's louder.

'Hyenas,' Lele breathes.

Then, nothing. I count the seconds of silence.

'Are they gone?' Ginger whispers.

'Shhhh, Ginger,' I hiss. 'Don't –'

Lele shrieks as a louder sound fills the room – a sound that turns my limbs to water.

I didn't know that animals could scream.

———————

Ginger mumbles in his sleep as I gently lift his head from my shoulder and ease to my feet. The muscles in my back pop as I stretch my arms over my head. Lele is curled into a ball below the bar counter, Ash's jacket draped over her. But where *is* Ash? Not here, that's for sure.

Now that morning light is streaming in through the broken windows the lodge doesn't look half as sinister as it did last night, but the place is still a dump, and the musty smell of the rotten thatch makes me want to sneeze. And then I remember what else might be scurrying around in here – what else with eight legs. Trying to block the images from my mind I hurry outside.

Ash is crouching by the remnants of the fire, a cigarette in his fingers. For once I don't feel like chastising him. Our stuff's scattered all over the stoep – the lions didn't hold back last night. I nudge the tatters of one of our rucksacks with my foot. That bag could have been one of us; the clothes and cans strewn all over the place could have been bones and pieces of flesh.

'Morning, Ash.'

He looks up at me. 'Don't come any closer.' He gestures towards the edge of the stoep. 'You don't want to see that, Saint.'

But of course I have to look.

One glance is enough to convince me that Ash was right to warn me. It is not pretty. Flies crawl over a grey shape the size of a large dog, which lies just below where we were sitting last night. The ground around it is stained a dark reddish brown, tufts of gory fur dotted in the grass.

I turn away. 'What sort of animal is that?'

'A hyena, I think,' he says, standing up and sliding his sunglasses over his eyes.

I drop to my haunches and poke through the clothes, cans, tampons and toiletries, checking what is salvageable. I pick up the remains of the map book. It's still readable, but the pages are torn. I chuck it at Ash.

'Last night really put things in perspective for me,' he says.

'What do you mean?'

'This trip. How dangerous it could get.'

'You want to go back?'

'No. It's just ... ' He crushes the cigarette under the heel of his boot, and his eyes flick towards the lodge. 'Forget it.'

'It *is* just the journey you're worried about, right?'

'What's that supposed to mean?'

'Don't be coy with me, Ash. Hello? You and Lele? Ginger's starting to call you Lashle.' He sighs and sinks down onto a log. 'Look, Ash, if you are going to go there with Lele just make sure it's what you both really want. Or someone's going to get hurt.' I remember the Brangelina conversation Ginger and I had last night. 'And ... look, this is awkward, but have you thought about more practical issues?'

He glances up at me. 'Huh?'

Great, it looks like I'm going to have to spell it out. 'Protection. Do you want to get her pregnant?'

Ash recoils. 'No!'

'I'm just saying.'

'Hang on. You and Ginger have been pushing for this for ages, Saint. I thought you wanted me and Lele to get together?'

I shrug. 'Yeah, but we only want what's best for both of you. What do you want, Ash? If you made a mistake, rather tell Lele now.'

'Tell me what now?'

We both start guiltily as Lele emerges out of the lodge, rubbing her eyes. Ginger pads at her heels.

'Nothing,' Ash says quickly, getting to his feet.

Ginger spies the trashed equipment. 'Oh no! Our stuff!'

Lele races forward and grabs at her bag. She digs through it. 'Well, they ripped up the clothes and the food, but they didn't touch my sketchbook.'

'I'm happy for you, Lele,' I say, 'but we can't eat art, can we?'

'Ginger, will you check the rondavels for any supplies?' Ash says. 'The rest of us will see what we can salvage.'

There's no answer.

Ginger's standing with his back to us, his shoulders slumped.

Dammit. We've forgotten to warn him about the gory sight just metres away. I walk over and put an arm around his shoulder.

'Do you think it saved us, Saint?'

'What do you mean?'

He doesn't reply, so I give his arm a squeeze and turn back to help the others.

———————

'Blimey, guys! You are not going to believe this!'

I look up from where I'm packing the bike to see Ginger running towards us. He's cradling something in his arms, and as he gets closer I realise it's a bundle of dark brown fur the size of a basketball. 'Ginger, put that dog down, it could have rabies!'

Ginger's smile fades. 'It's not a dog, Saint.'

A head emerges out of the fur ball. I take in the blunt black muzzle, round dark eyes and large satellite-dish ears. 'What the hell is it then?'

Ginger looks sheepish. 'I think ... It's a hyena, okay?'

'I'm sorry. Let me rephrase that. Ginger, put that wild animal down before it takes your arm off.'

'It's just a baby, Saint.'

'Have you forgotten what happened last night?'

'But he needs us. I found him all alone in one of those round house things.'

'Well put it back! What if its mother is looking for it?'

'It won't be though, will it, Saint?' Ginger nods back towards the main building. 'His mother died, didn't she?'

'I hope you don't think you're taking that thing with us, Ginger,' Ash says.

'Of course I do.'

'No ways. That is *not* going to happen.'

Bright spots of colour appear on Ginger's cheeks and his jaw clenches. 'He'll die if we leave him here, Ash. His mum saved us from those lions and –'

Ash snorts. 'Yeah, right, Ginger. Dream on. They're just animals.'

'I'm taking him and that's bloody final.' I cannot remember seeing Ginger looking so determined about anything before. This could turn ugly.

'You really want to leave it here to die, Ash?' This from Lele.

'Thanks, Lele, at least someone here has a heart,' Ginger says, leaning forward so that she can stroke the hyena's head.

I motion for Ash to follow me away from the others. Ginger's staring at us defiantly, the wriggling animal clutched firmly in his arms. It's nipping at him but he's acting as if he doesn't feel a thing.

'Let Ginger take it, Ash.'

'It's a wild animal, Saint. It's not some stray puppy.'

'So? He's right – it will die out here if we just leave it.'

'It'll die if we take it with us. Then how's he going to feel?'

I really do not want to lug a wild animal around with us, but the last thing we need is a fracture in the group. 'Look, Ash, you don't need to feel that you have to take care of us all the time. You don't need to make our decisions for us. You're not Hester.' He glares at me – if Ripley is my sore spot, Hester is his. 'Let Ginger make up his own mind.'

Ash sighs, shakes his head and turns on his heel. 'When it dies, you deal with it, Ginger,' he says, without looking in Ginger's direction.

'Fine.'

Ash stalks over to his bike and starts angrily tightening the ropes around the remaining equipment.

'Thanks, Saint.' Ginger grins at me gratefully. 'He won't be any trouble, I promise.'

'There's a more practical problem though, isn't there, Ginger?'

'What do you mean?'

'How are you going to carry it on the bike?'

Ginger thinks for a second, his eyes narrowing in concentration. 'Got it. Lele,' he calls, 'can you chuck me my bag? Or what's left of it, anyway.'

Lele smiles at him and throws it over.

Gently setting the hyena on the ground Ginger begins to poke through the bag, pulling out a large black hoody that's only slightly ripped.

'You're going to boil in that, Ginger.'

'I'll be cool.'

The hyena snuffles at my feet and I step back instinctively. A little larger than a terrier, it stands on bandy legs, the front two almost twice the length of the back ones. The hair on the ridge of its spine stands up like a Mohawk, and black spots are spread over a mixture of tan, dark brown and grey fur. It stretches its long neck and shakes its stubby tail. It's so unfortunate-looking I can't help but find it cute.

'Aw,' Ginger says, 'look how tame he is. He's not even trying to run away.'

As if on cue the hyena ducks its head and darts forward, trying to make a break for it. Ginger yelps and scrambles after it, but the animal bounds out of his reach. Ash surprises us all by stepping forward and picking it up.

Ginger quickly shrugs himself into the hoody and holds his arms out.

'This is a really bad idea, Ginger,' Ash says. 'What are you going to feed it for a start?'

'I'll make a plan,' Ginger says. 'Don't stress about it, Ash. Now, hand him over.'

Ash hesitates and then passes the furry bundle to Ginger.

'Ginger,' I say, kicking the bike's saddlebags. 'You have a choice. The hyena or the chainsaw. You can't have both.'

'Oh, what?'

'There's not enough room.'

Ginger shrugs, grins and pulls the chainsaw off the back of the bike.

Lele laughs and shakes her head as Ginger cradles the hyena to his chest and zips it into the hoody, the animal's head poking up though the opening. 'Now that I thought I'd never see.'

Ash catches my eye. Maybe he's right. But then I take in Ginger's face. He's beaming down at the hyena, and I'm reminded of our conversation last night, the one we didn't have a chance to finish. If Ginger can't find himself a hot geek, then maybe a four-legged companion is the next best thing. I can't take that away from him.

'Have you thought of a name for him?' Lele asks as she climbs on the back of Ash's bike, wrapping her arms around his waist.

'Yeah. Bambi, of course.'

'What?' I say.

'Bambi,' Ginger shouts over the sound of Ash starting his bike. The noise doesn't seem to bother the hyena; it's busying itself by gnawing on the hoody's zipper.

'But Bambi was a baby deer, wasn't it? Aren't hyenas predators?'

'*Duh*, Saint,' he says. 'Bambi's mum also died, innit. He's the world's most famous orphan.'

Scowl still in place, Ash guns the bike and he and Lele zoot off towards the highway, a dust cloud trailing in their wake.

'Thanks for sticking up for me, Saint,' Ginger says, voice wobbling with emotion. 'That was cool of you.' He scratches the hyena's head and murmurs something to it in baby language.

'Let's go.' I jump on the bike, making sure that he can't see my face. He's already way too attached to the animal, and if Ash is right, and it doesn't survive, I'll only have myself to blame.

I'm far more comfortable with the bike now, but I'm still struggling with the gears. I keep hitting the space in between first and second and making the engine scream as if it's scolding me.

Ash and Lele zoom ahead of us. I'd like to think that Ash is finding the going easier because he doesn't have a hundred kilos of zombie slayer and a wild animal wedged on the bike behind him, but I suspect he's still seething about the hyena issue, and is taking it out on the bike.

We're approaching a wide concrete bridge, its surface free of the branches and debris I've been forced to contend with since we left Cape Town. I rev the throttle and whiz across it, for once enjoying the sensation of speed.

'Stop, Saint!' Ginger yells in my ear.

Without thinking, I squeeze the front brake hard, and the wheel locks beneath me. Shit! The bike feels like it wants to turn to the right, so I try and compensate by jamming my right foot on the back brake. For a horrible second the handlebars feel weightless and I have no control; it takes all of my strength to keep the bike upright, and then, suddenly, I have it back. Pressing the brakes with more care this time, I bring it to a stop.

'What the hell, Ginger? We almost crashed!'

But even before the words are out of my mouth he's jumped off the back of the bike with the hyena still zipped up in his hoody. 'I saw something!' he yells, looking like the father of the world's ugliest baby.

My legs are rubbery and it takes several seconds for me to gather myself before I join him at the side of the bridge.

He's leaning over the edge, holding on tightly to his new pet. 'Bloody hell, Saint. Check this out.'

A chasm yawns beneath us, a river glimmering far below. But it is not the view that has Ginger so excited. There's another bridge parallel to this one – not more than a couple of hundred metres away. It's constructed out of criss-crossing metal struts, and there's something hanging from a cord attached to a platform in the centre of the structure.

'It's a Rotter!'

'It can't be, Ginger.'

But he's right. It is. It's hanging upside down, the rope attached to its feet, its head just metres from the river bed. It's wriggling from side to side, flapping its arms like a large rotten bird.

'Who on earth would bother to do that to a Rotter?' I say, still taking in what I'm seeing.

'I don't think anyone did do it, Saint,' Ginger yells over the howl of Ash's bike heading back towards us.

'What do you mean?'

'I think it did it to itself.'

He points to a buckled sign stuck to the metal cage above the platform. It's spattered with rust but I can still make out a word: *Bungee.*

'You've lost me, Ginger.'

'Well, duh, Saint. It was bungee jumping –'

'What's going on, guys?' Lele says from behind me, making me jump. She peers over the side. 'Holy crap! Is that what I think it is?'

'We can't just leave it hanging there like that,' Ginger says.

'Why not?'

'I bloody hate Rotters, you know that, Saint, but I dunno, it doesn't seem kosher leaving it there. And anyway, we haven't seen any people near here, so it's not as if it can run off and start attacking anyone.'

'Found another stray, Ginger?' Ash says. 'I hope you don't think we're going to be taking a Rotter along with us as well.' But I'm relieved to see that he says this with a smile.

'Can I borrow your panga, Ash? I want to go cut it down.' Ginger moves to pass me the writhing bundle of fur.

'No ways, Ginger,' I say.

Lele sighs. 'I'll go.'

Ash hands her his panga and we wait while she jogs to the end of the bridge and disappears behind a bunch of thorn bushes. A couple of minutes later she reappears on the other side and begins picking her way past the metal struts before lying down on her stomach and shuffling forward to reach the rope.

'Careful!' I yell across to her. 'Don't fall!'

The Rotter moans, the sound bouncing off the steep cliffs either side of it.

'Get a move on, Lele,' Ginger calls. 'What's taking so long?'

'Shut up, Ginger,' she shouts back. 'It's really tough and –'

But before she can finish the rope suddenly snaps and the Rotter falls the final metres into the shallow water below. Its feet are still tied together, but it manages to crawl towards the bank.

'Wait there, Lele!' Ash calls. 'I'll drive round and get you.'

'Does that count as our good deed for the day?' I say to Ginger as the Rotter scrabbles into the greenery next to the river bank and disappears from sight. 'Can we go now?'

'Just think, Saint,' Ginger says. 'He's probably been hanging there for ten years. Must've been turned just before he jumped. Imagine that, think you're off for a day's adventure and then . . .'

I shudder. 'Horrible.'

Ginger shrugs. 'I can think of worse ways to go.'

'Oh yeah, like what?'

'Being turned into one of them Guardian things for a start.'

BWAAAAAAAA-POP-POP – the engine sputters, and the bike shudders. I press the accelerator again, and this time the engine groans like a dying mechanical elephant.

Dammit.

Doing my best to keep the bike from toppling over I pull to a stop and wait for Ginger to climb off. I don't bother with the kickstand and let it crash to the ground. Somehow I don't think we'll be using it again.

'What's up, Saint?'

'I think we've run out of petrol, Ginger.'

'Oh, bummer.'

'You can say that again.'

Ginger unzips the hyena from its makeshift pouch and places it on the grass at our feet. I wait for it to dart away again, but it doesn't. Perhaps it's too hot. I don't know how Ginger can stand it – his forehead is beaded with sweat from having to wear the hoody in this heat – but I know he won't complain.

'Still,' Ginger says, breathing in deeply. 'We could have run out of petrol at a worse place, innit? I mean, it's gorgeous here.'

Directly in front of us a wide bridge spans a lagoon, the sky reflected in its glassy surface. The only signs of habitation appear on distant rocky hills to our right; a scatter of white houses clinging to their sides. Ash and Lele are powering on ahead. I wave my hands above my head to attract their attention, but Ash appears to be too busy enjoying the smooth tar of the bridge to notice that we aren't behind him. He only finally slows the bike when he reaches the road on the other side of the bridge.

'What are we going to do now?' Ginger asks as Ash swings the bike around and heads back to us.

'Like I know. Just make sure your friend there doesn't drown.'

The hyena is snuffling at the edge of the water. Ginger looks down at it with the fond eyes of a parent who believes his child can do no wrong. 'Reckon there's another one of those petrol stations near here?' he asks.

'A lot of good that will do us.' We've come across plenty of service stations en route, but without electricity the petrol pumps are useless, and try as we might we've been unable to prise open the manhole covers that cap the fuel stores – they have either been rusted over or locked tight. Ash insisted on trying over and over again, though with every failed attempt he withdrew further into himself.

Ginger delves in his bag and offers me a piece of biltong.

I mime throwing up. 'You've got to be joking, Ginger.' We may not have found any petrol, but against all odds he managed to find a packet of vacuum-packed biltong in one of the service station shops – miraculously untouched by the legions of rats, baboons and other scavengers that had trashed the place. Its sell-by date of January 2011 hasn't put him off. I just hope he doesn't feed any to the hyena. It looks too young to be eating solid food, and Ginger's already collected a number of foul-smelling stains on his hoody.

I drop to my haunches next to the water and splash some on my face, then crack my spine and jump up and down to get the feeling back into my bum. The last few kilometres have been exhausting, the road flanked by large trees and dense foliage that have littered the tar with ten years of dead branches and decomposing leaves. In places it was like travelling through a damp green tunnel, as if the trees were greedily swallowing up the road bit by bit, spitting out rotten limbs onto the tarmac like a monster discarding bone fragments.

And through it all still no sign of life. Human life, that is. There's been plenty of animal action – posses of baboons who refused to budge from the centre of the highway as we zoomed through them, flocks of ostriches loping across the veld and a fair number of mongooses and other rodents. This area must once have been thriving, a prime destination for holidaymakers, if the signs advertising luxury accommodation and water sports are anything to go by. But there's not much to write home about now. Approximately an hour ago we passed a massive crater ringed with heaps of buckled metal – the remains of some kind of processing plant. The inferno must have been quite a sight –

even the tar on the road next to it had melted. But that wasn't the worst of it. At one stage the road widened out into a triple-lane highway that was free of dead vehicles and potholes, and as we topped a rise and whirred downwards I caught a glimpse of the sea spreading out before us. I had been convinced that this time we'd find an enclave of some description, but the town, harbour and informal settlement on its outskirts were the casualties of ten years of bush fires – yet another dead city.

'Hey, guys,' Ginger calls to Ash and Lele as they pull up and park next to where I've dumped my bike. 'How pretty is this place?'

Ash ignores him. 'Petrol?' he says to me.

I nod. 'Petrol.'

'Just great.'

'It looks likes it's on foot from here on in.'

Ash pulls a hand through his hair. 'Lele, you wait with the others. I'll go ahead and see if I can find some fuel.' He looks hopefully towards the houses in the distance. 'There has to be some somewhere.'

'Shouldn't I come with you?' she asks.

He shakes his head. 'I'll be cool.'

Before she can argue he leaps back onto the bike, guns the engine and heads back towards the bridge.

'He's in a bit of mood, innit?' Ginger says.

'You can't really blame him, Ginger. This trip was his idea. Can you imagine how awful he's feeling? We've travelled hundreds of kilometres and, so far, no survivors, no fuel and the only Rotter we've seen has been hanging from a bridge for the last ten years.'

'He'll cheer up when we find a settlement,' he says.

'If we ever do.'

'Whole areas of the country, dead,' Lele says. 'What happened to all the people? All the Rotters?'

'I reckon the Rotters only hang about where there *are* people,' I say. I think of the thousands of the walking dead that surround Cape Town; the Resurrectionists idiotically feeding more hosts to that parasitic spaghetti stuff.

'Should we walk for a bit?' Lele says, gazing towards the other side of the bridge.

What I really want to do is lie down and sleep, but the chances of Ash scoring any fuel are slim and I suspect we have a long walk ahead of us. May as well make a start. 'Yeah. Why not.'

Ginger gathers the hyena into his arms, and I help him shoulder his rucksack – or what's left of it – before Lele and I gather up the rolled-up sleeping bags and the water containers.

Together we ramble over the bridge.

'One of you guys want to carry Bambi for a bit?' Ginger asks hopefully.

I snort. 'He's all yours, Ginger.'

The forest has continued to eat up the road on the other side, but there's a walkway right next to the lagoon. The corpses of half-submerged boats litter the water and far to our right I spot the remains of a buckled railway bridge – from here it looks like a neglected child's toy.

Ginger puts the hyena on the ground. It raises its head and shakes its body.

'You sure you want to do that, Ginger?' I say.

'He won't run away.'

'That's not what's worrying me.' There are several ducklings paddling near to the bank below us. 'Just watch it doesn't –'

Too late. The hyena perks up and scurries towards the edge.

'Bambi! No!' Ginger shouts. He barges past me and rugby tackles the hyena, grabbing it around its torso before it can snap at the baby ducks. It yelps in shock and whips around, clamping its teeth down on Ginger's hand. 'Ow!' Ginger yells, but he doesn't drop it.

'Oh crap,' Lele mutters, and she races over to him.

'I knew this would happen,' I sigh.

'Take Bambi, Saint,' Lele says.

I back up. 'No thanks.'

'Just do it, Saint.' There's a panicky look in her eye – Ginger's injury isn't that serious, is it? Rivulets of blood run down his fingers, but he doesn't appear to be in that much pain. I decide to humour her and take the still-writhing animal out of his arms. It immediately calms down and looks up at me with round black eyes. I'm not stupid enough to think I've got some magical way with wild animals – even Bambi must realise that the ducklings are out of his reach; they're now happily swimming away next to their mother.

Lele grabs Ginger's hand. 'Careful,' he says.

'Sorry.' She looks down at it and confusion flits over her face.

'What's up, Zombie Bait?'

'Nothing. It doesn't look too bad.' She pulls her water canteen out of her bag and washes the blood away.

'Whoa, Bambi's jaws are well strong,' Ginger says proudly. 'You can see the teeth marks and everything.' He waves his injured hand in my direction. Small puncture wounds mark the soft flesh between his thumb and forefinger.

Lele rips off a piece of her shirt and wraps it around Ginger's hand. 'You're going to have to keep that clean, Ginger.'

'Now will you see sense, Ginger?' I say, passing Bambi back to him. 'It needs to go back to the wild.'

'He didn't mean to do it, Saint. He was just scared.' The hyena cocks its head to the side as if it knows that we're talking about it.

'Well, don't come crying to me when you get rabies and we have to put both of you down.'

Late afternoon sun beats down on us as we carry on trudging along next to the lagoon. On the left-hand side of the road several houses fight to be seen through the greedy foliage, the shards of their broken windows catching the sun; ivy gobbles up rotting signs advertising guest houses and holiday accommodation. We round a bend and find Ash untying the equipment on the back of his bike.

'You run out of petrol too, Ash?' Ginger asks.

''Fraid so. Not that we could have gone much further anyway.'

'What you on about?'

'You'll see. Come on.'

He strides off without even checking to see if we're going to follow behind him like good little Mall Rats. I'm getting sick of his downbeat attitude. We're all drained and his moody emo behaviour is not the way to deal with it.

Lele hurries to catch up to him, but I hang back with Ginger. A section of the cliff next to us has vomited rocks and dead trees onto the road, and we slowly pick our way over them, checking for snakes and other critters. Then I see what Ash was talking about.

The highway is blocked by a mishmash of cars, a bus, lashed-together planks and garage doors. The barricade extends from the sheer cliff face on our left to the walkway's railings on our right. It's too high to see what might be behind it. Ginger and I put on a spurt of speed and catch up with the others. I can't help it – I feel the beginnings of hope stirring inside me.

'You know what's behind this, right?' Ash says.

'Yeah,' Lele says. 'It's gotta be some sort of enclave.'

'Well, what are we waiting for?' Ginger asks. 'Let's go check it out.'

The only way through the barricade is through the bus that makes up the main part of the blockage. Ash has cut through the wire which covers the bus's door, and I pull myself up and into it, following him out through a broken window on the other side. As I land, my feet slide out from underneath me – the tarmac is hidden beneath a mixture of fishy-smelling silt and black mud and I have to steady myself against the bus. The edge of my T-shirt catches on a piece of metal and I hear the sound of fabric ripping. *Dammit.*

Lele jumps down next to me. She looks as defeated as I feel. If there is life here I can't see any sign of it. Yellow bone shards and scraps of plastic peek up through the mud, and the buildings around us are trashed – most are little more than burned-out skeletons.

'Saint!' Ginger calls from behind me. 'Take Bambi.'

I reach up and he drops the hyena into my arms. It writhes and I brace myself for it to nip at me, but it settles down and sniffs the air instead.

Ginger's fighting to fit his body through the bus's window. Finally he's forced to pull himself through head first, landing face down in the filth.

He jumps to his feet. 'Oh, what?' he whines, using the bottom of his T-shirt to wipe his face and hands. 'This place is toast.'

I pass Bambi to him.

'We don't know that for sure, Ginger,' Ash snaps. He is standing a few metres away, his back to us. 'Don't be so negative.'

I've had just about as much of Ash's moody behaviour as I can take for one day. 'How can you accuse Ginger of being negative? He's just being honest. Get real, Ash, this place is another dead end.'

I wait for him to turn on me, but he simply swears under his breath.

'Hello? Aren't you going to apologise to Ginger?'

'It's cool, Saint,' Ginger says. 'I don't mind if Ash wants to take it out on me.'

'Well I do mind. Mr Superior needs to be taken down a peg or two.'

Ignoring me, Ash stalks off down the street.

'Fantastic,' I call after him. 'Run away from your problems, Ash. That will work.'

'Should I go after him?' Lele asks.

'Nah. Just let him cool off.'

'Shall we go see what's what?' Ginger asks.

I tie the ripped pieces of my T-shirt together. 'Yeah. Come on.' But all I can think is: What's the point? Ginger's right, this place is toast – burnt toast.

We trudge past the melted remains of a garage forecourt; there's no way Ginger's going to source any biltong from its collapsed One Stop shop. Across the road from it there's a mall-type structure, its innards hanging exposed to the elements – piping, wiring and thick yellow insulation fabric spilling from its collapsed ceiling.

'Check this out,' Lele says. She's staring through the doorway of a glass-fronted coffee shop, a red Vida e sign peeling above it. Its window is fortified with rusty wire and rotting planks. I peer past her. There are a couple of mattresses coated with black mould on the floor, an upended table and a tatty sofa. 'Looks like someone used to live here. Like they converted it into some kind of house.'

'Ugh.'

Other shops and restaurants also appear to have been made into makeshift homes at some stage, and as I wander past the town square, its cobbles clogged with more silt and mud, I notice that the derelict buildings that surround it are also covered with chicken wire. The side streets around us are blocked by old cars, pieces of metal and corrugated iron, isolating the high street from the world outside.

'What do you think happened here?' Lele asks.

'That,' Ginger says, pointing to one of the barricades which block off the side streets. Part of the fence is missing, as if it's been swept aside by a giant hand. 'Rotters probably got in.'

'So where are they now, then?' Lele asks.

I shrug. 'Your guess is as good as mine. I think we should find somewhere to camp for the night. It's getting late.'

'Not here, though,' Ginger and Lele say almost simultaneously.

'Shall we go back?' Ginger says. 'Camp next to the lagoon?'

'Yeah. Let's catch up with Mr Moody and head back.'

'Where is he though?' Ginger asks. The street ahead is empty.

There's the squelching sound of approaching feet and Ash appears from behind the blocky structure of an apartment building. 'Guys!' he shouts. 'I've found something.'

It's rare to hear Ash excited – he hardly ever raises his voice – and Lele and I are off and running, feet sliding in the mud, before he's even finished his sentence, Ginger at our heels.

We join him at the back entrance of the building, where he points to a vehicle that's parked a few metres away, just in front of the fence that severs the street from the outside world.

'So what? It's just a car, Ash,' I say.

'It's not a car, it's a bakkie.'

'A what?'

'Like a pickup truck.'

'Whatever. So what's the big deal?'

'Duh, Saint,' Ginger says. 'It's the first one we've seen in here, right? I mean, that hasn't been used to build the fences. And anyway, it's in pretty good nick.'

Ginger's right. The vehicle's tan paint is pitted with rust, and the metal of its flanks is dented and buckled, but other than that it looks perfect. It's in a better state than any car or truck I've seen since the War.

'But that's not the point,' Ash says. 'Look at the ground.'

Twin grooves mark the mud beneath the car's tyres, and they lead back to the main road and stretch into the distance.

'Holy crap,' Lele says, moving forward towards the bakkie. 'Tyre tracks.'

'So where's its driver?' Ginger asks as we approach the vehicle.

I cup my hands around my face and peer into the car's interior. The seats are empty, but something on the floor of the passenger side catches my eye.

'No way!'

'What?'

'There's a gun in here.'

'Guys!' Lele breathes.

I hear the squeal of hinges and look up in time to see the building's back door creaking open.

'Uh-oh,' Ginger says as a figure steps out into the light.

I make out a mass of curls and wide terrified eyes. It's a girl. She's clutching several planks of wood to her chest, but as soon as she sees us she lets them fall as if she's readying herself to run.

'Blimey,' Ginger breathes. 'That is one good-looking Rotter.'

'Wait!' Lele says. 'We aren't going to hurt you, honest.'

The girl freezes.

Her eyes flit to the car. She must be kicking herself for leaving the gun behind.

'Do we look that dangerous?' Ginger murmurs to me.

'Probably,' I say. We're all covered in mud, our clothes are ripped and there's a huge knife strapped to Ash's back. I nod my head in his direction, and he gets the picture. He unsheathes the panga and throws it away from us.

The girl takes in a shuddering breath. 'Oh Goddess! I can't believe it. Where are you *from*?'

'Long story,' I say.

Ginger coughs nervously, and busies himself scratching Bambi's head. He's turning redder by the second. She's tall – almost as tall as Ash – her bare legs are well muscled. Her hair is a couple of shades darker than Ginger's and feathers and flowers are woven through her curls. But her personal style isn't the cause of Ginger's embarrassment, it's the fact that she's wearing very little – a pair of khaki shorts cut high on her thighs and a tight black tank top that doesn't leave much to the imagination.

'Is that a dog?' The girl asks.

'He's a hyena,' Ginger says, still struggling to look her in the eye.

'Oh wow!' she says. 'That's –'

'Ridiculous?' I say. 'We know.'

'He's so cute,' she says.

'You think?' Ginger manages to grin at her.

The girl laughs nervously. 'I'm Megan.'

'I'm Saint. This is Lele, Ginger and Ash.'

'Lekker names,' the girl says. She looks me up and down. 'Saint – wow, that totally suits you.'

Ginger, the one responsible for our nicknames, grins proudly.

Megan pops a lock of hair into her mouth and chews on it – a nervous gesture if ever I saw one.

'Are there other people around here?' Ash asks.

'Ja, of course. Well, not *here* exactly. But ... Are you from a settlement?' She frowns. 'I thought all the ones near here were overrun years ago.'

Ginger opens his mouth to answer her, but Ash nudges him. 'Something like that.'

We haven't discussed what we'd actually say if we came into contact with anyone. Perhaps Ash is wise to be cautious, but it doesn't look like Megan poses any threat. In fact, now that's she getting over her shock she's fidgeting excitedly from foot to foot.

'But I don't understand,' Megan says. 'How come the Old Souls didn't take you?'

'Old Souls?'

'The dead,' Megan says. 'Sorry, Old Souls is what Father calls them.'

'Just lucky, I guess,' Ash says quickly, before Ginger can blurt out his freak-of-nature spiel.

'Yeah,' Ginger says. 'We're really good at running.' He blushes again. Ginger's as rubbish at lying as he is at hiding his feelings.

'We haven't seen any Rotters – I mean – Old Souls around here,' Lele says. 'Are there some in the area?'

'Oh, ja,' Megan says. 'Loads and loads. But not here, of course, they left years ago.'

'What exactly happened here?'

'Oh, there was a big flood – you can tell by the mud, right? And one of the fences was washed away. The Old Souls got in, and ... ' She falters.

'We get the picture,' I say. I nod towards the truck – the bakkie. 'So this is your car?'

'Ja,' she says, looking pleased with herself.

'It's in good condition.'

'Thanks. I do all the maintenance myself, but Land Cruisers are hardy anyway.'

'You know where we can get some petrol?' Ash asks.

'Goddess, no. Well, not around here.'

Ash gives her one of his rare charming smiles. 'You couldn't spare any, could you?' He nods back to the main barricade. 'We've had to dump our bikes back there.'

'What kind of bikes do you have?'

Ash looks at me and I shrug back at him. How would I know? 'Um ... ones with two wheels?' I say.

She laughs. 'In any case the Land Cruiser runs on diesel, so that wouldn't work in your bikes.' She bites her lip. 'Vegetable oil might work.'

'Seriously? You got any of that?'

'No, sorry.'

Dammit.

'Are there other survivors around here?' Ash asks.

'Oh, ja. Course! But ... how far have you come?'

Ash catches my eye. 'May as well,' he says.

'We're from Cape Town,' I say.

'Cape Town? No ways! Are you ... Are you here to rescue us? Is everything back to normal in the city? Are –'

'No,' Ash says, interrupting her. 'Far from it. It's a long story. You think we could meet everyone else first?'

She glances at us all individually again, then seems to come to some sort of decision. 'Ja. It'll be dark soon. Oh! Wait.' She turns back to collect the wood, and Lele hurries to help her. 'Thanks,' she says, smiling up at her. Her teeth are very, very white.

Dumping the wood in the back of the bakkie she walks

around to the driver's seat. 'Well, hop in! Goddess, no one will believe it when they see you!'

But there's a very important question we've neglected to ask her. 'Hang on,' I say. 'How come the Old Souls don't get *you*?'

She toys with her hair again and grins at me, 'I'm also very good at running.'

Maybe she isn't quite as naive as she looks.

With absolutely no warning Megan yanks the wheel to the left, and for an instant I'm sure we're going to crash into the trees that border the whole road out of the ruined settlement. But before I've had time to brace for the impact I'm sure is coming the car has barrelled through a mask of branches and thumped off the highway onto a narrow forest track.

Now that we're in the forest proper I'm hit with a thick peaty odour, and the trees press in on us as if we're entering a damp, green mouth. Huge ferns spread their fingers over the track, twisting tree trunks coil around each other, and dull red mushrooms and diseased-looking fungi push up from the forest floor. Ugh. I flinch as something large crashes through the bushes in the distance.

'What the hell was that?'

'Oh, don't worry. Probably just an elephant.'

Great. 'What the hell are we doing here?'

'You'll see!'

Megan changes gear, and over the growl of the engine I hear something else: the moaning of Rotters. So *this* is where they are.

'This place is full of Old Souls,' Megan says, reading my mind.

'Yeah, about that. Seriously, how come they don't attack –'

A Rotter lunges out from behind a thicket and falls into our path. Megan brakes sharply and swerves around it, branches scraping the side of the car. I hear the muffled sounds of Ash, Ginger and Lele thumping into the back of the cab and swearing behind me. There's a glass window in between where we're sitting and the open back section, and Megan reaches behind her and slides it open. 'Sorry!' she calls, speeding up again, the back wheels skidding on wet leaves.

Megan rounds a bend and pulls to a stop in front of a tree trunk, its bark shaggy with ivy. The murky shapes of Rotters flit between the surrounding undergrowth, but there's no sign of anything that could be a fence or the edges of an enclave.

'Now where?'

Megan leans down, giving me a great view of her chest, and retrieves the gun. She shoves it in her bag and smiles at me. 'Come on, I'll show you.'

I climb out of the car and sling my rucksack over my shoulder. Lele sidles up next to me. 'Is this the part where she kills us?' she murmurs.

Megan grins at all of us in turn. There are several Rotters lumbering around, but they completely ignore her.

'Megan,' I say, 'have you got a twin by any chance?'

'No,' she says. 'Why would you ask that?'

Bang goes that theory.

'Hey!' Ginger says. 'Maybe all redheads are immune to Rotter attack. How cool would that be? Think about it: ginger power!'

'I don't think so, Ginger,' Ash says.

'So why do you think the Rotters don't attack you?' Lele asks.

'Mother says that maybe I've got special pheromones or something.'

'Special whattames?' Ginger asks.

'They don't like the way I smell.'

'You smell fine to me,' Ginger says, turning scarlet again. To cover his embarrassment he puts the hyena down on the forest floor while he shrugs on his hoody.

'Not a good plan, Ginger,' Ash says, eyeing Bambi. The hyena is making a curious grumbling sound in his throat. 'If it runs off we'll never find it in here.'

'He won't run off, he knows who his mummy is,' Ginger says. 'Anyway, it's only for a sec.'

Megan looks serious. 'Listen. Stay close to me. And I should probably mention that –'

The bushes rustle and a rabbit darts in front of us, making me jump. The hyena gives a high-pitched *yip*, and before any of us can spring for it, takes off after the rabbit, its strange bandy legs propelling it into the bushes.

'Bambi!' Ginger yells, dumping his bag and fleeing after it.

'Shit!' Ash hisses.

I race after Ginger, spurred on by the vision of spending the next three days combing the forest for the two of them. Lele flies past me, her bag thumping on her back.

'No! Please! You mustn't run ahead without me!' Megan yells after us.

I hear the rustle and snap of Ginger blundering through the trees – he sounds as cumbersome as that elephant, and then: *CRACK*.

That was way too loud to be a breaking branch.

Lele stops dead and turns to face me. 'You know what that was, right, Saint?'

Suddenly it's difficult to swallow. 'Yeah,' I say. 'A gunshot.'

LELE

Ginger's standing stock-still, staring up at the leafy canopy above us. He's managed to catch Bambi, and the hyena is wriggling in his arms and nipping at his jacket. I'm so relieved to see him that for a moment I forget about the gunshot – and, more importantly, that where there's a gunshot there has to be someone with a gun.

Saint and Ash arrive behind me, breathing hard, as I follow Ginger's gaze up into the trees. Someone's staring down at us – someone with a shaven head, angry eyes and a rifle in their arms. He or she – it's hard to tell which – is leaning over a long wooden bridge, so camouflaged by the leaves and branches that we could easily have walked underneath it without noticing it.

'Put your hands in the air where I can see them!' It's clear from the voice that it's a woman, and we all do as she says, except for Ginger, who's still holding Bambi close to his chest. 'I *said*, put your hands in the air!'

'Don't shoot! I have a hyena!'

'You've got a *what*?' Her grip tightens again on the rifle.

Something warm and wet drips onto my cheek, making me flinch. I risk wiping it away, and my fingers come back bloody. Oh *gross*. There's a dead rabbit swinging above my head, a snare around its neck, hanging from a wire attached to the bridge's wooden railing.

'Wait! Don't shoot! They're with me!' Megan says. 'Please, Moreka, put the gun down. They aren't a threat, I promise.'

'And how do you know that, Megan?' the woman says, without moving an inch.

'I just do.'

'Not good enough.'

'Please, we're –' Ash slams his mouth shut as the gun swings in his direction.

'I don't remember asking you a question, *boy*.'

'Moreka – please,' Megan says. 'Trust me, they're cool.'

Moreka's eyes flick to each of us; she seems to be paying particular attention to Ginger and Ash. And then, finally, she lowers the gun.

'I've got a bad feeling about this,' Ginger hisses.

Megan smiles reassuringly. 'It's fine, really, you can trust me.' She gestures towards a large tree a few metres away from us. Its branches droop over the bridge. 'Come on, it's easy to climb up.'

Moreka points at Ash 'You. Boy. Leave that knife on the ground.'

Ash does as he's told, and throws the panga away from him.

'Meggie, you checked the others for weapons?'

'Really, Moreka. They're cool. I swear on Mother's life.'

I've been so tense that I haven't noticed that the number of Rotters has increased. They bumble around us, collecting under where Moreka is standing.

'Let's go,' Megan says.

'No ways,' I say, not caring that Megan can hear me. 'Do we really want to go up there? Can we seriously trust this chick?'

'What have we got to lose?' Ash says.

'Er ... how about our lives, Ash?' Ginger says. But Ash is already heading for the tree.

Saint catches my eye and raises her eyebrows. 'Come on then.'

Ash goes first, closely followed by Saint. Ginger zips Bambi into his hoody and follows suit. Then it's my turn. It's not difficult to haul myself from branch to branch, and although the bridge groans as I throw myself up and onto it, it seems quite solid. I steady myself and move across to give Megan room to climb up.

Moreka eyes all of us in turn. She's way shorter than she looked from down on the ground, but her bulk makes up for her height and all of it appears to be muscle. She's wearing a tight black T-shirt and khaki combats, and her forearms are scored with scars.

'Not bad,' Saint whispers to me. 'The first survivors we meet, and they're gorgeous Amazons. I can live with that.'

Bambi pushes his head out of the top of Ginger's hoody.

Moreka snorts. 'You really weren't kidding about the hyena.'

'They're from *Cape Town*,' Megan says as if she's been bursting to say the words.

'Cape Town?' Moreka frowns. 'Impossible. Meggie, these kids are lying to you, sweetheart.'

'We're not lying,' Saint says.

'And they're like me!' Megan says. 'The Old Souls don't get them!'

'Don't call them that,' Moreka snaps, spitting over the balcony at the Rotters below. 'The dead have no souls.' She turns back to us. 'One wrong move and you'll be sorry.'

Saint looks her straight in the eye. 'We'll behave as long as you don't point that gun at us again.'

Moreka and Saint stare at each other for several seconds. Then Moreka shrugs. 'This is on your head, Meggie.' She leans over the railing, snags the snare's wire and drags the dead rabbit towards her. Then she strides off down the bridge. There's a tattoo of a scorpion on the back of her neck, the words *Never Surrender* written underneath it.

'Sorry about that.' Megan grins at us. 'I did try and warn you. Moreka's cool – she just doesn't trust people easily.'

'I would never have known,' Saint says.

We follow Megan along the bridge. It leads into the heart of the forest and connects to other, thinner rope and wood constructions that disappear off into the gloom in several directions.

'So you live up here?' Ash asks. 'In the forest canopy?'

'Ja.'

'Clever,' Ash says. 'Rotter-proof. Too high up for the dead to reach.'

'It was built years ago,' Megan says. 'I think it started off as some sort of holiday place, but no one really knows.'

The light is diminishing fast, and now that it's getting darker I'm finding it hard to see exactly where to place my feet. Saint swears under her breath behind me. I peer down at the forest floor. We must be three or four metres above the ground.

'How far do these bridges go?' I ask.

'Oh, quite far. We can't use all of them, though. A lot of them keep breaking.'

'Excellent,' Saint mutters.

'That's why I was collecting wood from the old settlement. They need a ton of maintenance and Mother is trying to build more so that there's a bigger area to hunt from.'

'It's like *Mad Max*! No, like *Avatar*!' Ginger says, 'But without them blue cat people and –'

'Enough with the move refs already, Ginger,' Ash hisses.

'Sorry, but I keep expecting to see Ewoks or something.'

Megan turns round and laughs. *'Return of the Jedi?'*

'Yeah! How do you know that?'

'I loved *Star Wars* when I was little.'

Saint snorts behind me, and I turn around to catch her eye. 'True love,' she mouths.

A faint glow shines through the branches ahead. A fire?

'Nearly there,' Megan says.

'Whoa ... ' Ginger points to a structure that's appeared out of the shadows to our left. It's a sophisticated version of the tree houses the kids in the Agriculturals used to build during the summer, and I can see other similar buildings set further back in the trees. A more substantial bridge leads to a huge wooden platform ringed with a solid balustrade. Sparks shoot up into the air from a fire burning in a metal container in the centre of the platform. I can make out Moreka's unmistakeable stocky silhouette and the shapes of a number of other people sitting around it.

'Nice,' Ginger says. 'Tree people.'

'Everyone!' Megan says. 'You won't *believe* it!'

She waves us forward. There are five other people in all – two men and three women. The women give off the same threatening vibe as Moreka – their hair is also cut close to their scalps, and they all look to be around the same age as the Mantis. The two men stay seated. One of them has a bundle in his arms, and it's only when it moves and makes a mewling sound that I realise it's a baby swaddled in some kind of fur blanket.

Ginger offers his hand to the woman closest to him; she's skinny and white and her lips are like razors. She ignores it.

'Don't worry, everyone,' he says, undaunted. 'We're cool. We're not going to hurt you.'

Thin Lips laughs humourlessly. 'I'd like to see you try.'

'Awesome welcome,' Saint mutters.

'Is Mother back yet?' Megan asks.

'She's checking the east-side traps,' Moreka says, crouching down and starting to skin the rabbit she took from the snare. There's a wet rip as she pulls its fur from its body in one go. Thin Lips and the other two women continue to ignore us. They look like they might be sisters; they're both plump and are wearing identical strappy tops that show off impressive biceps.

Ash taps my shoulder and motions the three of us away from the group. Thin Lips shoots us a suspicious glance, but no one tries to stop us.

'Well, this is interesting,' Saint says when we're out of earshot. 'What the hell is up with these freaky tree people?'

'No idea,' Ash says. 'You think they could be dangerous?'

'Are you kidding?' Saint says. 'Have you seen the arms on those women? On the bright side, though, it doesn't look like there are any Guardians here.' She pauses. 'I hope.'

I feel a chill creep up my arms that has nothing to do with the dank forest air.

'They're not all bad,' Ginger says. 'Their set-up is pretty cool.'

'Really, Ginger?' Saint says. 'I reckon even the Resurrectionists would give us a warmer welcome.'

'But you have to admit Megan is seriously awesome.'

Saint rolls her eyes and peers back at the people sitting around the fire, 'Well, they've had their chance to kill us and they haven't taken it, so I think we're safe enough for now.'

'Let's find out what the hell is going on,' Ash says. 'Megan,' he calls. 'Can we talk to you for a second?'

Megan turns away from Moreka and hurries over. 'I'm so sorry,' she whispers. 'They're just a bit ... nervous of you.'

Thin Lips looks over to us and says something to Moreka. She bursts out laughing.

'Right,' Saint says. 'They're acting like they're petrified.'

'So,' Ginger says, turning to Megan, 'there are no Guardians here, right?'

'No what?'

Ginger screws his mouth to one side as if he's thinking about what to say. 'Where we're from there are these, well, actually they're teenagers, and we think they've been taken over by the spaghetti stuff, you know, the stuff that's inside the Rotters, and it turns them into, like, these robot people. But they're not like Rotters, they're more ... You know, like in *Terminator II*, when Arnie is a robot, but he's not actually a robot, so he acts like he's human even though he isn't a human?' He catches his breath. 'Make sense?'

'No,' Megan says. 'But I can safely say that there are no teenagers here. I'm the only one.'

Ash looks thoughtful for a moment and then walks back to the fire. Saint elbows me and we hurry to catch up to him. 'Have we offended you somehow?' he says to Moreka.

'You haven't offended us,' Moreka says, eyes still fixed on the rabbit, which is now perfectly skinned.

'You don't want to know where we're from?' Ginger says. 'And what mission we're on or anything? What's going on in the world?'

Moreka tosses the rabbit carcass to Thin Lips, who catches it neatly. 'You aren't the first to pass through here, and unfortunately you won't be the last. We don't need the trouble.'

'You've had other visitors?' Ash asks. 'When and how many?'

No one answers him.

'We're clearly not welcome here,' I say to Ash. 'Maybe we should just leave.'

'No!' Megan says. 'Please don't. Why don't you sit down and I'll get you some food. You must be starving.'

Ginger grins at her. 'You can say that again.'

I expect the others to object to sharing their resources with us, but they don't even glance our way. The two men still haven't said a word.

'Please, sit,' Megan says.

We have no choice but to squash in around the fire. There are no chairs; Thin Lips and Moreka squat on their haunches, the plump sisters are sitting cross-legged and the men appear to be sitting on tree stumps – wrinkled tree stumps with large white ... toenails. Oh gross. I nudge Ginger. 'Are those ... elephant feet?' I whisper to him.

He checks them out, blanches and cuddles Bambi closer to his chest.

Megan skips over to a large stoneware pot placed on a stand next to the fire. She collects up several wooden bowls and starts spooning a sloppy brown mess into them. It looks like crap, but it smells okay – like herby mutton stew.

Ginger looks up at the man holding the baby. Unlike that of the shaven-headed women his hair is fairly long, gathered into a ponytail at the nape of his neck. The baby mewls and Ponytail's companion – a slight guy with shaggy dreadlocks – fusses with the blanket. 'Nice place you've got here,' Ginger says. 'What's the baby's name?'

'Artemesia.'

'Oh, cute name!'

Ponytail manages a watery smile.

Ginger beams at the group of women. 'Which one of you is her mum?'

Moreka laughs. She nods towards the guy with dreadlocks. 'That would be Tumi there.'

Still unfazed, Ginger unzips his hoody and lets Bambi jump down onto the platform. The hyena cracks a yawn and starts snuffling at Moreka's feet. The first hint of a smile we've seen from any of them touches her lips and she reaches out to stroke its back. At least someone's getting a warm welcome. The other three women take it in turns to make a fuss of Bambi and even Thin Lips smiles. Only the two men seem to be immune to Bambi's charms. When the hyena pads over to them the guy with the ponytail stands up and cuddles the child protectively to his chest.

'It's cool,' Ginger says, forgetting completely about the bandage on his hand. 'He doesn't bite.'

'I must put Artemesia down for the night,' Tumi says to no one in particular, and Ponytail smiles at him fondly as he hands the baby over.

Megan passes a bowl of stew to each of us. I'm so hungry I don't actually care what I'm eating, but I still try not to look at the snakeskins drying over the side of the balcony. Mind you, it doesn't taste too bad, and I'm fairly sure the chunks of flesh in it are rabbit, not reptile.

'Delish, thanks,' Ginger says, leaving a mouthful in his bowl and sneakily placing it on the ground where Bambi falls on it.

Thin Lips chuckles and throws a chunk of meat in the hyena's direction. Ginger catches her eye and grins at her. She actually smiles back. Looks like baby hyenas are perfect ice-breakers. The women aren't exactly brimming with joy, but the atmosphere seems to have thawed.

Megan sits down next to Ash. 'So, tell me everything. What is it like in –'

'Megan!' A voice barks from the darkness.

I squint into the gloom and see a woman striding towards us. She's Saint's height, super-skinny and there's a bandanna tied around her scalp. Something droops from her right hand, and as she steps into the light I realise she's holding three limp guineafowl. A deep scar bisects her forehead and her eyes are deep-set and watchful. She has the same delicate bone structure as the Mantis and gives off the aura of being just as formidable.

'What are you thinking, bringing outsiders here?'

Megan jumps to her feet as the woman surges forward like a freight train and dumps the guineafowl into Ponytail's lap. 'I can explain, Mother,' she says. She looks close to tears, but to her credit she faces the woman without flinching.

'She's not your real mother, right?' Ginger looks from Megan to the woman and back again. 'I mean 'cos she's, like, African, innit, and you're a whitey. Unless ... Hey, is your father a ginger?'

Saint nudges him sharply. 'Shut up,' she hisses.

'I tried to talk her out of it,' Moreka says quickly.

'Well, you didn't try hard enough,' Mother replies, her voice hard.

Ash stands up slowly, palms raised. 'Look, we don't want any trouble. Really, if you want us to leave, we will.'

'Yes. I *do* want you to leave.'

'Mother!' Megan cries. 'Please! When I ran into them back in Old Knysna they could have hurt me then, and they didn't.' Megan looks down at her feet. 'I mean ... I left my Glock in the car and –'

'You did *what*? How many more times do I have to tell you? It is not safe out there!'

'I know. I'm sorry! But that's what I'm saying. They could have hurt me, stolen the gun, taken the Land Cruiser, but they didn't. You can trust them.'

Mother sighs, although it is more of an angry exhalation. 'The damage is done.' She glares at Ginger and Ash. 'They can sleep in the guest house tonight. Take them there now.'

'But we've only just got here!'

Ash nudges him. 'Let's just do what she says, Ginger.'

'Well, thanks for the food anyway,' Ginger says, picking up the hyena. 'Appreciate it.'

No one responds. It looks like we've lost whatever ground we'd managed to gain in the women's good books.

We follow Megan back the way we came. She leads us towards one of the wooden houses set back in the trees. It's fully dark now, but Ash holds his Zippo in front of him, the tiny flame providing just enough light for us to see our way across another narrow rope bridge.

The guest house is constructed from half-logs, and even though the floor creaks as we step up onto the porch in front of it, the platform it's built on looks sturdy enough to take our combined weight. Above us a flurry of bats flick off into the trees.

'Our very own tree shack,' Saint says. 'Just what I've always wanted.'

'What was that all about, Megan?' Ginger asks. 'Back there?'

'Sorry,' she says. 'In the past they've had visitors who weren't so ... ' She glances at Ash. 'Cool.'

'Don't worry about it,' Ash says. 'It's natural that they'd be suspicious of us. But is that everyone? All the survivors?'

Megan nods. 'Here at least. You still have to meet Father and his family. They live a few kilometres away.'

'You mean in another settlement?'

'Ja. Maybe we can go tomorrow.' She wraps a lock of hair around a finger. 'If Mother says it's okay, of course.'

'That reminds me,' Ginger says. 'What was up with those

blokes?'

'Sorry?'

'The guys with the baby.'

'Oh! Tumi and Stefan! They're brilliant parents, really. Artemesia is *so* lucky to have them –'

'Megan!' Mother shouts.

'I have to go. I'll see you in the morning.' She blows us all a kiss. 'Thank you, *thank* you for coming.'

We watch as she skips back down into the darkness.

Saint peers into the shack and shudders. 'There had better not be any spiders in here.'

'Bambi and I will check,' Ginger says. Ash hands him the Zippo and Ginger disappears inside. 'There're a couple of candles in here. They look old, though ... Hang on ... Oh, awesome.'

'And spiders?' Saint asks.

'Um ... Nah. Doesn't look like it.'

I follow Saint and Ash inside. It's roomier than it looks from the outside, and the candles, which must be made of some sort of animal fat, judging by the smoky aroma that fills the space, provide a surprising amount of light. The wooden walls are covered with feathered wall hangings, there's a table carved out of a tree stump and several books, swollen with moisture, are stacked up on a shelf to one side. Ash picks one up and flips through it. Two large straw mattresses covered in rabbit-fur blankets lie in the middle of the room. Saint lifts up the tree-trunk table and a nest of scorpions scuttles out, but oddly they don't seem to bother her at all. Using one of the books, Ginger gently takes them outside.

'Home sweet home,' Saint says, slumping down on one of the mattresses. 'So, let's face it, it doesn't look like these people are going to be much help to us.'

'At least it's a good place to stay the night,' Ash says. 'Beats camping. And who knows, maybe Mother *can* help us.'

'How, Ash? You think they've got motorbikes stashed here that we can use? Hey, maybe they've got a car carved out of wood. Unless you want to take Megan's.'

'Very funny, Saint.'

'But it's a weird set-up, don't you think?'

'I thought you liked strong women?'

'I do. Just not ones who look at me as if they want to kill me.'

'We can't blame them for being cautious.'

'I guess.' She kicks her boots off.

'What do you think Father is going to be like?'

'Who knows? Probably the male version of those hard-core chicks. And how are their names? Mother and Father. Imaginative, right?'

Ash chuckles, and I try and catch his eye and grin at him. He smiles at me, but then turns back to the book.

Ginger gently takes Bambi out of his hoody and places him on the floor. The hyena yawns and curls into a ball on the floor next to Saint's mattress.

'If he messes in here, I'm throwing him out,' Saint says.

'He's already been,' Ginger says.

'When?'

'On that platform.'

Saint laughs. 'No wonder Mother was pissed off with us, Ginger.'

'Yeah, yeah,' he says. 'Anyway, at least we know there are other survivors outside Cape Town.'

'Yeah, good-looking redheaded survivors, right, Ginger?' Saint says. 'How was that outfit Megan was wearing? I swear, she might as well have been naked.'

'I don't know what you mean.' Ginger says. Even though it's

too dark to be sure I'm certain he's blushing again.

'And how come she's immune to Rotter attack? Theories, anyone?'

'Maybe she does have some freaky pheromones,' I say.

'Yeah!' Ginger says. 'Maybe we both do. Hey, there could be loads of people like us out there who smell funny.'

'You've only been smelling funny since we left that lodge, Ginger,' Saint says, looking pointedly at his hoody.

'Which mattress should I take?' Ginger asks

I glance at Ash, but he's still paging through the book, his back to me.

'I mean, is it boys together and girls together, or Lele, do you and Ash want to sleep together? I mean ... not like that ... but you can if you want to, if you're quiet –'

'Ginger!' Saint says. 'You don't need to spell it out.'

'Ash?' Ginger asks.

'Whatever you want, Ginger,' he says. The atmosphere suddenly feels awkward. What's going on with him?

Ginger finally decides to plonk himself next to Saint.

'Keep that bloody hyena away from me,' she says, sounding like she's already half-asleep. None of us got much sleep last night, or the night before, come to think of it.

'Ash?' I say. 'Aren't you tired?'

'I think we should take turns staying up,' he says. 'Just in case.'

'I'll stay up with you then.'

'No,' he says quickly. *Too* quickly? 'You get some sleep, Lele.'

Is he regretting what happened between us at the lodge? He's been grim all day, but we've had a lot to deal with, so maybe he's just stressed out. But you don't do what we did if you're not serious about someone, do you? I can't help but wonder what would have happened if we hadn't been interrupted, how far we would have gone. Neither of us wanted to stop – of that I'm sure. I've never felt like that before – completely lost in the moment – and I know Ash felt the same. It was as if we couldn't get enough of each other.

Fighting to think about something else – I won't get any sleep otherwise – I lie back on the mattress, every inch of my body sighing with relief. Saint is already snoring softly and Ginger and Bambi are both on the verge of passing out.

I feel my eyes closing, and then, nothing.

What the hell is that noise?

It sounds like a giant rat is trying to gnaw its way through a tough piece of meat.

I sit up, still half asleep, and it takes me a few seconds to figure out where the hell I am, the last wisps of a dream muddying my thoughts. Thabo. I was dreaming about Thabo. I shake my head to clear the cobwebs out of my brain, and then the smell of wood and stale candle smoke brings it all back to me. There's another, fouler odour in the air, and I think I have a fair idea of where it's coming from.

Bambi looks up at me, his tongue lolling out of his mouth. Just great. He's almost chewed right through the sole of my boot. I grab it from between his paws and chuck it at Ginger. 'Wake up!'

'Wha –?'

'Look what Bambi's done!'

Ginger lifts his head, then drops it back down onto the rolled-up jacket he's using as a pillow. 'It's not his fault. I've run out of biltong.'

Saint sits up and sniffs. 'That's not all he's done. It *stinks* in here.'

'Where's Ash?' I ask.

'Dunno.' Saint yawns and nudges Ginger. 'Let me see where that bloody hyena bit you, Ginger. I want to make sure it's not infected.'

'His name's Bambi,' Ginger gripes. 'Not "that bloody hyena".'

'Whatever.'

He holds his hand out and Saint peers at it. 'It's just a scratch. You're such a baby.'

I jump up, pull on my gnawed boots and head outside.

Birdsong melds with the occasional Rotter moan and I breathe in deeply. The air is damp and cool, and after the fetid stink in the cabin it smells deliciously clean.

In the light of the fire last night the place seemed gloomy and threatening, but now, in daylight, it looks welcoming and homely. Some of the knotted rope bridges are frayed and decaying, but the main platform's planks look well cared for. The huts set back into the trees have the same comforting air as our cabin, and as long as I don't look too closely at the animal carcasses hanging from the branches it's almost idyllic.

Saint joins me, stretching her arms behind her. 'Where do you think the bathrooms are?'

'Bathrooms, Saint?'

'Yeah. I know, I know, stupid question.'

We make our way back to the main platform. Thin Lips is sitting next to the fire drum, whittling a piece of wood.

'Morning,' Saint says to her.

Thin Lips nods curtly, then focuses her attention back on her work.

'I still can't get over the fact that they don't seem to be curious about us,' Saint whispers to me.

'I know, it's weird,' I say, looking around for Ash.

Then I spot him. He's following Megan across one of the bridges on the other side of the platform, their arms full of wood. She says something to him over her shoulder and he laughs. For an instant I'm hit with the acidic burn of anxiety. Megan seems to fizz and crackle with life and energy, her hair catching the morning sun. She's wearing the same outfit as yesterday, though if anything the shorts seem even shorter, her tank top even tighter. She spins, stretches out a long shapely leg and points her toes. I can't quite see from this distance, but I swear that Ash's eyes drop to her chest.

Ash catches sight of us and starts. Does he look guilty?

Megan dumps her armload of wood on the platform, waves and jogs over to us.

'Morning,' I say, my smile artificial.

'Hi!' Megan says, rushing forward and enfolding me in a hug. I'm not expecting it and I take a step backwards, but she doesn't seem to notice. She smells of flowers and garlic. Next she throws her arms around Saint, who clearly enjoys the experience far more than I did. 'How did you sleep?'

'Great,' I say.

'Bambi!' Ginger roars, thumping his way towards us, the hyena skittering in front of him. 'Someone stop him!'

Before any of us can move, Megan steps forward gracefully, bends down and gathers him in her arms, giving us all a good look at her chest as she does so.

'Thanks,' Ginger says, colouring bright red again.

I notice that Bambi doesn't nip at Megan. In fact, he seems completely at home. 'I didn't know you could keep wild animals as pets,' Megan says.

'Neither did we,' Ash says, catching my eye. I smile back at him and the jealousy fades.

'Where've you been?' I ask him.

'He's been helping me unload the Land Cruiser,' Megan says.

'Why didn't you wake me up?'

'You were sleeping so peacefully,' he says. 'Seemed a shame to wake you.'

Did he even get any sleep last night? His eyes have lost their defeated look, but they're still ringed with dark circles. He didn't wake any of us to take over lookout duty.

Megan grabs one of the dried snakeskins and fashions it into a makeshift lead. She ties it around Bambi's neck and hands the end of it to Ginger. 'We don't want him to fall off the edge.'

Ginger grins. 'That's so cool of you.' He points towards the bridge Ash and Megan had been walking along. 'Hey, what's through there?'

I follow his gaze and make out the edge of another platform through the trees. I hadn't noticed it last night in the dark.

'Oh, that's where we grow our vegetables. We hunt mostly, but Mother says we also have to eat some green stuff. You want to see it?'

'Sure.'

We follow her towards it, Saint not looking charmed at having to make her way over yet another rickety bridge. This platform is covered with wooden pots and piles of old car tyres, out of which sprout lettuce, spinach and potatoes. A cloud of fruit flies hovers above us.

Saint wrinkles her nose. 'Nice smell.'

Megan laughs again and gestures to a small wooden structure at the corner of the area. It looks like some sort of outhouse.

'You mean that's where you ... ?' Saint asks.

'Ja. Fertiliser. Nothing goes to waste here.'

'Even the waste. Lovely.'

'How long have you guys lived in this place?' Ginger asks.

Megan scrunches up her nose in a way that even I can see is

cute. 'I'm not sure. We don't really keep track of time. Mother says she thinks we've been here for two or three years.'

'And that settlement back there? The one where we found you? Did you used to live there?'

'Ja.' She sighs.

'And that's how you knew you were immune to Rotter attack, right?' I ask.

'Ja. It was –'

'Meggie!' Moreka is making her way over to us. 'Mother wants to see you – all of you.'

'Right away,' Megan says. 'Come on.'

As she walks quickly back to the bridge I grab Ash's elbow and indicate that we should hang back.

'Shouldn't we get out of here soon?' I say to him as quietly as possible as the others begin to cross back over the bridge. 'We don't want to leave it too late, and it doesn't look like they're going to want us to stay another night.'

'Let's just play it by ear. The least we can do is prove to this Mother woman that we aren't dangerous, that Megan didn't make a mistake bringing us here.'

'You think that's a good idea?'

I don't miss his eyes moving to follow Megan as she makes her way effortlessly back to the main platform. 'Yeah. I trust her, Lele,' he says.

I smother another stab of anxiety as he moves to catch up with the others

———

Mother is seated on one of the stuffed elephant feet, her muscled forearms resting on her knees, a putrid-smelling hand-rolled cigar cocked between her fingers. Thin Lips and the other women stand behind her like bodyguards, their rifles held loosely in their arms.

Mother motions us towards her. 'We need to have a little chat.' She takes a long drag from the cigar, and I smother a cough as the exhaled smoke hits my lungs. 'Moreka says that you told Megan that you are from Cape Town.'

'Yes,' Ash says.

'And you really expect us to believe this?'

Thin Lips lifts her gun and rests the barrel against her shoulder. I get the message loud and clear – we need to watch our step. I'd better keep my big mouth shut; it has a knack of getting us in trouble.

'Well, yeah,' Ginger says. 'That's 'cos it's the truth, innit.'

Mother blows a plume of smoke in his direction. 'Who sent you?'

'No one,' Ash says. 'Leaving was our decision. Things are … difficult there.'

Megan steps forward. 'He's telling the truth, Mother. They *are* from Cape Town. Ash told me the whole story –'

'Did he now?' Mother says, and I don't like the way she focuses the full force of her gaze on Ash. And I like the fact that he's been filling Megan in on the details of our situation even less.

'They're looking for survivors,' Megan says. 'They need help –'

Moreka snorts with laughter.

'You think that's funny, do you?' Saint says, pointing a finger right in Moreka's face. 'You know what? Screw you.' She looks at each of the women long and hard, her stare lingering longest on Mother's face. 'Screw all of you. We don't want – or need – your help.'

Mother takes another drag of her cigar, her eyes fixed on

Saint's. 'Ha!' she says, getting slowly to her feet, a smirk on her lips. 'I see one of you has balls.'

'Actually,' Ginger says. 'She's not the only one who –'

Mother holds up a hand to silence him. 'What do you need?' she asks Saint.

'Petrol.'

Mother shakes her head. 'We have no petrol here.'

'Do you think Father's got some stashed away somewhere?' Megan asks.

Mother picks a piece of tobacco or whatever it is she's smoking off her bottom lip. 'Who knows? He could have anything in that dump of his.'

'I could take them there to check it out.'

Mother's eyes shift back to Ash. 'Just because I haven't shot them does not mean I'm willing to let you get in a car alone with them.'

'But they don't know the way!'

Mother shoulders her rifle. 'That's why I'm coming with you.'

Gross. The bakkie's cab clunks of Mother's cigar smoke, and I'm seriously regretting accepting Megan's offer to sit up front with them. I hadn't exactly wanted to in the first place, but I couldn't think of a way to politely turn her down. Besides, as the car bumps along the road and my thigh brushes up against Megan's, I'm glad it's me and not Ash sitting between the two women.

I'm too busy trying not to gag from the stink of the smoke to attempt conversation, and Mother isn't exactly the chattiest person on the planet. She's seriously brave, though. I'm still impressed by the way she hared through the forest, vaulted onto the roof of the car and slipped inside through the window, nimbly staying out of the Rotters' reach as they swarmed around the vehicle. Clearly this isn't the first time she's risked attack to leave her settlement. She didn't even flinch when one of the Rotters grabbed onto the bakkie's window; she merely bashed the door open with her shoulder to dislodge it.

I glance in the rear-view mirror as we trade the forest track for the highway. A bunch of Rotters spill out of the trees and totter after us like children terrified of being left behind. They grow smaller and smaller as Megan steps on the accelerator.

'So,' Mother says, twin streams of smoke jetting from her nostrils. 'Do your parents know that you're on this adventure?'

I think about Dad back in Cape Town. I wonder if the Mantis told him that she'd seen me and that I've left the enclave. 'Actually, it was my stepmother who suggested we leave. It ... It wasn't safe for us there anymore.'

She raises her eyebrows. 'Really? Interesting how it is always the women who make the difficult decisions, isn't it?'

I wait for Mother to quiz me further, but it's as if she's lost interest – she merely stares out of the window, her cigar trapped in the corner of her mouth.

Megan looks over at Mother and shoots her a half-affectionate glance.

'Is Father's settlement far from here?' I ask her.

'No,' she says. 'You'll see it just now.'

We swing down a hill, and I'm treated to an excellent view of the sea, the sunlight shimmering across it. There's evidence of another town to our right but, like the others we've passed, the telltale signs of devastation are everywhere – staved-in roofs, the sooty remains of a mall, yet another ramshackle service station. And then I see the first Rotters. There are several hanging about at the side of the highway like forgotten hitch-hikers.

'There it is,' Megan says, pointing to the beginnings of a high concrete wall that runs parallel to the highway on the opposite side of the road. It's topped with strands of barbed wire, starlings perched in a long line across the top of it. Below it, the Rotters stand in loose groups, their hands scraping at the wall's rough concrete as if they're begging to be let in.

More and more Rotters emerge out of the stinkwood trees and bushes around us as we drive on. I spy an ancient sign, pockmarked with bullet holes, which reads *Private: Members Only*. It's hanging at a skew angle from a tree, but a couple of hundred metres beyond it I make out the top of a security booth and a gate.

'Here's good,' Mother says. She digs in the bulky bag at her feet and pulls out a sheet of thick grey leather that looks like it might be elephant hide.

As soon as Megan pulls the car to a stop Mother flies out of the passenger-side door and darts to the back of the bakkie. The lurking Rotters jerk like puppets on strings; almost as one they turn and start towards us.

Oh crap. What the hell is she doing? I leap out after her.

'You,' Mother points at Saint. 'Follow me.'

Saint doesn't hesitate; she leaps off the back, closely followed by Ginger, Ash pausing only to retrieve his panga that he'd rescued from the forest floor before we climbed into the car.

'You won't need that,' Mother says to him, and then she's sprinting for the wall, Saint hot on her heels.

'Don't worry,' Megan calls, head out of the window. 'She's done this hundreds of times.'

A particularly gross Rotter lurches ahead of the swarm, only metres away from Mother and Saint. I don't know what's worse, the fact that it's nearly on them, or the outfit it's wearing. It's clad in bright, yellow-checked trousers, the remains of what were once white shoes, and a grubby pink sweater.

Mother throws her bag and rifle over the wall, and then chucks the skin on top of the wire. Without being asked, Saint cups her hands and boosts her up.

I hold my breath as Mother grabs the lip of the wall and heaves herself over it in one smooth motion, Saint disappearing from view as several Rotters slam into the concrete, their hands waving as they grasp at the air.

Pushing through the howling Rotters, Saint jogs back to us. 'That woman is incredible. Did you see that?' she pants.

'Tune in next week when Mother fights lions,' Ginger says in his best American accent, 'with her bare hands.'

Megan laughs, making Ginger blush. He's looking very pleased with himself.

Saint grimaces and wipes a hand down the front of her shirt, 'Ew. I think I got some Rotter on me.'

Megan nods towards the knot of Rotters moaning at the fence. 'We need to get through the gate while they're distracted.'

'How did what's-his-name – Father – have time to build these walls if you didn't have any Guardians protecting you?' Ginger asks.

'He didn't,' Megan says. 'It was already here. He just took it over.'

'So what was this place?'

'A golf estate. The whole thing was fenced already.'

'Oh, that was lucky, innit.'

'Father's always saying that South Africa must be one of the best countries in the world for surviving a zombie apocalypse,' Megan says seriously. 'It's full of security estates and high fences.'

'Oh yeah? Dunno about that, mate. I reckon Britain managed

okay. Not that we'll probably ever know.' Ginger drops his head, jumps onto the back of the bakkie and cuddles Bambi to his chest. Despite the fact that he's destroyed my boot, the hyena is growing on me; he pushes his head into Ginger's hand as if he's trying to comfort him.

With the Rotters still clawing at the wall, it's easy to slip through the gate without any stragglers following us in. Ginger and Ash do the honours, slamming it behind us before vaulting back onto the bakkie.

We cruise along a driveway flanked by dead and dying palm trees, the grass around us topping the height of the bakkie's tyres. The settlement must be enormous; miles of overgrown rolling landscape unfolds in every direction. Every now and then the grass gives way to what looks like a series of half-hearted attempts to create vegetable plots. Most of the mealies are rotting on their stalks, and the other beds are overrun with weeds. The sight makes me cringe; you'd never see so much waste and neglect in the Agriculturals – Gran would have freaked out. But maybe they don't need to bother with growing their own food. After all, the place is crawling with Egyptian geese – they explode into the air in a flurry of feathers and wild honking as the car passes them.

To our left I make out the glint of water through the palm trees and grass, and a large lake shimmers into view. A thumping sound floats through the windows.

'Are those drums?' Saint calls through the partition.

'Ja,' Megan says. 'Father always has a morning drum circle.'

'Okaaaaay,' Saint says. 'Who doesn't?'

'He says it calms the Old Souls.' For a second she looks

embarrassed as if she's said something she shouldn't.

'Oh cool, tribe-lings!' Ginger shouts, pointing at the lake.

Three small children wearing nothing but little leather loincloths jump out of the reeds and race alongside the car, laughing and waving sticks. Megan slows to a crawl so that they can keep pace with us. Bright paint is smeared over their skin in designs they've clearly made themselves and long matted hair hangs down their backs – they look as wild as the overgrown settlement.

We head towards a low whitewashed building that sits next to a car park, its tarmacked surface almost entirely reclaimed by grass and wild flowers. Megan parks the car next to a decrepit golf cart and the moment she climbs out of the driver's side the children throw themselves at her, their thin arms wrapping around her thighs. I'm hit with a stab of longing for Jobe, swiftly followed by a flood of regret that there's no chance he'll ever race around and laugh like these kids.

I step away from the car, struggling to swallow the lump in my throat, and focus my attention on the goats and chickens that are wandering around the edge of the water.

'Lele!' Ginger calls. 'Check it out.'

One of the kids, a small girl with startling blue eyes, has climbed up onto the back of the bakkie and is jumping up and down on the bumper, waving her stick in the air.

'Oh, hey there,' Ash says, smiling at the girl. He catches my eye and we share a look full of understanding. He must also be thinking about Sasha.

The girl's dirty face splits into a grin, her eyes lock on Bambi, and she starts howling at him like a giggly wolf.

'Aw, looks like you have an admirer, mate,' Ginger says, stroking the hyena's back.

The girl's grin snaps off, she looks straight at Ginger, and then she jabs forward with the stick, clearly aiming for the hyena.

'Oi! Don't do that!' Ginger grabs the stick out of her hand and throws it into the grass. She sticks her tongue out at him and dives after it.

Saint's looking down in disgust at the two boys who are viciously scraping their sticks along the sides of the bakkie, leaving grooves in the dust that coats its sides. 'Um ... do they bite?'

'No,' Megan says, ushering them away. 'They just get excited when they see the Land Cruiser.'

The children chase each other around the car before taking off back to the lake.

'Come on,' Megan says to us. 'Let's go meet the others.'

We follow her towards the building and onto a limestone patio. From the car park the structure's whitewashed walls and red-tiled roof looked impressive, but up close it's clear that the place is barely hanging together. The window frames are swollen and warped from water damage, roof struts show where tiles are missing and the double doors are hanging off their hinges. Weirdly, although the place is falling to pieces, woven dreamcatchers and wooden wind chimes hang from hooks hammered into the walls, and freaky sculptures made out of bird skulls and feathers are scattered everywhere.

Megan leads us across the patio and down a shallow incline to a less-overgrown grassy area. A group of men and women sit in a ragged circle around a single seated figure, large rustic drums cradled between their knees.

'That's Father,' Megan whispers to us.

The rhythmic beat stutters to a stop as, one by one, the drummers notice us. They stare up at us dreamily as if they've all just snapped out of a daze. Not including the figure in the middle, there are seven of them – five men and two women – all sporting feathers in their long hair and wearing very little – the men clad in tatty loincloths and the women in painted hides that cover the bare minimum of flesh. With the exception of one man with a long mangy beard, who's well past his sell-by date – older even than Gran had been before she was sent out to join the Rotters – they appear to be around the same age as the women back at Mother's enclave.

The man in the centre stands up, throws back his head, claps his hands and spreads them out as if he's imitating a large bird. Unlike the others he's fully dressed in a long smock and a tatty red velvet cloak. Beads are threaded through his beard, and feathers and scraps of fabric are woven into his greying hair.

'Ah, Megan! How wonderful!' he says in a sing-song voice that carries above the far-off moans of the Rotters. 'We weren't expecting to be treated to the sight of your beautiful aura for another month.' He walks over and envelops Megan in a hug. As he does so his eyes sweep over us. They're a strange muddy blue colour, and for a moment his smile falters. 'And you bring us guests! How marvellous! Gaia has truly blessed this day!'

'Freak alert,' Saint whispers in my ear.

Ash steps forward. 'I'm Ash,' he says, holding out his hand. 'And this is –'

'Given names are unimportant,' Father says, ignoring Ash's hand. 'Just energies and souls. Don't you agree?' Ash is taken aback, but Father doesn't seem to care. He gestures to the drumming circle. 'Please, join us.'

Bambi whines and Father jerks his head in the animal's direction. 'What is that?'

'It's a hyena,' Ginger says. 'Cool, isn't he?'

Father flinches. 'We don't believe that nature's creatures should be confined.'

'But if I let him off his lead he'll probably kill your chickens.'
Saint coughs into her hand to hide a laugh.

Father pretends not to hear her and stretches out an arm. It jangles – beneath his sleeve he's wearing a good kilo of silver bracelets. 'Before we share with our treasured guests, I think it would be beneficial if we ask those who are not with us to join us. All of you, think of someone who is not here with us right now and say their name out loud. I will start.' He closes his eyes. 'Hunter,' he says theatrically.

'I thought he said names are unimportant?' Saint whispers to me.

The other people all seem to be doing the same, and I catch the names Poppy, Sage, Parsley and Frodo.

'Share with us,' Father says. It's more of a command than a request.

'Um ... Angelina Jolie?' Ginger says.

Saint coughs into her fist again, and I know that if she starts giggling she'll set me off, and I won't be able to stop.

'And you?' Father focuses his gaze on me.

'Um ... Jobe,' I say. And just saying his name stops the laughter in its tracks.

Saint and Megan murmur names I can't catch. 'Sasha,' Ash says.

'Good. Their energies will join us shortly. Now we will open our hearts and minds and listen to what they tell us.' He reaches into a bag tied to his robe and pulls out a collection of chicken bones, shiny stones and beads. He throws them onto the ground, then he sinks to a crouch, waving his hands over them and swaying his entire body. He closes his eyes, and the drummers and Megan follow suit.

There were a couple of sangomas and traditional healers back in the Agriculturals, but I don't remember them being quite so ... showy. This looks fake to me.

'Cut the crap, Gerald,' a voice barks from behind us.

Father jerks to his feet, his little show with the bones completely forgotten.

We all turn to see Mother striding towards us up the lawn. Father's eyes track her approach, a grim set to his mouth. He turns on Megan. 'Why didn't you tell me *she* was here?'

'Sorry,' Megan says. 'I meant to, but –'

'That fence is falling to pieces, Gerald.' Mother barrels towards him. 'You have a responsibility to keep these people safe. You need to keep this place properly maintained.'

With the exception of the guy with the mangy beard, the drummers start drifting away. 'We thank you for your concern ... ' Father takes a step back from her and seems to recover some of his confidence. 'But I do not need you to tell me how to run my own homestead.'

'Like hell, you don't.' Mother kicks one of the drums over. 'Is this all you do all day? Bang your drums?'

'Of course not,' Father says, a defensive note in his voice.

'And there were children swimming unsupervised in the dam again.'

'We do not believe in confining our young,' Father says, looking to Mangy Beard for support. 'It smothers their souls and their creativity.'

'Well,' Mother snarls, 'I don't want Megan coming here if you can't even keep your own water supply clean.'

Father flinches like he's been slapped across the face. 'I don't think that is your choice to make.' He turns to Megan, a forced smile on his face. 'You like it here, don't you, Megan?'

Megan's eyes dart between Mother and Father. It's obvious that this is not the first time she's been caught in the middle of one of their fights. 'I –'

'Don't you dare drag her into this,' Mother snaps.

I shift uncomfortably, and even Saint looks embarrassed.

'You have no right to deny us Megan's company,' Father says.

'If it puts her in danger I have every right.'

Father places a hand on Megan's head. 'Do you feel unsafe here, Megan?'

'Don't answer that, Megan!'

Megan drops her eyes, and I open my mouth to tell her that she doesn't need to listen to this, but Mangy Beard toddles forward and points a grimy finger in Mother's direction. 'How dare you disrespect us in our home,' he says to her, his jaw working furiously. 'Father has taken care of all of us for many years ...'

'Thank you, Lavender,' Father says, 'but it is fruitless trying to explain to those who have not opened their hearts to listen.'

'Lavender? No ways!' Ginger snorts with laughter.

'Shut up, Ginger,' Saint hisses.

'I will not fight with you, Mother,' Father says, straightening himself up to his full height and finally looking her in the eye. 'Not in front of our visitors. Negative energy has no place here.'

Mother grunts. 'You're going to have a lot of negative energy on your hands when the dead break in.'

'Megan,' Father squares his shoulders, 'why don't you show our guests around while Mother and I talk?'

Judging by the look on Mother's face I won't be surprised if there's a new Rotter lurching around the wall in the near future. One dressed in a smock with bangles jangling on its arms.

Megan seems to have lost some of her usual energy, and she walks quickly away, leading us towards the lake. Ginger holds tightly onto Bambi's lead – there are far too many distractions around here. I can't see any sign of the children; maybe Mother chased them away.

'Do they always fight like that?' Ash asks Megan, his voice gentler than usual.

'Sometimes, but it's harmless really.' Megan picks up a stone and skims it across the water. 'I like to think that it's just because they miss each other so much.'

Somehow I doubt this, but I keep my mouth shut.

'Why do they live so far apart, then?' Saint asks.

'They were together once. Back in the old settlement, I mean. They kind of ran it, but everything changed after the Old Souls broke in and we had to escape. There weren't many survivors left, and Mother wanted to do things a certain way, and Father ... Well, he discovered his love for nature.'

'So he hasn't always been like ... ' Ginger pulls a stupid face and mimes Father's over-the-top greeting.

For a second I think he's offended Megan, but then she smiles. 'No, he used to be as hard as Mother, if you can believe it. After the break-in we managed to get one of the buses to start, and we all fled here. But after a while Mother couldn't take it anymore. Knowing that I wasn't going to be infected by the Rotters, she asked me to help her and her followers find another place to live. She knew about the tree houses from years ago, and I took them there and helped them set it up.'

'Wow,' Ginger says. 'That's pretty young to be taking that much responsibility.'

She shrugs. 'It was only a couple of years ago.'

'So she risked infection just to get away from Father?' Ash asks, incredulous.

'Can you really blame her?' Saint mutters.

'And you're caught in the middle,' I say.

Megan sighs. 'I don't mind. I get to split my time between two completely different worlds. And I get to help both of them out by bringing them luxuries and supplies from the outside.'

'So, basically, they're using you,' Saint says.

'No, it's not like that.' Megan picks up another smooth stone and skims it with a little more force than necessary. Instead of skipping across the surface of the water it lands with a loud splash. 'So,' she says, pulling her hair back from her face and tying it into a knot at the nape of her neck. 'I think we should go and see if we can find you guys some petrol.' She smiles sadly. 'Otherwise you're also going to be stuck here.'

Holy crap, is he never going to shut up?

I've drawn the short straw. Father has chosen to plonk himself down next to me and use me as his sounding board. Everyone's sitting in a circle around a bonfire that a couple of the drummers built as night began to fall. Before they lit it they said a lengthy prayer over the wood, asking for forgiveness for causing environmental damage – I couldn't look at Saint in case we both exploded from suppressed laughter. For the last hour Father's been prattling on about Gaia and the 'natural order'. I can't get a word in, so I haven't been able to correct his utterly crap theories behind why it is that we're immune to Rotter attack – most involve 'the power of positive thought', 'natural energy' and some kak about crystals. It wouldn't be so bad if he didn't sound so patronising – he's speaking in the same preachy tone the hard-core Resurrectionists always use.

'You see, Lele,' he's saying, 'Gaia has blessed you with a rare and treasured freedom and you must not waste it ... '

He goes off on another tangent and I tune him out. Next to me, Saint is similarly trapped in conversation with Mother. At least it doesn't sound as dull as the monologue I'm enduring – from the few words I can catch they seem to be swapping War stories.

'I may have seemed surprised to see you and your friends when you first arrived,' Father drones on, 'but the truth is that I have been seeing signs of your arrival for weeks. Just yesterday I saw an eagle swooping ... '

It's getting late, and the feral children we saw when we first arrived are curled up next to two skinny women who are weaving dreamcatchers. (How many do they need?) A waft of ganja smoke drifts my way – Lavender, the other folk around the fire and Father and Mother have been puffing on hand-rolled joints all night, and even Megan's taken a drag or two.

I try and catch Ash's eye for the thousandth time, but he and Ginger are deep in conversation with Megan. She's sitting between them, and from here it looks as if they're vying for her attention. Would it be rude if I just stood up and joined them? Probably. But how can Ash just ignore me like this? Megan says something to him, and both he and Ginger laugh. My stomach twists – and I know I can't put it down to the tasteless mush we were served for supper. Ash really has no reason to look so cheerful and relaxed – without petrol we're all screwed. We spent hours searching the filthy garages next to the old clubhouse, where rusting golf carts and other junk was stored, but all we unearthed was half a can of syrupy oil. Our only option is to walk to the next town, hope it isn't a burned wreck, and see if we can source some bicycles. I'm not looking forward to peddling all the way to Bloemfontein or wherever. I haven't ridden a bike since before the War, and I doubt we're going to find one with training wheels.

'Don't you agree?' Father says to me and I nod automatically, hoping desperately that I haven't just agreed to join his drumming circle.

Father claps his hands, stands up and glances at Mother. 'It has been a long day. We should all get some sleep.'

'Where are we sleeping?' Saint eyes the dark building behind us. I know what she's thinking: it looks like spider heaven.

'Under the stars, of course!'

Great.

I wait for Ash to stand up and move across to where Saint and I are sitting, but he doesn't. Lavender hands woollen blankets to each of us in turn. Mine smells like wet sheep, and Saint's obviously isn't much better because she sniffs at it and pulls a face.

'Night, Lele! Night, Saint!' Megan calls from the other side of the fire. 'Sleep tight!'

I try to smile, but my muscles don't seem to want to move. Ginger waves at me and snuggles next to the hyena, and now the fire's dying it's too dark to make out Ash's expression. He rolls his blanket into a pillow and lies back, arms behind his head.

Mother stands up, murmurs something to Father and moves away from the fire. Saint shuffles up next to me. I think about asking her what I should do about Ash, but she's already breathing deeply. I replay the night we spent at the game lodge over and over in my mind, trying to convince myself that I'm being paranoid. But I still can't shift the sick feeling that lurks in my belly.

'You're a bloody fool, Gerald!' Mother's voice shatters the early-morning calm.

I turn over just in time to see her storming out of the clubhouse, pulling a shirt over her head.

Megan is already on her feet, Ash is sitting up and wiping

sleep out of his eyes and Ginger rolls over and groans. Next to me Saint swears under her breath. The others lying around the dead fire barely stir. Maybe they're used to this kind of wake-up call.

'What's going on?' Megan asks.

'We're out of here,' Mother snaps. 'I can't spend another moment in this place.'

'Mother!' Father bellows. 'Lerato! Wait!' He comes jogging out of the building, awkwardly wrapping a leather hide around his hips.

'Don't you have a drumming circle to organise?' Mother spits at him. She gestures to Megan. 'Let's go.' She starts marching across the grass, but Megan doesn't move to follow her.

'Wait, Mother! I can't just leave my friends behind.'

Mother halts and whirls around. 'Friends? They're strangers. Strangers who will be on their way soon.'

'Nice,' Saint murmurs. 'So much for our sisterly bonding session last night.'

'How can you say that?' Megan says. 'They *are* my friends!'

Mother looks over at Father and something passes between them. 'Megan,' he says, 'Mother and I may have our disagreements, but she is right, you should do what she says.'

'But they need our help.'

'What they need is to continue on their way.'

'Well, maybe I want to go with them!'

There's a shocked silence. I glance at the others to see how they've taken this. Ginger is grinning from ear to ear, Saint is staring at Mother in disgust and Ash is watching Megan carefully. Has Megan mentioned this to him before?

'Excuse me?' Mother says, her voice cold.

Megan seems just as surprised as the rest of us by her sudden outburst. 'You don't need me here. Not really. I want to see some of the outside world. I . . . I want to go with them.'

'It's not safe out there!' Mother says. 'You know this. How many times have we had this conversation?'

'We'll look after her,' Ginger chips in.

Mother turns on him. 'This is all your fault! Filling her head with lies about adventures!'

'It's her choice,' Ginger says. 'I mean if Megan really wants to come with us, why would you want to stop her if it'll make her happy?'

'Yeah,' Saint says. 'She's not a child. She can make her own decisions.' She glares at Mother. 'And it's not as if you guys are perfect role models.'

'You just want Megan for her car,' Father says.

I'd have thought that the man who believed in letting his young run free would have wanted Megan to leave and 'see the world'. But I'm not getting a worried parent vibe from him. I'm getting a possessive vibe, like he's scared he's about to lose a prize horse.

'No, Father,' Megan says. '*You* just want me for my car. Can't you see? There's nothing for me here, no one my own age. I don't want to spend the rest of my life ferrying useless stuff between the homesteads and listening to you fight.' Mother and Father exchange another look. 'I promise I'll come back. I won't be gone for long. I'll regret it if I don't go.'

'You've really disappointed me, Megan,' Father says. 'How can you be so ungrateful?' He shakes his head mournfully. 'After all that Mother and I have done for you.'

'No! I . . . I'm not ungrateful!'

'Well, you have a nice way of showing it,' Mother growls. 'Wanting to take off at the first chance you get.'

Megan drops her eyes and stares at her feet, guilt written all over her face.

'We're your family, Meg,' Father says. 'We gave you a roof over your head.'

'Some family this is,' Saint mutters.

'Let's go, Megan,' Mother says. 'You're safe with us, and your ... friends have told you how dangerous other places can be. That's why they left Cape Town in the first place.'

'Well maybe they can stay here, then. Live with us!'

Father shakes his head. 'You know resources are stretched, Megan. And you are still so young. Maybe you can have a little adventure when you're older.'

'But ... but I should at least take them to the next town.'

Father's eyes are hard blue stones. 'I don't think that's a very good idea, Megan. You know we have to conserve the diesel.'

Mother puts her arm around Megan's shoulders. 'Come on, let's get home. I bet Tumi and Stefan will make you one of their goat-cheese omelettes if you ask nicely.'

Megan seems to deflate. Part of me wants to stand up for her – the way Mother and Father are treating her reminds me of the kak the Mantis and Dad put me through when I first went to live with them after Gran died. But another part can't imagine feeling the way I did last night another second, and this is the part that makes me keep quiet.

'Can ... can I say goodbye first?' Megan whispers, her eyes glistening with tears.

'Of course,' Father says, spreading his arms out expansively, forgetting about the hide around his hips. Fortunately he grabs it before it slips too far.

'Don't worry, Megan,' Ginger says, 'we'll visit you on the way back.'

'You promise?'

'Course. You're our mate.'

Megan throws her arms around him, Ginger nearly losing

his grip on Bambi's lead, then she hugs the rest of us in turn. I try not to flinch when she wraps her arms around Ash's neck. 'Good luck, guys. I know you'll find people who can help you.'

Ash grabs her arm as she turns away from us, ignoring the furious look Mother gives him. 'Megan, if you want to come with us you're more than welcome.'

'Yeah, mate,' Ginger says. 'We'd love to have you along.'

She smiles and a tear wobbles down her cheek. 'Thanks. But Mother's right. I belong here.'

Mother puts her arm around Megan's shoulders again – tighter this time – and leads her away. Neither of them turn to look back.

'I think you've outstayed your welcome here,' Father says to us. 'I have to ask you to leave.'

'You don't have to ask us twice, mate.' Ginger says, gathering Bambi into his arms. 'I wouldn't stay with you lot if you paid me.'

———————

It feels like we've been walking for hours, and we've only just reached the gate that leads to the outside world. We trudge through it, pushing aside the Rotters hanging around the security booth, and make our way back onto the main road. The settlement's wall seems to stretch along the highway for kilometres; it's going to be ages before we see the back of it.

None of Father's people said a word to us as we packed up our stuff, and as we headed back along the palm-lined track I could hear the sound of drums beating – the circle had obviously started up again. Out of sight, out of mind is clearly Father's motto. Ash and Saint are subdued, but Megan's hasty departure an hour ago seems to have hit Ginger the hardest. He drags his feet and keeps looking in the direction of Mother's settlement. 'Can we stop for a moment?' he asks.

Ash rolls his eyes. 'We've hardly even started, Ginger.'

'Yeah, but there's something in my boot.'

We cross the road and stop under the shade of a stinkwood tree. Saint and Ash flump down on their bags as Ginger starts the lengthy process of untying his laces.

'Well, that was a complete waste of time,' Saint says. 'So much for finding helpful survivors.'

'We found Megan, didn't we?' Ash says. 'So that has to be a good sign. And like Ginger said back at Mother's, at least we know now that there are other people alive out here.'

'Yeah, trigger-happy psycho women and a bunch of guys who do nothing but play the bloody drums all day. I almost prefer the Ressers.'

Ginger tips his boot upside down. He wasn't lying about the stone in his shoe – it looks like half of Father's enclave is tumbling out of it. 'Bummer Megan didn't come with us,' he mumbles. 'First person I've ever met who's like me – you know, a freak of nature or whatever.'

'Cheer up, Ginger,' Saint says. 'You never know, there could be another smoking-hot freak of nature just around the next corner.'

'Wish I knew *why* we were immune though,' Ginger says.

'Don't we all.' Saint sighs. 'But let's face it, we could find a hundred people like Megan and there's no reason why they'd feel the need to throw their lot in with us.'

'Don't say that, Saint,' Ginger says. 'We've got to believe that we're going to find someone somewhere who's going to give us a hand, otherwise this whole trip is a waste of time.'

'Yeah, yeah, I know.'

Something catches my eye on the wall opposite. A bunch of

Rotters are reeling around it, but when they wander away I see a flash of blue paint partially hidden behind a bush.

No *ways*. It's that star symbol again.

'Hey! Look!' Saint says, jumping to her feet.

'Yeah, I know,' I say. 'I keep seeing it. I wonder what it means?'

'What?' Ash says.

'That blue star.'

'No, not that,' Saint says. 'Tell me I'm not imagining things.'

The heat's already started to kick in, the road shimmering as the sun blasts down on it, but despite the heat haze I can make out a blurry image in the centre of the highway, and it's moving quickly towards us. Then I hear the sound of an engine.

'No way!' Ginger yells.

'Yes way,' Saint says.

Ash, Ginger and Saint run into the centre of the road and wave their arms above their heads. I struggle to force a smile onto my face.

Megan brakes sharply in front of them, leans an arm out the window and flashes us one of her smiles. 'Hey, you guys need a ride?'

She jumps out of the bakkie and Saint pulls her into a hug. 'Took you long enough!'

'How did you get away?' Ash asks. 'Did Mother change her mind?'

'No, I ... ' Megan's smile slips. 'I dropped Mother off and I just couldn't do it. I couldn't go back there and pretend that none of this had ever happened. So I left.'

'Blimey, mate,' Ginger says. 'That was brave.'

Megan shrugs. 'Not really. I can always go back, can't I?'

'Yeah. Course you can. This is so cool, though! And hey, if you're coming with us, that means we have to make you an honorary Mall Rat.'

'A what?'

'That's what we call ourselves. You know, it's like our gang name, innit.'

Saint snorts. 'Yeah, right, Ginger.'

'And that's not all,' he says. 'You need a nickname.'

'I do?'

'Course. All of us have nicknames.'

'I don't,' I say, looking at Saint. 'You said it was bad luck.'

'You're Zombie Bait, remember?' Saint says.

'But I love your name, Lele,' Megan says. 'It suits you.'

'Seriously?'

'Ja. Megan is so ... boring.'

Ginger clicks his fingers. 'How about ... Hit Girl?'

'What?'

'Yeah, from *Kick-Ass*.'

'I don't think so, Ginger,' Saint says, rolling her eyes.

'How about Ember?' Ash says.

'Ember?' Ginger says, repeating the word.

'Yeah. Like the colour of her hair.'

I turn away and fumble in my bag for my sunglasses.

'I like it!' Ginger says. 'Ember and Ginger. Nice one!'

Yeah, Ginger and Ember go well together, but I'm trying not to think that Ash and Ember has a better ring to it.

Megan giggles. 'Ember works for me. What do you think, Lele?'

I return her smile, glad of my sunglasses – I know it doesn't reach my eyes. 'It suits you.'

'Brilliant. That's sorted then. Ember it is,' Ginger says, moving to the passenger door.

'You're in the back, Ginger,' Ash says.

'Aw, what?'

'Can't have Bambi messing up the upholstery, and I need to read the map.'

'I'll get the bags then, shall I?' I mutter, collecting them from beneath the tree and chucking them into the back, on top of the spare fuel containers.

Saint and Ginger vault over the sides of the bakkie and make themselves comfortable, and I'm just about to join them when Ash sticks his head out of the window. 'Why don't you squeeze in here, Lele?'

I think about it, but then I remember how cramped it is in the cab with three people squashed together on the seats. Do I really want to watch Ash's leg brushing against Megan's – Ember's – thigh as we head towards God knows where? No thanks. 'It's cool,' I say, trying to keep the edge out of my voice. 'I'll be fine on the back.'

'So where to?' Megan asks.

'Straight ahead, old chap,' Ginger says in a posh British accent, 'and don't spare the horses.'

SAINT

Dense forest hems us in, the highway's surface buckled and cracked where roots have snaked under the tarmac, fighting for any available space. The car bumps and jolts over the humps and fissures, and I'm relieved that I don't have to navigate this stretch on that bone-shaking bike.

Ginger and Bambi peer over the sides of the bakkie, the wind blowing the hyena's ears back, mirroring the way Ginger's hair is flattened against his head. Whenever the bakkie thumps over a particularly large lump in the road, Ginger whoops and laughs. His mood has lightened considerably since Ember rocked up. And it isn't just Ginger. Even Lele looks like she's perking up. She hasn't been acting like her normal self – she can be moody, sure, but she's more likely to lash out than sulk – and Ash hasn't been helping. He hardly said a word to her when we were at Father's settlement, and it can't be because he's still wracked with worry over what we're going to find out here. Stumbling across Megan – aka Ember – someone else with our talent for avoiding Rotter attack, must now make him feel like his decision to leave Cape Town is justified.

The car slows, and we pull into the forecourt of a large petrol station. It's ringed with dilapidated fast-food outlets, and to our right I make out the shape of a large white bridge that spans another gorge. I bloody hope we're not going to find another semi-suicidal bungee-jumping Rotter there.

Ash and Ember climb out and we jump down to join them.

'What we doing here?' Lele asks. 'I thought Megan brought along a ton of spare diesel.'

'Yeah, but we should try and see if we can get more. Ember's going to show me how to get fuel out of the storage tank.' Ash points towards a rusty manhole cover next to one of the pumps.

'You can do that?' Lele asks. 'We've tried before, but didn't have any luck.'

'Ja,' she says, digging in a box in the back of the car and pulling out a crowbar and something that looks like a manual pump. 'It might be all dried up though. It depends how full it was before everything happened.'

'You need help?'

'Under control,' Ash says, without even glancing at Lele. I glare at his back. Way to be sensitive, Ash. 'Why don't you guys go see if you can find any food?'

'Oh, I brought some supplies,' Ember says.

'We can never have too much,' Ash says. 'Not with Ginger around.'

'Don't worry, I get the hint,' Lele mumbles. She marches away, heading in the direction of the bridge.

Dammit. I'd better go after her.

Ginger's spotted a store on the far side of the complex, the word *Biltong* in plastic letters above its window. 'Me and Bambi will check that out.'

'Oh, there's a surprise.'

I hustle to catch up with Lele – she's disappearing down a pathway hidden between a trashed fast-food joint and a bank of public toilets. 'Wait up!'

The path leads out onto a large wooden platform, benches and the remains of picnic umbrellas dotted around it. Lele is leaning over a balcony, staring towards the bridge. The view from here is staggering. The bridge balances between two sheer cliffs, and when I look down at the river far below, a hollow feeling yawns in my stomach.

'Okay, what's up, Zombie Bait?' I say, sitting down on one of the benches.

'Nothing.'

'Don't lie. You and Ash haven't fallen out again, have you?'

'No.'

'I mean, because back at that game lodge you seemed to be getting on okay.'

'Whatever.'

'Come on, spill. I'm not going to stop bugging you until you tell me.'

'It's just that … it's convenient isn't it?'

'What do you mean?'

'We find a survivor and not only is she six feet tall and mysteriously immune from Rotter attack, but she also has a car we can use.'

'So? Aren't we due some luck sometime? What's gotten into you?'

Lele turns around and tries to smile. 'Ignore me, Saint, I'm just being a bitch. I'm tired is all.'

'We all are.'

'And I guess I'm still worried about Jobe.'

'I'm sure he's fine. Your stepmother won't let things get out of hand.'

'She can't run the whole enclave, Saint.'

'Really? She seemed like she could manage it with her hands tied behind her back. Besides, we've only been gone for four days.'

'I guess.'

'Score!' I hear Ginger yelling. 'Ember! Check!'

'I think Ginger is in lurve.'

Lele snorts. 'I'm not sure she feels the same.'

'Yeah. I guess he is a bit of an acquired taste.'

'What do you think of Megan – I mean, Ember?'

'She's pretty cool. Giggles a lot, but I can handle it.'

When we first encountered her I thought she might be a breezy, shallow girl like the ones I used to know back in the enclave before Hester found me – girls who didn't seem to worry about anything other than boyfriends and clothes and how many children they were planning on popping out. But she's smarter and more resourceful than she looks, and it must have taken some guts to leave her home. I'm not sure I'd be so quick to disobey Mother.

Lele turns to lean over the balcony again. 'When I first joined you guys you gave me a seriously hard time.'

'That was different.'

'How?'

'You know how, Lele. Hester wanted you to be part of the team. And we didn't know at first that we could trust you.'

'So how do we know that we can trust her?'

'Oh, come on, who is she spying for? The bunny-killing butch women or the dreamcatcher-weaving hippies?'

Lele shrugs.

'Come on, Zombie Bait, it's not like you to be moody.'

Lele looks over her shoulder and grins at me. 'You being sarcastic?'

'Of course.'

'It's just that ... Ember's all happy and smiley and she can drive cars and she's hot.'

'But she's not you.'

Lele sighs. 'That's probably why Ash digs her so much.'

'Don't be like that.'

But she's already turning away from the bridge and heading back to the car.

As we cross the forecourt Ember says something to Ash and he throws his head back and laughs. I've known Ash for many years – Hester took me in when I was barely a teenager and I've always thought of him as my family – but even I've never seen him acting so unguarded.

Night has crept up on us, but I know we cannot be far from our next destination – Port Elizabeth – a far larger town than any we've come across so far. According to Ash it's right next to the ocean, not that we'll be able to see any sign of it tonight. The moon is swathed in a shroud of cloud, and until it clears we have to depend on the bakkie's headlights.

'You really think we should be heading into the city at night, Saint?' Ginger asks.

'Ash says there's a better chance of spotting survivors this way, Ginger,' I say. 'If there are people around we'll see lights or fires.'

I hope Ash is right. It's getting chilly on the back of the bakkie – the wind has picked up and it howls in my ears and buffets against the side of the car. And now I am not sure which is worse, the gluttonous forest or the darkened shapes of the buildings that line the highway. Around us the dead traffic is thickening, most of the vehicles pointing away from the city. Not a great sign.

'You think there are people alive around here?' Ginger asks.

'Probably not,' Lele says. 'The Cape Town enclave is away from the actual city, isn't it? But we're going to have to be on our guard, whatever the case.'

'You think, Lele?' Ginger says. 'We haven't seen any Rotters for ages.'

'It's not the dead I'm worried about so much. Can you imagine what would happen if a bunch of strangers rocked up in Cape Town? The kind of welcome they'd get from the Resurrectionists?'

'Or the Guardians,' I add.

'Sheesh,' Ginger says. 'I hadn't thought of that.'

The car screeches to a stop, and I slide forward and then back, bashing against the wall of the cab.

'Sorry!' Ember calls.

Ash opens the partition. 'We can't go any further. Road's blocked.'

I peer through the cab. The headlights illuminate a twisted mass of metal shapes – the remains of an ancient car crash.

'We'll have to go back, take an off-ramp.'

Ember reverses, turns the car and then hangs a left. Bridges criss-cross above us, and I try not to think of the weight of all that concrete. We pull into a wide boulevard; plastic bags floating around us like ghosts. I look through the partition to see what's ahead of us. The headlights flick over a huge billboard displaying a blown-up photograph of a woman in her underwear, the words *You're Worth It* still visible above her head. It's black with spots of decay, making her look far more like a Rotter than an airbrushed model.

We drive through intersection after intersection, abandoned

vehicles providing a maze through which Ember slowly navigates.

'Hey!' Ginger finally calls. 'Slow down!'

Ember pulls to a stop and Ash turns around in his seat. 'What?'

Ginger stands up and points towards a blocky row of buildings that sit on top of a slight rise to the right. The cloud lifts and for a second I'm able to read familiar signs stuck to their walls: *Pick n Pay Hypermarket*, *Mr Price* and *Game*.

It's a mall.

'Can we go check it out?'

'I can't see any lights coming from it, Ginger,' Ash says.

'Yeah, but we are the Mall Rats, right?' He looks down at his filthy hoody. 'Wouldn't mind getting some new gear, and if there's a Pick n Pay, we might find some –'

'Biltong,' I say. 'I know, I know.'

It is nothing like our mall back in Cape Town. The shops are laid out in a long line facing a rubbish-strewn parking lot, their glass doors bouncing the headlights back at us as we drive around.

Ember parks metres from the entrance of an enormous supermarket, and I clamber off the back of the bakkie, jumping as a shopping trolley glides towards us on skew wheels, propelled by the howling wind. Empty plastic cooldrink bottles bounce across the parking bays. 'Let's make it quick, you guys,' I say. 'This place is giving me the creeps.'

'You can take the torch, Saint,' Ginger says, handing it to me. 'Why don't you, Lele and Ember see if you can find us some new gear, and me and Ash'll hit the supermarket.'

'Fine by me,' I say. I really don't like the look of the pitch-black hypermarket and the possessed shopping trolleys that dance around it.

I lead Lele and Ember towards a Mr Price shop. There's just enough space to slip in between the glass doors and I shine the light around the interior. The clothes nearest the entrance are covered in furry mould, but the further we head inside, the more wearable they appear. Ember stares around her, running her hands lovingly over the racks of dresses and scarves. It's obvious that it's been years since she's set foot in any kind of clothing store and thanks to Father's unconventional approach to fashion the poor girl has been subjected to the sight of ratty loincloths for much of her life. 'May I borrow the torch, Saint?' she asks. I pass it to her and she picks through a pile of T-shirts, pulling one out and handing it to Lele. 'Lele, this looks like it's your size!' The words *Drama Queen* are scrawled across the back of it.

'Oh ha ha,' Lele says, but she's smiling, which makes for a pleasant change.

'I'm going to see if I can find a replacement for the world's most disgusting hoody,' I say as Ember hands the torch back to me. I pick my way over to the men's aisle. It stinks in this section, some kind of animal has made a nest under the underwear rack, clumps of fur and gnawed bones are scattered among shredded boxer shorts printed with cartoon characters. I grab a couple of pairs of jeans that will hopefully fit Ash, a pair of XXL surfer shorts for Ginger and a lime-green hoody that should be large enough for one boy and his hyena to wear simultaneously.

I head back to the women's section, but pull up short as I catch a glimpse of some badass skinny jeans. Perfect. I dig out a small size in black for Lele, a medium dark-purple pair for me and a red pair for Ember. Grabbing a few T-shirts and tank tops I make my way back to the others. 'Here you go, guys,' I say, chucking the scavenged clothes in their direction. 'Knock yourselves out.'

I place the torch on the top of a shelf where it will provide us with the most light, drag on the jeans and pull a black tank top over my head. The fabric feels scratchy and stiff, but it's wonderful to be out of my mucky old clothes. Lele scurries behind a rack to get changed, but in contrast Ember unselfconsciously strips off.

There's the sound of running feet.

Lele reaches the door before me. 'Ginger? That you?'

'Yeah!' he thumps into the store, sending a clothing display toppling to the floor. 'Sorry,' he says, stopping dead as he catches sight of Ember pulling her T-shirt over her head.

'What is it, Ginger?' I ask. 'Are you and Ash okay?'

'Course,' he says, shrugging off his embarrassment, though I know his face must now be the colour of a tomato. 'I wanted to show Ember what I found.' He holds up the axe he's brandishing in his left hand. 'Ember, you should see what I can do with this.'

'The mating ritual of the big Ginger zombie killer,' I whisper to Lele.

She snorts.

We join the others under the canopy in front of the supermarket's doors, doing our best to shelter from the relentless wind. Ember hands out dried apricots and Ginger pours the last of the goat milk she'd thoughtfully brought along into a bowl for the hyena.

'Ember, you look really cool in your new clothes,' Ginger says.

'I do?'

'Course.'

'Hey,' I say. 'What about the rest of us?'

'Yeah, but I'm used to seeing you guys ... um ... dressed.'

He looks down, embarrassed again. 'I was just saying ... '

Ash laughs and punches him on the shoulder. 'It's cool, Ginger. We know what you meant. And anyway,' he says, grinning at Ember, 'you're right.'

'This is so much fun,' Ember says.

'It is?' I say, ripping a label off my new stiff jeans.

'Course! It's an adventure.'

The wind suddenly drops, and I sigh with relief.

'So, what now?' Lele asks.

Ash shrugs. 'Onwards, till we find more people.'

'And how long is that going to take? What if while we're all out here travelling around, having adventures and making new friends, Jobe and Sasha are in danger?'

Ash groans. 'Not this again, Lele.'

'Yes, *this again*, Ash. I'm serious. I think we need to –'

'Shhh!' Ember says.

Lele turns on her. 'Don't tell me to –'

'No, Ember's right,' I say. 'Listen.'

Now the wind has ceased I can hear a faint, but unmistakable sound.

'Rotters,' Ginger says. 'For sure.'

It has taken us more than an hour to locate the source of the Rotters' moans – Ginger, Lele and I standing on the back of the Land Cruiser and straining our ears over the noise of the engine – but now that we've found it I suspect all of us wish we hadn't.

We've made our way down to the esplanade – leaving the bakkie in an empty bay outside a run-down hotel – and we're all gazing at the sight in front of us in silence, trying to make sense of what we're seeing.

We're lucky – or unlucky – that the clouds have drifted away from the moon. It shines down onto the sea, turning it a deep blue and flecking it with silver, but where the sea looks relatively calm in the moonlight, tranquil even, the beach in front of it is a seething mass of Rotter bodies. Behind them a pier juts out into the water, and looming next to it there's a colossal black shape. I realise that I'm looking at a ship, the front part of it lodged in the sand. It's tilting at a slight angle, and compared to it the Rotters are the size of ants.

I shiver, remembering the oil tanker we saw on the beach back in Cape Town when we were looking for a safe place to camp. I do not like boats, and I'm not really a fan of the ocean either. It's too vast, too unknown. Dad never took Atang and me on holiday to the sea, and the first time I saw it up close was during a school trip to the Waterfront Aquarium.

'Blimey,' Ginger says. 'There are hundreds of 'em, innit? They look like holidaymakers gone mad. Wonder what they're doing on the beach?'

'You reckon there are survivors around here?' Lele asks.

'Doubt it,' Ash says. 'I can't see any sign of a settlement nearby, and no one normal could survive that many of them.'

'Er, guys,' Ginger says. 'Look!'

A light winks on and off. And it's coming from the ship.

LELE

I'm out of breath from jogging across the sand, my thigh muscles burning like they used to after one of the hectic training sessions I had to endure with Hester and Saint. Thankfully it's fairly easy to avoid bumping into the undead that crowd around us – they aren't anywhere near as tightly packed as they looked when we spied them from the walkway that runs parallel to the beach.

Ember's keeping as close as she can to Ash, their shoulders practically touching, and I secretly give Ash the finger behind his back. Jealousy is nothing new to me, of course. I've been down this road at Malema High, when Thabo was the centre of giggling girl attention, but this feels way more intense – a panicky sensation that sits heavily in my chest. It doesn't help that Ember is everything I'm not: curvy, cheerful, long-haired. I wouldn't blame Ash if he did prefer her. Who wants a skinny, moody, sulky girlfriend when you can have one who smiles all day and can handle a car like a racing driver? What makes it worse is that she's impossible not to like. It would be so much easier to resent her if she was a shallow idiot like the girls who used to hang around Thabo.

Ash turns around, almost catching me flipping him off. 'Lele, you *are* keeping an eye for Hatchlings, right?'

'Yes, sir,' I grumble. He needn't worry, these Rotters are definitely past their sell-by date, knocking blindly into one another as they let out their trademark moans.

Now we're up close to the ship, the size of it takes my breath away. It towers above us, a huge metal monster.

'Has the light gone on again?' Ginger asks, peering upwards.

'No,' Saint says. 'Doesn't look like it.'

Soft waves roll in, lapping against the boat's hull, and for a second it feels as if it's going to wash forward and crush us.

'We didn't imagine the light, did we?' Ginger says. He shines his torch upwards and clicks it on and off.

'Guys,' Ash says. 'Check.'

A flickering light sparks above us, then dies. And then a man's voice calls out: 'Who's there?'

'Just us!' Ginger yells over the waves. 'Um ... ' he looks at Ash. 'What should I say?'

Ash shrugs. 'Dunno. I'm not sure what we're dealing with.'

'Hang on, I have an idea,' Ginger mutters. 'Friend or foe!' he shouts.

There's a pause, then: 'Friend!'

'Oh genius, Ginger,' Saint says. 'It didn't occur to you they might lie?'

'Hold on!' the voice calls. Something tumbles down towards us, slapping against the side of the ship. Ginger shines his torch on it. 'It's a rope ladder,' he says, reaching to tug on it. 'Should we?'

'What do you think, Ash?' Saint asks. 'The last thing we want is to get stuck up there if they're as screwed up as the Resurrectionists.'

'Why should they be?' Ginger asks. 'Ember's settlements were cool. Weird, but cool – no offence, Ember.'

'I'm just saying we should be cautious.'

'Come aboard!' the voice hollers.

'How many of you are there?' Ash replies.

There's a pause, then: 'There's two of us.'

Saint shrugs. 'Unless they have guns we could easily take them.'

'Someone needs to stay here just in case,' Ash says. 'Any volunteers?'

'Um ... me and Ember could hang back I suppose,' Ginger says. 'I should really stay with Bambi anyway. I mean, if that's okay with you, Ember?' Shame, Ginger sounds way too overeager.

'Sure,' Ember says. It's too dark for me to see her face, so I can't tell if she's happy about this or not.

'Awesome,' Ash says. 'I'll shout down to let you know we're cool.'

Ginger mock-salutes. 'Aye, aye, Captain.'

Ash yanks on the rope ladder, checking that it will hold his weight, and then starts the long climb.

'Remember, Ginger, you've got our backs, 'kay?' Saint says, following Ash.

I'm not sure what Ginger could actually do if we got trapped up on the boat, but what the hell.

It's harder than it looks. The ladder's nylon rope feels slippery and insubstantial and sways dangerously as I pull myself up onto its lowest rungs. Above me, Saint is almost at the top, and as she climbs off it and disappears into the darkness the ladder swings against the ship's side and I feel my jeans catch on the dried-out barnacles that coat its surface.

'Don't look down, Lele!' Ginger calls as I clamber past a row of round, darkened windows, stuck in the side like alien eyes.

But of course I can't resist doing just that.

Oh crap, I'm way higher up than I thought I was – the tops of the Rotters' heads look tiny from here. I cling on, fighting the panic as the strength drains from my legs. It's only desire not to look stupid and weak in front of Ember that keeps me going.

I finally reach a balcony, the irony taste of adrenalin filling my mouth. Scurrying over it I thump down onto a darkened deck. Getting to my feet I shift my weight to compensate for the slightly tilted surface, and the next thing I know someone has seized me around my waist.

I move instinctively, grabbing the hand of whoever's holding me and twisting it to the side. Spinning around I ready myself to follow up with a kick.

'What the *hell*, Lele?' Ash says.

I release my grip and step away from my would-be assailant. It's a guy – a stocky guy with shaggy light-coloured hair – and he's staring at me in confusion. Ash is shaking his head and Saint looks like she's trying not to laugh. There's a tall, well-built figure with long, straight hair standing next to her, holding a smoking tiki torch.

'What did you do that for?' Shaggy Hair says. 'I was only trying to help you.'

'Sorry.'

'Okay if I just shake your hand then?' His grip is strong and he pumps my arm up and down enthusiastically. 'I'm Scott.' The figure next to Saint steps forward. 'And that's Previn.'

'I'm Lele – sorry again about that.'

'It's my fault,' Scott says. 'I was a bit overeager. It's just –

you're the first people we've seen for ... ' He looks at Previn. 'How long's it been, bru? Six months?'

Previn shrugs. With his long, floppy hair he reminds me of Zyed – if Zyed was well over six foot and built like a kombi. They seem to be in their mid-twenties, but the light's not good enough to be sure. For some reason they're both dressed in dinner jackets and bow ties. 'Nice outfits,' I say.

'Huh?' Scott looks down as if he's forgotten what he's wearing and chuckles. 'Ja – I know. The guests, or whoever was on the ship before us, left all of their stuff and we just thought, why not?' He paces back and forth, running his hands through his hair. 'I can't believe it. We were just about to eat when Previn saw lights – torches, right? And we're like, "No ways, man! Are there people over there? I mean, real living people!"' He laughs. 'Listen to me, I'm babbling.'

'Why didn't the dead get you?' Previn asks. 'There are hundreds of them down there. There's no way you could have made it if –'

'Bru, don't be so rude,' Scott says. 'You can see they're not Death Eaters, check out their eyes.'

'Death Eaters?' Saint says.

But I've figured it out. 'He means Guardians.'

Previn looks as if he's about to say something else, but Scott jumps in. 'Where the hell are you from?'

'It's a long story,' Ash says.

'You guys on the run from a settlement or something?' Previn asks, still sounding suspicious.

'Something like that,' Saint says.

Thunder rumbles in the distance.

'Awesome,' Scott says. 'Looks like it might rain. Prev, did you take the tarp off the water tanks and Jacuzzi?'

'Course.'

'Thanks, bru.' He turns back to us. 'How about we all get inside?'

'We're fine here,' Ash says.

'We're not going to eat you, bru.'

A fat drop of rain lands on the top of my head and trickles down my cheek.

Ash murmurs something to Saint and she nods. He walks over to the ship's balcony. 'We're cool!' he shouts down to Ginger.

'Shall we come up?' Ginger's voice floats up.

'Nah. Wait there for us!'

'But it's raining!'

Ash sighs. 'Go back to the car then!'

'There are more of you?' Previn asks.

'Yeah. They're waiting for us.'

'So bring them up here,' Scott says. 'Let's get this party started.'

'Maybe later.'

'It's cool, bru. It's all cool.'

Scott grabs the smouldering torch from Previn and leads us through a heavy metal side door and into a dark corridor. I'm hit immediately by the overpowering stench of rotting fabric and fish. The ground feels soft and squishy beneath my feet – waterlogged carpet – and when I stumble on the slanting floor and reach out a hand to steady myself, my palm is coated in a slimy residue that drips down the walls. Without the torch we wouldn't be able to see a thing.

Saint slips her arm through mine.

'What's up?'

'Nothing,' she says. 'Just think we should stick together is all.'

'We stick to this deck and the top one,' Scott says. 'If you think it pongs in here you should smell the rest of the place. The ship took on water at some stage and most of the other decks are rot city.'

He turns a corner.

'Wow,' Saint breathes.

We've entered a large open area. Two identical staircases curl upwards on either side of the room, chandeliers droop from the ceiling and the walls are covered in murals, mostly depicting bearded guys in boats battling a series of giant jellyfish, whales and bare-breasted mermaids.

'If Ginger were here he'd probably start singing the *Titanic* soundtrack,' Saint murmurs.

Scott heads towards a pair of glass doors slotted between the staircases. 'Let's get comfortable and then we can swap stories.'

'What happened to all the other passengers?' Ash asks.

Scott shrugs. 'Gone. All the lifeboats are gone, too, so we reckon the ship must have run into trouble and they abandoned it before it washed up here.' He turns around and grins. 'Leaving it for us.'

———

'Ta-da!' Scott says, ushering us into a gloomy area. 'Home sweet home. This is where we mainly hang out.'

'What was this place?' Saint asks.

'It's one of the bars. There are six or seven on the ship. And there's a casino, but that leaks like you won't believe, so you're better off here.'

Scott moves around the space, lighting candles that are stuck in empty wine bottles on every available surface. Bit by bit the darkness gives in, and I realise that we're in a circular windowless room, a wide curved bar backed by a huge cracked mirror dominating one side of it. The light catches the rows of multicoloured bottles that stand in front of the mirror and dances over the crystal teardrops of another chandelier that hangs from the centre of the ceiling. Thankfully, the smell of candle wax smothers the odours of dank carpet and fish.

Scott gestures to a cluster of small side tables, padded chairs and sofas in the centre of the room, most of which are only slightly spotted with mould. Saint and Ash slump down in adjoining armchairs, I choose the largest of the couches and Scott sits next to me. Previn leans against the bar, his arms folded.

'Oh, wow,' Scott says, staring at me and then Saint. 'I didn't realise you were both so pretty.'

Ash's face hardens. 'Yeah, right,' Saint retorts.

'Sorry – let's just say it's been a while. This calls for a celebration. Prev, fetch the good stuff.'

Without a word, Previn leans over the bar and I hear the clinking of glasses.

Scott winks at me and I find myself smiling back at him. Now I can see him properly in the candlelight it's clear that he's quite a bit older than me – probably late twenties – and quite good-looking in a piratey kind of way.

''Scuse the stink. We've been experimenting with fish biltong.'

'Any luck?' Saint asks.

'Not really. We'd offer you some, but the last batch almost killed us.'

Previn passes a glass filled with dark liquid to each of us. It smells far more potent than the champagne.

'Johnny Walker Black,' Scott says. 'One thing about this place, the quality of the booze is top notch.'

I take a sip and almost choke. My throat feels like it's on fire, but when it hits my belly I feel a pleasant warm buzz.

'What do you do for food?'

'Some of the canned goods are still okay, but we mostly eat fish and shellfish, stuff like that. Sometimes we get lucky and catch a bird – Prev's good at that – and what we can get when we go out foraging.'

'You're able to leave here?'

'Not often, trust me. We've got an inflatable raft and when we're low on water we risk it. We've had quite a few near misses. There weren't half as many Deadheads on the beach when we first arrived.'

'What do you mean "arrived"?' Ash asks. He doesn't seem to have taken to Scott and Previn – he's been watching them closely since he sat down. 'Aren't you from the city back there?'

'Nah, bru. We're from Durban.'

'Durban?' Saint says. 'But that's miles away. How on earth did you make it this far?'

'Yacht. Well, more of a fishing boat, really. But it wasn't in great condition when we set out, and more by luck than anything else we made it to the harbour before it gave up the ghost. We weren't planning on coming here, I can tell you that. Thought maybe we'd try and get to one of the islands – Mauritius maybe – but neither of us knows anything about boats and sailing and navigation, so we stuck to the coast till we ran out of fuel.'

'Why leave Durban in the first place?' Ash asks.

'What is this, an interrogation?' Scott says, winking at me again.

'Were you at a settlement there?'

He nods. 'If you can call it that. It was more like a military base.'

'The army ran it?'

'Ja. With an iron fist.'

'And you said there were Guardians – Death Eaters – there?'

'Ja. Other people called them the kgo-kgo. Death Eaters is the name Prev chose for them.'

'Do you know what they are?' I ask.

'Most of the people in the enclave thought they were supernatural creatures – spirits of the ancestors or whatever. Me? I dunno. Evolved Deadheads probably. Never got to see beneath those robes they wore to be sure.'

I open my mouth to put him straight, but Ash jumps in. 'So, what happened to the settlement?'

'Cholera epidemic. It spread like wildfire. People panicked, the army tried to control them, set up a quarantine, but it still got out of hand. There was an uprising, and in the fighting the Deadheads got in.'

Saint shudders and I wonder if she's thinking about the Cape Town enclave break-in all those years ago.

'Didn't the Guardians – the Death Eaters – stop them?' I ask.

'I dunno. We took a chance and fled to the harbour. Didn't look back. Got lucky, jumped on the first boat we came to, and the rest is history.'

'And the others?' Ash asks. 'The other people in the settlement? What happened to them?'

Scott looks straight at Ash and drains his glass. 'Who knows? Now, enough about us, what's your story?'

I wait to see what Ash decides to tell them. He's still looking at Scott warily and I notice that he's barely touched his drink. But despite their weird dress sense, compared to Mother and Father, and, let's face it, most of the Resurrectionists, they seem to be refreshingly normal.

I decide to take matters into my own hands. 'We're from Cape Town,' I say, ignoring the pointed look Ash shoots my way.

'Seriously?' Scott says. 'This I've got to hear.' He reaches over and tops up my glass.

It's taken me the best part of an hour to sketch out the situation in Cape Town and the reasons why we left, and in that time I've lost count of the number of times Scott's refilled my glass. I'm getting used to the bitter burn, but that might just be because the alcohol's taken hold – the room feels like it's beginning to tilt.

'You reckon we could make it there?' Scott asks. 'To Cape Town, I mean.'

'You wouldn't want to go there, trust me,' Saint says. 'And I doubt it. The place is surrounded by Rotters.'

'And you think you're able to avoid the Deadheads because you've got twins? That's freaky, man.'

'Something like that,' Saint says, closing her eyes and leaning her head back against the chair – I'm obviously not the only one who's feeling the effects of the whisky.

'I wish I had a twin,' Scott says. 'It'd make things a lot easier. I'd be able to get the hell off this ship for a start.'

I knock back my drink. 'Weren't there people like us in Durban?'

'Another one?' Scott smiles at me.

'Maybe you shouldn't have any more, Lele,' Ash says. 'We'd better get back to the others.'

Yeah. I think. He's probably missing Ember. 'I'm fine, Ash,' I say. 'You're not my Dad.' I suddenly find this hilarious, and Scott laughs along with me. My glass slips through my fingers as I hand it to him. 'Whoops!' he says, catching it at the last second.

Scott fills the glass almost to the brim and I take a long sip, trying not to cough as it hits the back of my throat.

'Hey, why don't you stay here?' Scott says. 'Most of the

cabins on this deck are still kosher, right, Prev?'

I realise I've forgotten all about Previn. He's been lounging on a couch in a darkened corner of the room, and he's hardly said a word. 'They should be cool, ja,' he says.

'No,' Ash says. 'Like I said, our friends are waiting for us.'

'Oh, come on,' Scott says. 'I've had no one but this idiot to talk to for six months.'

'Don't be so lame, Ash,' I say.

'Lele, can I have a word?' Ash says, standing up. 'In private,' he adds as he heads for the glass doors.

'What's the matter with him?' Scott asks.

I shrug and wobble to my feet. 'I'd better go and see.' Oh crap, I'm not even sure I can walk straight. And as if I needed proof I bash into a table, almost sending one of the candle-holders flying.

Ash is waiting for me next to one of the staircases, his arms crossed.

'So, what is it, Ash? I'm just having fun. You got a problem with that?'

'I think you've had enough. That's all I'm saying.'

'Yeah, 'cos we all remember what happens when I drink, right? Like back at that game lodge.' Ha. Good, at least he has the grace to look uncomfortable. 'Do you remember that, Ash?' I hold my glass up in front of him and wiggle it, liquid slopping over the rim and onto the carpet, and then I take a deep gulp. 'Yum.'

'Look, Lele, we don't know these guys. Ginger and Ember will be wondering where –'

'Now we're getting to it. We wouldn't want Ember to *worry* would we?'

'What?'

'You know what I'm saying, Ash.'

'Hey, guys,' Saint says from behind us. 'What's the plan?' I turn around to face her, almost losing my balance in the process. 'Whoa, Zombie Bait, you're off your head.'

'I'm cool,' I say. But I don't feel cool anymore. The paintings on the wall are beginning to spin.

'You don't trust those guys, Ash?' Saint asks, smothering a yawn.

'They seem okay. I just reckon we should get back, is all.'

I open my mouth to speak but my tongue feels numb. The alcohol swirls greasily in my belly.

'Fine by me. This place stinks. Let's break the news.'

I follow the others back into the bar, placing my glass carefully on the nearest table. It's empty. Did I finish it? I can't remember.

'We're going to call it a night,' Ash says.

'You will come back in the morning, right?' Scott says. He laughs. 'You're not just going to leave us here, are you? Hey, maybe you could bring some supplies or something.'

'Of course,' Ash says, though I can't tell if he means it or not.

'I'll come with to see you off,' Scott says, getting to his feet and grabbing a torch.

Previn stays seated and waves languidly at us.

———————

Not good. This is not good. It almost feels like the ship is actually moving, and even though I'm concentrating on walking in a straight line I keep bashing into the slimy walls. My stomach is really churning now, and the fishy odour isn't helping. Saliva floods into my mouth and I swallow convulsively. I pray that I can make it outside. I don't want to be sick in front of Saint and Scott – and, most of all, Ash.

We finally reach the deck, and I drag in a lungful of damp

sea air.

'You going to make it down okay, Zombie Bait?' Saint asks.

I try to smile, but I can feel sweat prickling my forehead. And then I know I can't control the nausea any longer. My mouth fills with the bitter rush of bile, and I run as far away from the others as I can, scooting behind a pile of life jackets and coiled rope.

'Lele?' Saint calls after me.

The whisky rushes up and I bend double as it gushes out of my mouth.

I hear the thump of running footsteps. 'Oh, *Lele*,' Saint says.

'Saint?' Ash calls.

'Don't let Ash see me like this,' I say as soon as I can speak. 'Please, Saint.'

'I'm on it.'

My legs are shaking and I rest my hands on my knees while I get my breath back.

'You go, Ash,' I hear Saint saying. 'I'll make sure she's okay.'

'Shame, man,' Scott says. 'I'll get her some water.' There's a pause. 'Nice meeting you, bru.' He must be saying goodbye to Ash.

'You sure you'll be cool, Saint?' Ash says.

'Yeah. We'll be five minutes. She just needs some privacy.'

The nausea passes and I breathe in a lungful of air. I wipe my mouth with the edge of my T-shirt and try to stand up straight. My head feels clearer, so that's something.

'Can we walk a bit?' I say to Saint as she reappears out of the gloom.

'Sure.'

We walk slowly down the deck. With every step I feel a little better. I lean over the railing, letting the soft rain fall on my head. Saint puts her arm around me. 'You sure you'll be able to climb down without killing yourself?'

'I think so.'

She shakes her head. 'No more whisky for you from now on. You ready?'

I nod. She takes my elbow and starts to lead me over to the rope ladder.

Something slams into the base of my spine, sending me stumbling forwards. Before I can regain my balance, a hand grabs the collar of my shirt, wrenches me back, and I feel an arm wrap around my neck. 'Saint!' I scream. I can't see her – where is she?

'You're not going anywhere,' Previn says in my ear.

My stomach drops, but this time it has nothing to do with the whisky. I try and turn my head to see what's happened to Saint, but I can barely move. Previn's strong. Twisting my body around I try and slam the back of my boot down on his foot, but he increases the pressure on my windpipe and stars start to dance in front of my eyes. I scratch at his arm with my nails, but he grabs my wrists with his other hand and squeezes. When I stop struggling, the stranglehold slackens slightly and I can breathe again.

Scott moves into my eyeline. He's smiling down at the floor. With an effort, I follow his gaze. Saint is sprawled at my feet, clutching the back of her head. 'You blindsided me, you bastard,' she says. 'You're going to be sorry.'

'Looks like it's just you girls and us,' Scott says.

'Oh, really,' Saint says, struggling to her feet. 'You have no idea who you're dealing with.'

Something sharp and cold presses into the side of my neck. It can only be a knife. 'You want me to hurt her?' Previn says. It sounds like he's smiling.

Saint's furious expression shifts to one of dismay. 'Shit.'

Scott heaves the rope ladder back up onto the deck, and I hear Ash shouting something from below.

'Get inside,' Scott says. 'Back to the bar.'

'Like I said, you don't know who you are dealing with,' Saint says, but she does as she's told.

Without loosening his grip around my throat, Previn manhandles me down the corridor. I try and make it as difficult as I can for him, but he outweighs me by about fifty kilograms.

Scott pushes Saint through the glass doors. 'Now what?' Saint asks as we follow them into the room.

Scott waves her towards one of the armchairs. 'Have a seat, sweetheart.'

'I'm not your sweetheart.'

'Not yet, you're not.'

I'm waiting for Previn to loosen his grip enough for me to kick back at him, but if anything he's tightened his hold now we are back in the bar. Crap.

'Our friends are waiting for us,' Saint says. 'They'll know something is wrong.'

Scott laughs. 'So? What they gonna do? They can't climb up here without the ladder.'

'What the hell do you want?' Saint says.

'You didn't think we'd let you leave us here, did you?'

'Who said anything about leaving you here?'

Scott smiles. 'We're not idiots. We knew you wouldn't be coming back after tonight. Why would you?'

'There were people like you in Durban,' Previn says. 'Traitors. They said they'd help us, but they left the settlement and didn't come back. We're not letting you get away so easily.'

'You're too valuable to us,' Scott says. 'If we've got you, your friends have to do what we say. Get us what we want. We can't go into the town for supplies, but they can.'

'Let her go,' Saint says. 'Let her go and I'll stay.'

'Oh, I think we'd rather have both of you as our special guests.' Scott moves closer to me. 'And while you're here, there's no reason why all of us shouldn't get to know each other a little better.' He's inches away from me now, and I'm hit with a blast of potent alcohol breath. How could I have ever thought he was good-looking? Up close his eyes are small and cruel.

'Don't you touch her, you bastard,' Saint hisses.

'If you move,' Scott says to Saint, 'she's gone. You understand? It would take less than a second to finish her off. Previn knows how to use a knife.'

'Shouldn't we tie the big one up?' Previn says.

'Where's the fun in that? What's she going to do? Lucky we got rid of that tall oke, though. Now *he* could have been trouble.' He traces a finger over my cheek and down my neck. I close my eyes and try to move away from him, but Previn's grip is too strong.

'Lele, I'm sorry,' Saint says.

I can feel him tugging at my clothes, Previn's breath hot and heavy in my ear.

I have to stop this. I can't let this happen. No one's going to magically appear and get me out of here. *Think*, Lele. Scott yanks at the buttons on my jeans. And then I get it.

'I don't feel so good,' I whisper, and then I pretend to gag – it's not too difficult to fake, I'm still feeling gross. Scott instantly recoils, Previn loosens his grip and I lean forward as if I'm going to throw up, the point of the knife moving from my neck. It's all I need.

I clench my fists and slam upwards with my elbow, catching Scott on the side of his face, and at the same time I lash back with my boot, feeling it connect with what I hope is Previn's knee. I hear him grunt. Good.

Scott pinwheels back and I drop to the floor, knowing that at any second Previn could slice down at me with the knife.

'Lele!' Saint yells, 'Stay down!'

Something whizzes through the air above my head – a bottle? – and shatters behind me. I leap to my feet and propel myself forward, but even as I do I feel Previn grab at my shirt, yanking me back towards him. I fall heavily, feeling the sharp bite of glass digging into my palm.

There's the sound of more glass splintering and the room is awash with the stench of alcohol – Saint must have thrown another bottle – and this time I hear Previn yelp in pain and surprise.

A boot clouts me in the stomach, forcing the breath out of my lungs. I look up and see Scott grinning triumphantly. 'You are going to be really sorry now,' he says, moving to kick me again, but as he does I brace myself, grab his foot, twist it and yank him towards me. He loses his balance, stumbles backwards, and, as I release my grip, he falls back, hitting his head with a clunk on the table behind him. I scramble to my feet, ready to drop-kick him if necessary, but he doesn't get back up.

Previn and Saint are circling each other. He towers over her, but I know this won't make any difference.

'Oh, I like it,' Previn says, waving the flick knife in front of him. 'A chick who thinks she can fight. Sexy.'

'Sorry,' Saint says. 'I'm not into guys.'

'I can change that,' Previn says. 'It wouldn't be the first time.'

Rushing forward he lashes out wildly with the knife, but even after who knows how many drinks Saint is more than a match for him. She catches his wrist and twists it so that he's forced to drop the knife. Then she spins and kicks him with full force in the groin. Previn yelps and drops to his knees. 'You were saying?' Saint says. 'Lele, find me some rope or something to tie up this asshole.'

'You're dead, bitch,' Previn says, blindly fumbling for the knife, his face contorted with pain. But Saint is way ahead of him. She boots the knife away from him and follows up with another kick between his legs. 'Call me names again, and I'll kick you even harder where it hurts. Get it?' she says.

I walk over to Scott, double-checking that he's not faking. I can see his chest rising and falling, but I'm pretty sure he's out cold. Blood drips onto the floor from my hand, and I hold it up to a candle flame. The gash is deep, slicing across the faint scar that's already there. Inside it I can make out the thin tendrils of the fine spaghetti stuff, knitting together and sewing up the wound.

My secret.

I quickly rip off a piece of my T-shirt and wrap it around my palm.

Looking around for anything we can use to restrain Previn, I spy the fancy plaited sashes tied around the curtains. They'll do. I yank them down with my good hand and throw them to Saint.

'Hey, you hurt, Zombie Bait?' she asks, checking out my crude bandage.

'It's nothing,' I say. 'Just a scratch.'

'You sure?'

'Yeah.'

'Are you going to be a good boy while I tie you up?' Saint says to Previn. 'Roll over onto your stomach and put your hands behind your back.'

Previn glares at her. 'Make me.'

'Okay.' She draws her foot back as if she's about to kick him again, but before she can follow through he does as he's told.

Saint nods at the knife and I jog over and pick it up. 'If

asshole here tries anything, use that on him, Lele.' Kneeling on Previn's back she makes short work of tying up his hands and feet. I've often seen Saint in fight mode before, but I don't think I've ever seen her so furious. 'Were you lying about Durban?' she says, standing up and looking down at him. 'Did they throw you out? Maybe for being ... What's the word I'm looking for here? Oh yes, total bastards.'

Previn turns his head towards her and tries to spit in her direction, but it lands on his chin.

'Come on, Lele, we're leaving,' Saint says.

Previn's expression changes instantly; he now reminds me of a dangerous animal trapped in a snare. 'You can't do that,' he whines. 'We can't stay here any longer. We just got drunk. Please don't leave us here!'

'You should have thought of that,' Saint says. 'I told you not to mess with us. Check you later, *bru*.'

Saint and I grapple to lift up the ladder and shove it over the side – it's way heavier and more cumbersome than it looks.

'You go first,' Saint says. 'You sure you'll manage with your hand cut up and everything?'

'Haven't got much choice.'

I push the flick knife into my pocket and get moving. I still feel dizzy and shaken, my throat sore from vomiting, and I almost lose my footing as I climb down the ladder – the rain has made the rungs even slicker and the nylon rope cuts into the wound on my palm.

Stumbling onto the sand I bash into a Rotter, the stench of it making my stomach tip over. A light blasts straight into my eyes. It must be Ginger's torch. 'Blimey, Lele,' he says. 'Are you okay, mate? We've been dead worried. Ash came and –'

Saint jumps down the last couple of metres. 'Where's Ash, Ginger? And get that light out of my eyes.'

'He's looking for a way to get back onto the ship.'

'Go and get him.'

'I'm here,' Ash says from behind me. 'What happened?'

'Long story,' Saint says.

'But you guys are okay, right?' Ginger asks.

'Lele – you're bleeding!' Ember says, grabbing my wrist. 'Here, let me look –'

I snatch my hand away from her. 'Don't touch me!'

Suddenly it's all too much – the last thing I want is to face Ash right now. I turn and stumble into the crowd of Rotters, and then I run blindly across the beach, ignoring the voices of the others calling after me, the ache of my muscles as I push through the wet sand, and the tears that are streaming down my cheeks.

———

I don't remember falling asleep, or even making it back to the car, but I must have passed out in the back of the bakkie at some stage. Someone has placed my rucksack under my head and draped a jacket over me to make me more comfortable, but neither of these things stops the sunlight from shearing into my eyes. My head throbs like it's gone ten rounds with Saint's fists, and my tongue feels like a furry piece of carpet. I fumble for my sunglasses and sit up. The sea is gone, and we're surrounded by arid bush. I'm alone in the back of the bakkie, which is parked by the side of the road in the meagre shade provided by a dead fig tree. I pull back the makeshift bandage that covers my palm. The ragged cut has already almost healed, and I can make out a pinkish strip of puckered flesh underneath it. There's no way I can let the others see this. It's healed way faster than is natural.

I dig in my bag for my canteen. As I take a slug of water I glimpse movement through the opening at the back of the cab. Saint and Ash have spread the map out on the bakkie's bonnet and are poring over it. 'So what do you think, Saint?' Ash says. 'Think they were lying about what happened in Durban?'

'Yeah. I think those bastards were lying about everything.'

'But they said there were Guardians at the Durban settlement. How would they know about the Guardians if they hadn't seen them?' Ash pauses to consider this. 'And if they were telling the truth about the Guardians, then maybe they were telling the truth about the cholera. Maybe Durban is toast.'

'So what do you want to do?' Saint asks.

'Okay, well I reckon we can assume that there have to be settlements and pockets of survivors all over the place, but what help are they going to be? We need to get to a big city.'

'We've just been to a big city, Ash. It was screwed. And if there were Guardians in Durban then what's to say that they won't be in the other cities?'

'We don't know that they'll be there for sure, Saint. What about Bloemfontein or Johannesburg? We can cut up here, go through Grahamstown.'

'Yeah. Johannesburg could be a good bet.'

They don't say anything for several seconds.

'What is it, Saint?'

'It's just ... Look how close Johannesburg is to Botswana.'

'You think your family's still there?'

'I dunno.' Another few moments of silence. I wish I could see Saint's face. 'You think we've got enough fuel to get to Bloemfontein or wherever?'

'Probably. Ember will have a better idea.' Of course she will.

Good old *Ember*.

'Saint, I've been thinking. About Ripley.'

'What about her?'

'Something that Ginger said, back at that game lodge. Look, don't take this the wrong way, but maybe she helped us leave the Deadlands because she didn't want us to be in a position to help the ANZ. You know, we were the only people who could leave the enclave. Maybe the Guardians were worried that we'd bring weapons into the city. Help overthrow the Resurrectionists.'

'Maybe she helped us leave because there's something she wants us to discover out here. Ever think about that?'

'Maybe.'

'Sheesh, Ash. You're the one who wanted us to leave, right?' There's a brittle edge to Saint's voice. 'You can't have it both ways.'

'I'm just putting it out there, Saint.'

'So what are you saying? You want to go back?'

'No. But after what happened last night ... '

'Not every survivor we're going to meet is going to be like those guys. Ember's people were cool, weren't they? Freaky, but not screwed in the head like those guys.'

'We shouldn't have been so stupid. I should have known better.'

'Don't be crazy, Ash. It's not your fault. It's no one's fault.'

'How do you think she's doing?' Ash says, meaning me, obviously. I duck back down so that they don't catch me eavesdropping.

'Lele's tough. She's been through worse.'

'But they didn't –'

'No,' Saint says. 'But go easy on her.'

'Why wouldn't I? It's just ... she's been moodier than normal since we left Ember's place.'

Saint sighs. 'And you can't guess why?'

'Guys!' Ginger yells. 'Great news, Ember's found some guinea-fowl eggs!'

Which means that I don't get to hear how Ash would have answered Saint's last question. Great.

We're moving faster now – there's no traffic and the road is less overgrown. It's easy to imagine that nothing has happened here, that the War never kicked off at all.

Saint and Ginger have been doing their best to snap me out of my funk, but now even they've given up. Ginger lies down next to the hyena, and Saint rests her head against the back of the cab and closes her eyes. I hide behind my sunglasses, crouching in my corner of the bakkie, watching listlessly as the world slides by. It helps to think of the car as some sort of ravenous monster, eating up the distance. We pass rusty gates, overgrown side roads and distant farms that have the aura of long abandonment. The desolate landscape mirrors how I'm feeling inside, which is one level below totally crap.

Even worries about Jobe have taken a back seat to the kak that's running through my head. I can't make Ash like me again, I can't stop him feeling what he does for Ember, I can't change what happened with those two assholes on the cruise ship and I can't do anything about the mess Cape Town's in. Not from here at any rate.

I find myself thinking about Thabo. Wondering how he would have dealt with Previn and Scott. If he'd been there would any of it have even happened? Would I have stupidly drunk myself into a stupor? Would we have left Cape Town in the first place? Thabo had thrown all his energy into fighting for 'the people';

he would never have run away from his problems.

And if Ash and I are supposed to be together, what the hell am I doing thinking about another guy?

But we're not together. That much is obvious. Whatever happened between us back at the game lodge is ancient history.

We pass a dilapidated bus abandoned next to the road, *St Martin's School* stencilled across its side. Its tyres are flat, its windows are covered in chicken wire and its windscreen is staved in. I'm hit with an image of a bunch of terrified survivors, driving onwards, desperate to get to safety, feeling exposed and alone and wretched with no one to help them. Maybe they'd been trying to escape from somewhere like Cape Town; leaving one horrible situation for something far worse.

'Oh no!' Ginger cries.

Saint jerks awake. 'What?'

'It's Bambi. He's had a little accident.' He rummages in his backpack and pulls out a plastic bag.

'Oh gross, Ginger. You need to house-train him or something.'

'He's a wild animal, Saint.'

'It's what you're feeding him that's the problem.' She shakes her head and bangs on the partition glass. 'Pit stop,' she yells.

The car shudders to a stop. 'I'd better see if he needs to go again,' Ginger says. He play-punches my shoulder. 'Come on, Lele, why don't you come with me?'

'I'm cool, Ginger.'

'Aw, come on. I need a wingman in case Bambi decides to run off.'

We both know this isn't true; if anything, the hyena seems to get tamer each day, more subdued. I hope he's not getting sick. His diet of scraps can't be doing him much good.

I jump down and we walk away from the bakkie. Cosmos flowers poke up from the thorny scrub around us and a black-shouldered kite whirls in circles overhead. Bambi lollops away from us and sniffs at the ground just like a puppy.

'You okay, mate?'

'Sure.' I try to smile for Ginger's benefit. 'That alcohol last night's just making me feel a bit kak is all.'

'Yeah.' He fidgets with the zipper of his hoody. 'Sorry, about what happened, Lele.' Tears spring to my eyes. What the hell is wrong with me? *Stop being such a moody bitch.* 'Saint told me about what those guys did. It's not your fault, you know that, right?'

'Course.' But I keep thinking: What if I hadn't got drunk? What if I'd listened to Ash? Stupid. I wish I could climb outside my body and give myself a good shake.

'Lele ... Um, can I ask you a question?'

'Sure.'

'I know you're not feeling so hot, but ... do you think ... do you think I've got a chance with Ember? I think we really connected last night, and we've got loads in common. She totally thinks *The Empire Strikes Back* is the best *Star Wars* movie. She hasn't seen it for years, but she could still quote lines from it and everything.'

He's looking at me eagerly, and there's no way I can hurt his feelings. 'Why not?' I say. 'She'd be crazy not to. You're great.'

He throws his arms around me and lifts me off my feet. 'So are you.'

And then the tears come, and I can't stop them.

SAINT

It's scorching inside the bakkie's cab, but after hours of sitting on my rucksack on the hot corrugated metal in the back the comfortable passenger seat is a godsend. Ash offered his place in the front to Lele, but she turned it down, and with Bambi's current spate of digestive troubles there's no way Ginger can sit in here.

Ember casually adjusts the steering wheel with her left hand, her right elbow resting on the edge of the open window. We cruise up a gently curving mountain pass, the undulating road a welcome change from the miles of flat thorny landscape we've been travelling through for the past few hours. More spiky aloes cling stubbornly to the sides of the rocky outcrops. Ginger's dubbed them Triffids – the dead leaves that droop like drying tentacles around the base of their stalks creep him out.

'You want me to drive for a bit, Ember?' I'm not sure I'd be able to figure out the gears, but then again the bakkie can't be harder to master than the bike, can it?

'No, I'm fine. Thanks, though, Saint.' Without slowing down, she swings the car around a small rockfall.

'Who taught you to drive?'

'My dad. I've been driving since I was eight. This was his vehicle. He kept it running when we were in the settlement back in Old Knysna. He thought we might need to use it eventually.'

There's no way she means Father. I can't see the guy we'd met at the golf estate doing anything as practical as car maintenance. 'You mean your real dad?'

'Ja.'

I don't know if I'm straying into personal territory. I've assumed that Ember is a 'what you see is what you get' kind of girl, but we all have our own secrets and pain locked away inside. Even Ginger. 'Well, he did a good job.'

She clears her throat. 'Ja. He was a good guy. He ... When we all tried to escape ... He didn't make it.'

'I'm sorry.'

'Thanks. My ma didn't make it through the war, so for years it was just the two of us.' She puts both hands on the wheel and hunches forward, concentrating on the road ahead. 'It was horrible.' She clears her throat. 'And the thing was, when he was ... When he was taken, for months afterwards I felt guilty. It wasn't fair. I mean, why was it that I survived and he didn't?'

'You can't think like that, Ember.' She doesn't respond. Dammit. I'm no good at this spilling-your-guts-out personal stuff – I never know what to say. 'Look, I know what you went through. There was a Rotter break-in at the Cape Town enclave a few years ago. I was right in the middle of it.'

She winces. 'I couldn't believe how fast it happened.'

'Yeah. The Rotters don't mess around, do they?'

'I hate them.'

As we reach the top of the pass I catch a glimpse of our next destination – Grahamstown – an urban sprawl sitting in a bowl-shaped valley to our left. From here it looks untouched, perfect, but I know better than to allow myself to hope.

The road ahead is flat and straight, flanked by more dry aloes and a few junked cars crouching among the thorn trees, the heat shimmering off it. 'We're almost there,' Ember says. 'I hope this time we're going to find –'

Oh *shit!* 'Watch out!'

A figure rushes out from behind a corroded kombi and into the road in front of us. I'm expecting Ember to swerve and slam on the brakes, and I reach out instinctively to brace myself against the dashboard, but she doesn't. There's a thump as we hit the body, it disappears beneath the car, and then, sickeningly, there's another thud as the back tyres run over it.

Ember hits the brakes, and the car slows to a halt. We sit for a few seconds, listening to the sound of the engine ticking over. 'That wasn't a person, was it, Saint? Tell me it wasn't a person,' she says finally, white-knuckled hands gripping the steering wheel. 'I knew if I swerved we could be in trouble, so I just kept going . . . '

'Stay here.'

I join Ginger, Lele and Ash – they are already by the side of the road, staring down at something lying on the parched grass, next to a ditch. 'Well?' I say.

'It's a Rotter,' Lele says. She stands back as it gets to its feet. It's one of the soggy ones, as Ginger calls them; too decayed for me to tell if it was once male or female. It's dressed in a pair of filthy jeans and a hoody. It moved so fast that for a second there even I was convinced we'd hit a survivor.

Ember approaches shakily, hugging herself as if she's cold.

'That was good driving, Ember,' Ginger says, nodding at the ditch. 'If you'd swerved we could have been gonzos.'

She doesn't seem to hear him. I hope she's not in shock. Ash puts his arm around her, and I can't bring myself to look over at Lele. 'You okay to go on?' he asks.

'Sure,' she says, managing a weak smile.

We watch the Rotter limp away, dragging its leg after it. 'You know what this means,' Ginger says. 'Where there are Rotters, there are people.'

Lele snorts. 'Oh, good. Because that's worked out so well for us so far.'

Several more Rotters stumble across the highway as we approach the town's periphery. Most are skeletal and in far worse condition than our Cape Town variety; it looks like the area's dry heat has sucked every ounce of moisture out of their skin, withering their flesh to their bones.

A hulking concrete building – some kind of featureless office block – sits imperiously on top of a small hill to our left. There's something gloomy and cold about it, and I'm glad to see the back of it as Ember pulls off the main thoroughfare. The tyres pop over the tree branches littering the overgrown slip road. Above our heads there's a faded *Welcome! 2010* banner – another reminder of the World Cup that never happened.

'How you holding up, Ember?'

She manages to grin at me. 'I'm fine,' she says, taking another turn at random, a church spire towering above the trees.

We coast down a leafy street. It must have been nice here years ago, a residential area full of neat houses and walled gardens. Many of the buildings have an old-worldy feel to them, with wrap-around porches and solid doors. It's a refreshing contrast to the burned and shattered towns we've passed through since we left home.

'It's like this place is sitting in its own a time warp,' I say as we swing into a wider street.

'Oh Goddess,' Ember breathes, slowing to a stop and leaning across me to stare out of the passenger window.

I've spoken too soon. This town is anything but untouched.

Behind a sagging fence cobbled together from rusted metal, wood and coils of spiked wire I can just about make out a cluster of once-imposing red-roofed buildings and the top of a boxy clock tower. The bushes and plants in front of them are scorched skeletons, and soot stains the walls above the few windows that are visible.

'This must have been a settlement once,' I say, stating the obvious.

'The fire must have happened recently,' Ember says.

'How do you know?'

'The plants and grass. They're still burned. Nothing new has had a chance to grow here yet, and it wouldn't take long for weeds to appear.'

I slide open the partition glass. 'Guys,' I say. 'Keep an eye out for Hatchlings.'

'Way ahead of you, Saint,' Ash says.

Ember takes a deep breath. 'Which way now?'

I point to our right and Ember drives towards an imposing church positioned in the centre of two wide streets. It looks untouched, and for some reason it makes me think of the Resurrectionists. But compared to this building, with its spire and arched windows, the Cape Town Embassy is as insubstantial as cardboard. I poke my head out of the window to check out the intricate towering spire – the one I saw as we drove into the town – its clock forever stopped at 3 p.m.

The rest of the street hasn't fared so well. The double-storey buildings lining both sides of the thoroughfare house trashed shops and restaurants, a few also the victims of rogue fires. The pavement is strewn with overturned chairs, tables and broken glass. But they must have been pretty once – the facades of the surviving structures are decorated with complex patterns that make me think of the doll's houses some of my friends had when we were kids.

Ember parks underneath a shady tree a hundred metres or so from the church, squeezing between two forever-stationary saloon cars. One of them has a *Furkids on Board* sign still visible in the back window.

I breathe in a lungful of sweltering air. My lips feel chapped – it is far drier here than in Cape Town. Ginger passes his water bottle to me and I take a sip. The water's warm and a bit slimy, but it's all I can do to stop myself downing it in one go.

Ash and Ember are checking the front of the bakkie for Rotter damage. Lele moves to stand a little apart from them and I amble over to join her. 'Hey,' I say. 'You cool?'

She shrugs. 'I will be.' She wanders out into the centre of the street.

'How was that settlement place we saw back there?' Ginger says. 'You think that's where the Rotters came from?'

'No idea,' I say. 'I hope not.'

His face is burned bright red, but there's not much chance of getting hold of any sunscreen. Something else we forgot to source from the mall back in Cape Town.

Ginger pours a bowlful of water for the hyena and places it in the back of the bakkie. Bambi laps it up, then jerks his head up and stands absolutely still.

'What is it, mate?'

'Rotter alert!' Lele calls, pointing towards one of the shops. A rotund figure bumbles out into the street. 'Holy crap! Is that ... Is it dressed like a clown?'

The Rotter is wearing baggy striped trousers, and its red jersey is still decorated with multicoloured pompoms. Another far skinnier one approaches it from a neighbouring building. It's dressed in what looks to be a black full-body leotard. They moan together – two undead circus folk shooting the breeze.

'Freaky,' Ginger says. 'If that's how the residents dressed I'm not sure I would have wanted to see this town *before* the apocalypse.'

'At least we can assume that there have to be survivors around here somewhere,' Ash says.

'But most of the Rotters were concentrated near the main highway,' I say, fishing in my bag for my sunglasses. 'You think there's a settlement outside the town?'

'Must be.'

'I would kill for a swim,' Ginger says. Then his eyes widen. 'Uh-oh. You hear that?' Seconds later I catch it too – the faraway rumble of an engine. And although it's difficult to tell exactly where the sound is coming from – the town seems to mess with the acoustics – there is no doubt it is getting louder.

And then we see it, approaching from the direction of the gutted buildings at the end of the street. It's not a car, but a bike. It roars straight towards us and for a second I'm positive that it's going to hit us. I instinctively step back, but at the last second it skids around, stopping just metres from the bakkie. It's being driven by a well-built guy dressed in black jeans, boots and a T-shirt with cut-off sleeves. I can't see his face – his eyes are hidden behind giant mirrored sunglasses; a blood-red bandanna is tied over his mouth and nose – but his muscled arms are darker in colour than his hands and neck, and then I realise why: they're covered in tattoos.

The engine cuts out, and without its roar the town feels eerily silent.

Ginger clears his throat. 'Hi. Um, friend or ... Oh *bugger*.' Ginger backs up and raises his hands. The guy has reached behind his back and is now pointing what looks like a crossbow at us. 'We don't want any trouble, mate.'

The guy walks towards us, keeping the crossbow level and steady.

The two Rotters, who are now milling around the church, ignore him. Not good. Could he be a Guardian? The sunglasses make it impossible to tell.

'What do you want here?' he says. His voice is accented – French most likely – and it doesn't sound as dead and emotionless as a Guardian's.

'Like I said, we don't want any –'

'Jack?' The guy pulls down the bandanna that covers his mouth. 'Jack? Is that you?'

'Whoa,' Ginger gasps. 'Isn't that your real name, Ash?'

'Ash?' I say, keeping my voice steady. 'What in the *hell* is going on?'

The guy laughs, but I cannot tell if he is finding the situation genuinely hilarious or is laughing for effect. 'Have you not told your friends about me, Jack? I am disappointed.' He whips off his sunglasses, and I breathe a sigh of relief. His eyes are dark, but the irises aren't flat and dead like Paul's. Or Ripley's.

'I know you,' Ember says. 'I've seen you before.' She turns to me. 'He visited Mother's place. With another guy. About a year ago.'

The crossbow is now aimed straight at Ash's heart. They are both still staring at each other, as if they're in the middle of some sort of macho bullshit competition.

'This is between you and me, Lucien,' Ash says. 'My friends have nothing to do with this.'

'*Bien*,' Lucien says. 'If that is how you want it.' He narrows his left eye and his arm muscles tense up.

'If you hurt him I will kill you,' I say, using everything I've got to keep my voice level. 'You can't shoot all of us at once.'

There's an agonising few seconds, and I ready myself to rush at him if I have to.

Lucien doesn't give an inch. 'Tell me, Jack. Where is Hester? Still back in Cape Town making herself rich?'

'He knows *Hester*?' Ginger whispers to me.

'She's dead,' Ash says, deadpan.

Lucien's expression changes. It doesn't soften exactly, but the fight seems to leave him. He lowers the crossbow and I breathe out. 'How?'

'She was sick. Cancer. She was in a lot of pain at the end.'

Lucien mutters something under his breath.

'Got that out of your system now, guys?' I say. 'Testosterone levels back to normal? Now, tell me how the *hell* you know each other, or I'll finish the job myself.'

Lucien glances at me, raising an eyebrow. 'I like her.' Then he turns back to Ash. 'How is Sami, Jack?'

'He's fine,' Ash says.

'He is the same?'

Ash nods. 'They all are.'

'Who's Sami?' Lele asks.

'My twin,' Lucien says.

Lele gasps. 'Of course. I never thought of that. I'm so stupid.'

'Thought of what?' Ginger asks.

'The other kids at Mandela House, of course. The twins! There has to be another half for all of them. I mean, there's Sasha and Jobe, and –'

'You all have twins back in Cape Town?' Lucien interrupts.

'Not me,' Ginger says with his usual pride. 'I'm a freak of nature. Ember's the same. We're thinking it's 'cos people with red hair are special.'

Lucien snorts. 'I see. That is an … interesting theory.' He shifts his attention back to Ash. 'Things must be serious in Cape Town if you have left Sasha.'

'You left Sami,' Ash says.

'*Oui*, but I did not have any choice, as you well know.'

'Neither did we, Lucien. Neither did we.'

Lucien pulls a silver cigarette case out of his pocket and pops a short brown cheroot between his lips.

'So, Lucien, are you French or summut?' Ginger asks.

Lucien smiles sardonically. 'Is it not obvious?'

'First things first,' I say. 'How come you know each other?'

'We fought together in the War,' Ash says.

'Seriously?' Ginger says. 'So you were like a child soldier as well, Lucien?'

'*Oui*.'

'And you knew Hester?'

'I stayed with her for a time, yes.'

'You did? When?'

'Before your time, Ginger,' Ash says.

Lucien blows a plume of smoke into Ash's face. He doesn't react.

'Where's Jova?' Ash asks.

'Who's Jova?' Ginger's not as talented as the rest of us at hiding his feelings, and his expression switches almost comically from wonder to confusion.

'Another child soldier, as you call us,' Lucien says. 'Jova is not here. He is gone.'

'Why didn't you go with him?'

'I had my reasons.'

'Hester never mentioned you to me,' I say. 'Why not?

'Let us just say that I did not agree with Hester's … economic policy, among other things.'

'Not getting you, mate,' Ginger says.

But I know what he means, and so does Lele. She'd also objected to the 'useless crap' we'd collected from the mall for Hester to sell on the black market. Lele was adamant that as the only people able to leave the enclave we should be helping people, not benefiting from everyone's misfortune.

'So you used to work with Hester?' I say to him.

'*Oui.*'

'You used to be a Mall Rat?' Ginger says. 'Wicked!'

'A Mall Rat? What is this?'

'But I don't get it,' I jump in before Ginger can answer. 'What are you doing here? When did you leave Cape Town?'

Lucien shrugs. 'A couple of years ago.'

'And why did you leave?'

Lucien stares straight at Ash. 'Like I said, Hester and I disagreed on several issues.'

Why do I feel that there's something he's not telling us?

'This is amazing!' Ginger says. 'I mean, it's like a wicked great big coincidence. We're out looking for other Mall Rats, and we find you! It's awesome.'

Lucien laughs. 'Now, I think it is time for introductions. You know my name, but I do not know yours.'

'I'm Ginger, Ash – Jack – you know of course, and that's Ember, Saint and Lele.'

Lucien looks me up and down. 'Saint? That is your real name?'

'It's not her real name. Her real name's –'

'Ntombi,' I say.

'It is a pleasure, Ntombi.' His eyes crawl over me, but his gaze isn't pervy exactly, instead I get the impression that he's assessing which of us he should watch.

His eyes flit to Ember. 'You said you have seen me before?'

'At the settlement in Knysna.'

Lucien frowns, then he nods and smiles as if he has just remembered something. 'Ah! The strong women who live in the trees.'

I snort. 'That's one way of putting it.'

Lucien's gaze lingers on her tight T-shirt and short denim cut-offs. 'But I do not remember you. And you are not someone it would be easy to forget.'

Ember blushes and lowers her eyes. 'Ja. Mother said I should keep out of sight. Just in case you were dangerous.'

Lucien laughs again.

'I'm originally from London,' Ginger cuts in. 'You can probably tell that, right? Lele's from Cape Town and Saint is from Botswana.'

'But Ntombi is a Xhosa name, is it not?'

He's sharp. 'Yes,' I say. 'My mother was South African. She knew that one day I'd probably go to school in Cape Town, so she gave me a Xhosa name so that I wouldn't stand out as a foreigner.'

Lucien smiles. 'She was wise.'

'There are Rotters here,' Lele says. 'If you're like us – immune to Rotter attack, I mean – there must be other survivors in the area. As far as we can tell, the Rotters don't hang around if there aren't people nearby.'

'*Oui.*' He nods in the direction of the charred buildings at the far end of the street. 'The main settlement was once in the grounds of the university, but it was destroyed by fire. And not so long ago.'

'But people got away, right?'

'Some.'

'Where are they?'

'Not far from here. Would you like to meet them?'

'It depends,' Ginger says. 'They're not freaky-ass weirdoes, are they? It's just that we've had more than our fair share of those.' He glances at Ember. 'No offence.'

Lucien laughs again and this time I am sure that it's genuine. 'No. They are not.' He throws his cheroot butt out into the street. 'Follow me.'

We're heading for the blocky concrete building that had gave me the creeps when we approached the town. Scores of Rotters mill around it and as Lucien skilfully weaves his bike between them they whip their heads towards the sound of the engine, but they don't try and grab at him.

Ember edges the car slowly through the Rotter forest, nudging them out of the way. A flimsy-looking chain-link fence, topped with a double layer of curled razor wire, is the building's only defence against the horde. Behind it an overgrown brick driveway curves up towards the structure.

Lucien digs in the leather satchels attached to the side of his bike and pulls out two collapsible water containers, sloshing with liquid. 'This way,' he calls.

Ginger throws his pack over his shoulder and gathers the hyena into his arms.

'You have a dog?' Lucien asks.

'Hyena, mate,' Ginger says with his usual pride.

Lucien recoils. 'You know what the hyena means to many people on this continent?'

Ginger shrugs. 'Nah.'

'Many people believe that they bring bad luck. Because they are thought to eat the dead.'

Ginger's smile drops. 'Bambi would never do that. Besides, he's brought us good luck.'

'He has?' Lele asks.

'Yeah, course. The Guardians haven't got us yet, have they? We found Ember, didn't we?'

There's a metal security gate bolted into the fence, and Lucien pushes between the Rotters and opens it wide enough for us to sneak inside. Now we're up close the building is even more forbidding; it seems to be entirely constructed out of windowless concrete rectangles slapped carelessly on top of each other.

I notice that Ash is hanging back. I'm not sure Lucien is trustworthy, and hell, I don't even know about Ash any more. How could he keep this from us? What's worse, I am positive we haven't heard the whole story.

'What was this place?' Ginger asks.

Ahead of us I can make out a dark statue of a man who would have been holding something above his head if someone – or something – hadn't sheared off his arms.

'A monument to the settlers.'

'The whattames?'

'The English who settled in South Africa.'

'Oh, cool. Like me.'

I roll my eyes at Ginger. 'Not quite. You got stuck out here by accident.'

'Ironic, is it not?' Lucien says. 'That this where the last survivors in the city are living?'

Ginger doesn't have a clue what Lucien is talking about. 'I guess,' he says. 'Who built the fences and stuff? I thought you said the survivors were at the university place?'

'*Oui*. They were. But at some time another settlement must have holed up here.'

I look back. The Rotters are pressing against the makeshift fence. 'It doesn't look very secure.'

Lucien sighs. 'It is not. We have had many break-ins. But it is safer than the city itself.'

'Hey!' Lele says. She points up to a wall behind the statue. There's a blue star shape spray-painted across it. 'It's that tag again.'

I swing round and try to catch Ash's eye, but his gaze slides away from mine. Lele glares at him accusingly. 'Something you want to tell us, Ash?'

Lucien pulls down the collar of his T-shirt. Just above a knot of scar tissue there's a blue star tattoo. It's not as bright as the symbol on the wall; his skin is too dark for it to show up well. He nods at the symbol on the wall. 'It is something Jova did, when we first left the enclave – his way of making his mark wherever we went.'

'Cool,' Ginger says. 'What's it mean?'

'It is a badge of honour. So that we never forget what we endured during the War.'

'But you don't have one, do you, Ash? And you fought in the War with Lucien, didn't you?'

'*Non*,' Lucien says with a smile that looks cruel to me. 'Jack does not have one.'

There's the patter of running footsteps and a skinny girl of about eight or nine races around the building, stopping dead when she spots us. She's wearing an oversized T-shirt, a belt clinching it in at the waist, and clutching a battered teddy bear. A chubby toddler follows behind her, and he also pauses when he sees us, hiding behind the older girl's legs.

'*C'est bon*,' Lucien calls to them. The girl hangs back, but the toddler runs into his arms.

I find myself instantly reassessing Lucien.

'Hello, mate,' Ginger says to the toddler, who stares at him for several seconds before bursting into tears.

Lucien laughs and pats the child's back. 'This is Kobu,' he says to us. He smiles at the girl who's watching us seriously. 'And that's Nelly.'

'And the other survivors?' I ask.

'This is it.'

'Where are their parents?'

'They are dead. I found the children when Jova and I came through here. I could not leave them alone, and we could not take them with us on the bikes, not with the number of the dead that are here. I have tried to start a car, but it is impossible.' He sighs. 'Eleven years is a long time.'

'So the children are why you didn't go with your mate?' Ginger asks.

'Oui.'

'That was good of you, mate.'

'What else could I do?'

'How long have you been with them?'

'Six weeks or so. I am not sure.'

'But I thought you said you left Cape Town two years ago?' Ember chimes in.

Lucien hesitates. 'I have been elsewhere.'

'Oh, yeah?' I say. 'Like where?'

'All over. A settlement in the Valley of a Thousand Hills.'

'Where's that?'

'Near to Durban.'

'But we heard that Durban was toast, mate,' Ginger says. 'Isn't that what those assholes on the cruise ship said, Lele?'

She drops her eyes and shrugs.

So, just as I thought, Scott was lying. Unless Lucien is lying. But after seeing the kids, I'm more inclined to believe what he says.

'The settlement was far from the city. Very rural. Hard for the dead to reach.'

'What was it like?' Ginger asks.

'It was successful, but poor. I did not think it was fair to place an extra burden on the people's resources.'

'So how long were the children alone?' Ember asks, smiling down at Nelly.

Lucien seems to relax. Is he more comfortable with this subject? 'For at least six months. It is incredible how Nelly managed to take care of her baby brother all by herself.' He smiles fondly down at her.

Kobu stops crying as he spots the hyena in Ginger's arms. He blinks at Ginger as if asking for permission, and then stretches a pudgy hand in Bambi's direction.

'You can stroke him, mate. But be careful. He's only a baby, but he's got sharp teeth.'

Lucien says something in French to Kobu and the toddler giggles. They move closer, and while Ginger tightens his grip on Bambi, Kobu gently touches the top of the hyena's head.

'He likes you, Kobu,' Ginger says.

'Come,' Lucien says. 'Let me show you where we live.'

We walk past the front of the structure, Kobu peering over Lucien's shoulder, eyes still glued to Bambi.

'We're not going inside?' Lele asks.

'*Non.* The children refuse to go in there. They say it is haunted.'

We follow Lucien around the corner, and across to where a ring of colourful tents is staked out in a pleasant garden. Beneath an open-sided awning attached to the wall of the building there's a rough kitchen – a grill placed over a square of bricks, a foldaway table and chairs, plastic buckets and a pile of tinned food and fresh fruit. I spot several petrol containers, a few cheap-looking children's toys and, under the table, a stack of books. Ash stares at them greedily. He was never without a novel when we lived with Hester, and it looks as if Lucien shares his love of mouldy old books.

Kobu wriggles in Lucien's arms and Lucien gently deposits him on the ground. He toddles towards Ginger, pointing and smiling toothily at Bambi. Nelly is still looking unsure, and she sticks close to Lucien's side. 'I worry about the children,' he says. 'Nelly has had to grow up far too fast.'

Lele rummages in her rucksack and hauls out her sketchbook and coloured pencils. She lays them on the grass next to one of the tents. 'You want to draw with me?' she asks Nelly.

Nelly looks down and rubs one of her feet in the dirt.

Lele smiles at her and beckons her over. 'Come.'

Shyly stepping forward, Nelly drops to her knees on the grass.

'We're going to need fuel at some stage, Lucien,' Ash says. 'Any idea where we could get it?'

Lucien shrugs. 'I have searched most of the city. I found some petrol in private homes, but not much. Most of the fuel is corrupted after all this time.'

'We need diesel, though.'

'The best place is probably the farms around here.'

'You think it's worth checking them out?'

'Perhaps. I must go and get the children some milk later, so one of you could come with me then.'

'Can we also get milk for Bambi? The hyena, I mean,' Ginger asks.

'*Bien*. But of course.'

Kobu is edging closer and closer to Bambi. He looks like he might be intent on grabbing his tail.

'Watch him, Ginger,' I say. 'We don't want any nasty bites.'

'I'm on it.'

'Ash,' I say. 'A word.'

Grabbing his arm I lead him away from the others, stopping next to a statue of a man, woman and child wearing old-fashioned clothing. We're higher up than I thought and the town is spread out below us. 'Okay, Ash, it's just us now. Why haven't you told me about Lucien before?'

He drops his head, hiding his eyes behind his long fringe. 'I didn't see the point. I didn't even know if he and Jova were alive.'

'But you knew that they had left the enclave, right?'

'Yeah.'

'And that blue star symbol, you knew it was connected to them?'

'Of course.' He finally looks up at me, but he doesn't hold my gaze for more than a couple of seconds.

I watch him carefully. I know Ash well and he's hiding something. 'What's the real reason you fell out with Lucien, Ash? Why did he look like he was happy to shoot you when we first ran into him?'

'Like he said, he fell out with Hester.'

'And the real reason?'

'That is the real reason, Saint.'

He runs his hands through his hair – his trademark nervous gesture – and now I'm convinced he hasn't told me the full story. 'Fine. If you won't tell me, maybe Monsieur Frenchy will.'

I turn away from him and start heading back to the camp.

'Saint, wait!'

'Screw you, Ash.'

Lele and Nelly are engrossed in their drawing, and Lucien, Ember and Ginger have their hands full trying to persuade Kobu not to pull on Bambi's tail. 'Hey, Lucien,' I say. 'How about we go and see if we can find some diesel?'

'Now?'

'Absolutely.'

He looks up at me and shrugs. 'If you wish.'

I don't bother looking back at Ash. It's not as if he can stop me anyway.

LELE

I've drawn a sketch of Bambi for Nelly to colour in, but it's taken a lot of coaxing to convince her that she's welcome to use the pencils.

'That's so cool!' Ember says, peering over our shoulders as Nelly signs her name at the bottom of the picture in large, careful letters. 'I wish I could draw.'

Nelly smiles shyly up at her.

Pulling her hair out of its ponytail Ember shakes it around her shoulders. Wild curls cascade down her back. Even I have to admit it's gorgeous. 'Hey, Lele,' she says, 'I meant to ask earlier, you want some buchu water to clean your hand? You know, where you cut it?'

The gash is completely healed, but I've decided to keep the filthy T-shirt bandage wrapped around it – though if I actually did have an open wound I'd probably have gangrene by now. 'No. I'm cool.'

She gives me one of her perfect smiles. 'You sure?'

I try and smile back at her. 'Thanks, though.'

Why does she always have to be so nice?

Ash ambles over, and for a second I think he's come to see what Nelly and I are up to. But no, of course he hasn't. 'Should we check on the fuel situation now, Ember?'

'Course!'

She skips off with him and Ginger plonks down onto the grass next to me and Nelly. He's out of breath from running around with Kobu, who clearly finds him fascinating. I rip a piece of paper out of the sketchpad and hand Kobu a pencil. He immediately puts it in his mouth.

'You okay, Lele?' Ginger asks.

Why does everyone keep asking me that? 'Yeah, fine. How's it going with Ember?'

Ginger's smile loses some of its wattage. He shrugs. 'Okay, I guess. But, hey, I've been thinking about it, and you know who she reminds me of?'

'No idea.'

'Milla Jovovich in *Resident Evil*.'

I look at him blankly.

'Milla's gorgeous. She's not *always* a redhead, but she's a kick-ass zombie fighter who's also really kind and helps people out and stuff.'

'Wow. She sounds almost too good to be true.' So just about spot on, then.

Bambi lollops past, and Kobu lunges to grab at his tail again.

'Ginger, watch Kobu. Those teeth are sharp.'

Ginger grins and waves his bitten hand in the air. The bite marks are scabbing over nicely, but they haven't healed anywhere near as fast as the injury on my palm. 'Don't I know it.'

The hyena skitters out of reach and flops down in the shade of the building's overhang. 'Bambi's perking up,' Ginger says. 'I thought he was getting sick, but I reckon he's cool.'

'Yeah. But I'd still go easy on the biltong.'

'Don't worry,' he sighs. 'It's all gone.' He rolls onto his back and stares up at the sky. Seconds later Kobu toddles over to him and does the same.

I sketch an outline of Nelly's bear for her and she smiles at me and starts colouring it in.

'It's not as bad as we thought,' Ember says from behind me. 'I thought water had got into one of the containers, but it's cool.'

'Great,' I mutter.

I hear the growl of Lucien's motorbike over the Rotters' ever-present moans.

'Saint and Lucien weren't gone long, were they?' Ginger says, sitting up. 'Maybe they got lucky and found some diesel.'

'Ash!' Saint shouts, striding towards us with a look of such exaggerated fury on her face that for a second I think she's joking around.

'Saint,' Ash says as Lucien appears behind her, his arms crossed, his sunglasses dangling from a finger, a mixture of regret and satisfaction on his face. 'Listen –'

'Come with me.' She marches away, Ash trailing after her.

'Watch Kobu and Nelly, Ginger,' I say to him. He's staring after Saint, eyes wide.

I hurry after them. There's no way I'm missing this.

'Is it true, Ash?' Saint asks as soon as they round the corner of the building.

'Is what true?' I say. 'Saint?'

She ignores me. 'That the reason the Rotters broke into the enclave five years ago was because of you, Ash?'

What?

I'm about to ask Saint if she's gone mad, when Ash says:

'Yes. It's true.'

I thought I'd seen the full extent of Saint's fury back on the cruise ship, when she'd floored Previn, but that was nothing compared to the punch she throws at Ash. She hits him right in the stomach, and he doubles over and falls to his knees. 'People died because of you!'

I've felt like punching Ash a thousand times since Ember joined us, and there's a small, nasty part of me that's happy to see him on the floor, but then I come to my senses and push myself between them. 'Stop it!'

Saint is still glowering at Ash, but she isn't about to fight both of us.

Ash gets to his feet, a hand placed over his stomach, clearly winded.

'What did Saint mean, Ash?' I ask.

He looks at Lucien, who has appeared around the side of the building, his sunglasses still dangling from his finger. 'You told her everything?'

'*Oui.*'

'Get Ginger, Lele. You all need to hear this.'

Ash wipes a hand over his face. 'Where do you want me to start?'

'Why don't you begin where you, Lucien and your other little friend decided to start the ANZ?'

Ginger shakes his head. 'What? Don't be daft, Saint. Ash didn't start the ANZ.'

Ash sighs. 'She's right, Ginger.'

'But, I don't get it, mate. Till we hooked up with Lele, you were always dead set against the Anti-Zombians. You said that they made things worse in the enclave, made the Resurrection-ists come down harder on people. I mean, I get that you guys all knew each other during the war. You, Lucien and this other fella –'

'Jova,' Lucien says, lighting up one of his cheroots.

'Yeah, him. But after that all you did was work for Hester, right? You did what we did – fetch stuff back from the mall to sell.'

'That's not all we brought back, Ginger,' Ash says. 'We could see what was happening in the enclave, that what had started off as a stupid cult was growing into something far more dangerous. The Resurrectionists were influencing more and more people, working with the Guardians to spread their poison.

'So at first, yeah, we did just as you said. We collected clothes and what food was still edible and brought it back into the enclave for Hester to sell, careful not to take too much of any one thing that couldn't be replaced from the mall's storerooms. You know the drill. But Jova suggested that we were in the perfect position to do more. He was well connected and he gathered together a group of people who also felt the same about the Resurrectionists. One of them – Paula – gave us the recipe for making rudimentary explosives. And we knew we could find most of the materials we needed in the mall. We decided to experiment with them first, out in the Deadlands.'

Saint snorts in disgust. 'But not far enough away from the fence, right, Ash?'

'I thought I could handle it,' Ash says. 'I really thought I knew what I was doing. But one of the bombs exploded in the very area we didn't want it to. We didn't realise it had compromised the fence at first, or even that the Rotters had got in. Jova and Lucien were badly injured in the blast and I was desperate to get them some help. We fled to the mall, and it was only afterwards that I saw what I had done.'

'So it *was* an accident then,' Ginger says.

'No, Ginger,' Ash says. 'There are no accidents.'

'That's why you fell out with this other fella – this Jova? Because you almost killed him?'

'*Non*,' Lucien says. 'It was because, after that, Ash became a coward.'

'A what? No ways, mate.' Ginger's expression darkens. 'You can say lots of things about Ash, but he's no coward.'

'Oh, really?' Lucien smirks. 'After this accident, as you call it, he refused to help the resistance. Hester was furious with us, and said that we had to choose. Stay with her, where we would have a home and could make money by selling rubbish to the very people in league with our oppressors, or make our own way. You know what choice Ash made.'

'You can't blame Hester for being angry, though, mate,' Ginger says. 'Loads of people were zombified because of you lot.'

'*Oui*, but there is always a sacrifice to be made in any fight. Hester did not see that. We had no home, and we knew that Hester would betray us to save herself if we stayed.'

'*Our* Hester?'

'She never betrayed you.' Ash looks over at Saint. 'After the Rotter break-in she had others she had to consider.'

'And Jack here took her side.'

'I was thirteen years old, Lucien.'

'You had fought in the War, Jack. You knew how to fire an AK, but you did not know the difference between right and wrong?'

Ash doesn't respond.

'So what did you do next?' I ask.

'We stayed with other resistance members while we recovered

from our injuries, but we could not stay for long without putting them in danger. After the break-in the ANZ was scattered and everyone was wary, fearful. We lived out in the city ruins for a while. You know the cable-car station up on Table Mountain? We made that our home for many months. It was hard being away from our friends. Away from Sami. But we didn't have a choice. Then, for a time, we lived in the Agriculturals.'

That's weird. I thought I'd met almost all of the farmers and families who'd lived and worked in that area. 'I don't remember seeing you. I grew up there.'

Lucien dismisses this with a shrug. 'We were hardly going to call attention to ourselves. And anyway, it is a big place. There are many places to hide. But after a time we decided to ask Hester one last time to help us. We did our best to change her mind, make her see that selling goods to the Resurrectionists was wrong – morally wrong – but she refused to listen. So we told her that we were leaving Cape Town for good.'

'So you travelled around a bit – and then Jova left you here with the kids?' Ginger chips in.

'*Oui.*'

'Where did he go?'

Lucien shrugs once more. 'The idea was to travel as far up-country as we could. Eventually to Johannesburg.'

Ash looks over to Saint. 'I should have told you about this years ago, Saint.'

'Why didn't you?'

'I was ashamed.'

She stares at him intently for several seconds and then she nods.

'Yeah, but look on the bright side,' Ginger says. 'If the break-in hadn't happened, then Hester would never have discovered me and Saint. Well, she probably wouldn't have.'

Saint has transferred her gaze to Lucien. 'You told me this because you knew that I would go for Ash, right?'

He shrugs.

'I don't like being manipulated.'

'I am sorry,' Lucien says. 'I did not think he would tell you himself. And he wanted to tell you. Didn't you, Jack? Why else would you have come to find me?'

'He didn't come to find you, Lucien,' Ginger says. 'It's a coincidence, right, Ash?'

Ash digs in the pocket of his jeans and hands Lucien a piece of paper.

'What's that?' Saint asks.

'It's a letter,' Ash says. 'From Hester.'

Lucien takes it, but Saint snatches it out of his hand. 'You've got a letter from *Hester*?'

'She gave it to me just before she died. She wanted me to find Lucien. And Jova. I think it was her last wish.'

I read it over Saint's shoulder. She shakes her head in disbelief. '"The others are out there somewhere. You must find them; you must ask them to come back and help to stop this,"' she reads aloud. 'What the *hell*, Ash?'

'You wanted us to leave Cape Town to find your old war buddies, Ash?' I say, my voice hard. 'This is why you were so keen to flee the Deadlands?'

'I'm sorry, guys. I didn't know for sure that we would find Lucien. And if we hadn't run into him, then I didn't see any point in –'

'Lucien is right,' Saint spits. 'You *are* a coward.'

'Don't be like that, Saint.'

'Don't you get it, Ginger?' Saint snaps. 'Ash has had a letter from Hester all this time!' She waves it in front of his face. 'He kept this from us. He lied to us. All this time he's had a hidden agenda.'

For a second I'm convinced she's going to hit Ash again. 'Chill, Saint,' I murmur to her.

'So,' Lucien says. 'You came to find me. You have found me. What now?'

'The enclave is in trouble, Lucien,' Ash says.

'So, what is new?'

'We need you. We need Jova.'

'To do what?'

'What do you think? What you do best.'

Lucien smirks again.

'I don't believe you, Ash!' I say, unable to keep my cool any longer. 'When we left you said it was pointless to fight against the Resurrectionists.'

'I know. But after what happened to us there ... I don't think there's another option.'

I can't help but feel hurt. I've fought Hatchlings at Ash's side since Hester found me and trained me. And Ginger is obviously feeling the same – it's written all over his face. 'Hang on, mate. So, what are you saying, that we're not good enough to fight? You think we can't handle it? Like we're the B-team and your old mates are the A-team?'

'No, Ginger. It's not like that.'

'This fighting will not get us anywhere,' Lucien says. 'And now it is not just us – or Cape Town – we have to consider. I need to take the children to a better place. A safer place. An enclave where they will get what they need.'

'What about Ember's settlements? They were pretty cool,' Ginger says.

'*Non*. I think they must go somewhere that is safer. I am thinking maybe Lesotho. In the mountains. Where there are maybe schools, a society. You help me do this, and then come with me to Johannesburg to find Jova. In return we will come back with you.'

'Deal,' Ash says without consulting us, earning himself another withering glance from Saint.

'*Bien*. We will leave in the morning.'

Saint stalks off and even Ginger refuses to look at Ash. It's going to be a long night.

────────

We've done our best to clear away the Rotters who were loitering around the fence, but it's as if they can sense that something is up – they're livelier than usual, bashing into each other and scrabbling to get closer to the building. As soon as the children are on the back of the bakkie, Ember is going to have to floor it. If something goes wrong – if the car stalls – then it could all be over in seconds.

We've all been up since first light though, save for the children and Ember, I don't think any of us managed to get much sleep. We packed up the car in silence, the atmosphere spiky. Only Ember seems to be her usual self. Nothing seems to get her down. She must have a fault somewhere, but whatever it is, I can't find it.

Ash and Ginger stand in front of the gate, ready to jump in if anything goes wrong; Lucien and I wait behind it with the children, preparing to pass Kobu and Nelly to Saint. Ginger has insisted that Bambi ride up front with Ember, tying his lead to the door handle so that he can't get under her feet.

'Ready?' Lucien shouts.

Ember sticks her hand out of the window, gives the thumbs-up and revs the engine.

'Now, Lele!' Lucien says.

I heft Kobu over the gate and drop him down to Saint, Lucien doing the same with Nelly, who lands comfortably on one of the sleeping bags.

'Go, Ember!' Ginger roars.

The engine screams and the car surges forwards. For a second the back slides out – my heart freezes in my chest – then it corrects itself and rockets away. One of the Rotters manages to grasp the side, but Saint kicks it away easily, and others throw their heads back and moan, as if they've realised that their potential prey is forever out of their grasp.

Lucien vaults over the fence and races for his bike, and I climb down as quickly as I can and join Ash and Ginger. We all know that it won't be long before the Rotters rally, but so far only a couple of stragglers seem to have caught the scent, and they're too soggy to move very quickly. Horribly, one of them looks like the Rotter Ember ran over on our way into town. Lucien fires up the bike and zoots after the bakkie, the three of us following behind on foot.

We're out of breath when we finally catch up with them. They are gathered around the bakkie, Lucien smoking and Kobu and Nelly playing in the back of the vehicle as if they haven't just narrowly escaped being zombified.

'That was brilliant, Ember!' Ginger calls. 'You were amazing.'

She smiles shyly.

'Yeah.' Saint grins. 'Not bad.'

'See, Lele?' Ginger says. 'Told you she was just like Milla Jovovich.'

'Nice one, Ember,' I manage.

'It was nothing.'

'Can I sit in the front now?' Ginger asks. 'I mean, we know where we're going and Bambi's tummy is better. Kobu can come with.'

Ash shrugs. 'Just don't let Bambi do anything on the seat.'

Saint doesn't look too charmed about sharing the back with Ash, and it's pretty clear that it's going to be a bumpy ride in more ways than one.

'It's weird, innit,' Ginger says. 'All this time we've been hoping to see Rotters, and now we've got the kids they're the last thing we want to find.'

The back of the bakkie is too cramped for comfort, heaving as it is with tents, petrol and diesel containers, water bottles, five hot and dusty humans, and all our equipment and supplies. The relentless heat isn't helping matters either, but at least the atmosphere has improved now that Ash has taken over from Ginger in the front seat. Saint's fury seems to have endless depths, but she was right there when the break-in happened and I know she's battling to deal with the fact that her oldest friend – the guy she trusted more than anyone – was behind it. Lucien has repeatedly offered one of us a place on the back of the bike, but we've all turned him down – the memory of our uncomfortable hours on two wheels is way too fresh.

Whenever it looks like we're nearing a town, Lucien has zoomed ahead to do a Rotter recce, but so far so good. The places we've travelled through have been nothing like the size of Port Elizabeth, the land is becoming drier the further inland we travel and judging by the number of derelict shacks and one-room brick houses we've passed the area wasn't prosperous to begin with.

Ember pulls to a stop just before we cross a narrow metal bridge that spans a wide, brown river. Lucien skids to a halt just behind us. Ginger and I stand up to look down at the running water beneath.

'Oh, awesome,' Ginger says. He leans down and picks Kobu up. 'Check it out, mate. Looks cool, doesn't it?'

Almost directly below us there's a sprawling double-storey thatched building that reminds me of the game lodge, and to the side of it a playground containing a wooden jungle gym and swings.

Kobu shrieks in delight and claps his hands.

'Can we stop for a swim?' Ginger asks.

Lucien shrugs. '*D'accord*,' he says. 'Why not.'

'Score!' Ginger says. He holds his palm out for Kobu to high-five him, but the toddler just giggles. Bambi stands up and stretches, cracking his jaw in a wide yawn, and Kobu copies him exactly. Even Saint manages a smile.

We follow Lucien down an overgrown track and into a barren parking lot. The hotel or restaurant, or whatever this place was back in its heyday, has fared far better than the game lodge, and apart from a few tufts of rotting thatch it almost looks habitable. Lucien carries Kobu, and Nelly reaches out for me to take her hand as we pad past the main building and make our way down to the river bank.

Already the air is cooler down here. The grass is dry and brittle, but it's pleasant – like a sepia version of what it once must have been. I can imagine families coming here on weekends. There are dilapidated brick braai areas, and, way back in the trees, thatched rondavels that must once have been holiday cottages.

The white metal bridge above us casts a dark shadow over the water, but Nelly and Kobu don't give the river a second glance. They race towards the jungle gym, Lucien hurrying after them.

'What you waiting for, guys?' Ember says. She shakes out

her hair, rips off her boots and strips down to her underwear.

Ginger's eyes almost pop out of his head, and his skin turns a vivid red that has nothing to do with the dry heat. Ash hangs back, but Ember grabs his hand and drags him down to the edge of the water. He acts like he's reluctant, but I can tell he's faking. 'Hey! Wait for me!' Ginger calls.

Ash pulls his shirt over his head. He's lost weight. The muscles on his stomach stand out, and Ember's freckled skin looks blindingly white next to his. She shallow dives into the water and spins around so that she can splash him, the shirt she's wearing now completely see-through.

Ash dives in after her, ducking underwater and grabbing her legs, acting like he hasn't got a care in the world.

I can't watch this anymore.

'Where you going, Zombie Bait?' Saint asks, sinking down onto the grass.

'Just want to be on my own for a bit.'

'Don't be like that, Lele.'

'It's cool, Saint.'

Ember waves at me from the water. 'Hey, Lele! Come on in, it's awesome.'

Whatever.

Nelly grins down at me from the top of the jungle gym, and I do my best to smile up at her. I have to get my head straight. Be on my own.

I walk away from the others, following a choked path that weaves through the bushes next to the river bank. A sunbird flits in front of me, and I brush away a cloud of midges as I push my way into a clearing close to the water's edge. There's a bench here, a plaque on it reading: *For Esme, I will love you always.*

Just what I needed to see right now. Though to be honest I can't understand why the sight of Ember and Ash together still bothers me – he's already proved that he can't be trusted, so why can't I just let it go? I scrabble at my feet, pick up a handful of stones and skim them into the water, disturbing a kingfisher that juts its beak angrily at me before shooting away.

'You do not want to swim?' A voice says behind me, making me jump. Lucien. What the hell is he doing here? I didn't even hear him approach.

'Maybe in a bit.'

'May I sit?'

I shrug. 'Suit yourself.'

He pulls out one of his cheroots and lights up. 'There is something going on with you, Lele.'

'No, there isn't.'

'And I am not just talking about the situation with you and Jack.'

What? 'You know about that? Did Saint say something?'

'*Non*. But you don't have to be sharp to see this. Jack is not as good at hiding his feelings as he thinks. Remember, I have known him for many years.'

'Yeah? Well, I'm beginning to think I don't know him at all.'

Lucien laughs and nods. 'Don't be too hard on him, Lele.'

'Tell that to Saint. She's not exactly his biggest fan at the moment either.'

'So what is it that you are hiding, Lele?'

'Nothing. I'm not hiding anything.'

Lucien watches me through the smoke curling between us. He doesn't speak for several seconds, and there's no way I'm going to break the silence. I can still hear Ember shrieking and splashing. Maybe she and Ash will drown, and all my problems will be solved.

Nice, Lele. Way to stop being such a miserable bitch.

'You were very good with Nelly yesterday, Lele,' Lucien

finally says. 'Saint says that you are an artist.'

'That's what I wanted to be anyway. Fat chance of that now.'

He smiles, stands up and turns his back to me. And then he starts pulling his shirt over his head.

'Whoa – what do you think you're doing, Lucien?'

'What do you think of this?'

Holy crap.

I noticed the tattoos on his arms – and that blue star below his collarbone, of course. They're mostly tribal-looking symbols and criss-crossing swirls, but on his back there's an actual drawing, its detail astonishing. The outline is in the shape of an outstretched hand, but where the palm should be there's a cityscape. I make out a tall, modern building topped with a skinny spire, a blocky mall-type construction and a round tower ringed with tiny black windows. There's a figure depicted in each finger: a woman with long, flowing dreadlocks; a sangoma holding the head of a goat; a soldier with a scar across his face; a crying child clutching a large gun; and a robed figure, its face hidden in shadows – a Guardian?

'That's amazing. What does it mean?'

'You will have to ask Jova.'

'Jova did this?' Now I *really* want to meet him. 'How long did it take?'

'Many weeks.'

'It must've hurt, right?'

He laughs. '*Oui.*'

He turns around to face me, and I can't hold in the gasp of shock.

The front of his stomach is a knotty mass of raised scar tissue that bleeds down from the tip of the blue star tattoo. It's smooth and a lighter colour than his skin. He watches me looking at it.

An injury that caused that amount of scarring must have been severe.

I hold out my palm, showing off my own perfectly healed scars. 'You know?'

He takes my hand in both of his and traces the scar with his finger. I shiver. '*Oui.*'

'Is that scar from the explosion?'

'*Oui.* You can imagine how hard it was hiding how badly injured I was from Jova.'

'Huh? I don't get it. Why would you try and hide it from Jova?'

'He does not have this ... this affliction. He would have wondered why it was I healed so quickly. It was weeks before I could show him the scarring.'

'But isn't he a Mall Rat? Sorry, I mean, isn't he immune to Rotter attack?'

'He is.'

Then I remember the bite mark on Ginger's hand. I've known for a while now that we aren't all the same. I just haven't admitted it to myself, not really. Now I don't know whether to feel relieved or gutted. What if Lucien and I are the only ones with this 'affliction', as he calls it? But that can't be right. When we'd fought Paul and his cohorts back at the mall all those weeks ago Saint had injured her knee. And that had healed frighteningly fast.

'I haven't told the others, either.'

Lucien smiles at me. 'I understand.'

'You do?'

'*Oui.* There's a certain shame to it, is there not? Having this ... parasite living inside of us?'

Ugh. 'You mean because we're more like the dead?' After all, the silver tendrils are similar to the white spaghetti stuff that keeps the Rotters animated. 'One of the Guardians,' I decide not to mention it was Thabo, 'said, "When you die, you will live." Do you know what that means?'

Something flashes over Lucien's face. '*Non*.'

'This silvery stuff makes us heal faster than normal, right? It's like, I dunno, sophisticated. But I'm thinking, what if we get an injury that it can't heal? What happens then?'

'I do not know.'

'Do you remember being taken by the Guardians at the beginning of the War, Lucien?'

He shakes his head. '*Non*. But I know Sami was.'

'That's your twin, right?'

He nods.

'It must've been hard leaving him back in the enclave like that.'

'The hardest thing I have ever done.'

I think of Jobe, back at Mandela House. His gift from the Guardians was never to grow up. Mine was ... what? But Dad had told me that I was also taken by them – only I can't remember a thing about it.

Still, the knowledge that there's someone else who knows, someone else who shares my secret, is strangely comforting.

'Why twins, though?' I say. 'Why would the Guardians do this to us?'

Lucien gives another one of his expansive shrugs. 'I do not know. Many African cultures had twins at the centre of their mythology. They believed that twins had great power. Some cultures believed that twins were cursed, that they were evil. Many were slaughtered.'

I shudder. 'Maybe whatever power the Guardians have taken from our twins has been given to us. I mean, they don't seem to grow, do they? Whereas we ... ' I look down at the scar on my hand.

Lucien pulls his shirt back over his head. 'I think only the Guardians know the truth about this, Lele.'

I open my mouth to answer, but before I can, a high-pitched scream blasts our way. 'Guys!' It's Saint, and she sounds uncharacteristically panicky. 'Quickly!'

'*Merde*,' Lucien says, already on his feet.

And then I hear what I've been dreading – a Rotter's moan.

It's worse than I thought. There's not just one Rotter, there are at least six, and they're gathered around the climbing frame, lunging for the children who are balanced precariously at the top of it. Crap, it's nowhere near as solid as it looks – the structure wobbles as the dead bash into it. With no weapons to hand, Ember and Saint are doing their best to keep them at bay – Saint repeatedly punching and lashing out at them with her feet, Ember bashing them with a branch. But fists and sticks are useless against creatures that can feel no pain. Lucien pauses to pick up a brick next to one of the braai stands and throws himself into the fray.

Kobu screams. He's kneeling on top of the monkey bars, Nelly holding tightly to his arm, but it's clear that they can't hang on much longer. Then the climbing frame shakes and I see him tumbling forward, his sister's determined grip the only thing keeping him from being taken.

'Saint!' I call. 'Catch Kobu!'

Dodging under the arms of the nearest Rotter, she leans back just in time to grasp hold of the falling child.

Saint ducks under the swings, almost getting tangled in their ropes, but one of the Rotters has sensed that Kobu is on the move. It whips its head around and lunges towards them. It's in good condition, nowhere near as rotten as some of the ones we're used to seeing out in the Deadlands, and I know it will be able to move frighteningly fast.

I pull the knife I slicked from Previn out of my pocket and flip it open. Keeping absolutely still, blocking out the sights and sounds around me, I aim for the back of the thing's neck, and throw it, knowing I only have one shot at this. The Rotter stumbles back, falls to its knees and then collapses to the ground.

But another one has caught Kobu's scent. Saint is moving as fast as she can, but she'll have to put on an extra spurt to outrun it.

'Stand back!' Ginger roars, sprinting towards the jungle gym, Bambi scurrying at his heels. I'm relieved to see he's carrying his axe in one hand; Ash's panga is clenched in the other. Ash is also haring towards us from the direction of the river, water streaming down his body. Ginger throws the panga at Ash, and without even slowing polishes off the Rotter chasing Saint and Kobu. 'Get down!' he yells to the rest of us.

I grab Ember's arm and pull her out of the way, ducking as Ginger swishes the blade above his head, dispatching two of the Rotters in one neat stroke. Ash makes short work of the remaining two.

Lucien reaches up so that Nelly can fall into his arms. He sets her down, and she clings to his legs.

'That was amazing,' Ember says. 'You guys were incredible.'

Ginger grins proudly, wiping the sweat from his forehead. 'It's what we do, innit.'

Kobu holds out his arms for Lucien to take him, and buries his head in his shoulder. Bambi makes a low grumbling sound and steps tentatively towards the Rotter bodies that lie at the base of the jungle gym. I move to retrieve my knife.

Lucien looks over at Ash. 'You have learned some new moves, I see.'

'Let's get the kids out of here,' Ash says, ignoring him.

Saint takes Nelly's hand and leads her away from the jungle gym, and Lucien rubs the sobbing Kobu's back until he calms down. 'Where the *hell* did they come from, though?' I say.

Ember looks down at the ground. 'It's my fault.' She motions towards the rondavels hidden amongst the trees. 'I was looking for a bathroom, and I found one of those big communal ones way back there. I heard a noise, and I guess I assumed an animal was trapped inside. I opened the door and they moved so fast I couldn't do anything about it. Goddess, I'm so, *so* sorry. '

'It's cool, Ember,' Ash says.

'Yeah, mate,' Ginger adds. 'You didn't do it on purpose.'

I can't believe what I'm hearing. 'That was so stupid! You could have got the kids killed!'

'I know. I'm sorry.'

She turns away, back to where she discarded her clothes.

Ash shoots me a warning look. 'Leave it, Lele. How could Ember have known? We didn't hear them or see any sign of them, did we?'

'Whatever,' I say.

We head back to the car in silence.

Ginger takes Kobu from Lucien, and places him in the back next to Bambi. The toddler is still tearful but he's calming down remarkably quickly. Nelly gives him a hug and then snuggles in next to Saint, her bear clutched protectively in her arms.

'Okay?' I say to Nelly and she looks up at me and nods. I smile at her, but she doesn't smile back. Nelly must've been through far, far worse than this during those months of being alone, single-handedly taking care of her brother. I'm suddenly swamped with shame. Talk about putting my stupid self-obsessed feelings about Ember and Ash into perspective.

'Guys!' Ginger says, tapping on the partition glass and snapping me out of a doze. I have no clue how far we've come from the river, but it's now dusk, and the dust in the air has turned the sky a fiery pink. Mountains loom in the distance, their peaks like ragged teeth.

Ember pulls over to the side of the road.

'What's up, Ginger?' Saint asks blearily. She's also been napping.

Ginger leans over the side of the bakkie. 'What the bloody hell *is* that?'

The road is flanked by fields of vlei grass, intermingled with clumps of wilting sunflowers, and in the middle of the expanse on our left there's some kind of fence constructed out of lumpy silhouetted shapes. Ginger and I have made a nest of sleeping bags for the children and I do my best not to disturb them as I leap off the back of the bakkie. 'Don't wake them up,' I say to Ginger. He puts Bambi on the ground, and the hyena pads towards the sagging barbed-wire fence next to where we've stopped, but doesn't venture further into the field.

Lucien parks the bike behind us, and Kobu stirs at the sound of the engine. Ginger leans over and rubs his back. 'Shhh,' he says. 'S'all right, mate.'

'Are those ... scarecrows?' Saint asks as she, Ember and Ash join us.

'It cannot be,' Lucien says. 'Why would there be so many of them?'

'Stay here,' I say to no one in particular. 'I'm going to check it out.'

'Are you mad, Zombie Bait?' Saint asks. 'Shouldn't we just get out of here?'

'I'll just be a minute.' Before she can change my mind I duck under the fence and jog across the uneven ground, the dry grass swishing against my jeans.

I need to see this up close.

Every summer when Jobe and I lived in the Agriculturals with Gran we'd help her make a scarecrow to keep the birds away from our little patch of mealies. We'd stuff hessian sacks with chaff and straw, and dress the scarecrow in whatever old clothes were too far gone to be repaired. Our scarecrow never looked even vaguely human, but whoever made these has done a skilful job.

But there are no mealies out here. No crops that need protecting from greedy birds. There's not much of anything.

I edge closer to the one on the end; its head is drooping onto its chest and a ratty straw hat hides its face.

I can't stop myself. I reach over and touch the filthy jeans that clad its legs.

It lifts its head, as I knew it would, and seems to stare right at me out of eyes as dry as peach pips.

'Lucien!' I call. 'Don't let the kids see this.'

'What's going on, mate?' Ginger asks.

'These aren't scarecrows, Ginger,' I shout, as the other figures raise their heads and swivel them in my direction, a choir of moans floating towards me. 'They're Rotters.'

SAINT

There are more than twenty Rotter scarecrows staked in the field, their outstretched arms tied to wooden posts, their legs secured with wire. I'm relieved that the children are still sleeping. They may have grown up in a world where most of the population is made up of walking corpses, but I would hate them to see this. It's just ... *wrong*.

'They must have been here for ages,' Ash says, pointing at the weeds that are spiralled around the scarecrows' legs. Their shoulders are spattered with bird droppings, and their clothes are nothing but rags. Most are in poor condition, the white tendrils of that spaghetti stuff coiling around sallow bones.

'Who would do this?' Ginger says. 'It's so cruel.'

'I thought you hated Rotters, Ginger,' Lele says. But it is clear that she knows what he means. We all know what he means.

'The thing is,' Ash says, '*someone* did this. The Rotters didn't get here by themselves. But why would anyone bother?'

One by one the Rotters cease moaning, leaving us in silence that is somehow creepier.

'Let's get out of here,' I say. 'I don't want to –'

An ear-splitting crack shatters the stillness. Ember screams and the whole field erupts as hundreds of birds shoot into the air. 'Get down!' Ash yells as another crack fills the air, and I throw myself to the ground, covering my head with my arms.

A male voice bellows something at us in Afrikaans, and I can hear Kobu crying in the background. Slowly, I raise my head. I have to distract whoever it is, get them away from the children.

Expecting to feel the punch of a bullet at any moment, I carefully get to my feet, holding my hands above my head. There's a man walking towards us, a shotgun or rifle pointed straight at me. His skin is as puckered and brown as a raisin, and he could be anywhere from forty to eighty years old. He shouts something else and I shake my head. 'Please,' I say. 'We have children with us!'

'Put the gun down,' Lucien says from behind me. He sounds calm, and there is no mistaking that he means what he says. 'Or I will shoot you, old man.'

There's a tense few seconds, then Ember says something in Afrikaans, her voice wobbly and unsure. I recognise the word for 'please', but that's about it.

There's a pause and then the man answers her. He lowers the gun and gestures for the others to stand up. 'Kom,' he says, turning his back on us and walking towards a rutted track next to the field. He says something else, and Ember responds.

'What did he say?' Ash asks.

'He wants us to go with him to his house,' she says.

'Uh-uh, no ways,' Lele says, pointing at the Rotter scarecrows. 'Anyone who does that for a hobby isn't someone I want to hang out with.'

'Yeah, mate. You never seen *The Texas Chainsaw Massacre*?' Ginger adds. 'We're asking to be chopped up into tiny pieces and stashed in a basement.'

The man turns around and waves impatiently at us.

'I think it'll be okay,' Ember says.

'Why?' Lele asks.

'He says he wants us to meet his wife.'

'*That's* why you think it'll be okay?' Lele says.

Ember shrugs. 'He didn't shoot us, did he? He put his gun down as soon as he knew we had the kids with us.'

'Ember does have a point, Lele,' Ginger says.

'What happened to being chopped up into tiny pieces?' she snaps.

'Yeah, there's that, but, like Ember says, I reckon if he was going to shoot us he would have done it by now.'

'You guys stay here with the kids,' Ash says. 'I'll go check it out.'

'Seriously?' Lele says. 'Just because Ember thinks it'll be fine you want to go running after a guy who just shot at us?'

Ash shrugs, refusing to rise to the bait. 'Maybe they've got some spare fuel.'

Lele snorts and shakes her head. 'As if that's likely.'

'What do you think, Lucien?' I ask.

He shrugs. 'Up to you. But do not be long. I do not like it out here.'

'If I'm not back in an hour, come and get me,' Ash says.

'No ways, Ash,' I say. 'I'm coming with you.'

He's not sure how to take this, but after what's happened between us he can't say no.

Ginger gently transfers Bambi into Ember's arms. 'Me three.'

Lele opens her mouth. 'Stay put,' I say to her. 'If you're right, we're going to need someone to get us out of here.'

She looks like she's going to argue, then turns on her heel and stalks back to the bakkie.

Our would-be assailant may be getting on a bit, but he walks at a cracking pace, and we have to hustle to catch up with him. I'm regretting not bringing Ember along. He hasn't responded to any of our questions, so either he doesn't speak English or he's the silent type.

'Just in case we *are* about to get murdered,' Ginger says to me, 'you guys are friends again, aren't you? I mean, you've forgiven Ash for being all secretive, right, Saint?'

'"Being all secretive" is one way of putting it, Ginger,' I say. 'Being a lying asshole is another.'

''Cos, like, it would be a real shame if you guys fell out for good, 'cos you've known each other for years and you've been through, like, *tons* of stuff.'

'I'm working on it, Ginger,' I say. But Ash's betrayal still burns, and I'm not sure how – or if I even want – to bridge the distance between us. How could he hide so much from me for so long? I thought we shared everything. After Ripley disappeared I spent hours with him – talking to him, crying with him. He was endlessly patient with me. It's not even as if I'm feeling angry anymore. I managed to get most of my fury out in that one punch. It's more of a crushing disappointment. A sadness. I'm sick of lies, of hidden agendas. But at the same time I know that Ash has been carrying this secret around for years; it must have festered inside him like an abscess.

The road rises and dips and then, straight in front of us, there's a large farmhouse with a wrap-around stoep, a neat barn next to it. A well-maintained if ancient tractor is parked at an angle in the driveway.

'They might have diesel, after all,' Ash says.

'Have you noticed, guys?' Ginger says. 'No anti-zombie

fences. It's like the War never happened here. I mean, apart from the freaky-ass scarecrows obviously.'

'Kom,' the man says again, beckoning us towards the house. We approach cautiously, and step up onto the stoep. There's a porch swing next to the door, and herbs and flowers spill out of clay pots. It looks like somebody's *home*.

Ginger takes in a deep breath. 'Smell that?'

The rich odour of herby gravy wafts out of the house and my stomach grumbles.

'Well,' he says, 'if they are planning on chopping us into little pieces, I hope they feed us first.'

The front door opens and a woman steps out, a double-barrelled shotgun slung under her left arm. She's rotund and white, and although she's probably around sixty or so her skin is unlined. Her bright-blue button eyes don't look like they miss much.

The man says something to her in Xhosa, and she rattles something back at him.

'Hello,' Ash says. 'You speak English?'

'Ja, I speak English if I have to. What do you want here?'

'We were just passing; we don't want any trouble.'

Her eyes dart to each of us in turn, and then she seems to come to a decision. 'Come with me,' she says, turning back towards the house.

We follow her into a dark hallway – the delicious smell of cooking meat infusing every inch – through a doorway and into an enormous kitchen. Despite the temperature outside, a wood-burning stove in the corner kicks out waves of heat – a giant potjie pot squatting on top of it. Everything is well worn but spotlessly clean. A scuffed wooden table the size of my old bedroom back in our hideout fills the room, and there are vases of sunflowers everywhere.

'My name is Mariska.' She nods to the man, who's leaning against the door frame. 'That is Wiseman. He speaks only Afrikaans or Xhosa.' Her eyes flit to mine, as if to imply that because I'm black I should have no trouble conversing with him. 'Sorry.' I shrug. 'English or Tswana.' And I haven't spoken Tswana for so long that I'm not even sure I could hold a conversation in it. Stupid Resurrectionists and their insistence that English be the dominant language.

Wiseman pushes past us, sits down at the kitchen table, pulls a filthy rag out of his pocket and starts cleaning his gun.

Mariska wipes her hands on her apron. 'Where are you from? And where are you trying to travel to?'

Even Ash realises that there's no point being cagey with this woman, and he outlines the reason we left Cape Town, and why it is that we're looking for other survivors. Unlike the vile Scott and Previn she doesn't question how it is we're able to evade the Rotters. Maybe because in this area, with the exception of the ones staked out in the field, there aren't any.

'Sit,' Mariska says as soon as Ash is finished, ushering us towards the table.

Wiseman grunts something in Afrikaans and Mariska chuckles. 'Wiseman says that you don't like our friends out there in the field, nè?'

'They are a bit ... disturbing,' I say. But they're worse than that.

'Why did you put them there?' Ginger asks.

'To warn us.'

'Warn you?'

She nods. 'Ja. They let us know if anyone comes. Listen.' I can just about make out the faint sound of the Rotters' moans. 'They make a different sound if there are other dead – or even living – people nearby.'

'Seriously?' Ginger says. 'They always sound the same to me.'

Mariska smiles, but her eyes stay hard. 'You're not listening carefully, my boy.'

'Let me get this straight,' Ash says. 'You keep the scarecrows as ... an early warning system? An alarm?'

'Ja.'

'I notice you don't have any fences,' Ash says. 'Aren't you worried about being attacked?'

She shakes her head. 'Like I say, they told us you were coming.'

'You think there are lots of settlements like this one?'

Mariska shrugs. 'I like to think so. I don't see why not. We have survived, and if you are used to hard living and hard work you can get by. It is the people in the cities who are not so lucky, I think.'

She has no idea how right she is.

'Are you hungry?' she asks.

'Starving,' Ginger says. 'What you cooking there?'

'Lamb,' she says. 'We have plenty. I always cook too much.'

'There are more of us,' I say.

'How many?'

'Um, quite a few,' Ginger says.

'I will make some bread.' Mariska says something to Wiseman and he stands up and makes for the door.

'No offence,' Ash says, 'but I think it's best if I go.'

Mariska bustles into a pantry that leads off the kitchen and Ginger and I peer past her. It's heaving with hanging slabs of meat, ropes of dry wors and jars of pickles and preserves. She definitely keeps busy. There's enough food in there to feed the Cape Town enclave.

'Do you and Wiseman live alone?' I ask as Mariska re-emerges with an earthenware pot and a basket of potatoes still dusted with earth.

'Ja. Just us,' she says, placing the provisions on the table. Her eyes stray to the dresser against the wall. Framed photographs jostle for position on the top shelf. One of them is of a younger, prettier Mariska in a frilly white dress. Next to her stands a round-faced burly man who couldn't look more different from Wiseman. The others are mainly of children – boys mostly – and there's a large colour shot of Mariska standing in the middle of a group of broad-shouldered young men, all of whom seem to have the same beady eyes as she does. Her sons?

'Can I give you a hand there?' Ginger asks.

Mariska hands him a knife and sets him to work peeling potatoes. 'We have a shower,' she says to me. 'But the water is cold. You are welcome to use it.' She nods to a door that leads out into a dark passageway.

'A shower?' My stomach may be empty, but the desire to be clean overrides the hunger. 'That would be great, thanks.'

Leaving Ginger to his spuds I slip into the hallway and try the doors that line the dimly lit corridor. They each open into a bedroom: one with a double bed covered with a patchwork quilt, another containing bunk beds and a third with two single beds. All three rooms smell of lavender water and furniture polish; the walls decorated with watercolours – most of cows, sheep and pastoral scenes – and framed cross-stitch sayings, all of which are in Afrikaans.

I try the final door. 'Oh, thank you,' I say, taking in the flushing toilet, the shower cubicle and the lump of handmade soap next to a basin. 'There is a God.'

When I make my way back into the kitchen, clean and feeling a hundred times more like my old self, I hear the sound of the others arriving. Ginger introduces Lele and Ember to Mariska as Lucien walks in carrying Kobu, Nelly holding tightly onto his hand.

Mariska's eyes lose their hard edge when she catches sight of the children. 'Ag, shame.' She waves them towards the kitchen sink and hands Lucien a cloth. 'Here. You can clean them up. Poor little things.'

Ember hands Bambi to Ginger.

'What have you got there?' Mariska says to Ginger as the hyena raises his head and sniffs at the air.

'A baby hyena.'

I'm waiting for the usual 'a *what?*' exclamation, but Mariska doesn't seem that surprised. 'Ag, he's cute. We take in lots of orphaned animals here, but we have never had a hyena. A wild dog pup once, and quite a few buck. Put him on the floor and I'll get him some milk.'

'You have milk as well?'

'Ja, of course. We have cows, goats, pigs. And some horses.' She bends down and scratches Bambi's ear. 'What have you been feeding him?'

'Scraps, whatever we can get.'

'You are lucky he didn't get sick.'

'He's tough. Like I am,' Ginger says. 'I can eat anything.' He eyes the stove hopefully.

Mariska chuckles. 'Supper won't be long.' Disappearing back into the pantry she returns with an earthenware jug. She pours thick creamy milk into a bowl and places it on the floor. 'We miss our dogs,' she says as she watches Bambi fall on it.

'What happened to them?'

'Most were killed protecting us.'

'From the Rotters? I mean, the dead?' Ginger asks. 'They don't go after animals, do they?'

'No.' She turns back to the wood stove. 'We don't get many of the dead anymore.'

'So who attacked you?'

Still with her back to us, Mariska says, 'Travellers. People who were escaping settlements. Others.'

'So you've encountered other survivors?'

'That's what you call them? I call them skelms.'

I wonder what happened to these skelms, and if any of them met their end staked out in the middle of that field.

'But we have not seen any for many months now,' Mariska continues.

Kobu and Nelly follow Lucien to the kitchen table, both of them sticking as close to him as they can get. Mariska says something to Wiseman and he leaves the room, returning with a wooden box. He places it on the floor in front of Kobu and turns it upside down. It's full of toys – cars and blocks and jigsaw puzzles – and even Nelly gasps in delight. 'They belonged to my boys,' Mariska says. 'I knew they would have a use one day.'

Mariska starts dishing stew into large bowls. She serves Wiseman first and then ushers the children to the table. Kobu and Nelly stare down at their food as if they're not quite sure what to do. 'Eat up,' Mariska says. 'You are all too thin.'

Ginger looks like he's in heaven, and he dives into his food. 'Oh Goddess,' Ember says. 'This is the best meal I've ever had.'

The stew tastes as good as it smells. I take a piece of yeasty bread to dip in the delicious gravy as Mariska passes around blocks of rich butter, bowls of potatoes and dishes of thick yogurt. The bread is straight out of the oven, and it's so hot that I almost burn my fingers.

Kobu grabs a handful of gravy and potato and shoves it into his mouth. Most of it lands on the floor, where Bambi makes it disappear.

Mariska clucks her tongue and hands Kobu a spoon. 'No fingers. We are polite here.'

'They are just hungry,' Lucien says.

'I know this,' Mariska says, smiling at Kobu and gently wiping his mouth with her apron. 'Where are you taking these children?'

'Somewhere safe. Lesotho, maybe.'

She shakes her head. 'It is not a good idea to travel with them. Not with the skelms and the dead out there. They need stability.'

'There is no stability in this world, mama,' Lucien says.

Mariska sighs. 'This I know well.'

We eat in silence; Ginger, Ember and Ash all manage third helpings.

Ember tears off a piece of her bread and passes it to Ash so that he can mop up the gravy on his plate. 'How sweet,' Mariska said, nodding to them. 'It's nice to see people in love.'

There's a moment of such awkwardness that I can almost taste it. Lele freezes mid-mouthful. 'Wrong,' I say before I can stop myself. 'It's the other chick he's been screwing.'

Ash glares at me, and Lucien laughs into his hand.

Mariska chuckles. 'Ag, sorry,' she says. 'Too long with just me and Wiseman, see. Not used to being around other people.'

Ginger has coloured crimson again. 'I'd better take Bambi outside, just in case,' he mumbles.

Ember gets to her feet. 'I'll come with you,' she says, and Ginger gives her a smile of such gratitude it nearly breaks my heart.

Kobu looks up from where he's bashing his spoon on the side of his bowl and yawns.

'Shame,' Mariska says. 'The children are tired.'

'They can sleep in the back of the car,' Lucien says.

'No, we have plenty of space. It is a big house. I have a room for the children, you men can sleep in the barn and the girls can have my boys' old room.'

I glance at Lele. She shrugs. 'Thanks,' I say to Mariska. 'That's kind of you.'

'It is nothing.' Mariska stands and reaches down to pick Kobu up. Then she holds out a hand to Nelly, who takes it after the smallest hesitation. 'Kom,' she says to them. 'I will tell you a story.'

Lucien pushes himself back from the table, but the children look like they are quite happy to go with Mariska, and he sits back down. Wiseman scrapes his chair back, picks up his gun and heads outside.

Lele is still staring down at her plate.

'Ash,' I say. 'You and Lucien clear the table and do the washing up.'

'Where are you going?' Ash asks.

I grab Lele's hand and pull her up. 'None of your business.'

I lead her down the corridor and into the bathroom. 'Check it out, Lele. A shower.' I close the door behind us, and sit down on the toilet seat. 'Listen,' I say. 'Don't worry about what Mariska said. She got it wrong, that's all.'

Lele wipes her palms over her face. 'Maybe she didn't. But don't stress, Saint, I'm cool. It's Ginger I'm worried about.'

'Why?'

'You know why. He's got a major crush on Ember.'

Again I think back to what Ginger told me at the game lodge – about how lonely he is. I have no idea how Ember feels about him, but Ash must be aware of Ginger's feelings for her. And there's no way that Ash would come between them ... is there?

'You sure you're cool, Lele?'

'Yeah.'

'You haven't developed a thing for Lucien instead, have you?'

She snorts and gives me the finger, but I notice she hasn't denied it. 'It's just ... to be honest, Saint, I don't know what to think about Ash any more. Not after what he's told us.'

'Yeah,' I say. 'I know exactly what you mean.'

———————

Footsteps thump across the floorboards outside the room I'm sharing with Ember and Lele, followed by the sound of raised voices.

I jump up, instinctively reaching for my chains that are still somewhere in the bowels of the Embassy. The room is pitch black, so I know for sure that it is still night-time.

'What is it?' Lele whispers.

'I don't know.'

Ember is still fast asleep – she's obviously not as attuned to danger as the two of us.

Despite their gruesome Rotter alarm system, the generosity Mariska and Wiseman have shown us has convinced me that they can be trusted. But after the assholes on the cruise ship and what Mariska said about the 'skelms', I can't help but wonder if the majority of people out there aren't dangerous in some way – like the survivors in Ginger's apocalyptic movies, who all seem to dress in leather trousers and have rape on their minds.

I crack open the door, readying myself to fight if I have to. Wiseman strides past without sparing me a glance, Mariska scurrying behind him, wrapping a shawl around her shoulders.

'What is it?' I ask her.

'Listen,' she says. 'There is someone, or something, out in the field.'

I can't hear anything except the usual velvety night-time sounds, and the whir of insects. Then I make out a barely audible chorus of Rotter moans.

Lele joins me outside the room, hopping on one leg as she pulls on her boots. 'Let's go.'

'The men will handle it,' Mariska says.

'No offence, Mariska,' I say, 'but in my experience that leads to nothing but trouble.'

Mariska clucks her tongue, but she doesn't look as if she disagrees with me.

Ash, Lucien and Ginger are waiting at the side of the barn, their eyes clouded with sleep. Wiseman is already striding down the track that leads to the road, his shotgun slotted under his arm.

Lele grabs my shoulder. 'You hear that?'

All I can hear is my heart pounding in my chest. I keep absolutely still, doing my best to control my breathing.

And then I catch it, the sound of an engine – a bike, or maybe a car.

I hold my breath and strain my ears, but it's receding, and in seconds it's gone.

'Guardians?' Lele says to me.

I don't answer her. All I can think is: *Ripley*.

I haven't slept in such a comfortable bed for what feels like forever, but I still couldn't get back to sleep after last night's incident. While Lele and Ember have been snoozing I've been lying awake, head filled with thoughts of what that engine sound could mean, my mind refusing to shut itself off. I can hear Mariska bustling around the kitchen, but my stomach is a clenched fist, and even the yeasty smell of home-baked bread and sizzling bacon can't spark an appetite.

I pad down the corridor. Mariska has already laid the table and is setting out platters of cold meat, hard-boiled eggs and rusks.

'Môre,' she says.

'Morning.'

'Breakfast is nearly ready. Will you go and wake the boys?'

She hands me a steaming mug of milky tea, and I step outside. The air is already warm with the promise of summer heat. I spot Ash over by the Land Cruiser, the map spread out over the bonnet.

He glances up at me and tries to smile. Things are a little better between us, but they are still awkward. I don't know if they will ever be the same. I slip my sunglasses on as I walk over to him. 'What are you thinking?'

'We have to assume the worst.' He hasn't slept either by the looks of things. The strain he's under shows in the dark rings around his eyes.

'You really think the Guardians would follow us all this way? And if it is them, why didn't they show themselves last night?'

He shrugs. 'Maybe they didn't know we were here.'

'You think they're waiting for us up ahead?'

'It's possible.'

'If it even *is* them.'

'It could be other survivors. Maybe the skelms Mariska keeps mentioning.'

But I don't believe this, and it is clear that neither does Ash. We haven't encountered anyone else on the road, and we've seen first-hand how difficult it is to source fuel and vehicles.

'So we have a choice,' Ash says. 'We can carry on to Johannesburg, or we can head back to Cape Town.'

'What do you want to do?'

'I reckon we carry on.' He waves me over to him and nods down at the map. 'If we head off the main drag and stick to farm roads we could avoid them.' He traces a route with his finger.

'Okay. Let's do that.'

I move to go back inside the house. 'Saint?' he says. 'Are we cool?'

Are we? I don't know. 'You lied to me, Ash.'

'Yeah. I know, Saint ... I'm really sorry. I screwed up, okay?'

I turn around look into his eyes. What's the point of stressing about ancient history? If I dwell on his past actions I may as well end our friendship right here and now. And, like Ginger says, it was an accident. An accident I suspect Ash has been paying for ever since. 'Yeah. We're cool, Ash.'

He sags with relief. 'Thanks, Saint.'

'Come on. Let's go break the news to the others.'

———

I'm still too wound up to eat, and Ash and I hang back by the door while the others tuck into the spread. Mariska moves around the table, topping up mugs with tea and helping Kobu cut his bacon into manageable pieces. Bambi lies underneath Kobu's chair, lapping at a bowl of milk and gazing up hopefully in case any morsels come his way.

There's someone missing. 'Where's Wiseman?'

'He is out in the field,' Mariska says, bending to the oven and pulling out a tray of hissing sausages. 'He will be able to read the tracks of whoever came here last night.'

I hope we haven't brought trouble to her door.

Ash nudges me, and I turn around to see Wiseman entering the room. He says something to Mariska in Xhosa.

'Well?' Ash says.

'Two motorbikes,' Mariska says. 'They stopped at the end of the road, then left very quickly.'

'Dammit,' Ash says under his breath.

'Ag, it's probably just skelms. Like I have said. Every so often we get people coming past here.' I hope she's right.

Lele looks up and catches my eye. 'It's time to leave, right?'

'Yeah,' Ash says.

Mariska steps around to the back of Kobu's chair and places a hand on his head. 'Listen to me. I think you should leave the children here.'

Lucien shakes his head. '*Non*. No way. That is not going to happen.'

'There is something going on with you,' Mariska says. 'I can see that. You are not bad people, but you are in trouble. Why would you want to drag the children into that?'

Lucien pushes his plate away. 'I cannot leave them.'

'These children need a home. They are safe here.'

Lucien snorts. 'Safe, maybe ... but what is out there in the field, it is not right.'

'We do what we can to survive,' Mariska says. 'We've made sacrifices like everyone has.'

The exact same words Lucien used not so long ago. And for some reason this makes me think of the Resurrectionists, and the hold they have over the people in the city. Are the citizens – the Comrades – who follow their skewed religious dogma just doing what they have to do to survive as well?

'They should be with me,' Lucien says.

Lele clears her throat. 'I think Mariska might be right,

Lucien.'

'*Non*, I will make sure they are safe.'

'It isn't forever, Lucien. You want to see if you can find your friend, right?'

'*Oui*. That is important to me, but so are the children.' He bends his head to the table and rubs his hands over his shorn hair. He looks at Mariska, then at Kobu and Nelly.

'We'll be back, I can promise you that,' I say to him. 'We're not saying we'll be leaving them here forever.'

'I do not know.' He stands up. 'I need to speak to them. See what they think.' He picks Kobu up and motions for Nelly to follow him outside.

'You'll need supplies,' Mariska says to Ash as soon as Lucien is gone. 'Food. We have plenty to spare.'

'Biltong?' Ginger says hopefully.

'Ja,' Mariska says. 'I will pack you a box.'

'I don't suppose you have any diesel, do you?' Ember asks.

Mariska shakes her head. 'We used to have a store, but it is running very low. You might find some on the farms closer to Bloemfontein, if you are heading in that direction.'

Lucien walks back in, closely followed by the children. His eyes are red-rimmed, as if he's been crying. Mariska looks at him expectantly. 'Kobu often wakes up in the middle of the night – he has nightmares,' he says. 'And Nelly may be the oldest but she likes to keep her bear with her. Do not try and take it away from her, please. I think it is important that she be allowed to be a child for as long as possible.'

Mariska nods. I look over at Wiseman, and for the first time since we've been on the farm his face cracks into a broad smile.

'You're doing the right thing,' Lele says.

'Am I?' Lucien says. 'We will see.'

We've only known them for two days, but it's harder to leave Kobu and Nelly behind than I thought it would be. Mariska and Wiseman walk with us to the edge of the property, where Lucien picks the children up in turn and whispers in their ears. Then he climbs on his bike, guns the engine and roars off without looking back.

We take it in turns to hug the children. It's Nelly especially that I feel for. I can't get the thought of her looking after her baby brother for all those weeks by herself out of my head. Taking responsibility for him. Even Bambi allows himself to be squeezed one final time by Kobu, and when Ginger gently takes back the hyena there are tears rolling down his face.

Mariska picks Kobu up and the five of us climb into the bakkie, Ginger and Bambi hopping into the front with Ember.

'Bye-bye' Nelly whispers. 'Bye. Bye.' It is the first time I have heard her speak.

Ember drives away, beeping the horn as we pull onto the smoother surface of the road. As we pass them the Rotters' heads swivel towards the sound of the engine, as if they are begging us to cut them down. Mariska and Wiseman may have fed us and helped us out, but still ...

Ash mumbles something. He's also looking back at the Rotters, and I suspect he's reading my mind. 'What is it, Ash?'

'I was just thinking. It's a good job we judge people on how they treat the living, and not on how they treat the dead.'

LELE

There's more room in the back of the bakkie now that the children are no longer with us, but the hours of traversing miles of often washed-away, uneven farm roads haven't been easy on any of us. Thankfully we're only kilometres away from Bloemfontein, the next large town.

The car pulls to a stop, and now that we're stationary I'm hit with a blast of dry heat.

'We there?' Ginger asks, turning around to peer through the partition as Lucien growls up behind us in a cloud of orange dust. 'Thanks a lot mate,' Ginger mutters, brushing dirt from Bambi's fur.

Bambi's not the only one who's coated in grime. It's wormed its way into every crevice and line on Ginger's face, making him look like an ancient version of himself. He takes a gulp of water and passes the bottle to me. I down mouthful after mouthful. Even my teeth feel gritty.

Handing the bottle to Saint I jump down to get a better look at our surroundings. The road ahead is blocked by a line of cracked red-and-white plastic cones and rows of army trucks. The vehicles' tyres are flat, their canvas roofs frayed and torn and their windscreens swathed in thick powder. A fat monitor lizard of some type skitters out from beneath one of them, disappearing behind a sign which reads *Danger Gevaar Ingozi. Quarantine EC Sector 17.* There's a blood-red skull and crossbones beneath the writing.

As the dust kicked up by the bakkie and bike finally disperses I make out a series of tents behind the trucks, their brown canvas as ragged as that of the vehicles' roofs.

'No Rotters,' Saint sighs, ruffling her hands through her hair and causing her own mini dust storm.

'Let's check it out,' Ash says.

Ginger's pouring water into a bowl for the hyena. 'Wait for me!'

'You can catch up,' Saint says.

Saint, Lucien, Ember and I follow Ash into the first tent. It's like a heat trap, the air full of the stench of rotting canvas. Piles of automatic weapons are littered over wooden trellis tables inside it, and more spill out of packing crates dotted around the floor. They look like they were dumped here in a hurry.

'Someone was expecting a serious fight,' Saint says.

Ash picks one up and weighs it in his hands. He looks over to Lucien. 'You think we could still use these?'

So says the guy who supposedly hates guns.

'I would not risk it,' Lucien says. 'These have not been oiled for years. Have you not learned your lesson about faulty weapons, Ash?'

Saint shakes her head at Lucien. 'Very subtle.'

Ash ignores them and pushes through a flap in the back of the tent which leads into another behind it. It's like travelling through a canvas labyrinth. Several of the tents contain rows of foldaway beds, the mould-spotted sheets and rotting pillows now home to insect life. I catch a glimpse of a particularly large sand-coloured spider that I hope Saint doesn't spot. We come across another, larger tent that houses a makeshift kitchen, the pots, gas canisters and stove thick with rust, and another with a red cross stitched to its roof in which a dead generator squats next to a bank of cracked lights that are all focused towards a stainless steel bed. Gross. It looks like some sort of operating theatre. The final tents were clearly used as bathrooms; the toilet stalls nothing more than planks of wood with holes cut out of them balanced over a ditch.

It's a relief to be outside again, away from the heat and the smell of rot. Behind the tents there's a wood and razor-wire fence. Judging by the uneven joins in the slats it was built in a hurry, but it's still too high to peer over. A few metres away there's a lookout tower, a canopied turret at the top of it.

'It doesn't look like their quarantine was very successful,' Saint says. 'No sign of life anywhere.'

'We don't know what's behind the fence though, Saint,' I say. But she's right, even if there is anyone alive behind it, surely there would be Rotters nearby?

Ginger blusters through the tent behind us, the panting hyena clutched in his arms. He places Bambi on the ground next to the fence and fans himself with his hand. 'That was not fun. Thought I'd got myself lost for a while back there. And it's too bloody hot. It never gets this hot in Cape Town, innit?'

'Complaining won't help, Ginger,' Saint says. But she also looks the worse for wear. 'I'd bloody kill for a cold shower right now.'

'I'm not holding out much hope that there are survivors behind that fence,' Ash says, rubbing his neck as Ember pours a little of the water in her canteen onto a cloth and wipes her face with it. She offers it to Ash and he takes it with a smile.

How *sweet*.

Lucien catches my eye and winks at me.

I slip my sunglasses on and peer up at the wooden tower. 'I reckon we could see for miles from up there.'

'Count me out,' Saint says. 'It has to be a hundred degrees out here.'

'I'll go,' Ember says.

'It was my idea.'

Saint sighs and gives me a pointed look. 'Here's an idea, why don't you *both* go?'

Thanks a lot, *Saint*. I shoot daggers at her but she ignores me.

'Fine by me,' Ember says.

'I'll come with,' Ash says.

'*Non*,' Lucien says. 'There is no need. Lele is perfectly capable of looking after herself.'

Ash looks like he's about to argue, but Lucien shakes his head at him.

The dry heat is making my skin feel like it's been sandpapered, and Saint has a point – climbing to the top of the tower is not going to be fun. I'm trying not to think about that horrible trip up the cruise ship's rope ladder. But I can hardly do a U-turn now, not without looking like a complete wuss.

'You sure you want to do this, guys?' Ash asks, but I notice he looks at Ember first when he says this.

'Absolutely!' Ember says. 'It will be fun.'

'Just make sure the wood isn't rotten or anything,' Saint says. 'The last thing I feel like doing is picking up body parts. We've had enough drama as it is.'

I stride ahead, meaning to go first. The ladder feels secure and although my palms are slippery with sweat it's a million

295

times easier to climb than the rope ladder. And this time I don't look down.

Sweat runs into my eyes, but I blink it away as I pull myself up onto the observation platform. There's a rusty machine gun attached to a plinth on the chest-high balcony, and bullet casings, the remains of crushed drinks cans and cigarette butts litter the floor. I lean on the railing and stare out over the city.

Or what's left of the city.

Every once in a while a fire would start on Table Mountain, the smoke filling the sky, but the blaze would always die out somewhere in the dead city before it managed to threaten the enclave. But this city hasn't been so lucky. Whole areas of what must have been a thriving residential area are scorched black as if an inferno has raged through it. There's a large black-earthed crater next to the skeleton of what was probably a soccer stadium, the shattered remains of warehouses, office blocks and shopping malls scattered around it. The devastation spreads far into the distance, and I can't see a scrap of greenery anywhere. Nature hasn't bothered to reclaim this city. It's as if it knows the earth has been poisoned.

Rivulets of perspiration trickle down my sides, and I regret not bringing any water with me. I hear Ember climbing up behind me. 'See anything?' she asks.

'Look for yourself.' I turn away from her and gaze back the way we came. I don't want to stare at the lifeless city any longer.

'What do you think happened here?' Ember asks.

'Well, *duh*. Isn't it obvious?'

'Hey!' she pushes my shoulder and I stumble forward.

I spin around, ready to give her a mouthful. 'What did you do that for?'

Her mouth is set in a hard line. I've never seen her angry and she almost looks like a different person. 'For being such a total bitch to me! What have I *ever* done to you?' Tears are glistening in her eyes, and one spills over and starts to roll down her cheek, leaving a track mark in the dust that coats her skin. That's something we have in common – I always cry when I lose my temper. She brushes it away with the back of her hand.

For a couple of seconds we just stare at each other, and now the surprise is fading I start to feel the first stirrings of rage. 'Why do you think, Ember?'

'I don't know.'

'Ash,' I say. '*That's* what you've done to me.'

'What are you talking about?'

'Don't play that game with me. You know exactly what I'm talking about. "Oooh! You fancy a swim, Ash?"' I say, putting on a little girl voice. '"Oooh, Ash, look at me with my see-through T-shirt." Sound familiar?'

She scrubs tears away from her cheeks. 'I don't know what you're –'

'Don't lie. You know very well. You've been flirting with him non-stop! And what about Ginger? He's got a major crush on you and you've just been ... playing with his feelings.'

'I have not!'

I shake my head in disgust and turn away from her.

'So ... you're in love with Ash, then?' she says to my back.

Am I in love with Ash? What I'm feeling for Ash at the moment is something between anger and disappointment. I'm not sure any of us have come to terms with the fact that he's hidden so much of his life from us. I turn around and open my mouth to speak, not actually sure what I'm going to say, but she jumps in first. 'Because you don't act like it. You've been moping around like a moody bitch since I've known you. But I'll tell you something, Lele, I wasn't trying to get with Ash.'

I snort.

'I won't lie, I like him a lot, but the last thing I want after seeing the crap Mother and Father go through is a boyfriend.' She sniffs loudly. 'And if I *did* it wouldn't be Ash.'

'Really? Why?'

She shrugs. 'Not my type. He's too ... I dunno, intense.'

She has a point. 'Honestly?'

'*Ja*. How many more ways do you want me to say it?'

I wasn't expecting this and the anger drains away as fast as it came upon me. Shame starts to creep in. 'I really have been a total bitch, haven't I?'

'Ja. You really have.'

'Look, Ember, I'm sorry. I was jealous. I was jealous of you, okay? Now you've made me admit it.'

'Really? Jealous of *me*?'

'Yeah.'

'Why? How can you be?'

'Oh, I dunno. 'Cos you're gorgeous, and you make Ash laugh, and you can fix cars, and you never complain about anything, you just get on with it.'

'But I'm just trying to fit in, Lele. You guys, well, you have a history.'

'Some history.' Full of secrets and lies.

'But you're a team. You all know each other – you're like a family. I feel like an outsider, like I don't belong anywhere.'

And then I realise that I know exactly what she means. I think back to when I first joined the Mall Rats, how I'd also felt like an outsider, having to play catch-up to all their secrets and in-jokes. They'd given me a really hard time at first – Saint especially – and I wonder if this is the real reason why I resent Ember. The others seem to have instantly accepted her as part of the group, whereas it took weeks before Ash or Saint would even share a kind word with me.

'I really am sorry, Ember,' I say. And then I find myself telling her about my own Mall Rat initiation. How I'd hated Saint and Ash and their stupid nicknames at first; that it was only because of Ginger and Hester that I'd decided to stick it out. It all pours out – and then I move on to Thabo. About how I'd had a major crush on him at Malema High, before he'd left me to join the ANZ and fight against the Resurrectionists. How the Mall Rats had betrayed me – something I realise still stings after all these weeks. And maybe that's another reason why I haven't shared my secret with them. Because of their betrayal. I thought I'd forgiven them, but obviously not.

'We've got more in common than you think, haven't we?' Ember says. 'And, Lele, I didn't mean to ... you know ... flirt with Ash.'

I believe her.

'It's cool, Ember. Ash and I aren't exactly the couple of the year, anyway.' He's been off with me since that night at the lodge when we'd almost ... But I don't want to think about that. Maybe Ash and I are just too similar. We're both moody secret-keepers – Ash with his hidden agenda, not telling us about Lucien and his past, and me chickening out of telling the Mall Rats my own secret. Maybe we're not meant to be together at all.

'Hey! You know what Mother would say? What advice she'd give you?'

'What?'

She grins at me. 'She'd say "a woman needs a man like a zombie needs a flag."'

I smile back at her. 'That could practically be Saint's motto.'

'You think we can be friends?' Ember asks, pulling up her T-shirt and wiping the drying tears off her face.

'Actually, yeah, I do.' And I mean it. Ember's cool. She's

always been cool. I'm the one who's been the dumb-ass.

She holds out her hand. 'Shake on it. I'll teach you how to drive if you teach me how to fight. Deal?'

'Deal.'

'And you really think Ginger likes me?'

'Are you kidding me? How could you not have known? He practically faints every time he's near you.' I smile at her. 'Anyway, he told me.'

'He did? What did he say?'

'Lele!' Saint is standing at the bottom of the tower. 'What the hell are you guys doing up there?'

'We're coming.'

'See anything?'

'Nothing,' I shout down to her. 'The city's toast. We'll have to drive around it.'

We climb down and shake the dust off our clothes.

Lucien looks from me to Ember and smiles. 'You are friends now, I see?'

'How did you know we weren't friends?'

He pulls his sunglasses down and peers at me over the top of them. 'There is not much I do not see, Lele. But I am very happy that you have connected. You will do each other good.'

I roll my eyes. 'Lucien, you're cool and stuff, but sometimes you can be *seriously* patronising.'

Lucien and Saint laugh as Ember holds out her palm for me to slap it. I glance at Ash. Even he's smiling.

———

We drive along a rutted road that skirts the edge of the city. In some places Ember is forced to slow to a crawl to avoid gaping potholes and sections where the tar has disintegrated. Shacks and one-roomed houses flank the road; they're in far better condition than the once-substantial buildings in the razed city.

'Check!' Ginger says. He points to our right, but I can't see what he's talking about – it's hard to see anything through the dust haze kicked up by the tyres. 'Smoke! Someone's burning summut.'

Ember pulls off the main drag and we thump along another narrower road, ending up in front of a high chain-link gate. There are buildings far behind it – low, windowless face-brick structures that look utilitarian – and fifty metres or so from us a gatehouse and another fence.

Now that the dust has settled I can see grey smoke billowing up into the sky.

Lucien skids to a stop behind us and kills the bike's engine.

'Should we go in?' Ember asks.

'I do not think we can get past this gate,' Lucien says. 'It is locked.'

Jumping off the back of the bakkie Ginger walks up to it and nudges it with his boot. It swings open, screaming on rusty hinges. 'No it isn't.'

Lucien shrugs. '*D'accord*. After you.'

Ginger hurries to collect Bambi from the back of the car. The hyena's tongue lolls out of his mouth and I know just how he feels.

'What is this place?' Ginger says as we approach the gate-house. 'Talk about security overkill.'

'There's your answer, Ginger.' Saint points to a sign that reads *Correctional Services*. 'Lovely. You've brought us to a prison.'

'Should we even bother checking it out?' Ash asks. 'I mean, there're no Rotters around here, so it's unlikely there are any survivors.'

'Aw, come on, mate. What we got to lose?'

Saint catches my eye – the memory of our near miss on the cruise ship is never far away from either of our thoughts.

Ginger rattles the gate next to the gatehouse. 'Aw, what? It's locked.'

'Back to the car,' Saint says.

'Hellooo!' Ginger shouts. 'Anyone there?'

'Come on, Ginger,' Saint says. 'It's too hot to mess around.'

'Wait,' Ember says. 'There must be survivors. Look. Someone takes care of that.' She gestures to an area to our left and I peer past her. Set back from the fence there's a cultivated garden, complete with a scarecrow – one that is clearly not a Rotter, thank goodness – dressed in a bright orange jumpsuit. It's hard to be sure from here, but it looks like someone's planted – and watered – rows of mealie plants, spinach and sugar snaps. Chickens and a clutch of guineafowl peck around the plants.

'Heeellllloooooo!' Ginger yells again, and this time the squat figure of a man hurries around the side of the building, waving his hands above his head and shouting something in Xhosa. My stomach flips – I can't help it – but as he gets closer it's clear that he's smiling at us. And this guy is definitely not a Guardian. His stomach bulges in front of him, and he's dressed in a pair of faded dungarees and rubber boots, a fraying straw hat balanced on his head. He toddles over, clearly out of breath, his round brown face dripping with sweat.

He greets us in Xhosa and Ash does his best to respond. When the man chuckles and shakes his head, Ash grins apologetically. 'You speak English?'

'Yes, but you will have to excuse me, I am rusty.'

'You sound perfect to me, mate,' Ginger says.

The guy beams at Ginger, showing off large stained teeth. He doesn't look like someone who might be dangerous, but we all know how great I am at judging people.

'Come in, come in. Let's get you out of this heat,' he says, unlocking the gate and waving us through. I hesitate, but the others don't seem to be concerned so I follow, the gate clanging shut behind us. 'I do not want my chickens to escape. They can be naughty.' He offers his hand to Ginger. 'I am Mr Philiso. I am the warden of this facility.'

'Didn't know chickens needed prison guards,' Saint mumbles in my ear.

We all introduce ourselves, but I notice that Lucien hangs back. Mr Philiso blinks at him. 'Have I seen you before, sir?'

'*Non*,' Lucien says with one of his charming smiles. 'I think I would remember.'

Mr Philiso clicks his tongue and throws up his hands. 'I can be so absent-minded.'

'You burning something?' Ginger asks.

'Oh! Yes. Just my garbage.' He leans forward conspiratorially. 'Once the rats get in there's no stopping them. It's the best way to dispose of leavings.' He pulls a lacy handkerchief out of his pocket and rubs it under his hat. 'Is that how you knew I was here?'

'Yeah,' Ginger says. 'I saw the smoke.'

'What luck! I get so few visitors these days.'

Bambi squirms in Ginger's arms – he's spotted the chicks. 'Please,' Mr Philiso says. 'If I could ask you, do not let your dog chase my chickens. They do not lay when they get upset.'

Ginger opens his mouth to go into his 'it's not a dog, it's a hyena' spiel, but Saint nudges him. 'Don't worry,' she says. 'He's very well behaved.'

'Excellent.'

'What happened to the city?' I ask.

The warden wipes his face again. 'You do not know?'

'Nah, mate,' Ginger says. 'Not from around here.'

I wait for Mr Philiso to ask us where we're from, but he doesn't. In fact, he doesn't seem that surprised to see us at all. I hope it's just because he's eccentric and not for any other, more sinister reason.

'They tried to quarantine it many years ago,' he says. 'Then they tried many explosive devices to wipe out the infection. But it did not help, of course.'

'And all the people?'

'The ones that survived fled. Most live out in the Karoo now, I think.'

'So why didn't you leave?'

He straightens his back. 'I have my responsibilities, of course,' he says as if this is a stupid question. 'I can't just leave.'

'Is it possible to get around the city if we follow the road towards the mountains?' Ember asks.

'Yes. That is possible.'

'Great. Thanks.'

'But it is getting late. To where is it that you are travelling?'

'Johannesburg.'

'Ah. The road in that direction is very bad. Many wild animals live there.'

'Wild animals?' Ash says.

'Yes. Before the quarantine they released the animals from the zoo. Sometimes you can hear them at night.'

Saint glances at me. 'Great,' she mouths. I'm not sure I believe him, though. Hard to imagine anything surviving in this dry terrain.

'Why do you not come and be my guests for the night?' He rubs his hands together and bounces on the balls of his feet. 'Yes! That would be lovely! I could give you the guided tour!'

'I don't think so,' Ash says. 'We should really get on.'

The warden's face falls.

'Oh, come on, Ash,' Ginger says. 'If the you-know-whats are following us, what could be safer than a prison?'

'Ginger,' Ash says, a warning note in his voice.

'I could do with a break from driving,' Ember says, and Ginger beams at her.

Ash sighs. 'Let's check it out first.'

'Yes?' The warden says. 'You will stay?' He claps his hands like a child. 'Come, come. Follow me.'

'Why don't you guys go in,' Ember says as Mr Philiso waddles towards the low building without checking to see that we're following him, 'Ginger and I will wait outside with Bambi.' She catches my eye and breaks into a grin.

'Don't let the hyena get the chickens, Ginger,' Ash says.

'You don't need to tell me that,' Ginger says as seriously as he can, but he looks like he's about to explode with joy.

'I will also wait here,' Lucien says. Good on Ginger, he manages to hide his disappointment at losing out on some alone time with Ember.

Ash shrugs. 'Okay.'

Mr Philiso shepherds us past an open barred gate and through wide wooden doors. It's gloomy in here, but at least we're out of the blazing heat. We follow him down a corridor and into an area painted the colour of old ladies teeth, a long scuffed counter along one wall, chipped wooden benches pushed to one side. Next to the edge of the counter stands a sagging drinks machine with its door hanging off, its shelves empty. There's a sign tacked up on the wall that looks like it was put up yesterday, but is obviously a legacy from when the prison was full of people. It reads: *VISITORS' ALLOWANCES: one tube of toothpaste (see-through packages ONLY), one cool drink, one pie, NO family size chip packets.*

'Now,' the warden says with another grin, 'let me show you around.' He's definitely more than a little bit eccentric, but I'm beginning to warm to him.

Mr Philiso unlocks a heavy metal door and waves us towards a long corridor. It's way darker in here, the only light filtering in from tiny windows set high up in the walls, and the place stinks of disinfectant. It's really quiet too – too quiet almost, the only sound the squeak of our footsteps on the rubbery floor.

'Are you sure this is a good idea, Ash?' I overhear Saint asking him.

'Ginger's outside, isn't he?'

'Why doesn't that make me feel better?'

I know what she's thinking – if we get locked in here, there's no way Ginger will be able to break in.

We follow the warden through a barred gate and down another passageway, this one punctuated with more solid metal doors, and out into a spacious area. Thankfully it's brighter in here; the windows are barred but far larger. Two long metal tables are set up in the centre of the room, and a pile of folded-up chairs and tables slant against the walls.

'This is the recreation room and canteen,' the warden says.

'It's very nice,' Saint says. 'Shall we go back outside now?'

'Oh no. You have to see C-Wing.'

He unlocks a gate that opens out into a walled courtyard containing nothing but a drooping basketball hoop, and we cross it to yet another hefty metal door.

'They'll be so glad to see you!'

'Whoa,' Saint says, stopping dead. '*What*? Who will? I thought you were here by yourself?'

He chuckles. 'Of course I am not here by myself. I have to look after my prisoners. They are my responsibility.'

'*Prisoners?*'

My fingers move to the knife lodged in my pocket.

'Of course there are prisoners. Although I do not like to call them that. I prefer "clients".' He turns to smile at us. 'Would you like to meet them?'

'Shit,' Saint says in my ear. 'You think we could be in trouble?'

But it's too late. He's already opened the door.

And then I hear it. The moans.

'I keep the difficult ones in here,' the Warden says, pointing towards a wider corridor that's lined with small barred cells. 'The ones who need extra care.'

A raggedy hand lunges through the bars.

'No ways!' Saint jumps.

I'm not sure if I'm disgusted or fascinated, and I find myself stepping forward.

'You keep Rotters here?' Saint says, recovering her composure.

But the warden isn't listening. 'Julius,' he says, directing this at the Rotter in the cell closest to us. 'Look who is here! Visitors for you.'

'Were they always here?' Ash asks. 'I mean, right from the start of the War?'

The Warden nods. 'Yes. When the infection spread in here I saved as many as I could. Some ... escaped, of course. But it is my duty to look after them, see that they get proper care. And when I feel that they are ready, that they have paid their debt, I release them.'

'What?' Saint says. 'And they don't attack you?'

'Of course not! They know that I only have their welfare at heart.'

Mr Philiso stops outside another cell. Weirdly there's a Rotter lying on a bed inside. It looks like it's chilling out – there are even books and magazines strewn on the floor next to a grubby sink.

'And, um ... how do you know when they are ready to leave?'

'Oh, I know. I have been in this business for many years. You can see by the number of empty cells what a high rate of success I have had.'

'Whoa,' Saint murmurs to me.

'Say we do decide to stay,' Ash says. 'Where would we be sleeping?'

The warden laughs. 'Oh, not in the cells, of course! There is an area that the members – the guards – used to sleep in. It is near to the canteen. Do not worry, I will not lock you in.'

We follow him back into the courtyard.

'What do you think?' Saint asks me.

'The warden may be nuts, but I honestly don't think he's dangerous.'

'And we can take it in turns to keep watch outside,' Ash jumps in. But Saint's still not looking too keen. 'We're all exhausted, and seriously, Saint, do you want to be camping outside if the Guardians are around?'

Saint looks like she might find it preferable.

We head into the dining room, the warden pushing through flexible double doors that lead into the largest kitchen I've ever seen. It's spotless in here; the stainless steel surfaces and white tiles look freshly cleaned, and it hums with the smell of cleaning fluid.

'It is best to eat early. It can get very dark in here,' the warden says, trotting towards a fridge the size of a shack. 'I am afraid I only use the generator on special occasions, and gas is very hard to find. There was a large store of it here, of course. But I do not like to go into the city to forage, as it means leaving my clients for too long.'

He drags out a sack of putu.

'You don't have to feed us,' Ash says. 'We've got supplies.'

'Yeah. We'd be happy to share with you,' I say.

The warden smiles at me. 'Oh, it is not for us,' he says. 'It is for the clients.'

'The Rotters? I mean – the dead?' Unlike the zombies in Ginger's movies, who all seem to have insatiable appetites for brains and other innards, I've never seen a Rotter eating or drinking anything. I guess I assumed it was the spaghetti stuff that needed to feed – and it did that by controlling its host.

Mr Philiso cocks his head to one side and stares into my eyes. 'You see,' he says, 'if you feed them, they will eat.'

There's no moon, and the stars are hard, bright pinpricks above me. I sit outside the main entrance, ears straining for any sound other than the click and burr of insect noise. There's no indication of the wild animals the warden mentioned earlier, but that doesn't stop me imagining a tiger slinking through the night, hungry eyes watching me.

But there are real dangers to worry about. Could the Guardians be following us? Why though? I can't really see it. Ripley wanted us to leave. Why else would she have left the bikes for us? Unless it's Paul. But again, I can't think of a reason why he would come after us. We're in no position to help the ANZ out here, so why would he bother?

And that warden. Has being alone all this time turned him crazy? It's incredible that the Rotters haven't taken him yet. What are the chances?

The gate clangs behind me and I leap up, my hand unconsciously grabbing the flick knife out of my pocket. A figure moves towards me. My stomach flips, and I surprise myself by hoping that it's Lucien. But it isn't – it's too tall, and I make out a shock of dark hair as it approaches. Ash.

Great.

I sit back down. I've only been out here for fifteen minutes or so, so he can't be here to take over the watch from me.

He clears his throat – a very un-Ash-like thing to do. Is he nervous? 'Hi, Lele.'

'Shouldn't you be asleep?'

He shrugs. 'Can't sleep.'

There's the flick of his lighter and I'm hit with a waft of smoke. He waves it away. 'Sorry.'

I don't answer.

'So ... how are you doing?'

Now he asks me? 'Fine,' I say. If he wants us to have a conversation he's going to have to work for it.

He sits next to me and takes several drags on his cheroot. He must have begged one from Lucien. 'Um ... Look, I think I owe you an explanation. After the night at the lodge I know I've been ... ' He sighs. 'Dammit.' He takes another drag. 'What I'm trying to say is that I know I've been distant.'

'Oh yeah, you think?' There's an empty hole in my gut. Nervousness? Anticipation? I can't pin down how I'm feeling. 'Why didn't you just say: "I was drunk, I made a mistake, Lele." Instead of shutting me out?'

'Because it wasn't a mistake. It just ... it just ... happened.'

Brilliant. 'That the best you can do?' The empty hole is starting to fill with the beginnings of anger.

'You've also been ... um ... I dunno, moody.'

'Are you surprised? One moment you're all over me, the next you're shutting me out and laughing and joking with Ember as if you don't have a care in the world. What the hell is up with that?'

He starts. 'What do you mean?'

'Oh, come on. I know you like her, Ash. And that's fine. Just don't hurt Ginger, okay?'

'You've got it wrong, Lele. I do like Ember, sure, who wouldn't, but not in the way I like you.'

Just two days ago I would have given anything to hear him say this. I would have felt overwhelmingly relieved, elated. But now it leaves me cold. And in any case, I'm not sure I really believe him.

'I've been acting like a real idiot, haven't I?'

'Idiot isn't the word I'd use, Ash.'

'I shut people out when I get close to them, Lele.'

Yada yada yada. As if that's an excuse. 'Oh really, Ash? I've heard all this from Saint a million times, but it doesn't help me, does it?'

'I want us to be friends again. I ... I *need* us to be friends again.'

'I don't know that we were ever friends, Ash. I can't read you. Friends don't mess with each other's feeling like this. Or treat them like absolute crap.'

I'm expecting him to stalk off, angry Ash-style. But he stays where he is. He crushes the cheroot under his boot, then reaches over to take my hand. He squeezes it, but I don't reciprocate. I let it flop there like a dead fish.

'So what do you want from me, Ash? You want us to ... be together, that it?'

'I'm saying that I'm sorry, that we should get through the journey first. Then we can see after that.'

No. No, I think. More weeks of uncertainty, of obsessing, of not knowing what he's thinking? I've been eaten up with jealousy, with insecurity, and I don't want to go through that ever again. Part of it is my fault, sure. I didn't have to tear myself up over a guy, but the lion's share of the blame still lies with Ash. And he doesn't even realise it. 'Actually, Ash, I don't think so.'

'What?' He sounds like he can't believe what he's hearing.

'I think we should just be friends. End of.'

'You really mean that?'

Do I? *Do* I? And then I know for sure. 'Yeah.'

He stands up. 'I don't know how I feel about this.'

And I think: *good*. Welcome to my world.

And I feel free again.

SAINT

''C'mon, Saint, rise and shine.'

I open my eyes to find Lele sitting on my bed, grinning down at me. I can't believe I finally dropped off. I tossed and turned for hours, listening to the echo of the Rotters' moans drifting down the corridors, trying to fight the claustrophobia. Even the fact that the door was propped open did nothing to stop the swirls of panic as the dark crept in.

Lele nudges my leg. 'Time to get up, lazybones.' She looks far more cheerful than I've seen her for ages.

'How come you are in such a good mood?'

She shrugs. 'I dunno. I think I've sorted things with Ash.'

'You have? When?'

'Last night. While we were keeping watch.'

'And?'

'It's over.'

I sit up. 'What? You serious?'

'Yeah.'

'It's not because of Ember, is it?'

'No. Ember's cool. I was wrong about her and Ash. Well, I hope for Ginger's sake I was, but I just can't deal with all the tension anymore. We have enough to deal with as it is.'

'You feeling okay about it?'

'Yeah. Actually, I'm more annoyed with myself than anything. I mean, he's been treating me like crap since we left Cape Town, and I just took it like an idiot.'

I'm still wondering if it was the talk I had with Ash after the night at the lodge that made him cut himself off from her, but I decide not to mention this. There's been enough trouble between us all for one trip, and it is almost a relief to think that the Lashle soap opera is over.

'What are the others doing?' I ask, sensing that Lele is ready to change the subject.

'Lucien and Ash are messing with the bike, and Ginger and Ember are off somewhere with Bambi.'

'And that warden fellow?'

'I dunno.' Lele puts on a deep voice: '"If you feed them, they will eat."'

'What if he's right though? What if there is some kind of humanity left in them?'

'How can there be, Saint? They're dead.'

'Well, remember out in the Deadlands how some of them would approach the fire as if they wanted to get warm? And then Mariska said she could tell the difference between their moans.'

'I don't want to think about it, Saint.'

'Don't blame you. Gah. I need something to drink. Is there any tea?'

'There should be some left. Come on.'

Lele waits while I pull on my jeans and boots and then together we head down the corridor and into the canteen.

Sunlight filters in through the room's large barred windows, but somehow the room's atmosphere remains cold – the Rotters' moans are louder in here.

'Check it out,' Lele says, motioning towards one of the windows.

There's a group of twenty or so Rotters hanging about in the walled courtyard, all dressed identically in orange jumpsuits.

'He must've let them out there early this morning.'

'I can't believe they haven't infected him yet.'

'I know. It's freaky.'

It's worse than that. 'I'll be glad to get out of here.'

I push through the doors and into the kitchen. There's a pot of tea sitting on the stove and Lele hands me a scuffed metal mug.

'More!' the warden calls from the rec room as Lele scoots up onto the serving hatch ledge, letting her legs dangle. I wave at him. Today he's dressed in a smart black suit and tie, and for some reason he's carrying a basket full of tennis balls.

Lele glances at me. 'What do you think he's up to?' she whispers.

'No idea,' I say. I take a sip of tea and struggle to swallow it without throwing up – it's bitter and cold.

The warden strolls towards the gate at the side of the room. Hang on – that gate leads out into the courtyard.

'Oh crap,' Lele says. 'Hey!' she shouts to him. 'Hey! No! No! Don't –'

The warden smiles at her, pulls a bunch of keys from his belt and starts fiddling with the lock.

Lele swings her legs through the hatch's opening, jumps down and flies after him.

But it's too late. Before she's halfway across the room, he's through.

'No *ways*, Saint,' Lele says as we shut the gate behind us. 'It can't be.' The warden is standing in the middle of the courtyard, sunlight bouncing off the top of his bald head. He's surrounded by Rotters, but they're acting as if he's not there. 'Why the *hell* aren't they attacking him?'

'I have absolutely no idea, Lele.'

He waves to us. 'You see? If you treat them well, they will respond. They must like you too. The last time we had visitors here, they were not so lucky.'

'Do you think that's right?' Lele asks. 'That they won't attack if you act as if they're still ... human?'

'Can't be.' There has to be some other explanation. 'He's too old to have a twin, right? The only people we've met who don't get attacked are our age.'

'There's Ginger and Ember, though. They don't have twins.'

'True.'

'And what about all those stories we've heard about survivors – the skelms, the people who came through Mother's settlement?'

'Other freaks of nature?' Lele sighs. 'Who knows?'

'What *is* he doing now?'

He grabs one of the tennis balls out of the basket and throws it at one of the Rotters – a relatively fresh-looking specimen with tufts of grey hair sprouting above its ears like a clown's wig. The ball bounces off its chest and it moans.

The warden grins at me. 'I will teach them, you will see. It is only a matter of time before they learn.'

He picks up another ball and rolls it towards the feet of a Rotter. More by luck than anything else it takes a step forward and kicks it. 'You see?' the warden says triumphantly.

'Blimey!' The gate clangs behind us as Ginger and Ember join us in the courtyard. Ginger's mouth is hanging open in surprise. 'Why the bloody hell aren't they going for him?'

The warden fishes a ball out of the basket and chucks it into the air, catching it one-handed.

I feel the inkling of an idea tickling the back of my brain. It can't be. If I'm right, though ... There is only one way to find out.

'Mr Philiso!' I call. 'Can you throw me a ball, please?'

'But of course! You want to join in? How lovely.' He lobs a tennis ball in my direction. His throw is weak, but I manage to catch it.

I spin to face the others. 'Ember!' I shout. 'Catch!' I chuck the ball at her and she instinctively reaches up and plucks it out of the air.

She giggles. 'What did you do that for?'

'Throw it at Ginger!'

She gives me a strange look, but does as she's told. She aims high, and Ginger has to leap to catch it.

I knew it.

The implication of what I've seen – and what it could mean – hits me with such force that my legs turn to water and I have to drop to a crouch.

'Saint?' Lele says. 'Are you okay?'

'Get the others. You are not going to believe what I've just figured out.'

'What the hell you talking about?'

'Just do it, Lele.'

She must have picked up on the urgency in my voice because for once she doesn't argue.

———

'Bullshit, Saint,' Ash says. 'So you're saying that if you're left-handed you're immune to Rotter attack? Can't be.'

Everyone is seated around one of the canteen tables, staring up at me. I cannot sit still; I pace up and down. My hands are shaking and I dig my nails into my palms to make them stop. 'How do you explain it then, Ash?'

'Well, we always said that Ginger's a freak of nature. Maybe there are other freaks of nature as well?' It is typical of Ash to play devil's advocate, but I don't blame him. If the roles were reversed I know that I'd be thinking that he'd lost his mind.

'I'm with Saint on this one,' Lele says. 'Think about it. Ember, Ginger and the warden are all immune to attack, right? But none have twins, and the warden must be, like, I dunno, a hundred years old or whatever, so even if he did have a twin, the Guardians wouldn't have ... messed with him or her or whatever they did at the beginning of the War. Being left-handed is the only thing all three have in common.'

Lucien is watching me carefully. He lights one of his foul cheroots. 'And it's not just that. Remember that family?' I say, waving the smoke away. 'The family we rescued in the Deadlands?'

'Yeah. Course.'

'And how the Rotters seemed to ignore the old man?'

'That was just a fluke,' Ash says, but now he's not looking so sure.

'But someone would have figured this out sooner, wouldn't they?' Ginger says.

'Why would they? Think about it, the War happened fast, remember? And we only found out that we were immune by accident – Hester found us after the Rotter break-in. And we knew Lele had a "special" twin, and that's why we recruited her.'

Lucien is still watching me through the smoke dancing in front of him.

'What we do know for sure is that those of us who *do* have twins are immune,' Lele says. 'That one of our twins doesn't grow, as if their energy has been transferred to us.'

'So what does that have to do with being left-handed?' Ash asks.

'What do you think, Lucien?' Ginger says. 'You know tons of stuff, innit?'

Lucien gives one of his shrugs. 'I do not think what Saint is saying is impossible. And there *is* a connection to the twins.'

'Go on,' Ash says.

'Some scientists believed that left-handed people did have a twin originally, and that it died before it could develop properly in the womb.'

'Seriously?' Ginger says. 'You mean I had a brother or sister who didn't make it? That sucks.'

Lucien shrugs. 'Some believed that left-handed people absorbed – or ate – their twin in utero.'

'Aw, what? No way!' Ginger says.

'I am just repeating what I have read.'

Ash still doesn't look convinced. 'So, theoretically, there could be hundreds of people trapped back in Cape Town with no idea that they could leave the enclave whenever they wanted to?'

I nod. 'Exactly.'

'I ate my twin?' Ginger says. 'I ate my twin? I think I'm going to be sick.'

'*Enough*, Ginger,' I snap.

'So what percentage of the population is left-handed?' Lele asks.

'No idea,' Ash says.

'Say, I dunno, ten, fifteen percent. If I'm right, that's enough people to really make a difference.'

'But we've been through so many deserted enclaves. Wouldn't we have seen more survivors?' Ash asks.

Ash isn't going to give up, and while I don't blame him I'm desperate for my theory to be right. 'We're not immune to the newly dead, though, are we, Ash? Hatchlings move fast, they could account for loads of fatalities.'

'True.'

'And, in any case, it's not just the Rotters people have to worry about. There's disease, starvation, violence.' Again I think of those bastards on that ship. 'Survival is a hard business. And if people are smart they're not going to live near the cities. They could be miles away from the main road. For all we know we could have passed hundreds of successful settlements. Lucien, you said you've seen other enclaves where people are getting along okay, right?'

He nods.

'Yeah,' Ginger says. 'If there's one thing this journey's taught me, it's that Africa's bloody huge, innit.'

'But how would you test this theory, Saint?' Ember asks. She's been strangely quiet, and I wonder if she's trying to remember if any of the people in her home settlements are left-handed.

'Easy,' Ginger says. 'Just throw a ball at them.'

Ember punches him playfully. 'I didn't mean that, Ginger! I meant, how do we test their immunity to the Old Souls before we're sure about this? We can't just send people into the midst of the dead and hope for the best.'

She's got a point. 'Honestly, Ember, I haven't thought that far ahead, but we've got a long drive to figure it out.'

The excitement is catching and Ash gets to his feet. 'Okay,

let's pretend for a second that I agree with you, and that there is a significant portion of the population which is immune to Rotter attack. That means that the only thing stopping them from living a normal life is the Guardians.'

'Yeah, and the Resurrectionists. In other words, people's stupidity. But think about it, if we find a way to stop the Guardians then the left-handed people can almost take their place. And if the Rotters do eventually disintegrate completely then –'

'We're sorted!' Ginger says.

'Don't get ahead of yourself, Ginger,' I say, smiling at him.

'If the ANZ had this information we really could have a chance,' Ash jumps in. '*Everyone* could have a chance.'

'We should get back to Cape Town as soon as possible,' Lele says. 'This could change everything.'

'But we're so close to Johannesburg,' Ginger says. 'And Lucien wants to find his mate. We did say we'd go with him.' He grins at Lucien. 'He's like part of the team now, innit?'

Lucien is looking into the far distance. 'I think it might be a good idea if you do go back to Cape Town.'

'Slight problem,' Ember says. 'We don't have enough fuel to get us back there – or even back to Father's homestead. We should do what Mariska suggested, maybe check out some farms, see if any of them have a watertight diesel store.'

'We could do that on the way back,' Lele says. 'And maybe we could convince Mariska to part with some of her diesel this time.' She pauses. 'Hey, did anyone notice, were they left-handed?'

Lucien shakes his head. '*Non.*'

'Whoa, mate? You noticed that?' Ginger says.

Lucien nods. 'Lele is right. You have a duty to return. I will go on alone. Or Ash and I could go together, perhaps. Catch up with you later.'

'How about a compromise?' Ash says. 'We'll travel on a little bit further, see if we can source some fuel, then head back.'

Lele doesn't look so sure, but I am undecided. Botswana is temptingly close to Johannesburg. What if Atang *is* still alive there? What if Dad is holed up in a settlement somewhere?

And there's something else too. Do I really want to go back to Cape Town anyway? It's not as if the people there treated us well when we were taken by the Resurrectionists. It's impossible to erase the memory of that crowd of jeering citizens, laughing at us, calling us names, throwing rotten fruit at us. Sure, there are good people among them, but ...

I make my decision. 'Lele, we've been gone little more than a week. What harm can it do?'

She shakes her head. 'It feels like we've been away forever.'

'And think about it,' Ash says. 'Now that we know what to expect – and which areas to avoid – we can get home in a matter of days.'

'I guess.'

I realise I've forgotten about the warden outside with his band of Rotters. He's laughing at something, then I hear him shout: 'Goooooal! Laduuuuuma!'

'Do we tell him about this?' Lele asks.

'Nah,' Ginger says. 'Let him believe what he wants. If it makes him happy, who cares about the truth?'

LELE

It's time for Saint to take over lookout duty, but I decide to let her sleep on. There's no way I'll manage to drop off again – my mind's racing like a toddler who's been at the sugar – and in any case, it won't be long till dawn. The sky is morphing from black to dark blue and I can hear the first faint chirrups of early-morning birdsong.

If Saint's outlandish theory is right, then we've actually done what we set out to do. We've found a possible solution to freeing the enclave from the Guardians and the Resurrectionists. If people are able to take control of their own lives and support themselves then things could change radically. Of course, there's still a mountain to climb. I can't see Nkosi, Zyed and the other power-hungry citizens loosening their hold on the city without a fight (not to mention what the Guardians will do to stop us), but it's a start.

If people believe us, that is. And if Saint is actually correct.

I chuck another couple of logs on the fire, poking the dying embers to spark them back into life. I don't need the warmth, but the firelight helps banish the shadow cast by the bridge above us. There's something seriously spooky about camping on the side of the highway, surrounded by the carcasses of abandoned vehicles, but everyone was way too exhausted after the day's hectic exertions to bother looking for a more comfortable spot to spend the night.

It had taken us most of the day just to traverse Bloemfontein's perimeter. Great chunks of the road have crumbled away leaving yawning craters, and we were forced to search for logs and debris to fill the fissures so that the Land Cruiser could negotiate them.

Still, despite slaving away all day under the energy-sapping sun, everyone, including Ash, managed to keep their spirits up. After our heart-to-heart the night before I was expecting a day of sulky asshole behaviour, but if anything he was more upbeat than Ginger, joshing with Saint and Lucien, and even shooting the odd grin in my direction. I can't help but feel a pang of dismay at how quickly he seems to have accepted that we're just not right for each other, but I push this thought from my mind. I've wasted way too many hours obsessing over Ash as it is.

Ginger murmurs in his sleep, rolls over and flings an arm over Ember's waist, disturbing Bambi, who's curled up between their sleeping bags. The hyena yawns, shakes out his body and pads over to me. He flops down at my side, and I run my hand over the rough fur on his back. Ember sighs contentedly and wiggles closer to Ginger. Saint spent the day unsubtly fishing for details about the status of Ginger and Ember's relationship, but it's pretty clear to everyone that it's progressing super-fast. They sneaked away from camp for an hour or so just after supper, and when they returned Ginger couldn't wipe the grin off his face and Ember's T-shirt was on inside out.

There's the scrape and hiss of a match igniting, and I turn

to see Lucien propped up on one elbow, the smoke from his cheroot drifting out of his mouth. 'You want that I take over the watch from you, Lele?' he asks.

'Nah. I'm cool.'

'You are sure? Tomorrow – or today, I should say – could be very busy.' He takes a deep drag and Saint coughs in her sleep as if she's unconsciously scolding him for smoking. 'We are not so far from Johannesburg now, after all.'

'Might not make it at all unless we find some fuel. And anyway, we haven't decided for sure that we're even going to go there yet.'

Ember reckons that if she drives carefully the diesel should last for another hundred kays or so, which will hopefully give us enough leeway to scout the nearby farms for fuel. But, whatever happens, I'm hoping I'll be able to convince the others to head straight back to Cape Town. It's not that I don't want to help Lucien out – there's definitely some sort of connection between us, although what it is I'm not sure – it's just that Johannesburg is a great big unknown, and the last thing we need is to run into more trouble. For all we know the survivors there could be more screwed up than the Resurrectionists.

'Aren't you worried about your friend, Lucien? About Jova? You don't think it's strange that he hasn't tried to find you after all this time?'

'I know Jova. He can look after himself.' He chucks the cheroot into the fire.

'So you think he actually made it to Johannesburg?'

Lucien doesn't say anything for several seconds. 'Lele, I really do think it is best for you and the others to return to Cape Town.'

Where did that come from? 'What makes you say that?'

He sighs and runs a hand over his face. 'You have a brother

back in Cape Town, you should be there for him.'

'So have you.' I look down so that he can't see my expression and stroke Bambi's back again.

'*Oui*. This is true.'

Bambi's body tenses under my hand, the hair along his spine standing up. Maybe he's sensed the presence of a porcupine or feral cat. 'It's okay, boy,' I murmur to him, but he scrabbles to his feet, making a low grumbling sound in his throat and trots away from us, ears pricked. Not good. The last time he acted like this was just before we ran into Lucien.

'What is the matter with him?' Lucien asks.

'I don't know. I think he's –'

'*Merde*,' Lucien says, staring wide-eyed at something behind me and getting slowly to his feet.

I turn around. Oh *crap*.

Two round yellow lights are drifting towards us, and they're moving fast – too fast. Seconds later, I hear the all-too-familiar growl of approaching vehicles.

'Shit!' Ash yells, instantly wide awake. 'Get to the car!'

Saint sits up groggily. 'Wha … ?' she says. But her sleepy expression instantly disappears as she registers the steadily increasing engine noise. 'Oh *shit*, Guardians!'

'In the car, Saint,' Ash hisses. 'Fast as you can.'

I don't need to wake the others – Ember is already scrambling out of her sleeping bag and Ginger is making a beeline for Bambi.

The hyena darts out of his reach, still making that strange sound in his throat. 'Ginger!' Saint shouts. 'Just leave him!'

There's a crack of what can only be a gunshot. It rocks my eardrums and I drop to the ground, skimming my hands on the rough surface. I hear Ash yell something that I can't catch as the air fills with the roar of engine noise and we're engulfed in a cloud of dust and the stink of petrol fumes.

Two motorbikes skid to a halt in front of the bakkie and I'm blinded as the headlights blast into my eyes. I blink to clear my vision. Two black-clad figures are approaching: one pointing a pistol at us, the other hefting a large automatic weapon like the kind we saw back in the tents.

'Don't move!' a woman's voice shouts.

Ginger leopard-crawls towards the terrified hyena and covers him with his arms.

'I said, do not move!' the woman bellows.

'Stop!' Lucien yells. He steps forward, arms raised. '*C'est moi.*'

The two figures hesitate, then slowly lower their guns. They step into the firelight and it's immediately clear that they're not Guardians, after all, but a guy and a girl, probably not much older than us. The girl's hair is plaited tightly to her skull – just like the Mantis used to wear hers – and the guy is short and stocky, his face blooming with painful-looking acne.

'Lucien?' the girl says. 'Seriaas? It's you?' Then she laughs. 'Where the *hell* have you been, man?'

'You *know* these people, Lucien?' Saint asks.

'Déjà vu,' I mutter, remembering Ash and Lucien's showdown in Grahamstown. I get to my feet, rubbing my stinging palms.

'*Ça va*, Pris?' Lucien says to the girl. 'What are you doing here?'

'Looking for you,' the guy says as he and Lucien engage in some kind of complex handshake.

'It is good to see you too, Sifiso,' Lucien says. 'How did you find me?'

'We've been following your tracks, bru.' He nods to the Land Cruiser. 'Lost the scent for a while, though, couple of hundred kays past Grahamstown. We were about to give up. Then that befok guy in Bloem said he'd seen you. Saw the light from your fire just now and thought we'd check it out.'

Crap. An icy chill dances up my spine as I remember Mr Philiso saying that he thought he recognised Lucien when we first arrived at the prison. Ash, Ginger and Saint are also staring at Lucien as if they can't believe what they're hearing, but where's Ember? I can't see her anywhere. Could she have made it into the bakkie? I hope she's got the sense to keep out of sight.

'We've been looking for you everywhere, Lucien,' the girl's saying. 'It's been a total mission. Jova sent us down the N1, but we cut across. We knew you wouldn't have gone that route after what happened in Die Hel.'

'You've been gone for weeks, bru,' Sifiso says. 'We thought you'd bought it.'

'I got sidetracked,' Lucien says.

'You can put your guns down now,' Ginger says, standing up and gathering the hyena into his arms.

The girl laughs. 'You're a big one, nè?' She turns back to Lucien. 'Nice haul. All Lefties?'

Lucien nods. '*Oui*.' I try and catch his eye, but he's refusing to look directly at any of us.

'Lefties? You mean you knew about the left-handed thing all along?' Saint spits at him.

Lucien nods. '*D'accord*.'

'*Bastard*.'

The chill extends its icy fingers to my gut. How could I have been so stupid? Lucien's tattoo – the hand-shaped tattoo on his back. I should have bloody well put two and two together when Saint discovered what Ember, Ginger and the warden all had in common.

Idiot.

'Tell me this is not what I think it is, Lucien,' Ash says, his fists clenched tightly at his sides.

'It is whatever you think it is, Ash.' Lucien shrugs. 'As a former ... Mall Rat, as you call yourselves, why would you be surprised? It is simple commerce that we are engaged in, after all. And, in any case, it was you who came to find me, remember?'

The girl laughs again. 'And you will be very valuable to us.'

Exactly what those assholes on the cruise ship said.

'What do you mean "valuable"?' Ginger asks.

'You'll see when we get you back to Jozi,' Pris says, looking Ash up and down. 'Sweet.'

'So you've been in Johannesburg ever since you left Cape Town?' Ash says bitterly.

'*Oui*. Except when I go out to find others like you. Like *us*.'

'And Jova? Is he also there?'

Lucien nods. 'He will be very pleased to see his old friend Jack again.'

'They know Jova?' Pris asks.

'*Oui*.'

'You've done well, Lucien,' Sifiso says, checking us out in turn. 'I thought we got the last of the Lefties back in Kimberley.'

'You're not going to let them shoot us, are you, Lucien? After all we've been through?' Ginger says. 'I thought we were mates.'

'I am sorry, Ginger,' Lucien says. 'But I did not expect to meet Ash again. And you others, you are a bonus. Call it ... luck, if you like.' He chuckles. 'You did say that is what Bambi has brought to you, *non*?'

'And Kobu and Nelly?' I ask. 'Were they also part of this ... this *act*?'

Lucien shakes his head. '*Non*. I was hoping that they were immune, but as you have seen they are not. I am not a monster.

I could not leave them to survive alone.' He smiles. 'And I am glad they are not coming with us to Jozi. It is better this way.' Lucien straightens his shoulders. 'Pris, Sifiso, it is good to see you. But these people are mine. I will deliver them.'

Sifiso shakes his head. 'No ways, bru. You can't manage this lot by yourself. We're happy to help.'

'Lucien, you saying that you're not going to share with us?' Pris pouts at him. 'After all the fun we've had?'

The two of them stare at each other for several seconds, something unreadable passing between them. Despite the dire situation I'm hit with a twinge of what feels bizarrely like jealousy.

Lucien shrugs. '*D'accord*. But they are not to be hurt.'

'That's up to them,' Pris says.

I check out our options. If we can't distract them for long enough to grab the guns then Ember's our only chance of getting out of this situation. But why hasn't Lucien told the others about the missing member of our group? Once again I try to catch his eye, but his gaze slides away from mine.

'Sifiso, tie them up and put them in the back of the car.' Pris strolls towards the Land Cruiser and kicks the tyres. 'I am going to enjoy driving this.'

'They got weapons?' Sifiso asks Lucien.

'Just him,' Lucien says, nodding to Ash. 'And the big one has an axe.'

Sifiso shakes his head in derision. 'An axe? What are you, seriously old school or something?'

Lucien knows I have the flick knife in my pocket. Has he forgotten about it? I sneak it out and slip into the back of my waistband.

Still keeping the gun trained on us, the girl reaches into her bag and pulls out a length of nylon rope. Sifiso shoves his gun in his waistband. 'Keep an eye on the big one, Pris.' He ambles over to Saint, looking her up and down and wolf-whistling. 'Turn around, bokkie.'

She spits in his face. 'Screw you!'

'Do what he says, chica,' Pris says. 'One less won't matter too much.'

Saint reluctantly does as she's told, and Sifiso binds her wrists behind her back, then does the same to Ash. I hold my breath as he knots the rope behind me, praying that he won't notice the knife in my waistband.

'Get in the car,' Sifiso says to us.

'How?' Saint snaps. 'Our hands are tied behind our backs. How are we going to climb in?'

'Figure it out,' Sifiso says.

I pull the knife out of the back of my jeans, flick it open, and, struggling with the awkwardness of the blade's angle, start sawing through the rope, nicking my fingers in the process. Too bad.

'Plan C?' I hear Saint mutter to Ash.

'Not this time, Saint. We're going to need a miracle to get out of this one.'

'Hurry it up!' Pris calls, her gun still trained on Ginger.

Taking their time, Saint and Ash struggle over the lip of the load-bed.

'Now you, sisi,' Sifiso says to me, grabbing my arm and shoving me against the side of the car. Doing my best to hide the knife from view, I step up onto the tyre, sling my torso over the side and roll into the back.

I try to yank my wrists apart, hoping that I've sliced through enough of the rope for it to snap, but it still holds.

'Come on, big guy,' Sifiso says to Ginger. 'Your turn. Put the dog down.'

'He's not a dog,' Ginger says. 'And no, I won't.'

Sifiso laughs and steps forward to grab Bambi out of Ginger's arms. The hyena's head snaps forward. 'Ow!' Sifiso yells, backing away and grimacing in pain. 'The bloody thing bit me!' He whips the gun out of his belt. 'He's dead!'

'Now, Ember!' Ash yells.

The Land Cruiser's engine suddenly growls into life and it leaps forward, heading straight for Pris, Lucien and the bikes. The abrupt movement sends Saint and Ash reeling into me, and I lose my grip on the knife as I'm slammed down onto the load-bed's metal surface, whacking my head against the bakkie's side. Everything happens at once – I hear the crack of a gunshot, Ginger bellowing, 'No!' and a scream that can only have come from Pris. There's an almighty crunch and the squeal of rending metal as the Land Cruiser crashes into the bikes, Ash's boot smacking into my jaw as the impact throws us against each other again.

'Ginger!' Saint yells as the engine cuts out.

'Over here!'

Untangling myself from Saint and Ash, both of whom are looking slightly dazed from the collision, I peer over the back flap. Ginger and Sifiso are grappling on the ground several metres away, Bambi nipping at Sifiso's feet. They're both trying to reach the gun that's lying next to one of the back wheels.

I pull against the rope with all my strength, and this time it gives. I'm about to spring over the side to retrieve the gun, but then the Land Cruiser roars into life again and I land heavily on my tailbone as it shoots backwards. 'Ember! Stop!' I scream.

The car jerks to a halt inches from Ginger's wildly flailing legs just as he finally manages to land a solid punch square on Sifiso's jaw.

'Get in!' Saint shouts at Ginger as Sifiso flops back, defeated.

Snatching up Bambi he chucks him unceremoniously into my arms, then vaults over the side.

'Ember! Go!' Ash bangs against the partition.

Pris weaves to her feet in front of us. Her face is slick with blood, but she's still holding the weapon in her arms. I can't see Lucien anywhere. Despite what he's done to us I hope he wasn't too badly hurt when the bakkie smashed into the bikes.

Ember revs the engine and the bakkie flies forwards, kicking up a hail of grit. Pris is forced to leap out of our path as the car rushes towards her, moving faster than I imagined possible. I look back to see her running after us, yellow flashes of light that can only be gunfire sparking around her. 'Get down!' I yell, curling myself into a ball. There's a *thwok* as one of the bullets hits the side of the car, but within seconds we're out of range.

'Shall I slow down?' Ember shouts through the partition. 'The headlights are bust.'

'Not yet,' Ash replies. 'Keep going just in case.'

'Whoo-hoo!' Ginger crows in delight. 'We made it!'

'We're not out of the woods yet, Ginger,' I say. There's still Lucien's bike, so it's possible that at least one of them could come after us. I strain my ears to detect any trace of engine noise, but there's no indication that they're chasing us.

I feel around in the back for the knife, finally locating it beneath Ember's equipment bag. 'Turn around,' I say to Saint and Ash, making quick work of slicing through the ropes binding their hands.

'Dammit, Ginger, I thought you were shot for a second there,' Saint says, rubbing her wrists.

'Nah, mate. Close call, though. I couldn't just let him shoot Bambi, could I? When Ember started the car I kicked the gun out of his hand and the shot went wide.'

'Nice work.'

'Not really. Ember's the one who saved our asses.' Ginger grins. 'Hey, Ember!' he calls.

She turns her head slightly, 'What?'

'You were totally amazing back there!'

'It was –'

'Watch out!' Ash yells.

I whip my head around in time see a large black shape filling the windscreen. Ember screams and slams on the brakes. The car swerves violently, and then the back drifts around smoothly as if it doesn't weigh anything at all, as if we're floating on air. The world slows down as an overturned truck glides forward in slow motion to meet us. I'm crazily aware of how beautifully crisp the dawn sky looks and then I'm flying and the ground is rushing up to meet me and –

Blood. I can taste blood. And my head feels too heavy for my neck, as if there's a large weight bearing down on it.

Someone is digging needles into my hand. I try to move it but pain shoots through my shoulder. With a gargantuan effort I turn my head. Bambi is crouching next to me, tugging on my fingers – his teeth the source of the needle-pricks. I shake my hand free, and he lopes away to pace back and forth in my eyeline. His grey fur is matted and covered in dark brown paint.

Not paint. *Blood.*

Oh no, oh shit, oh crap.

The crash.

The others. I have to get to the others.

'Ash?' My voice comes out as a whisper. 'Ash?' I try again. 'Ginger? Saint? Anyone?'

Bambi growls and he crouches down next to me, burying his

head between his paws.

'Yessus, Lucien, if they're dead Jova's going to be seriously pissed off.' The girl's voice – Pris.

'I could have driven them straight up to Jozi with no problems,' I hear Lucien say. 'This is on your head.'

'Ja, ja. Whatever. Where did you find them anyway?' This from the guy – Sifiso.

'They're from Cape Town.'

'Huh? Jova said Cape Town was off limits till we're ready.'

'I didn't *find* them in Cape Town, Sifiso. They were travelling up to Jozi when I came across them.'

'Lucky, eh, bru?'

'Perhaps.'

'I can't believe that bitch totalled my Ducati,' Pris says. 'Why the hell didn't you tell us there was another one, Lucien?'

'We have been through this, Pris. Because I did not know. I thought she had run away into the night. I did not see the point in wasting time trying to find her in the dark.'

'Whatever, Lucien.' Pris sighs. 'Help me check the car, Sifiso.'

The soft tread of approaching footsteps. A pair of black high-top Converse stops in front of me.

'Lele?' It's Lucien. He drops to his knees next to me. I turn my head and look up, see my face reflected in his sunglasses. My eyes look too large, my face shiny and wet. Blood?

'Am I dying?'

'No, Lele.'

My whole body tingles with pins and needles. I try to lift my left arm, but I can't make my muscles do what they're supposed to. I roll onto my back and will myself to sit up. The world tilts sickeningly – like it did when I was drunk on the cruise ship – and I look down to see a jagged tear in my jeans; the silvery threads intertwining and writhing, sealing the flesh beneath.

Lucien smiles ruefully. 'It wasn't supposed to happen like this, Lele. I really did want you to get away. Believe me.'

'Get away from me. You did this.' The anger helps. The pain recedes enough for me to breathe easily again.

'Let me help you, Lele.'

'If you touch me, I will kill you.'

I have to get to the others. I stagger to my feet, a bolt of agony bursting through my head, fire raging through my left leg. I put my weight down on it. It buckles, then holds. The world slides away from me for a second, then shimmers back into focus. I circle around, the landscape refusing to stay level. Somehow, dawn has made way to full daylight.

Holy crap.

The bakkie is lying on its side, its cab nothing but a scrunched mass of twisted metal and broken glass. Pris and Sifiso are inching Ember out of the debris, grunting with the effort. Her head lolls back on her neck as Sifiso drags her away from the car. Her face is a mask of blood, her red hair clotted with gore. Oh God. Please let her be okay.

'This one's out cold!' Sifiso calls. 'She's breathing, though.'

Limp with relief, I crouch down and gather Bambi into my arms. He whines and I run a hand over his body. I can't feel any broken bones.

'Bambi!' Ginger shouts, his voice faint. He's lying a few metres away from me, next to the charred remains of the truck we smashed into. Lucien stands back as I hobble over to him.

'Where's Bambi?'

'Bambi's fine, Ginger.'

I gently deposit the hyena on the ground next to him and help him to his feet. He falls to one side. 'Gah,' he says. 'I busted my leg.'

'Try not to move. Have you seen Saint or Ash?'

'Nuh-uh. How's Ember?'

'Okay, I think.'

I turn to see Sifiso helping Ash to his feet on the other side of the bakkie. He looks dazed, and is clutching his shoulder, early-morning light glancing off the silver tendrils knitting together the gaping gash just below his collarbone. But he looks to be in way better shape than Ember or Ginger.

'I've got the last one!' Pris says.

I whirl around, trying to locate her voice. She must mean Saint.

Then I see her. Saint's landed further away from the car than all of us, half-hidden in a culvert at the side of the road. Pris nudges her back with her foot.

'Get away from her!' I limp towards them. From here Saint looks untouched; I can't see a scratch on her, but why isn't she moving?

Pris prods her again.

'Don't you touch her!' The words explode out of my mouth, and even though she's the one with the gun – with the power – Pris stands back.

I throw myself onto my knees next to Saint, ignoring the inferno in my leg.

Saint is lying on her belly, perfectly still. *Too* still. I reach out and shake her shoulder.

'Saint!'

Should I roll her over? Maybe I shouldn't move her. *I don't know what to do.* I pray that the silvery strands are getting to work. The last thing I care about right now is the others discovering my secret. It's too late for that.

'Lele!' Ash calls. 'How's Saint?'

'I'm not sure. I think she's ... I think she's badly hurt!'

'Move away,' Pris snaps, training the gun on me once again.

'No.'

'I *said*, move.'

'Shoot me then, bitch. I'm not leaving her.'

I reach over and touch the side of Saint's neck, fingers shaking as I search for a pulse. This can't happen again. It just can't. I saw it happen to Thabo, I saw him die, and I will there to be a flutter of life in her somewhere.

I can't feel anything. I place my hand on her back, desperate to feel her chest rising and falling.

Nothing.

'Saint. Saint. Please. *Please*.'

My vision is swimming, the back of my head throbbing, blackness threatening to swallow me whole.

And all I can think is: *When you die, you will live*.

SAINT

Music. I can hear music. It's underscored by a steady pounding beat and I feel like I should know what it is ...

Words: *I get knocked down, but I get up again* ...

Of course!

It's my song – mine and Atang's. But where's it coming from? Who would be playing it?

Then it's gone.

Did I imagine it? Yes. That must be it.

And what's that smell? I breathe in deeply. Then I have it – it's burnt toast.

Bizarre.

My head is lying on something soft.

I open my eyes. It's shadowy in here, but it is clear that I am in some kind of low-ceilinged room. I lift my head to look around. There's something comforting about the shape of the furniture in here. A chest of drawers, a low desk, a wardrobe. Something sparks in my memory. I know this room.

It's warm in here, too warm, and there's something heavy

draped over my body. A duvet.

I'm lying in a bed.

But that's impossible, isn't it? I haven't slept in a comfortable bed since ... since ... since when? That house. The scarecrows. That's it.

I have to get up. Find out where I am. I yank the duvet off my legs and force myself into a sitting position, ignoring a wave of dizziness. I don't feel quite ... right. Not sick exactly, more as if my mind is numb, detached.

Think back, Saint. Think about how you got here. Wherever here *is.*

We were in the car. Me, Lele, Ash, Ginger and ... Ember. Trying to get away. From what, though? I can't remember – there's a blankness.

I hear the grumble of voices coming from outside the room. Another snatch of music.

My eyes are starting to adjust to the darkness and I make out more detail. The shape of an oval mirror above the chest of drawers. A dressing gown hung up on the back of the door.

I know where I am.

My bedroom.

My bedroom back in Gabarone.

On the wall in front of me, a poster of – *What is her name? Think, Saint* – Rihanna. I begged Dad to let me buy it. He didn't approve. And he exploded when I stuck stickers all over my wardrobe. They're still there. Cheap glitter stickers.

But how can I be here? Did I somehow make it through to Botswana?

I stand up, feeling the scratchy wool of the rug beneath my feet and falter over to the window.

Opening the curtains I look down onto our small garden. It's exactly as I left it: the patchy grass that refuses to grow whatever Dad does to it, the uneven paving slabs and empty plant pots where Mom used to grow herbs. The shell of the half-built townhouse next to ours. Atang and I heard a rumour that our new neighbours were going to build a pool, and we were excited about it for weeks. The sounds of the taxi rank two streets away. Traffic, honking, laughter.

The sounds of my childhood.

This cannot be happening.

I run my hands over my body and look down at my legs. I'm wearing pyjamas, pink pyjamas.

I don't feel panicky, though. That's the strangest part. I should. I'm aware that I should, but the disconnection is still too strong.

Feeling like a sleepwalker I pull open the bedroom door and pad down the corridor. I peer into the bathroom. It's all familiar: the rust stain in the basin, a cracked tile above the bath's tap. Mom used to nag Dad to get it fixed. A meaty spider skitters over the bath plug, but I feel nothing but a faraway twinge of disgust.

The smell of burnt toast is stronger now.

I drift towards the kitchen.

There's a man sitting at the table, a newspaper spread out in front of him. He looks up at me and clucks his tongue. 'There you are, Ntombi. Why are you not dressed in your school uniform?'

'Dad?'

'Yes, Ntombi?'

'*Dad?*' He is older than I remember – deeper lines around his mouth, his hair receding from his temples. And he looks smaller, less imposing. But it is definitely him.

Another blast of music, and Dad shakes his head. 'Atang! Turn that off!'

A teenage boy walks into the room. He's gangly, tall, his

jeans sagging around his hips. Like Dad he's wearing glasses, but his have thick black frames. 'What you staring at, maggot?' he says to me.

'Do not call your sister that, Atang. Show some respect.'

Atang?

No.

The last time I saw Atang he was a skinny seven-year-old, not this lanky guy with a rash of acne across his cheeks.

Suddenly it's like I'm floating somewhere above my body, looking down, as if this is a scene out of one of Ginger's movies. Knees weak I pull out a chair and fall into it.

'What is wrong with you, Ntombi?' Dad asks. 'You are ill?'

I have so many things I need to say, but all that comes out is: 'Cape Town.'

'What about Cape Town?'

'You sent me to school there.'

Atang shakes his head and twirls his finger next to his ear. 'You has gone mental,' he says in a fake British accent.

'Atang!' Dad snaps at him.

'What?'

'Ntombi, what is this? Do you have a temperature?'

'When I was seven you ... ' Because that's the other thing, isn't it? I'm me. Me as I am now. The last time I saw Dad I was seven years old, sitting here at this very table, my stomach churning as Dad and I waited for the taxi that would take me to the airport, Dad explaining that my mother's last wish was for me to go to school in South Africa.

'I'm fine,' I find myself saying. It's still easy to lie to Dad.

Atang snorts. 'You been smoking some good stuff or something, Ntombi?'

'Atang, I will not tell you again!'

Have I gone crazy?

Because there is too much detail for this not to be real: the creases in Dad's paper and the newsprint smudges on his fingertips; the jar of coffee, spotted with melted granules; the bread crumbs scattered over the melamine countertop. I run my fingers under the table, feeling the lumps of the chewing gum Atang and I used to stick beneath it – one of a series of tiny rebellions. The rust just above the handle of the refrigerator; the photo of Mom and Dad, their arms around each other, taken at their graduation.

Something splits inside my head.

If this is real, what does that mean?

Did I make it all up? *Did* I? School in Cape Town, the War, Hester finding me in New Arrivals after the Rotters broke in. Ash, Ginger and Lele. Ripley – touching her for the first time, and that moment when she said she felt the same about me. She never said that she loved me, but I knew. How could I have imagined that emotion?

The mall, the Resurrectionists, living out in the Deadlands, leaving Cape Town, meeting Ember ... All imaginary?

No.

No.

Has time moved on here while I have been somewhere else?

Dad's been saying something to me; Atang is looking at me as if I *have* gone crazy. There's a smudged fingerprint on one of the lenses of his glasses, another too-real detail.

'Do you need to go to the doctor, Ntombi?' Dad asks, now sounding genuinely concerned.

'I don't know.'

There's a knocking sound. Someone banging on the front door.

'Atang, I told you that your friends are not to come here this early.'

'It's not them,' Atang says. 'I just texted Mikey, he's meeting me by the Spar.'

'Well, find out who it is!'

'Ntombi can go.'

'Your sister is not well.'

'I'll go,' I find myself saying. Through the numb shroud I feel a certainty that whoever is knocking on the door is here for me anyway.

Dust motes hover in the pools of sunlight that radiate through the front door's glass panels. I glide along, the corridor feeling like it is twice the length I remember it being.

I open the door and I'm blinded by a white shock of sunlight. I feel myself fumbling for the security gate, but it's no longer there.

A small figure stands on the front step.

Atang.

Atang as I remember him. Right down to the glasses and his favourite Pingu T-shirt.

He stares up at me, no expression on his face.

'Do you want to go back?' He's speaking, but his lips aren't moving. Am I hearing his voice in my head?

'Back where?'

Atang points behind me and I hear Dad arguing with my brother – the older version. The *unreal* version.

'No.' And I mean it.

He holds out his hand. And I lean forward to take it.

It is as if a thousand-watt globe has been switched on inside me. As if every nerve ending, every synapse has been electrocuted and I feel the pull of a thousand – a million – invisible threads. Different voices, a multitude of languages: Zulu, Xhosa, French, Tswana and others that I don't recognise. A babble; connected but separate. One murmurs 'Did I leave the oven on? Did I leave the oven on?' over and over again, another repeats 'Sipho, don't leave me. Sipho don't leave me.', another 'It's not real, it's just a dream.'

The Rotters. I'm hearing the Rotters.

We are all connected.

And then I'm seeing what they're seeing, feeling what they're feeling, although it is not that simple – their senses are cloaked in a hazy mist; there is a numbness, a deadening. I recognise the fence that surrounds the Cape Town City Enclave, the pull of the living behind it an irresistible lure; a mass of heaving bodies surrounding an enormous barricaded shopping mall in a city I've never seen before; the towering hulk of the cruise ship, smaller and somehow less forbidding now that I'm seeing it in daylight; parched earth, a canyon cutting through mountains, the pulse of life emanating from caves cut into a high-up rock face; a city by the sea, the buildings around it smouldering, and a vague sense of emptiness and dismay that there is no life left there. Other places, other pockets of life and death.

And sparking through the connections, other, brighter threads.

My friends: Lele, Ginger, Ash and Ember. I can hear their thoughts, the things they've buried, the secrets they're hiding.

I can sense Lele crying, sobbing. She's lost something. Something she can't get back. Ginger, Ash and Ember, all blasting out waves of fear and pain and confusion.

I'm aware of Ripley's emptiness, the frayed edges of her personality still there inside her like an echo. Thabo's presence is even weaker – he doesn't have the strength that Ripley and I have, but he is fighting it, fighting to stop himself being swallowed up.

Paul. Another faint glimmer, but fading fast. And others. Others I don't recognise.

But in among the shooting sparks of life and energy there's something else. A dark, drifting presence.

It's ahead. In the city ahead. Where I know my friends are going to be taken.

And even through my own foggy mask, my own deadening, I can feel the horror of it.

And I know.

It is not the Guardians we have to fear. It was never the Guardians.

I open my eyes and hear Lele scream.

Much-more...
From

Much-in-Little

Turn the page for a sneak preview of

THE ARMY OF THE LOST

THE GRIPPING THIRD BOOK IN THE

DEADLANDS series:

// COMING IN 2014 // COMING IN

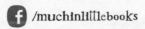 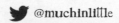

1

Tommy hangs back while Mooki, Jess and the other Newbies swarm out of the kombi and whoop their way towards the townhouse complex across the street. He waits until they've chucked their crowbars and shopping bags over the spiked metal gate, then heads in the opposite direction.

It's only his fourth day out in the suburbs without a supervisor, and he's determined that this time he's going to come back with *something*. He rambles along the cracked pavement, pausing every so often to peer through the long-defunct electric fencing. The chances of spotting an unlocked security gate are slim – he's learnt from bitter experience that most of the houses will be locked up tighter than bank vaults, and the crowbar and skeleton keys in his bag are useless against tungsten burglar bars and reinforced glass.

He finally decides on a small single-storey cottage with crumbling stucco walls that's set back from the street. It's flanked by sprawling Tuscan wannabe-mansions, and Tommy reckons that it was probably the shabbiest residence in the area even before the Dead took over Jozi. But that doesn't mean that breaking in is going to be a piece of cake. Even from here he can tell that its rusting burglar bars are made of good-quality metal, and the porch's overhang has protected the front door from water and sun damage.

Relieved that Mooki and the others aren't around to see him, Tommy struggles over the fence, the baggy sweatshirt he always wears to mask his gut riding up over his stomach. He lands clumsily in an overgrown garden buzzing with insects, the path smothered in moss and creepers. A garden gnome grins cheekily at him from its perch on the top step, and, remembering one of the tips he heard at Runner Camp, Tommy pushes it over with his foot, disturbing a nest of baby scorpions. There's a glint of metal in the circle of dust where the base of the gnome sat – a key. *Score!* Barely able to believe his luck, he picks it up and wipes it on his jeans.

The lock is stiff after eleven years of neglect, but after a couple of minutes of fiddling the door creaks open. Taking a deep breath, Tommy slips inside. 'Hello?' he finds himself saying, as if he expects an answer. He stills his breathing, listening for any sign that one of the Dead might be trapped inside. There's the scratch and scrabble of mice or rats in the ceiling, but that's it. He's heard horror stories from more experienced Runners about opening bathroom or closet doors only to find a walking corpse rushing out like a rotting jack-in-the-box. He doesn't know how he'd react if he saw one right up close. He'd almost puked when the kombi pulled out of the parking lot on their first day of training. Even Mooki had been stunned into silence at the hideous sight of the surging sea of decaying bodies lurching around Sandtown's high walls, everyone fighting not to gag as the overpowering musty stench of the Dead invaded the vehicle. It is one thing to hear their constant moaning – it's provided the soundtrack to eleven years of his life, after all –

quite another to come face to face with the reality of empty eyeholes and decomposing flesh.

Using the gnome to prop the door open – it's gloomy inside, the ivy growing over the windows blocks out most of the natural light – he creeps further into the hallway, his feet clunking over the dusty wooden floor. The house stinks of rot and rodent pee, but the ceilings are high, so the odour isn't overwhelming. He peers into the first room that leads off the corridor – a lounge dominated by a huge flat-screen television and heavy wooden furniture. A flash of movement in a shadowy corner next to a cabinet catches his eye, and his heart leaps into his throat. Steeling himself to run, he inches forward. Oh *gross*. One of the armchairs is alive with baby rats. He backs out, deciding to try the kitchen across the hall instead.

His old supervisor was always going on about how kitchens are usually the best bet for sourcing high-quality merchandise, but this one doesn't look too promising. There are two plates still smeared with the calcified remains of old food on the table in the centre of the room, along with a bottle of tomato sauce that's crawling with black mould. The chairs lie on their backs, as if they were pushed back in a hurry, and the sink is piled with dishes. His foot knocks against something – a dog's bowl, the name Teddy painted on the side. Goosebumps crawl up his arms. Tommy reckons that every house, every room, every shop probably tells its own story about the panicky minutes after the Dead swarmed through the city, stories that he would prefer not to think about. He fights a powerful urge to flee out into the sunlight; he's come this far and he can't allow himself to get spooked.

Trying not to look too closely at the faded and peeling photographs still stuck to the kitchen cupboards (most seem to be of a dark-haired girl wearing thick black make-up and cradling a white terrier in her arms) he roots through the cupboard under the sink, ignoring the cockroaches that gush out onto the kitchen floor. He pulls out a bottle of bleach, a tub of caustic soda and a can of WD-40 – one of the items on the Most Prized list. *Score again!*

Deciding to leave the lounge and its rat infestation till last, he wanders into the smaller of the two bedrooms. Its walls are painted dark purple, so it's even gloomier in here. The bed is covered in a moth-eaten duvet, spiderwebs loop from the light fixtures, and the chest of drawers is littered with dried make-up tubes. There's a creepy poster of a skinny cavorting fellow on the wall above the bed, a wildly grinning pumpkin where its head should be, and Tommy wonders what sort of person would want to wake up with that staring back at them.

Simo, Tommy's Handler (a spoiled ten-year-old Hiltonite whose whiny voice drives Tommy crazy), has ordered more plastic Transformers for his collection, but there are no toys in sight. There's a craze for iPods at the moment – the Handlers like to fashion them into necklaces and tie them onto their clothing – so he rummages through the drawers just in case, feeling weird as he roots through bras and underwear. He grabs several pairs of stripy socks, then scans the small bookcase next to the bed, even though the last thing Simo wants is reading matter. Most of the paperbacks fall apart in his hands, their pages fragile lace – the moths and silverfish have done their worst – but from the bottom shelf he pulls out a comic book protected by a thick plastic cover. *The Ballad of Halo Jones. Awesome.* He takes it out into the hallway where the light is better, carefully removes it from its covering and flicks through it. If he gets the rest of his shopping done quick sticks he'll have time to read it before he's due back at the kombi.

Tommy's been so lost in Halo Jones that Mooki and Jess are almost on him before he notices them. For the last half-hour he's been chilling out on the front porch, enjoying the shade, and it's only when Mooki sing-songs 'Hey, Piggy Piggy, guess who?' that he's snapped back to reality.

Stomach sinking like a stone, Tommy quickly shoves the comic book up under his sweatshirt to hide it, but it's too late to stash the rest of his haul.

'Check it out, Jess,' Mooki sneers, effortlessly vaulting over the gate, Jess close behind him. 'Little Piggy's found himself his own little sty.'

Jess giggles and flicks her glossy, straightened hair over her shoulder. Tommy may be sick with dread, but he doesn't miss the way her too-short T-shirt rides up, exposing her flat brown stomach. He's got a bit of a crush on Jess, even though she can be a total bitch, but he's wary of Mooki. Mooki's as mean as a dog with a sore tooth.

'What do you want, Mooki?' Tommy says, fighting to keep the wobble out of his voice.

'"What do you want, Mooki?"' Mooki scoffs. 'What do you think, Piggy? What you got in the bag?'

'Not much. Just crap really,' Tommy says, knowing that even someone as dumb as Mooki will be able to see right though him. He decides to try to diffuse the situation. 'How about you guys?' he asks, keeping his voice light. 'Get some good stuff?' He glances at Jess, willing her to help him out, but she's examining her nails, a cruel smile on her lips.

'Duh,' Mooki waves his empty bag in Tommy's face. 'Does it look like we got anything? Whole complex is locked up tight, and anyway, looked like there were JoJos inside.'

'It's *JuJus*, dumb-ass,' Tommy says before he can stop himself. He's heard Mooki trying to use Runner slang before, as if he's a swaggering old-timer instead of a Newbie, and he always screws it up. It's not *that* hard to get the gist of it, although Tommy has to admit that the first time he overheard a group of Runners chatting amongst themselves he thought that they were speaking in a foreign language. So far he's figured out that 'uKlevas' are the Handlers or the super rich, 'JuJus' are the Dead (although Tommy has no idea where this nickname comes from), 'Arbs' are non-Lefties, 'Pinkies' are much-prized items and 'ChomChoms' are Runners who have made it past their probation period.

'What you say?' Mooki says, his tiny eyes flashing with malice.

'Nothing,' Tommy sighs, hating himself for being such a coward.

Mooki reaches behind Tommy's back and hauls out the bulging rucksack. Tommy makes a half-hearted attempt to snatch it back, but he knows it's futile. He's no match for Mooki's bulk – Mooki's always bragging about how he's been able to get served in the shebeens since he was twelve. Mooki tips the bag upside down, and the tins and bottles clatter down the porch step. 'What's this crap?' Mooki says, kicking the plastic bottle of bleach.

Tommy shrugs, trying to act cool. 'All I could get. Told you there wasn't much.'

'Pathetic.' Mooki grins at Jess. 'Help yourself, Jessie.'

She curls her nose up at the tinned beans Tommy unearthed on his second swing through the kitchen, but picks out the WD-40 and the socks, as well as the antibacterial hand wash, the toothbrushes and the hand cream he discovered in a bathroom cabinet. She squirts a glob of cream over her palms and wipes it slowly over her fingers, glancing slyly at Mooki as she does so. Mooki helps himself to the rest – the tinned goods, a Woolworths shirt still in its packaging that was in the wardrobe in the main bedroom, an old *YOU* magazine and a sealed tin of paraffin.

Tommy tells himself that they can take what they want – he can always go back inside the house and restock – but when Mooki picks up the half-full bottle of Pantene shampoo he feels his anxiety turn to anger. He was saving that for Olivia, looking forward to seeing her face when he pulled it out of his bag. He won't be able to replace it; it's the only bottle in the house.

He stands up and tries to grab it out of Mooki's hand. 'Give that back!'

Mooki smirks, holds it up out of his reach, tips the container upside down and squeezes. It makes a farting sound as the last drop finds its way out of the bottle. 'Oh look, Jess, sounds like Piggy's pooped his panties.'

Jess squeals with laughter, acting as if this is the wittiest thing she's ever heard, but Tommy only has eyes for Mooki. Maybe it's because he's been reading about a couple of hardass girls who don't take any shit, maybe it's because he doesn't want to look like a weakling in front of Jess, but before he really knows what he's doing Tommy shoves his palms against Mooki's chest.

Mooki stumbles back, the surprise in his eyes instantly flicking into spite. 'You're going to be sorry, you fat *shit!*'

Big mistake. Tommy makes a break for it, dodging to the left, but Mooki's too fast for him. He grabs the collar of Tommy sweatshirt, yanks back hard, and Tommy trips over his own feet and lands heavily on his tailbone, a bolt of agony shooting up his spine and bringing tears to his eyes.

Tommy twists around onto his hands and knees and starts

crawling away, knowing that he looks stupid and pathetic, but unable to stop himself. He feels Mooki's full weight landing on top of his back, squashing his stomach into the path's paving stones and winding him. 'Get off!' He wriggles and twists, but Mooki's way too heavy to shift.

'Pull his jeans off, Jess!' Mooki shouts.

Tommy struggles again, kicking his legs to make it as hard as he can for her, but the weight on his back restricts his movements, and he can only draw in shallow breaths. As the fight drains out of him Jess snakes her arms under his stomach – every inch of him mortified at the thought of her touching the spare tyre that hangs over his waistband. 'Eeeeew! He's all sweaty,' she shrieks as her fingers fumble at his belt. Then, dragging his shoes off his feet, she lugs the jeans down over his legs. Despite the paralysing humiliation he's relieved that at least he's wearing a clean pair of boxers, but that doesn't stop the pressure from building up in his chest. He can feel the tears coming.

'Thanks, Piggy,' Mooki hisses in his ear. 'That was fun.' Then, suddenly, the weight is gone from his back and he can breathe again. He turns his head to see Jess skipping down the path, waving his jeans above her head like a flag, Mooki lumbering after her.

Tommy lets the tears roll down his cheeks, chest hitching with every sob. He stays where he is for several minutes, feeling the edge of the comic book digging into his chest, his heart thudding in his ears, the steady throb of his bruised tailbone. The sun beats down on the back of his bare legs and his insides feel like they've been scooped out and replaced with churned butter. How could he have been so stupid? He knew Mooki was planning on jumping him sooner or later and he should have been on his guard. But what he can't figure out is why Mooki decided to single him out as the runt of the litter in the first place. Tommy knows he's overweight and slow, but so's Kavish, and Kavish has specs and a lisp, which you'd think would make him even more of a target.

It's not the first time Tommy has been picked on, of course – Sandtown is teeming with wannabe gangstas and tyrants – but sharp-eyed Olivia put an end to any bullying before it got too hectic. But he can't let her fight all his battles. He's fourteen now. He has to stand up for himself.

Still, at least he managed to keep the graphic novel out of Mooki's claws, and for that he's grateful.

The kombi's horn beeps out the five-minute warning. Bad enough that he has to go back home without anything to show for it, but he'd rather be pegged a runaway than return pants-less.

Ignoring the pain at the base of his spine and the panic swirling in the pit of his stomach Tommy retrieves the key from where he replaced it under the gnome and races back inside the house, bare feet sliding on the dusty floor. He heads straight for the main bedroom. Most of the clothes he checked out earlier were covered in black mould and stank something awful, but beggars can't be choosers. He digs through drawers, chucking garments all over the floor, ignoring the silverfish swarming over his fingers. The jeans and trousers all look way too small for him, but he finally unearths a pair of tracksuit pants with only a few holes in the knees. He shakes them out and pulls them on. They're slightly too tight over his thighs and the elastic waistband digs into his gut, but they'll have to do.

The horn beeps again. Last warning. There's no time to restock his bag.

Tommy scrambles out of the house, pausing to pick up his shoes and socks, pitches himself over the fence and hightails it towards the kombi. He's completely out of breath when he thumps up next to it, sweat dribbling down his face.

Ayanda – today's supervisor – peers dubiously at Tommy's bare feet. 'Where the hell you been, man? You okay?'

Tommy nods, feeling Mooki's eyes burning into him.

Ayanda's eye's crinkle up in concern. 'You sure? What happened to your pants?'

Tommy feels a lump forming in his throat. He doesn't want to lie to Ayanda, but he knows he'll only make it worse for himself with Mooki if he squeals. 'I'm fine. Ripped my jeans on the fence as I was climbing over.'

Ayanda nods at the bag hanging limply over Tommy's shoulder. 'Didn't you find anything?'

Tommy shakes his head.

'Shame, man, Tommy. Hope you've got an understanding Handler.'

Tommy doesn't want to think about Simo right now. He'll worry about that when the time comes. But in any case, it's not really Simo's reaction he's dreading. It's Olivia's. He knows she won't tell him off, but the disappointment in her eyes will slay him. He owes her his life, and this is how he repays her? By being the world's worst Runner. *Awesome*. It's official. His life totally sucks.

'Nice pants, Fatty,' Mooki calls as Tommy climbs on board, and a gale of laughter follows him as he squeezes past the others. Tommy tries to catch Kavish's eye – they used to hang out in the old days – but Kavish's gaze slides away from his. Tommy doesn't blame him; he knows Kavish is relieved that he's not the one Mooki has singled out and he'd probably feel the same if he were in Kavish's position.

The only empty seat is in the back, next to Jacob. No one likes to sit next to Jacob and even the supervisors treat him like he's contagious. Unlike the rest of the Runners in the minibus, all of whom are Newbies on probation, Jacob is an Outsider, apparently picked up from some place in the Eastern Cape. Rumour has it that Jacob's tried to flee Jozi three times and is on his last warning. No one knows how old he is or why he's been put in with the Newbies, but judging by the lines around his eyes he has to be fairly ancient – at least thirty. Jacob huddles in his seat, mumbling to himself, blowing on the window and drawing spirals with his finger in the condensation. He stinks, stale sweat staining the air around him, but Tommy has to concede that he doesn't smell too sweet either – the raggedy tracksuit pants honk of mould and mildew. Tommy doesn't have a clue who Jacob's Handler is, but suspects he or she is probably a low-level stallholder or trader. He can't see one of the uKlevas sponsoring such a high-risk Runner. He has no idea why Jacob hasn't just been sent to join the Honey Wagon Committee, the dumping ground for the Lefties who are too old, useless, mad or dangerous to Run. You don't need to have your wits about you to empty Sandtown's septic tanks and dump the human waste out in the city, after all. Tommy glances at the floor and notices that Jacob's bag is full of shopping. Just great. Even a deranged Runaway is a better Runner than he is.

The minibus moves off, its front wheels jolting over the edge of the pavement as Ayanda executes a three-point turn. It won't take long to get back to Sandtown, worst luck. Now that the OutCasts are getting braver, and targeting the malls nearer to home, Jova's decided that for safety's sake Newbie Runners can only forage in the suburban warrens close to the Tri-Hotel area. Tommy almost hopes the OutCasts will strike – at least then he won't have to face Olivia's disappointment and Simo's whining.

Sitting back, Tommy tries to block out Mooki's voice. He's boasting again about how he's going to take the Trials as soon as he's paid off his sponsorship, how he'll ace the test and be welcomed into the Army of the Left with open arms. Tommy hasn't told anyone – not even Olivia – that this is also his dream. He knows that the AOL's first wave is already at the army base, fixing up the old fighter planes, preparing to wage war on the Dead, although Tommy isn't sure what sort of a war this will actually be – if you're a Leftie like him the Dead don't fight back.

The kombi nips through the streets, slowing occasionally to manoeuvre around the rusting skeletons of long-abandoned vehicles and the occasional group of lurching Dead. The anxious knot in Tommy's stomach tightens. The moans are increasing in volume – they're only minutes from home now – and he looks down at his hands so that he won't have to see the seething mass of the Dead swarming around Sandtown's outskirts.

Ayanda presses the brake, pulls off the main road into a side street and beeps the horn. The reinforced gate shudders up and a couple of Blues jog towards them, weapons at the ready in case any of the Dead attempt to dart inside. They're given the all-clear, and the kombi slides into the dark concrete mouth of the parking lot. Flicking on the lights Ayanda guns the engine and the bus speeds through acres of empty parking garage, heading lower and lower, sweeping the around the curving bends so fast that Tommy starts to feel dizzy.

Ayanda squeezes the kombi in between a Honey Wagon and a fuel truck and slaps the steering wheel. 'Everybody off! Catch yous tomorrow.'

Tommy gets wearily to his feet. All he wants to do is hole up in the room he shares with Olivia and baby Nomsa, lose himself again in the comic book and forget about Mooki, Jess and today's humiliation. He tries to formulate an excuse for why he's returning empty-handed, but can't come up with anything that Simo, or more importantly Simo's Dad, will buy. At this rate he'll be as old as Jacob before he manages to pay off his sponsorship – his dream of joining the AOL further out of his reach than ever.

'See you, Jacob,' he says.

Jacob peers up at him with rheumy eyes, then suddenly lunges forward and grasps Tommy's wrist.

Tommy yelps and looks around for help, but the seats around him are empty. He's worried about fighting back – he doesn't know if he should provoke Jacob. He could well be unhinged enough to be dangerous. He decides his best course of action is politeness. 'Um ... Jacob? If you don't mind, please could you let me go?'

'Wait,' Jacob croaks. He thrusts his free hand into his bag and pulls out a yellow-and-green soccer shirt still wrapped in its plastic covering. 'Take this.'

Tommy feels his mouth hanging open stupidly. 'What? But ... '

'Take it,' Jacob says, sounding almost angry.

'Um ... Thank you.' Tommy opens his mouth to say something else – he doesn't know what – but Jacob drops his wrist and turns back to the window, humming to himself.

Exiting the kombi Tommy follows the others towards the stairwell entrance. What just happened? He looks down at the shirt in his hand. Amazing. He's off the hook. It isn't a Transformer, sure, but at least he has something to show Simo and Olivia.

'Tommy!' the Blue at the gate shouts, waving at him.

Tommy starts guiltily – the Blues always make him feel like this for some reason – then he recognises Molemo, who used to own the sleeping bay two curtains away from him and Olivia. Tommy hears a derisive snort of laughter – Mooki and Jess are looking over at him and pulling faces. 'Nice friends you got, Piggy,' Mooki spits at him, pushing rudely past Molemo and disappears into the stairwell.

'You doing okay, my friend?' Molemo asks, clapping him on the back.

'It's *so* good to see you too, Molemo,' Tommy says, over-compensating for Mooki's behaviour.

'Tell me, Tommy, how is Olivia doing?'

'She's good, thanks.'

Tommy suspects that Molemo's got a crush on Olivia. In fact, he's pretty sure *everyone* has a crush on Olivia even though he has two wives, which is why he always feels uncomfortable when anyone asks him about her. It's not as if she's his actual mother – Tommy can't remember his real mom; try as he might he can't even call up the vaguest impression of her face – but Olivia's the closest thing to a parent he knows. He also suspects that Olivia is the reason he managed to secure such a wealthy Handler in the first place. She insisted on accompanying him to his interview, and Simo's father – a giant of a man who's high up in the Energy Committee – wasn't able to drag his eyes from her face. Since then Tommy's spied Simo's father hanging around in the corridor outside their room on a couple of occasions, and he can't come up with a reason why a man of his standing would bother to walk all the way up to the staff quarters. He's rich enough to have a whole floor in the first third of the Hilton, after all.

'She like it in the new place?'

'Of course!' Tommy hesitates. Molemo might have secured one of the few permanent jobs in the Tri-Hotel area, but he is still stuck for life in Sandtown, whereas he and Olivia are now free of its noise and stench and over-populated corridors. Tommy doesn't want to rub his good fortune in Molemo's face.

'I mean ... it's okay,' he says with a non-committal shrug.

Molemo leans closer. 'Hey, you hear?'

'Hear what?'

'Gonna be a market.'

'Today? But it's Tuesday, isn't it?'

'Ja. Special dispensation. The Army's found some more Outsiders.'

Tommy frowns. 'Seriously? I thought they weren't searching anymore? Not after what happened with the OutCasts.'

Molemo shrugs. 'Just repeating what I heard. Soon as my shift's over I'm going to head to the square, check them out.'

'You mean they're *sponsoring* them today?'

'Ja.'

'Wow. That's weird.'

'You going?'

Tommy shrugs. He knows that he should really head home as fast as possible – he doesn't want Olivia to worry – but if Molemo's right, and there is a market on today, then why shouldn't he go and check it out? It would only take a couple of hours, and he could always tell Olivia that Simo had sent him on an errand (although he loathes lying to her). The only Outsider Tommy has ever met is Jacob, and he wouldn't mind catching a glimpse of the fresh ones they've found.

Molemo steps back to give Tommy room to squeeze past him. 'Say hello to Olivia for me, nè?'

Waving goodbye to Molemo, Tommy starts to trudge up the concrete steps. Then he hesitates. Now that he's a Runner he's at liberty to travel through the well-patrolled service corridors used by the Handlers and their underlings, but he'll reach the square far quicker if he takes a shortcut through the Archies – the lower tunnels that cut right under Sandtown. Olivia hates him using the Archies; they're notoriously dangerous, especially for a Runner who may or may not be carrying goods that could be worth a fortune on the black market. The Blues who patrol the Tri-Hotels' service tunnels and the main thoroughfares are scarce down there, so if he runs into any trouble he'll only have himself to blame. But now that he's got the shirt in his possession he's feeling lucky, and besides, he knows the labyrinthine tunnel network like the back of his hand. He shoves the shirt and comic book in his bag, pulls it over his shoulders and ties it across his chest so that it's harder to snatch off his back.

Molemo is swapping gossip with one of the Honey Wagon crew, so it's easy for Tommy to tiptoe back down the stairs and slip past him without any fear that it will get back to Olivia. He heads deeper and deeper, feeling the hairs on his arms standing up as the temperature drops. The bored-looking Blue seated on a cracked plastic chair at the bottom of the staircase shoots him a suspicious glance, but as she's there to prevent Untouchables from sneaking upwards, and not the other way around, she waves him past without a word.

Stepping through the door Tommy pulls his sweatshirt up over his mouth to block out the stench of urine and mouldering concrete that rolls over him like a wave. The air down here is damp, the crumbling walls drip with green slime and effluence and he has to duck every so often to avoid being conked on the head by the kerosene lamps that hang from the curved roof, bathing everything in a sickly yellow glow. Hunched figures scurry past him, and he's forced to step over the bundles of rags that line the edges of the walkway. Family groups huddle in the gloom; wide-eyed children with dirty faces and naked torsos bob and weave between the passers-by, the offspring of the lowest of the low who can't even afford a bay in Sandtown and are forced to live in the service tunnels and old sewerage pipes that stretch beneath the city.

Tommy keeps his head down, refusing to catch anyone's eye. Inyangas practicing their outlawed trade, their wares hidden in the shadows of the tunnel's recesses, screech at him to stop, but he hurries on.

'Yo! Boss! My friend, my friend!' A scabby old man grabs at his sleeve. Tommy shakes him off and increases his speed, but the old guy jogs at his side, the tops of his ripped takkies flapping like angry mouths. 'You want a Runner, boss? Tell your parents I am good. Very fast. Don't eat much. Small, small appetite me. Tiny.'

'No thanks,' Tommy says, forced to slow his pace as the crowd thickens at an intersection.

'Please, boss, I'm a good Leftie. Ask anyone, they'll tell you.' The man pulls up his sleeve, showing off a seeping wound on his forearm. 'Look, boss, I got proof. Got the tattoo. Regular Leftie, me.'

Tommy hesitates and takes a closer look at the mark on the man's arm. The tattoo is clearly home-made – he must have sliced into his own skin with a razor blade, then smeared the cuts with cheap ink. It's weeping with yellow pus, and it looks more like a tree than the outline of a left hand.

Tommy realises that the guy's a Faker – the first one he's ever encountered. Without saying a word he rolls up his own sleeve, showing off his legitimate tattoo. It didn't hurt as much as he thought it would, and thanks to Olivia's insistence on covering it with plastic wrap it had healed within days. The old man grunts and takes a step back. 'Sorry, boss, sorry. You won't do a Benni on me will you, boss? You won't tell the Blues, boss?'

Tommy knows it's his duty to report this guy, but what would be the point? There's no way anyone is going to sponsor him, so there's no chance he'll put anyone in danger. Since

Jova implemented the punishments for the Runaways, Fakers and wannabe OutCasts there hasn't been a Faker incident for at least a year. Tommy can't imagine feeling so desperate to survive or leave Sandtown that he'd lie about being left-handed. Tommy's heard the horror stories, heard about the Runners who innocently set off into the city, unaware that one of their number wasn't actually what they claimed to be.

'I won't say anything,' Tommy says.

'Thank you, boss. Thank you. You spare me a few browns for a cup of rooibos?' His eyes skate greedily over Tommy's bag.

'Sorry,' Tommy says, diving into the crowd before the guy can accost him again.

Drifting along with the horde Tommy allows himself to be funnelled through one of the doorways that leads into the heart of Sandtown itself. News travels fast, and everyone and her dog seems to have decided to jack work in for the day and head to Mandela Square. Cooking smells fight with each other – curry and roasting meat and boiled samp – and he catches a whiff of the fertiliser from the open-air vegetable plots on the first floor. The air is filled with the noise of screaming babies, laughter and shouted conversations, and he spots a couple of men arguing over a plastic bottle of pineapple beer in one of the bays next to the escalators. He briefly considers heading down to the floor below and checking out his and Olivia's old bay, but decides against it. A month ago, after he passed the test, Tommy was delirious with excitement at the thought of escaping Sandtown's constant noise, odours and the ever-present spectre of disease. Their new room on the Hilton's staff level is small, sure, but it is a vast improvement on the tiny space they shared with three other families, a filthy curtain the only concession to privacy. And the Tri-Hotels had the unimaginable luxury of electricity for an hour a day, as well as running water, which, after years of queuing at the pump for hours every morning, still gave him a thrill. So Tommy's surprised at the jab of nostalgia and homesickness he feels for Sandtown's hustle and bustle.

The crowd streams into another narrow stairwell, coming to a standstill as a bottleneck forms at the top. Elbows poke into Tommy's sides, the people around him chatting and laughing good-naturedly, waiting patiently for their turn. Then, suddenly, he's moving again; the mass of bodies surges forwards and he's popped like a cork out into bright sunlight.

He's never seen the square so busy – not even on Freedom Day. It's teeming with Sandtown's dentists, hawkers, stallholders, doctors, muti-sellers, sangomas, tarot readers, hairdressers, leg-waxers and musicians, all taking advantage of a bonus day to hawk their wares.

A group of sweating Blues are busily keeping the Handlers' area next to the auction platform free from riff-raff, and Tommy shields his eyes and glances at the Nelson Mandela statue next to them. Olivia is always going on about how the real man was a genuine hero, but when Tommy was a kid the statue had featured in most of his nightmares. He'd endured months of night terrors as it came to life and chased him through Sandtown's tunnels and aisles. He suspects it's because there's something weird about the statue's proportions – he's never been able to figure out if its arms are too short or its head is too big for its body.

Pushing through the crowd Tommy finds himself a shady spot next to a stall selling a meagre selection of second-hand books, most of their covers ripped and tattered. The bookseller, an elderly woman with skin as dark and shiny as polished boot leather, smiles at him, mistaking him for a prospective customer.

Ahead he can just about make out two elderly men who have climbed up onto the platform: probably a couple of Lefties taking the opportunity to hawk themselves and convince the crowd to sponsor them. They both start speaking at once, much of their spiel swallowed by the cries of the hawkers and the screams of fighting children. One of them, a guy so wrinkled he looks like a naartjie left out in the sun for a week, is rambling on about his year working for the Energy Committee, boasting about the hundreds of litres of diesel he collected for the city. Tommy's sure he's lying. There's no way a Fuel Runner would ever have to sell himself in such a humiliating fashion. The other speaks way too fast in a mixture of Zulu, Afrikaans and English, but from what Tommy can make out he seems to be bragging about the time he found an intact shipment of Baby Soft toilet paper in a warehouse. Seconds later they're chased off the stage by a red-faced Blue, and he loses sight of them as they're pushed into the crowd.

Tommy's starting to feel uncomfortable – the bookseller's figured out he isn't a buyer, and she's shooting irritable glances in his direction – so he decides to edge closer to the platform. He inches his way through the tightly packed bodies, cringing at the black looks thrown his way. Feeling only a twinge of guilt for using his status to get what he wants he rolls up the sleeve on his left arm to reveal his tattoo, and the going gets easier as people melt back in reluctant respect.

He's only metres from the Handlers' area when he realises his mistake.

Dammit. Simo and his father are sitting behind the velvet rope that separates the Handlers' area from the rest of the square. He holds his breath, waiting for one of them to turn his head and catch him loitering, but they don't even glance at the commoners surrounding them. Fortunately, out here in the crowd of Untouchables, Tommy is invisible.

The crowd parts again and an immensely fat man dressed

in a white linen robe bobs towards the Handlers' section, the attendants carrying his chair grunting under the strain of his weight. The man waves a white feathered fan in front of his face, his bored expression accentuated by his hooded eyelids and downturned mouth. 'Who's that?' Tommy asks the woman next to him.

She clicks her tongue. 'Steven Coom, of course.'

Tommy whistles under his breath – even he's heard of Steven Coom. The Outsiders must be something special if someone of Coom's status is attending the auction. As the head engineer of the Energy Committee Coom's even more powerful than Sindiwe, the Tri-Hotels' top administrator, or Jova, Commander-in-Chief of the Army of the Left. Coom's team of specialist Runners is the stuff of legend – it's their job to scour the city's outskirts for the spare parts and fuel that keep the generators powered up. Only those from the very highest echelon of the AOL are chosen for this position – Fuel Running can be dangerous, especially now that the OutCast terrorists are upping their game. But Tommy's heard stories about Coom – that he's capable of twisted acts of cruelty; that he's above the law; that you don't want to get on the wrong side of him. That despite his standing in society and the unprecedented luxuries and power his Runners have access to, you don't actually want to be picked to be part of his team. Especially if you happen to be female.

Scattered applause ripples through the audience as Sindiwe approaches the platform. The gaudy pattern on her floor-length kaftan is so bright it hurts Tommy's eyes, and today the tresses of her long blonde wig are piled in a beehive that wobbles on top of her head. She flashes a toadying smile in the Handlers' direction before acknowledging the horde below her with a curt nod. In contrast there's an ear-splitting roar as Jova steps up behind her, and Tommy cranes his neck to get a better view. Jova raises his clenched fist above his head, eliciting another barrage of deafening cheers, then pushes his glasses up his nose and looks down at his ever-present clipboard. Tommy has never spoken to Jova – doubts he'll ever get the chance – but every time he sees him he feels some kind of invisible kinship, as if he knows that they're meant to be friends. Jova's skinny, his bones as delicate as a girl's, but Tommy can't imagine Jova ever allowing a dick like Mooki to push him around. A tall guy wearing mirrored shades, his arms covered in tattoos, climbs up gracefully next to him: Lucien – Jova's right-hand man.

'Welcome, good people,' Sindiwe says in her beautiful deep voice. 'Today, as you may have heard, we are to have a very special auction.' She beams down at the Handlers again. 'Thanks to the good work done by the AOL –' She's forced to pause as the crowd cheers again. '– three new Runners have been collected to help us fight the good fight! With time and training I am certain that they will add greatly to our ever-growing army, which will soon set us free!'

Tommy winces as the woman next to him screams joyfully in his ear. All around him people are chanting: 'Jova! Jova! Jova! Jova!'

Jova smiles modestly and waves a hand up and down as if to quieten the audience while Sindiwe stands rigidly, a fixed smile on her face. Gradually the chant dies away and finally Sindiwe opens her mouth to speak once more, but her words are cut off as the crowd roars again. Tommy's forced to stand on his tiptoes to see what's going on – everyone is straining to get a better look – and then there's a sudden hush as a group of Blues hauls the Outsiders up onto the platform.

They're younger than Tommy was expecting. Not that much older than he is, in fact. A small pretty girl with a shaven head and a tall guy with long straight hair and ripped clothes are fighting the guards who are dragging them across the platform, resisting with every step. But Tommy can't drag his eyes away from the third Outsider, who towers over everyone else, a cloud of bright orange curls framing his sunburned face. He's leaning on a crutch, his head hanging down. Unlike the other two, who look like they're about to explode with fury, the ginger-haired guy looks defeated – a felled giant.

Without looking up from his clipboard Jova raises a finger and Sindiwe scurries over to him. They share a brief whispered conversation, then Sindiwe barks an order to one of the Blues holding the dark-haired guy. The Blue nods, and he and his partner start manhandling the Outsider off the stage.

'Where are they taking him?' Tommy asks his neighbour.

She shrugs. 'I have no idea, my boy. Perhaps straight to the training camps.'

Impossible, Tommy thinks. Lefties always start off as Runners – they have to prove their worth and trustworthiness before they're allowed to take the Trials, everyone knows that. So what's so special about this guy?

Sindiwe holds up her arms for silence. 'Who will give me a hundred for the girl?'

Tommy watches the Handlers carefully, sees Coom run his tongue around his lips before languidly raising a hand. One of his attendants dabs at his master's sweaty face with a handkerchief, but Coom bats him away impatiently. 'A thousand!' he calls.

There's a stunned silence, followed by a collective gasp which turns into a rumble as everyone talks amongst themselves. A thousand rand as a first bid is unheard of – the girl will have to work for years to pay that back. Even Jova looks up from his clipboard in surprise. And as he does Tommy sees Lucien whirl on him, shaking his head and shouting something, his words lost in the crowd's excited babbling. He prods Jova in the chest, but Jova shakes his head and shrugs. For a second, Tommy is certain that Lucien is about to hit him, but then he turns on his heel, jumps down from the platform and stalks away.

'I have a thousand!' Sindiwe says, struggling to regain her composure. 'Do I hear more?'

'No chance,' the woman next to Tommy says. 'No one would dare bid against that bastard, even if they did have the bob.'

Tommy feels a wash of pity for the girl. If the stories about Coom are true, no one deserves that fate.

But she's not going to go easily. She arches her back, twisting her body and kicking out at the two guards either side of her. The guard on her left is forced to pull her arm up behind her back to stop her lashing out at him, and the crowd laughs as she turns her head and spits in his face. As she's dragged off the platform he hears her scream: 'Ginger!' And this time the giant raises his shaggy head, blinking at the mob in front of him as if he's only just noticed it. But this revival is only temporary and as the girl leaves the stage his head slumps forward once again.

Tommy feels a sharp pinch at the back of his neck and turns to see Mooki standing behind him. *Awesome.*

'What you doing here, Piggy?' Mooki asks. 'Shouldn't you be handing over all the stuff you collected today?'

'Piss off, Mooki,' Tommy says, feeling braver now that there are other people around.

Mooki wafts his hand in front of his nose. 'Smell that, Piggy?'

Tommy sighs. 'Smell what?'

'The shitty stink of the Honey Wagon calling you. All you're good for. Who wants a Runner who's fat and slow and cries like a baby?'

'Screw you, Mooki.'

Mooki grins nastily and nods towards the red-headed guy.

'You're the one who's screwed, Piggy.'

Tommy opens his mouth to answer back, but the words stick in his throat as he sees Sindiwe bending down to shake Simo's Dad's hand. Simo's grinning and jumping up and down in excitement, acting like a kid who's just been given a new toy.

'Looks like your Handler just got himself an upgrade,' Mooki sneers.

Tommy's blood runs cold. He has no idea what this means for him, but whatever it is, it can't be good.